THE SIGIL MASTERS

· RICK DUFFY ·

First edition 2020
Published by Greening River

ISBN 978-1-7351954-0-7 (paperback)
ISBN 978-1-7351954-1-4 (ebook)
ISBN 978-1-7351954-2-1 (hardback)

www.rickduffy.com

THE SIGIL MASTERS SERIES

The Sigil Masters

Dark Reckoning

The Last Nowen

Good books, good friends and a sleepy conscience
This is the ideal life

— *Mark Twain*

CONTENTS

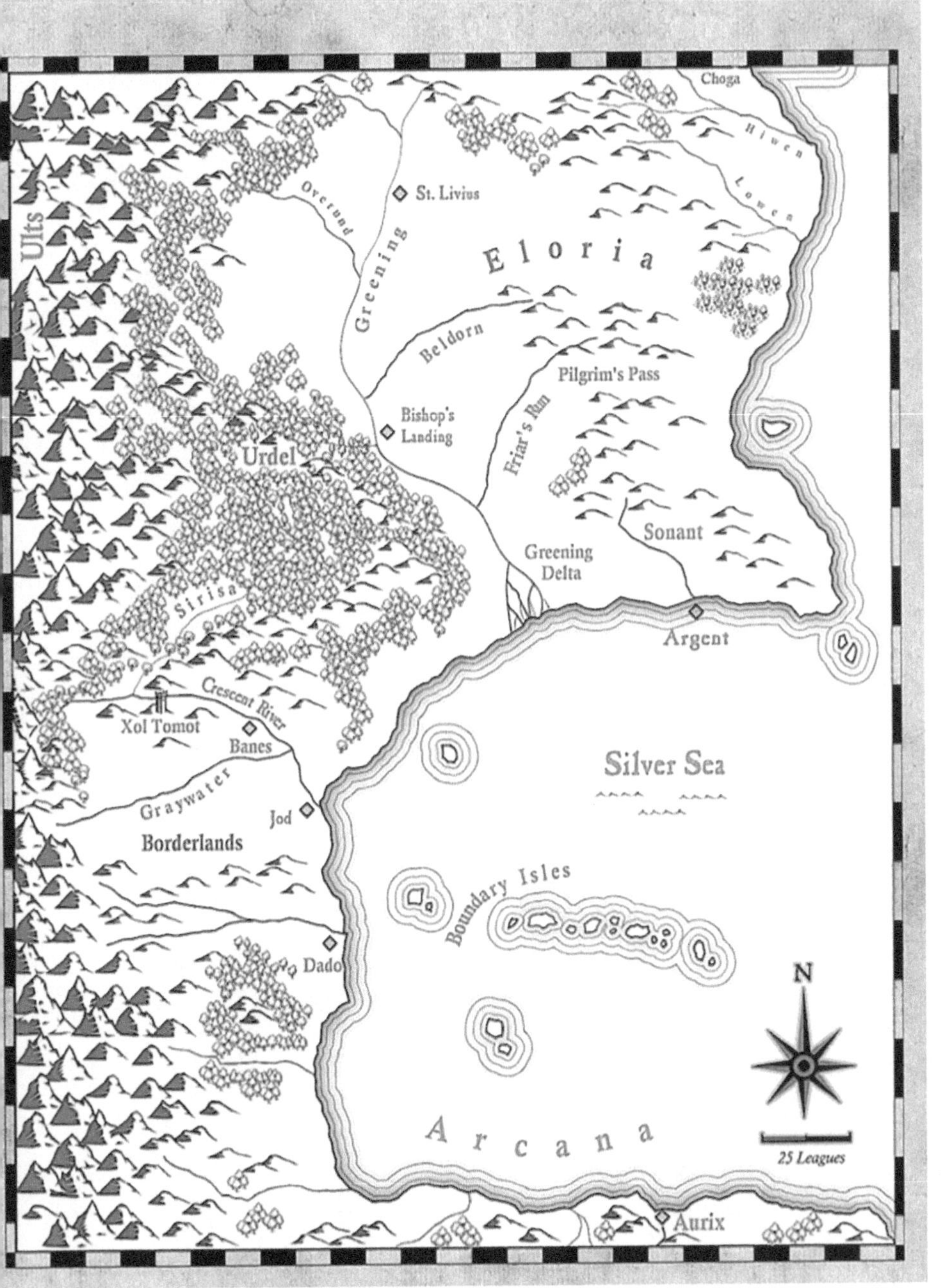

one league = three miles

Part One

The Abbey

CHAPTER ONE

OLEMN SINGING LEAKED from a passage across the cramped stone chamber. Par usually liked the singing. Now, every note filled him with dread. He couldn't have felt more doomed if he'd been buried alive.

A dozen other boys crowded close, all changing into the same white and orange robes, all whispering with excitement.

"I'll be the first to light," one of his classmates boasted, cinching the laces at his neck.

"Thank *gods* the classes are finally over," said another. "One more history and I'd combust—*without* an invocation."

"I liked the wars and stuff," a third objected. A hushed competition began over which battle with Arcana had been the best.

Par didn't join in. It was all he could do to keep breathing. Nearly every day for the past three years he'd walked up the squat hill of the abbey to receive his spiritual education—as the Rule demanded. Now, at last, their Lustering Day had arrived. The only ritual left was the invocation of a flame sigil, and they'd practiced that dozens of times. It would be no challenge at all. It wasn't meant to be.

Unless someone had cheated their way through the practices. Unless someone still couldn't invoke the gods for even the most basic of sigils.

Par swallowed. Like him.

The low chatter became thunder in his ears. His stomach churned like the Greening River in a spring storm. He grimaced, and when no one was watching backed away from his classmates—and from the gloomy passage to the temple—out the robing-room door.

A sinking sun lit a cavernous corridor through a long row of windows, creating harsh, blocky beams of drifting motes. Par crossed to a window, the stone floor cold beneath his bare feet. Outside and two stories below, a workman rolled a barrel across the abbey docks.

Par gripped the sill and inhaled the musky air. He could steal a boat, disappear down the river. Or hide until the ceremony was over. By now, he knew the abbey grounds as if he lived here. From the towers to the cellars. The brewery to the crypts.

But what then? He'd have to face things, eventually.

Someone slapped him on the back. "Gonna jump?"

Par spun. It was his best friend.

"What do you think?" Enio extended his arms. He posed in a white robe with overlays of orange flame, the same that Par and the other boys wore. Enio was on the skinny side, and the costume swallowed him alive. For the occasion, he'd tamed his black mop of hair into something manageable, but his eyes were as dark and fierce as ever. To top things off, Enio was smiling, and his disaster of crooked teeth—the broken ones on the side peeking out during expressions of joy—never failed to disarm Par.

"Fine," Par sighed. He turned back to the window. The low sun touched a distant snow-topped peak and cast long grey shadows among the hills and fields.

Enio joined him. He pointed to a canoe tied at the south

corner of the docks. "I fixed the *Sea Dog*. Flamed pitch over that crack in the bow."

Par stayed quiet.

"You're even paler than usual. You all right?"

Par brushed aside a strand of sweaty hair. "I'm trying to remember how you talked me into this."

"Stop worrying. We've practiced this cheat forever."

"But the gods still don't listen. What if I'm not *meant* to pass?"

Instead of answering, Enio elbowed him in the ribs.

Par yelped. "Hey!"

"Don't be thick." His friend glanced along the hall. "So what if you still can't invoke? People start at different ages."

"A lot younger than fifteen."

"It doesn't matter now. I've got that covered. And once we're through the ceremony we get"—Enio held up a finger as if giving a speech—"all the laws—"

Par forced a half smile. "Laws and freedoms of Eloria."

This was the crux of it. Once Lustered, he'd no longer be seen as a child, bound to his family or his hometown of St. Livius. His risk of being sent away for a Reckoning—to have his mind or spirit torn open, analyzed, fixed—disappeared. At least for now.

Enio dropped his hand. "Anyway, then you'll have more options. More time to figure out—"

They turned at the echo of footsteps. A man lumbered toward them. Ragged work clothes wrapped his swollen frame, and hulking shoulders balanced a pole of wooden buckets that hung from iron hooks. He was perhaps middle-aged or older. It was difficult to tell. His disfigured head and face were burned—melted—and his left eye stared pale and lifeless.

"Hi, Buckets!" Par said with Enio.

Buckets shuffled closer. His face twisted into an expression Par knew meant kindness and well wishes. The man passed with a gentle grunt. The boys ducked under the pails to keep from getting whacked.

They patted their mute friend on the back. The man continued to the robing-room, set his burden on the floor outside and carried in an empty bucket.

"The sun's almost right," Enio said. "We better get back—unless, you know, you don't have the buttons for it."

That was a challenge. Enio's face was still turned toward Buckets, but he watched Par out of the corner of his eye. Par appreciated the extra motivation. He squared his jaw. "Who doesn't have the buttons?"

Enio smiled.

As they left the window, Par's stomach tightened. "I just hope I don't get sick."

"On the altar?" Enio snickered. "I bet *that'd* get the gods' attention."

✳

They rejoined the others in the robing room. Par paused at a full-length mirror. Everything needed to be perfect. He straightened his neck lacings and made sure his hair was neat.

Enio came beside him. "You look absolutely lovely."

Par smirked. "Shut up, Enio."

His friend tugged his elbow. They sat on a bench near their everyday clothes, which hung on wall pegs.

"Stay calm," Enio said. "Don't act suspicious."

"I know."

"And remember"—Enio leaned in—"the closer we're together, the easier this will be. For me, I mean. You just stand still and look enlightened."

"Right." Par tried to breathe slow and easy, but his heart drummed on. He wouldn't be here if it weren't for his friend. Enio had gotten a sigil from a river merchant to flick a flame from one place to another. Whenever Par's parents or teachers suspected something was wrong with him, Par and Enio used their trick to fool everyone into thinking Par *could* invoke the gods to light a candle. But everything led to today. Could he fool the Prior, and in front of the congregation?

Par wiped his damp palms on his robe. "Enio, no matter how this goes, I owe you."

"Yeah, uh…" Enio peered past Par's shoulder.

"What?" Par turned.

Buckets was trying to retrieve a pail from underneath a bench. Two boys sitting there slid their legs to block him.

Before Par could say anything, Enio had moved there too. He addressed the larger boy, bulkier than any in the room. "Cut it out, Gorlo."

The two boys continued. Enio kicked Gorlo's leg. "Cut it out."

Gorlo curled his puffy lips. "Or what?"

"Or you'll wear that piss pot."

The others gathered around. Buckets had backed against the wall. The mob blocked Par from getting closer.

Gorlo rose from the bench. He frowned down at Enio. "Yeah? You worthless river rat. I'll—"

"You'll what? You can't touch me in the abbey."

"Maybe not. But my father can buy and sell *your* father. So *back off,* or one day you might just wake up an orphan."

Enio's face split into his wide, broken smile. "Promise?"

Gorlo didn't seem to have expected that. As he hesitated, Enio punched him square in the face.

Par pushed through the group. "Enio, no!"

Gorlo fell back, holding his nose. The boy beside him jumped Enio. Adult hands pulled them apart.

"He punched me!" Gorlo sniffled a bloody drizzle.

Two men in brown robes were now among the boys—Brother Marcus, a thin man with an angular face, and Brother Gaius, the very image of a monk with a taste for the abbey's beer. Brother Marcus took Enio by the collar. "Both of you, with me. The rest follow Brother Gaius. It's time."

Brother Gaius led the group into the narrow, bent passage. Par's last glimpse of the room was of Enio scowling while Brother Marcus performed a healing invocation on Gorlo's nose.

The singing grew louder. Incense like musty roses filled the air. The wall sconces here were not lit, and a glow ahead created broken angles of light and shadow.

Brother Gaius lined them along the wall. "Ready?" he squeaked in a high voice. "Bring your sigils to mind. And no fooling around. Remember, you'll be on the high altar."

Par looked again for Enio, then leaned against the cold hard stone. What had he done to deserve any of this?

Nothing, that's what.

He'd studied more than anyone. He'd had to, ever since the abbey had told his parents that the trouble with his invocations might be spiritual unworthiness.

And he'd served the gods harder than anyone. His father had seen to that, volunteering Par's free time to work at the abbey. Anything to avoid a Reckoning, a ritual performed on the spiritually damaged, murderers or prisoners of war. It changed the way you thought and felt and remembered. Who you were inside. It made him sick just to think about.

Next to him stood a boy named Li, the shortest in class, and skinny, even more than Enio. He was trying to tie the laces at his neck, but one of his hands had been born palsied and he couldn't grip the strings.

Par took a breath. "Those are a pain, I know."

Li looked up shyly.

"There's a kind of trick. Want to see?"

The boy hesitated. "All right." But there was no trick. Par simply tightened the laces.

"Thanks," said the boy.

Par smiled. "At least we won't need these after today." Even as he said the words, a shiver ran up his spine. He'd get no second chance.

Chapter Two

THE SINGING ENDED. Brother Gaius marched Par and the others into the spacious temple. They filed behind a long marble altar spread with white linen. Stained glass panels in a great vaulted ceiling arched rainbow-like overhead, luminous with the last of the daylight.

Prior Dogam Secundus, second in charge at the abbey, stood before the altar, his back to the congregation. The tall, blond man wore a robe similar to the boys, but with extra flourishes. His eyes followed Par and the others as they arrived. The man was younger than Par's father, but his tight face exuded discipline and authority.

A small group of monks stood past the far end of the altar, there to help with the singing. Near them, in a high-backed chair, sat Father Abbot Cornelius Ianarius, a cadaverous figure people said was over one hundred years old. He wore vestments like the Prior, and a tall, three-pointed hat. Before this venerable figure rested a huge, unlit candle, thick as a man's leg and five feet high. The Father Abbot gripped it with both hands like a staff.

The boys took their positions, shoulder to shoulder, behind the altar. Fresh, unlit candles in golden holders waited on the table before them. Par stood just short of center stage, his heart pounding. He scanned the dim temple hall. The room could hold five hundred people, but now only a few dozen clumped near the front—friends and families of those being Lustered.

He found his father, wearing an orange Friend of the Abbey robe. His mother held Par's new infant brother in her arms. He thought again of what they would do if he failed the ceremony. His stomach tightened another notch.

The congregation fell silent. Par looked back toward the dark passage.

No Enio.

Prior Dogam turned to the crowd and spoke with a loud voice. "The Sigil of the Living Flame was the first sigil bestowed upon man by Oä, Glory of the Gods. It represents the journey of our lives, from spark to flame to ember. Even as the smoke from its final exhalation ascends, so too shall we, on our last day, ascend to the eternal lights of the Higher Realms."

He lifted his arms. "In the name of his Eminence Pompeius Maxima Arcalus, Fondiscate of the Divine, and in the sight of our patron, Saint Livius, and with the blessing of the councils and of the High Sigil Master of Eloria, we invite our newest companions to join us on our journey."

Par glanced again at the passage. *Enio, where in the purple hells are you?*

The Prior turned to the boys and gave a solemn nod.

Along with the others, Par grasped his candle in both hands—except for Li, beside him, who could only hold it in one.

I should just tell them now I can't invoke. Why go through—

A shuffling came from the passage. Brother Marcus led Gorlo out to the altar, followed by Enio, who tried to continue toward Par. But the monk placed him next to Gorlo. Enio was at the very end of the altar, at least ten feet away—farther than he'd ever secretly flicked a candle flame for Par.

Brother Marcus joined the other monks near the Father Abbot. The last of the setting sun dimmed from the high windows, and a bell, far up in the abbey's bell tower, echoed through the temple. Par caught a quick, worried look from Enio.

"Begin," said the Prior, and bowed his head. Par turned to his candle, frantically going over everything he'd learned from the temple classes about the gods and invocations. Everything the others seemed to understand almost without effort.

Everything that continued to elude him.

He focused his attention on the candle, on its whiteness, its purity. He felt its slender shape under his fingers, the cool, soft beeswax. With a shaky breath, he summoned the feeling of beseechment, of worship, into his whole being, and whispered the sounds that helped beginners with their invocations. Once he'd completed the preliminaries, he closed his eyes and brought to mind this invocation's sigil—a simple spiral with an upward reach.

Slow now, step by step. Par mentally traced the shape that filled his internal vision. He summoned the thoughts and feelings of the invocation, guiding them through the sigil, letting the sigil guide them in return. As he did, he imagined that it brightened like a rising sun, golden and glorious, until the shape blazed in splendor. And at its peak of brilliance he pushed the radiant sigil from his mind, through his chest and arms and into his fingers, then up through the beeswax. With the faith of closed eyelids he saw the wick smolder, then leap to life with a fire granted from the gods.

A commotion sounded down the altar. He opened his eyes. The hem of Gorlo's sleeve had caught fire. An amused murmur ran through the crowd as Gorlo slapped it out.

The Prior cleared his throat. The room again fell silent. Several of the other candles had already lit, even Li's, using only one hand. Par's candle stood as cold and dead as ever.

It was as he feared—Enio was too far to help. Par closed his eyes and started again, summoning the flame sigil, summoning the light.

Please hear me. Just this once.

He was sure there was nothing wrong with his simple sigil. His father had first bestowed it upon him. Then his mother. And his teachers. Even Enio had once tried, awkwardly, to perform a bestowal ceremony. What was wrong with him? Why did the gods not hear? Maybe he should go over the lessons again, or the thoughts and feelings that infuse this sigil, or—

The light dimmed in his mind, and his hope went out with it. What was the point? Par couldn't do this. He would not be Lustered, would not claim his Enlightened name. He'd be a stain on the town, unworthy, a burden, foul, not able to do this or any other invocation, to purify a little water, heal a simple wound, take care of himself. The Reckoning was all that waited.

Again, the abbey bell tolled.

The ceremony was complete. Par experienced a strange relief as he opened his eyes. Whatever happened next, at least there'd be no more lies.

He looked along the altar. Every candle was lit.

Including his own.

While he stared in disbelief, the Prior turned to the crowd. "Welcome, now, the new Lustered of our community, favored of the gods, and subject to all the laws and freedoms of Eloria."

Par was afraid to breathe, that he might blow out the flame or wake from a happy dream. Even from the very end of the altar, Enio had managed to light Par's candle! The congregation held up their own unlit candles. Halos of gold winked round the people's heads—the glory, visible in the gloom or, sometimes, in the light if the invocation were strong enough. One by one each wick flashed to life, creating an expanding globe of warm brilliance in the otherwise darkened room.

The Father Abbot remained in his chair, his head lowered.

The tall candle before him had not lit. Everyone waited. The Prior coughed, and the old man jerked. A circle of light flickered around his head, and his candle lit.

The Prior turned back to the congregation, and he and the choir led everyone in a joyful hymn about the goodness of the gods. Par peered down the altar at Enio, expecting to see his friend's exuberant smile.

Enio was pale. Sweat matted his hair. A stain on his robe showed that he had vomited.

But though Enio's smile was slight, it was still there.

CHAPTER THREE

Prior Dogam, with the old Father Abbot leaning on his arm, led Par and the new Lustriants down the center aisle. The congregation filled the air with happy song. In the eyes of the Hierarchy, Par was officially Lustered.

Now for the last hurdle—his father.

Everyone continued to the vestibule, where paintings of the saints and of the Hierarchy decorated the walls. From the most prominent portrait, His Eminence, the Fondiscate to the gods, watched over the little parade. His wooly eyebrows and short, perfect beard made him seem both friendly and distant. Beneath him hung the image of a man with a long, ashen face, the High Sigil Master, second only to the Fondiscate in things spiritual, and overseer of the Ministry of Reckonings. The intense, accusing eyes followed Par across the room, and the mocking mouth appeared to be on the verge of exposing his cheat. Par picked up his pace.

The group proceeded out to the abbey's courtyard. Bright lanterns lit the cloistered walkways and painted the buildings with the congregant's moving shadows. They passed trimmed topiaries and the prominent statue of their patron, Saint Livius, a man with an angry, rugged countenance, said to have turned a flood and saved a village. Par glanced back, still numbed by his victory, and tried to locate his parents. A river of eyes sparkled in the cheery candlelight. Brother Gaius collected everyone's candles, promising the parents that, yes, their son's Lustering candle would be returned to them, along with a signed certificate.

At last they arrived at the dining hall, where the jolly group continued upstairs to a private gathering space. A festive fire crackled in the hearth. The tables brimmed with bowls of casseroles, and plates of meat and cheese and cakes, all brought earlier by the families. A barrel of the abbey's own beer sat on a table just inside the door.

Par crowded in with the others. While he waited for his family, he crossed between the tables to a window that overlooked the eastern wall. Below, a weedy cobblestone lane wound down the hill to join the road heading south into town. As lanterns there lit one by one in the evening gloom, someone gave him a hearty pat on the back. He turned, expecting Enio.

A barrel-chested man with bushy black hair and a beard framing a square face glared down. It was Par's father. His anxiety spiked. Had he fooled his father along with the rest?

The man broke into a grin. "Well done, Parynius Ignatious."

He had! This was the formal way for his father to address him after the ceremony, with Par's new Enlightened name tacked on the end. It was over.

His mother was there too, a plump, strong woman with chestnut hair tied back with a red ribbon. She held his baby brother snug in one arm, the small, inquisitive brown eyes—which his parents said were the image of Par's—swiveling up at him.

"Well done, Parynius Ignatious," his mother echoed with a tight grin. She didn't hide her worries as well as his father, and Par noticed how haggard her face had become.

With her free hand, she held out a coin-sized golden pendant, provided by the abbey and earned by each Lustriant with their new maturity. Carved onto its surface was the flame sigil. His mother had strung it on a thin gold chain. She tried to drape the chain over his head, but couldn't spread it with one hand. Par helped.

"Thanks." He smiled at them both. Then he remembered Enio. He looked past his parents. His friend was at the meat table. Enio's robe had been wiped off, which made the spot where he'd vomited look worse. His pendant dangled from a rough leather strip. Enio only had his father now, who hadn't attended the ceremony. No one had expected him to.

Par's father cleared his throat. "Well, then. Have you thought more about what you'll be doing now?"

Par focused back on his family. "A little." He touched the baby's tiny fingers.

"Still not interested in the smithy? It's the perfect place to improve your fire invocations."

"I might travel some."

"Travel? I have a friend in the Navigator's Guild. They're always looking for new recruits."

Par braced himself. "I meant, Enio and I were thinking—"

"No," his father said, the cheer gone from his voice. "Not with that one."

"But—"

"I've tolerated him because you studied together. But you have to know, son, that boy is trouble."

Par felt his face flush. He couldn't explain how much of their *studying* consisted of practicing their Lustering cheat. But Enio was his best friend, even if for some reason Enio never admitted it. "Dad, he's not—"

His mother interrupted. "It's not entirely his fault, Edwin. That father of his…"

Edwin sighed. "Still, I wouldn't be surprised if being around that boy retarded your spiritual development."

Par winced. He hated that phrase.

His father bent closer. "I've talked to the proctors here, and I think they'd let you in. You've got the head to be a teacher—if you'd apply yourself more."

Par's spirits rose, but only for an instant. To travel—to leave his home—without the ability to invoke, was, of course, a crazy dream. And despite his compelled extra studying and "retarded spiritual development," he *liked* the books and histories. Still, like most things, teaching at the abbey required the ability to invoke. Regardless of his newly gained freedoms, that was still beyond his grasp.

"Not as an instructor," Edwin continued. "Not at first. Maintenance, or helping in the brewery, that sort of thing, until you've proven yourself worthy of a position."

"I'll think about it." His father's suggestion might work, for a while. Even when the proctors discovered Par couldn't invoke, they might still keep him on. They'd kept Buckets on, a war hero who could no longer invoke.

But kept him on emptying piss buckets.

Par's little brother gave a tiny squeal. Edwin grinned at the baby and squeezed his wife's arm. "We were at our wits end with you," he said, not looking up. "Your invocations were so few, so…"

Par held still, trying not to give away any emotion.

His father went on. "A rumor started that an evil cursed our family. Longtime customers avoided the smithy. Your mother cried so—"

"I know." Par grimaced.

"We were afraid the gods had found you unworthy." His father's dark eyes bore into him. "I have to be honest. If the gods had not blessed you with a successful Lustering, we'd decided to send you for the Reckoning."

The old terror returned. Until this moment, he hadn't been

certain his father would have gone through with it. Now, all doubt disappeared. The man was absolutely serious.

But his father's face softened. "Thank the gods everything turned out the way it did. Still, you took much longer than the others. Why do you think—"

There was a commotion near the door. Par turned, relieved to be spared from some fresh lying.

"Hey, where's my boy?" A short, gangly man with a scraggly beard pushed into the crowd. Long, greying hair drooped over withered skin well beyond his age.

Tarley, Enio's father, had arrived.

"There he's at!" The man approached Enio, frozen at the buffet like a cornered animal, and knocked him on the shoulder. "Look at you, growed up so fast."

Enio glanced around, maybe for help, or escape. Par guessed both and stepped in Enio's direction. His own father's hand took his shoulder and stopped him.

Tarley reached for Enio's pendant. His words came slightly slurred. "What we got here—the medal? Got one myself once. It's gold, ya know. Pure—"

Enio snatched it away. "I'm Enius Marius now."

Fire flashed across the man's face. He glanced at the crowd, then smiled again. "Sure! Sure! A drink to my boy… where's the drink?" He staggered to the keg. People gave him ample space.

"Wait here," Par's father said, and walked toward the man.

Conversations resumed. Par strained to hear his father's words.

"Congratulations, Tarley."

Tarley drew beer into a wooden cup. "Is that Edwin? Thanks, Ed. Your boy here too?"

"Yep. We got two new men on our hands."

"And two bigger stomachs!" Tarley laughed.

Edwin nodded, "Isn't that the truth. We haven't talked lately. How're things at the warehouse?"

Tarley downed his cup in one gulp and wiped a sleeve across his mouth. "Used to run that place, you know."

Par's father put his thick arm around Tarley's shoulders and ushered him toward the door. "It's getting late."

"Now they got me working the docks! Can you believe—"

Tarley stopped short as they were about to exit the room. "Hey, what're you doing?" He pulled away. "Where's my boy! Where's—"

Prior Dogam and the Father Abbot were also in the room, sharing the festivities. The Prior had moved behind Tarley, and brushed the man's head. A brief glory flashed around the Prior's own. Tarley stopped speaking, and his face relaxed. Par felt sorry for Enio, but he had to smile. The Prior was using an invocation Par had seen his mother use, bestowed upon new parents to calm a baby. It was too weak to affect most adults, but in Tarley's intoxicated state, it worked even on him.

"Let's have a rest," the Prior said. Edwin transferred the man to the Prior, who walked a shuffling Tarley out the door.

Par's father returned. They stood silently for several awkward seconds while the rest of the room chattered around them.

"I should take your mother home before it gets too dark," his father said at last. "Stay out as long as you want. You're a man now. You've earned it, Parynius Ignatious."

His father held out a hand. Par shook it. Then he shared a brief kiss with his mother. It was the warmest moment Par could remember between them in a long time, and it brought a lump to his throat. The strain caused by hiding his secret had created a distance between himself and his parents. He swallowed hard as they left. Partly because of the closeness he felt to his family again. And partly because he now had the legal right to leave his home.

But he was still a fraud.

He had, in fact, earned nothing.

CHAPTER FOUR

Par eased through the lively crowd, looking for Enio. Near the fire, the Father Abbot demonstrated an invocation to create whimsical shadow animals, eliciting bursts of laughter as the shapes landed on someone's shirt or robe.

Enio had left, but Par allowed his smile to return. He knew just where to look.

Wrapping some meat and cake in napkins, he slipped back downstairs and through the dark kitchen to the cellars. Dim passages ran beneath the abbey. With his fingers brushing the cool stone walls, he made his way to where heavy oak doors opened onto the docks. Nearby, light spilled from a humble workroom. Voices escaped with it.

Par peeked inside. The room was lit by a lantern on a stout wooden table and a makeshift fireplace that vented out a window. Two cots rested against opposite walls. Enio sat cross-legged on one, his face buried in a tankard the size of his head. Buckets was at the table along with his brother John, a smaller man, perhaps a little younger, but with the grizzled look of an old workman. Food pilfered from the potluck was spread before them.

"Par!" John bellowed. "Come in!" Buckets smiled as best his melted face allowed.

"Thanks, John. Hi, Buckets." Par dumped his food onto the table, plopped next to Enio, and let out a long breath. It felt as though he'd been holding it for days.

"What was your fire-fly," Par asked. "Ten feet?"

Enio lowered his tankard and beamed. "Fifteen, if it was an inch."

"Feeling all right?"

"I won't be invoking for a while, but yeah, I'm good."

"You in any trouble for punching Gorlo?"

Enio snorted. "Nah. Now that the Lustering's over, everyone's happy never seeing me again. Besides, none of the monks like Gorlo, anyway."

John handed Par a small wooden cup of golden wheat ale and took away Enio's tankard.

"Hey!"

"Hey, yourself. That's for Buckets. And I don't care if you are men now. We'll have no drunken cavorts on my watch."

Enio pouted as John handed him a smaller cup like Par's. The man lifted his own beer and stood straight and formal. "First things first. A toast to our new Lustriants."

Par slid off the cot with Enio. Buckets watched from the table.

John cleared his throat. "Me and Buckets—me and Tommy— been here going on twenty years, so you'd think I'd know some fancy blessings. But maybe it's best to just say this: There haven't been any two better fellows walk into those abbey classes as kids and finish out as men."

Everyone had stopped smiling.

"I'll keep it short," John continued. "Here's to you both, Parynius—" John gestured to Par.

"Ignatious," Par said.

"Ignatious. And to Enius—"

Enio stuck out his chest. "Marius."

"Marius. And may the gods smile on you, and may all the laws and freedoms of Eloria be yours."

They cheered and bumped their cups and drank. Buckets took a mighty gulp from his tankard.

John looked to Par. "Doesn't Ignatious mean fire?"

Par nodded. "Dad chose it to inspire me."

"It's a fine name. What about Marius?"

Enio sat again on the cot, Par beside him. "My ma. She was Maria."

"Lovely," John said. "I expect you'll be moving on from here now?"

Enio took a drink. "I'll tie up some ends and hop a barge. Lots of work on the river."

"You're handy on the docks, there's no denying. And you, Par?"

Par lowered his gaze. He sensed everyone watching. "My father wants me to get on here at the abbey." He waited for Enio to bring up their travel plans.

Instead, Enio chuckled.

Par looked up. "What?"

"Remember when you used to be scared to crap of Buckets?"

Par gave a fast frown. "I'm not—"

"It's all right, Par," John said. Buckets kept eating.

Par shrugged, feeling sheepish. "Well, I didn't know him then. But he's the best. Plus, he's a war hero."

"The Grey Wars." Enio made a wet burp. "How, uh, what exactly happened to him, anyway?"

The conversation stopped. John's expression lost its cheer. He'd always steered them away from this topic—sometimes gently, sometimes not.

"Enio—" Par began.

"You've always been good to Tommy and me." John glanced

at his brother. "It's meant a lot, for both of us, even if he can't say it. And you're men now."

Buckets grunted and rose from the table to work the fire.

John took Buckets' place at the table. "Our father was a mason. I wasn't much at the stone invocations, so he set me to work on the water and the mix. But Tommy was born to handle stone. When the border wars got hot again, we joined up. It was natural they'd put Tommy to work the walls."

"As a builder?" Par asked.

John shook his head. "As a breachman."

Enio stifled another burp. "They break down gates, right?"

"More." John stood a thin slab of cheese before him on the table. "When you hear the stories of the castle battles, they tell of the great warriors charging in their shining armor on their thundering horses, swords flashing in the sun and missiles burning through the skies."

Par bent forward, captivated.

"But," John went on, "there's more to it. While most of us hold back and keep the enemy on the walls busy, the breachmen sneak around, feel out weaknesses deep in the stone and rot it. Breach it." He scratched a hole through the cheese. "After that, the rest of us can get in. I once told you we fought in the battle of Xol Tomot."

"You got rockshot," Enio said.

"I did. But Tommy was hit by a sorcerer's spell."

Par stomach sank.

"When the breachers split the walls, the sorcerer Tomot was waiting. But Tommy wasn't hit merely by one of their unholy Profana conjurations. He suffered a curse."

"A curse?" Par whispered through a suddenly dry mouth. He lifted his cup to his lips.

John's expression turned troubled. "They say it put a madness into him. He attacked everything. Yet he'd breached the wall, he'd done his job. There was plenty of fire and blood after that, but we prevailed. Tommy was restrained and brought to the regiment healers. But the field healers didn't know what to do with him. How could they? Arcana had agreed to the ban on curses in the second Treaty of Jod, and the Rule of Eloria has always prohibited curses by the dictates of the gods. So Tommy was sent to the nearest safe-hold and transferred back home, in hopes a Reckoning might help him."

Par choked on his drink.

"You all right, son?"

"Fine," Par managed. His heart had nearly stopped. A Reckoning?

Enio leaned in. "Why didn't they at least heal his burns before sending him home?"

Buckets poked the embers. The fire crackled.

"For a long time," John said, "that chapter of his life has been a blank. Lately, though—well, he still can't talk, but we've pieced a few things together. I'm given to understand it was like a nightmare, a fever dream. He remembers sailing toward the shining spires of Argent."

Par nodded tensely. "The capital."

"Yes, the seat of the Ministry of Reckonings. But then he remembers being in a cage, traveling through a wasteland of strange mists and black sands. He was brought to a circle of towering stones, and within those to a flashing pit. In that pit, he saw the sun."

"The... sun?" Enio said.

"He thinks someone took him to where the sun goes at night."

John dropped his voice. "He remembers being swung over the pit, lowered down. Then the burning came, deeper than any fire, even to his soul. Whatever they did to him, it took away his madness. But left him as he is—his mind, and his face."

Par exchanged a wide-eye glance with Enio. They each took a draw from their mugs.

John stood, went to Buckets and put a hand on the big man's shoulder. "Afterwards, the Hierarchy sent him here, to be cared for by the abbey. When I found him, I got on as a workman. It's been a good place for us."

Par gathered the courage to ask, "What has the Father Abbot said about all this?" Reckonings were bad enough, but this sounded like none he'd ever heard of. Was this a Reckoning for a curse? And what if the reason Par couldn't invoke was—

"Tommy's been against saying anything to the Abbot, and I don't know if he's wrong. Whatever happened, why stir it back up? What would it change? Where else could we go?"

John huffed and brightened. "Listen, boys. Don't you get dark about me and Tommy. We're good enough, and this is *your* day. Which reminds me. I have a gift."

Par left his interrupted thought unexplored. He shook off the chill from John's story. "You don't have to—"

Enio nudged him.

"It's not much," John said. "But with your permission, I'd like to bestow on each of you the rockshoot sigil."

Par grinned politely. He could accept sigils even though he couldn't use them.

But Enio didn't hide his enthusiasm. "Yes!" He jumped off the cot.

John held up a finger. "It won't do you any good unless you practice. And remember, rockshoot is a wartime sigil. Promise me you'll both respect it like one."

"We promise," Par said with Enio.

"Strictly speaking"—John rubbed the back of his neck—"you're only allowed bestowals from your parents and the priests, the people you work for, and like that. But I can't let you go off into the big wide world without something to help you along. Besides, we can bend the rules a little, especially on occasions like this, don't you think?"

"Definitely," Enio said.

"Fine. You first. We can skip the kneeling part."

John lit two small candles and brought them to the table. Enio joined him. They each grasped a candle. Then they leaned together until their foreheads touched and closed their eyes.

"Ready?" John said.

Enio cleared his throat. "By the will of the gods I beseech thee your bestowal."

"By the will of the gods I bestow upon thee." There was too much light to see a glory around John as he invoked, but Par caught a brief spark where their heads touched.

They sat back. For a moment there was a mark on Enio's forehead, glowing like an ember and shaped like a flame sigil with a small reach to the right. Enio rubbed it. When he removed his hand, the image was gone. "Got it."

"Now, Par."

Par went through the same ritual. As John bestowed, the golden sigil moved brightly into Par's mind, alive beyond what any drawing or sketch could capture. It faded into his memory along with the other sigils everyone got, and that he couldn't use.

Par rubbed his head. "Thanks John."

"Yeah, thanks!" Enio said.

"You're welcome. Don't go showing it off. Now, let's lighten things up."

From beneath the cot, John retrieved a battered fiddle. He plucked a few frayed strings and played. Buckets came back to the table, smiling.

As the evening went on, Par ate, and laughed, and sometimes even danced. It wasn't the beer that fueled his spirits, but the friendship. Eventually he was back on the cot, propped against the wall, watching Enio try to twirl Buckets in a jig. Par sighed happily, his problems forgotten. He drifted into a wonderful sleep, too content even to say his nightly prayers.

Chapter Five

E NIO WOKE TO the scuffling of boots. John and Buckets stood at the table grabbing leftovers. The window glowed with the light of early morning.

"Hey." Enio sat up, slumped back and groaned.

John put a finger to his lips and pointed at Par, still asleep at the end of the cot.

Enio nodded and eased off the bunk. He slipped out the door with the two men.

John spoke softly. "What's now for you, Enio?"

Enio smiled. "Nothing. Everything. I'll grab some stuff from home. Then we'll see."

"Well, best of luck, son." John gripped his shoulder. "Remember, there's a place for you here if you need it."

Before Enio replied, Buckets bent and hugged the air from his lungs.

"Careful, Tommy," John chuckled. "Don't breach the boy."

Buckets backed away, but not before Enio got in a quick hug of his own.

They parted there, John and Buckets to chores, Enio up to the robing room. Chanting drifted from its passage to the temple—the monks at morning prayers.

Enio changed from the ceremonial robe into his worn long shirt, trousers and boots, then kissed his Lustering medal. He'd once tried running away without this token of maturity. A boatman had turned him in, and things had gone badly, especially when they delivered him to his father. So he'd planned to steal a medal, but he met Par, who'd convinced him to go through the classes and make it official. Now, not only had Enio passed his Lustering, he'd just invoked his longest fire-fly ever! He was glad to have paid Par back, though for a moment during the ceremony, Enio thought he was about to pop an artery.

With his pendant tucked safely under his shirt, he made his way to the docks. His canoe, the *Sea Dog*, waited at the far corner of the landing.

Enio untied and pushed off. He paddled until he caught an easy current and let the murky green waters take him south. He cleared the abbey's low hill, the sun peeking through willows that sagged above the banks. The smells of fish and mud and old wet weeds filled his nose, and the chirp of insects shared the cool morning air with the song of a sleepy water bird. He lay back and drank it all in. A last visit to his home, and he'd leave his father, once and for all. Enio was free. He was the owner of the river. He was the ruler of the world.

Soon, he came to the pier where his father worked. Enio had been born in a riverside cottage. Now they lived in a two-room shanty. He had played on these docks, met the river merchants. There were good memories in these waters. But not enough to keep him around.

He maneuvered the canoe to the dock, lashed it, climbed onto the landing. His shack was nearby, through a line of cottonwood trees. He hurried there, crept to the riverside door and into the back room where he slept on the floor. If his father was home, he'd be passed out from drinking the previous night.

Enio gathered his few possessions into a rough woolen sack—his meager clothing, an extra ball of fishing twine. As he grabbed an old wooden comb, the last thing he had of his mother, the floorboards creaked. Before he could turn, bony hands grabbed his wrists.

"There's my boy!" Tarley was awake. And he was sober.

"Let go!" Enio squirmed. The comb fell to the floor. "I'm done with you!"

His father spun him around. "Yeah, I'll let you go. Straight to the abbey."

Confused, Enio stopped struggling. "What?"

"Them monks got me up this morning, said there'd been, what was it, an *irregularity* at your Lustering. Something about that boy's sleeve afire. They want to talk to you."

Enio hid his growing worry with a sneer. "So what do you care?"

Tarley released one of Enio's wrists but held the other tightly. He lifted a pouch from his own pocket, prompting the tinkle of coins. "Five silvers, that's what I care. Don't make no trouble. I can carry you hog-tied just as easy."

He yanked Enio into the front room, past a stained bunk near a table cluttered with bottles. It all smelled of liquor. A candle still burned in a wall sconce near the front door.

"Enius Marius, huh?" His father pulled him toward the door. "Where did you get that one?"

"Are you kidding? It's like Ma's name!"

"Maria? Boys don't take girl names. I could have done you something better."

Enio couldn't help but laugh. Parents often chose their children's Enlightened names. But the only things he'd gotten lately from his father were a roof and the occasional meal. Nothing had been the same after the man overturned their wagon, killing his mother and rearranging Enio's smile. That's when it had all gone bad, all the drunks, the beatings, everything.

And Enio was done.

As they passed the wall sconce, Enio invoked. He reached with his free hand and flicked the flame, sending its small blue heart flying to the cot. The sheets, marinated in liquor, caught.

"Damn you, boy!" His father threw him to the floor and ran to the fire.

Enio scrambled away, grabbed his bag and ran out the back.

Tarley bellowed after him, "You damn river rat! When I get ahold of you, there'll be nothing *left* for the abbey!"

Enio raced through the trees. He wasn't afraid of the monks. He'd been in trouble with them more times than he could count. But Gorlo's family had pull, and they'd cause him no end of trouble with his new life. Better to avoid the whole damn thing. He'd go downriver to Bishop's Landing. Then to the Silver Sea. Hop a ship. Sail the world. Everyone would forget he ever existed.

He reached his canoe. Besides, if the abbey caught him now— if they used a Confessor—they'd find out why he flicked his candle during the ceremony. They'd find out about Par.

Throwing his bag into the little boat, he slipped off the rope and jumped in. He floated in the cloudy green water, looking downstream to freedom and the rest of the big wide world.

Par would be fine as long as he didn't let his conscience out. As long as he kept up his lying. As long...

As long as he didn't say something stupid.

Enio shook his head. "Crap."

He spun the *Sea Dog* upstream, back to the abbey, and paddled as fast as his arms could pump.

Chapter Six

PAR WOKE TO distant chanting. He lay on the cot in the workroom, soaking up the rhythms and the tones. The music was sweeter than he'd ever remembered. Everyone else had gone, including Enio. His friend was like that, and Par would see him when he'd see him.

Now it was time to step into a new life.

He swung his feet over the edge of the cot, had a good stretch and grabbed a fistful of leftover cheese. As he nibbled his breakfast, he took a stairway back to the western hall. Close by the robing room, he found the set of narrow steps that climbed to the bell tower. The monks were at morning prayer, so no one would stop him from sneaking up.

He held his Lustering robe away from his ankles and jogged the two hundred and forty-seven steps—he'd counted them many times—and emerged panting at the top, sending a flock of pigeons fluttering into the morning sunlight.

Par loved the bell tower, his own private balcony to the world. A large bell and several smaller ones hung from the rafters, their ropes dropping through openings in the floor. Panoramic views opened between the stone columns that rose from the parapets to support the roof. The abbey stretched out below his feet: the walls and corner towers; the south gardens; the dining hall near the residence of the Prior and Abbot; the monk's dormitories. He'd been in them all. He'd *cleaned* them all. The stained-glass windows were collecting pigeon droppings again. The pigeons were the first thing he wouldn't miss. How many hours had he spent scrubbing off their crap?

Still, he hadn't climbed this tower for the view. Here he was alone, with no one telling him what to do—or judging him. Par had been slipping up here whenever he needed to clear his head, get a break from his worries. Even to practice his sigils. The monks said the closer you were to the gods, the stronger your invocations. Well, this was as high as he could get.

Par removed a chipped, loose brick from the bottom of the low stone wall. Inside the niche he had hidden a small candle. He set it on the eastern ledge in the bright morning sun. Like dozens of times before, he tried to invoke it to flame. Maybe with his Lustering, something had changed. Maybe he could invoke. In fact, maybe he *had* invoked. Maybe Enio hadn't lit his candle after all.

He tried three times, the same way he'd done it in the temple, except without Enio.

No flame.

So much for *that* theory.

Just down the road lay Par's hometown of St. Livius, spreading out to the south and east. People and carts and horses had begun their early routines. His town was growing into a city, with a thriving river commerce and the prosperity granted to the entire country of Eloria in the twenty years since the Grey Wars with Arcana. His gaze traveled over the distant buildings and statues and parks, soft and blooming in the early light. Sometimes he would try to find his own home from up here, off by the east canals near his father's smithy. He'd never succeeded.

After enjoying the view a little longer, he moved to the west side of the tower. The peaks of the Ult Mountains, so cold only the day before, looked friendly now, as if welcoming him into a larger world. The Urdel woodlands skirted their feet, dark forests stretching for endless leagues along the far hills. Many stories—probably to scare children—told of their strange beasts and ghouls and forest witches. He'd fantasied about exploring them anyway. Now, there was nothing to stop him.

Boats appeared on the river below, going about their business like the carts on the roads. Par picked up the candle. With all the strength he could muster, he cast it from the tower and over the walls to the river. As he followed its arc, he noticed a canoe splashing up to the landing. A figure jumped out and ran across the docks.

Enio?

Enio was his best friend, even if the guy never said it. But Par's father had a point: Enio might not be the best student, but he was a genius at getting into trouble. Par took in one more deep drink of the panorama, one more full breath of the free, elevated air, then left the tower to see what was going on. He still wore his Lustering robe, and when he reached the bottom of the stairs, he went first to the robing room for his everyday clothing. As he was lacing his shirt, Enio poked his head in.

"Enio, what—"

"Shh! There's a problem." Enio paced the floor and explained the run-in with his father.

Par felt the blood drain from his face. "That was you, Gorlo's sleeve?"

"Yeah. On my first try, that meat muffin moved his arm in the way."

"Oh crap, Enio! What do we do?"

"Nothing. I needed to tell you, so if they ask, you don't say something stupid. Tell them you don't know anything. If they try to stick it on me, let them. I'm leaving, so it won't matter."

Par nodded, his panic ebbing. "You'll be all right?"

"Sure. It only moves up my schedule." Enio looked around. "I guess that's it. I'm gonna cut."

Par didn't know what to say. The last time they were together in this room, he'd tried to thank Enio for his help, but never got out the words. He'd missed the opportunity again when they were with Buckets and John. This time, he went to his friend and hugged him. Enio flinched, and Par backed off.

"You did it, Enio. You saved me. How can I ever—"

"Just don't screw this up." Enio beamed his broken smile and turned to go.

A sudden sadness at this parting, so much sooner than expected, threatened to overwhelm Par. He forced a smile to hide it. "You think the gods really do hate me?"

"That wasn't the gods," Enio said over his shoulder. "Everything was going great until Gorlo's fat ass blocked my fire-fly."

"Is that so?" came a voice.

Par jerked to the sound. Prior Dogam stood in the temple passage.

"Uh…" Enio said.

"You were saying something about a fire-fly?"

Enio lunged toward the door.

"*Stop!*"

It was as if Enio had smacked into a wall. The invocation hit Par's mind too, and he couldn't have moved if his life depended on it.

"It's fortunate I've run into you." The Prior hung up his white chanting vestments, uncovering a common brown robe. "There's a serious concern regarding the ceremony, and we have a strict procedure to follow. It mostly involves Enio, but I think now I'd like you to come along as well, Par."

Two monks emerged from the passage. The Prior turned to them. "Brother Vortis, Brother Marcus, please escort these two newly Lustered to the Chapter Room. And ensure they stay there until I gather the other parties for a little chat."

As the Prior finished, the tower bell tolled, the signal to everyone within the abbey, and those in the town, that the hour of prayer and supplication was at an end. It was time to face the new day.

And hope that the gods had listened.

CHAPTER SEVEN

ONCE PAR COULD move, the monks escorted him and Enio down the hall to the Chapter Room, a lavish chamber reserved for important meetings and esteemed guests.

"Wait here," said Brother Marcus. The two monks closed the high double doors on their way out.

A long wooden table surrounded by tall, red velvet chairs took up most of the space. Simple benches set among gleaming cabinets lined the walls. Tapestries, presenting scenes from the sacred canons, swept beneath high decorative windows. Portraits of historical figures and of the abbey's more generous patrons filled the spaces between.

Everything was immaculate, and a flowery perfume floated in the air. Par had spent more time here than he cared to remember, scrubbing the polished latticed floors, and hanging on ladders outside the windows to clean off the pigeon droppings. Enio called the work "getting extra holy points." Right now, Par felt anything but holy.

Enio stared at the geometric frescos on the ceiling. "Kind of overkill for a little chat."

"Gorlo's father likes this room." Par sank onto a bench, feeling tiny in the chamber's splendor. "He meets in here when he visits the Abbot."

Enio sat next to him. "Remember, they can't prove anything. It's Gorlo's word against mine."

Par pointed to a large portrait of Gorlo's father.

Enio frowned.

"This is my fault," Par said. "I'll tell them I put you up to it."

"Don't be stupid."

"Their Confessor will find out."

"They'll only bring in a Confessor if they don't hear what they want to hear. And what they want to hear is that Enio is a rotten little sucking mud-maggot."

"But—"

"Listen," Enio said, "if they think I only did this to mess with Gorlo, they'll probably take away my Lustriance for another season, make me work the fields, or help around with Buckets and John. Whatever it is, the more I'm away from home, the better I'll like it. And if it makes you feel better, you can sneak me beer sometimes."

Par nodded slowly. "I'd do that."

"But if you run your tongue, I'll still get the same, your secret will be out, and everything we went through means nothing. And I won't get any free beer, see?"

It made sense. Par had hoped he'd be done with all the lies after he was Lustered. But anything was better than a Reckoning. "I'll make this up to you."

"You better."

Par smiled.

They waited, wandering the room, peeking into the cabinets. They even discussed stacking furniture to escape out the windows, but the panes were too high, probably to prevent nosey monks from eavesdropping. At last, the doors pushed open. Brother Vortis and Brother Marcus stepped in. They stood to either side while Prior Dogam, along with the Father Abbot, entered the room.

Gorlo followed with his father Festuvius, one of the richest men in St. Livius, and clearly supportive of the same diet as Gorlo. Par's father came in last, his face dark, his eyes locked on Par.

Par's stomach dropped. He hadn't expected his father.

Prior Dogam helped the Abbot to the far end of the table. The Prior motioned to two empty chairs along one side. "Par, Enio, please."

Par joined Enio at the table. Gorlo and Festuvius sat opposite. Par's father, his arms crossed and his jaw tight, sat next to Festuvius.

The Prior spoke. "Tarley is not yet here. But since Enio is now Lustered, I am permitted to ask, may we start before his father arrives?"

"Definitely," Enio said.

"Very good. Gorlorius may speak first."

"Go ahead, Gorlo," Festuvius prompted in a deep, smooth voice.

Gorlo filled his lungs and opened his mouth, but before he could get a word out, Enio spoke instead.

"Look, I did it. Gorlo was messing with Buckets and I got mad. So I punched him, and I guess I was still mad at the altar and…" Enio shrugged.

The Father Abbot, his bushy eyebrows rising in two white peaks, leaned forward and cleared his throat. "Am I to understand this was an emotional misfire?"

"Yeah," Enio beamed. "That!"

The Abbot started to laugh, then cough. When he recovered, he said, "I'm sorry. But do you know what I've just realized?"

"What's that?" asked Prior Dogam a little impatiently.

"We've never had this problem with the girls."

Par smiled, but after a glance at his father's cold grimace, sobered.

The Prior rubbed his chin. "I suppose emotions can—"

"He's lying!" Gorlo pointed at Enio. "He did it *after* his candle was lit. He did something to his flame. It jumped at me!"

"That doesn't sound like a misfire." The Prior turned again to Enio. "And it has the ring of truth. I don't believe someone of your age or ability could have invoked the fire sigil and ignited Gorlo's sleeve without physically touching him. But earlier today, you mentioned a fire-fly?"

Enio had become very interested in the table's woodwork.

"I see." Prior Dogam shifted his chilly gaze to Par. "Do you know anything of this, Parynius?"

Par hesitated. Enio knocked his ankle under the table.

Par shook his head.

"Very well." The Prior addressed the group. "I am still not satisfied we have the whole story. Perhaps a Confessor—"

"All *right*," Enio barked. "I was mad, and I did it on purpose. Is that what you want to hear?"

"That is, in truth, what I did *not* want to hear. You deliberately caused the flame from your Lustering candle to jump onto Gorlo's robe, do I have that right?"

"Yeah, I said—"

"Using this fire-fly invocation of yours?"

Enio nodded.

"Father Abbot," the Prior kept his eyes on Enio, "do you know of this invocation?"

The Father Abbot had fixed his eyes on the table and did not look up. "Perhaps it is not important. Some derivation of…" He trailed off with a frail gesture of one hand.

Prior Dogam waited a moment, then directed his voice toward the door. "Brother Marcus, please bring over a sheet of parchment, along with pen and ink."

The monk retrieved these from a cabinet and placed them in front of the Prior, who pushed them toward Enio. "Draw its sigil."

"I'm no good at drawing."

"Do your best."

Enio took up the pen and drew a crude shape, like a partial fire sigil, but stretching into a second, smaller spiral.

The Prior waited until he had finished. "Pass it here."

Enio pushed the parchment across the table.

The Prior placed his hands on either side of the parchment, studying it for what seemed an eternity. The Father Abbot took a glance, caught his breath and turned away.

Finally, the Prior said, "I am no Sigil Master, but this is wrong."

Enio threw up his hands. "I said I couldn't—"

"That's not what I mean. Its compass and gyre… What form of worship did your beseechment take for this invocation?"

Enio looked away. "I don't remember."

"Indeed. You don't remember because there wasn't any."

Par always assumed Enio beseeched Oä for his fire-fly, the same as for a normal fire sigil, though Enio had never said. Even when it wasn't one specific god, there was still a general beseechment—without that, no one's sigils would enlighten. And Enio's glory, when he used that sigil, had always been barely visible. Pale. Not golden at all.

A new fear clawed at Par's heart.

The Prior's voice came steely. "Who bestowed this upon you?"

Enio shrugged. "Some guy on the river."

Prior Dogam slammed his hand on the table. "*This* is why we have the Rule! *This* is why sigils are bestowed *only* by the priests, or consecrated delegates, like your parents!"

Par froze. Enio's voice cracked. "But—"

"Son," the Prior yelled down at him, "conjuring from the Profana is a crime!"

Par gaped. *Enio, what have you done?*

Prior Dogam composed himself. "The Profana is anathema to

everything which we believe. It comprises the forbidden incantations used by the sorcerers of Arcana, the enemies of the gods."

Enio muttered, "Well, I didn't know…"

The Prior leaned back in his chair, his fingers steepled, the muscles in his face iron tight. "I don't understand how you even managed it. Regardless, you have not the faintest idea the trouble you are in. There is not enough parchment in this abbey to set forth every penance that your atonement will require, Enius Marius."

Par heard Enio gulp. His own throat threatened to close up.

"If you boys would only learn to mind the Rule." Prior Dogam shook his head. "It's there to protect you. To protect everyone."

A knock sounded at the door.

"Yes?" called the Prior.

Brother Gaius poked into the room. "Excuse me, but Tarley—"

Enio's father pushed his way inside. "You found him? Whatever he's done, I ain't paying for it."

"We were just finishing, Tarley." The Prior rose from his chair. The others stood too. "I'll discuss it with you alone, but Enio will be spending all his time around the abbey for a while."

"He will? What about me? He's got work to do in the warehouses and—"

"Yeah?" Enio came out of his chair. He lifted his Lustering medal from under his shirt and held it out before his father. His words were bold and confident, like the Enio Par knew. "You don't have any more say about what I do."

"Well, we'll just see—"

"Stop!" barked the Prior. It wasn't an invocation that made everyone turn back, but the voice of deadly authority.

"Enio is correct," he said carefully. "He is now Lustered, a recognized adult in our community."

Tarley frowned.

Prior Dogam sat again and motioned to the others. They

hesitated, then returned to their seats. Tarley remained standing near the door. Enio's face reflected the new worry that Par felt.

The Prior continued, with the least amount of warmth Par had ever heard come from a person's mouth. "He became an adult the instant he invoked his Lustering candle. This means Enio was an adult when he performed his godless fire-fly. Not only did he conjure this unholy sigil as an adult, he did it before our high altar itself."

Par searched the faces around the table, but the Prior's words seemed to have frozen the air. No one dared breathe. Par broke the silence. "What does this mean? What are you going to do to Enio?"

"For a child to conjure such a thing, and do it in ignorance, he might in time labor toward atonement. But Enius Marius is not a boy. He is Lustered, and subject to all the laws and freedoms of Eloria."

"And?" Par rose from his chair.

"Par, enough," his father hissed, strict and urgent.

"And?" Par shouted.

Prior Dogam looked only at Enio. "He must therefore be tried as an adult. Tragically, the Rule specifies but one sentence for such heresy. Execution."

Chapter Eight

EXECUTION.

Par's muscles, his thoughts, crumbled like ash. He collapsed in his chair. The Prior's black words hung in the perfumed air with the stink of a corpse.

Enio sat unmoving, the blood gone from his face.

Gorlo's father leaned forward. "Execution?"

The Father Abbot laid a pale, freckled hand on the Prior's arm. "I realize you are administering the matter, but this all seems a bit of a technicality. Enio is only an adult in name."

"I am as distressed as you, Cornelius. But Enio is an adult *in fact*. He must face trial before the town's Judges."

"Surely—"

The Prior removed his arm from under the Abbot's hand, "The capital itself would demand it. The Rule is the Rule, and the gods make no provisions for the technicalities of men."

The Father Abbot sighed and retreated into silence.

"Prior Dogam," Gorlo's father spoke again. "This seems overly severe. Perhaps we could withdraw—"

"But *Dad!*" Gorlo whined.

"Shut it, boy."

Gorlo slouched, pouting.

"The issue no longer involves Gorlorius," said the Prior. "But if Enius is found guilty, supplication to the Fondiscate, to commute the penalty to a life of bound service, may be possible."

"A life…" Enio didn't finish.

Par closed his eyes. There was no choice anymore. "Wait." It was barely audible. He could barely breathe.

Gorlo and his father whispered together. Par's father mumbled something about right and wrong paths.

Par looked up. "Listen to me." His voice came cracked and dry.

Prior Dogam spoke to the Father Abbot. "I'll contact the town in the morning. I'd like the others to remain available as witnesses, though with what we've heard—"

Par slammed his fist onto the table. "Just stop!" The conversation halted. Everyone looked.

"You don't understand. Enio was helping *me*."

"You?" said the Prior.

The words burned in Par's throat. "This is all my fault. I… can't invoke. I never could."

"Son—" his father began.

"I asked him to help me, Dad. Even at home, Enio was by the window, helping me light my candles."

"Par," said the Prior, "you're telling me that Enio lit your Lustering candle from a dozen feet away?"

"Fifteen," Enio mumbled.

Par waited for his father to yell. To scream.

Instead, his voice came soft, resigned, and that hurt so much more. "I suspected, I mean I had hoped… We've done nothing but try to help you, son. And you—you've done nothing but lie?"

"I've done *everything* you ever asked," Par choked out the words. "But you were going to have me Reckoned!"

Edwin fell silent. His proud shoulders sagged, and the countenance of a capable smith became that of a weak, tired man. His stare was glassy, like the dead's.

Par's eyes welled up. He couldn't stand it. He sniffled and turned to the Prior. "So, this isn't Enio's fault. You can't—"

"Par," the Prior said. "You did not light your candle, therefore you are not Lustered. You can take none of the responsibility for his actions."

"Prior Dogam?" Edwin asked, a tremor in his voice.

"Yes?"

"Would you take our boy, get him help? We've failed with him. And in his… condition… we can't have him around the baby."

A knife stabbed into Par's heart. The thread of hope he'd clung to for so many years severed. He was falling.

"Yes, Edwin, I think that would be best."

Par's father stood and walked toward the door.

"Dad…" Par reached out. Tears burned down his face.

His father paused, his back to the room. When he spoke, he seemed on the verge of sobbing. "I'm sorry, Par. The gods be with you."

"Mom—" Par tried desperately. "She won't let you—"

"And thank you Prior Dogam." Edwin cleared his throat twice, then spoke over his shoulder as he disappeared. "His mother will have to understand. But I need to get back. I promised to… to watch the baby."

It struck Par like a bolt. Was that the reason his parents had another child so late, so recently? They must have suspected he was sick, that he was "broken." Now they had a replacement. Par's last hope went out like a storm-snuffed candle.

The Prior addressed the monks. "Brother Marcus, are any of the brethren doing penance in the south tower?"

"No, Prior."

"Very good. Please confine Enius Marius and Parynius Ig… and Par there for the night. We will handle what needs handling in the morning, and I will send word to the capital to expect a new candidate for a Reckoning."

Enio's father spoke. "That boy's been nothin' but trouble." Then more softly, "I get to keep the money, right?"

"Yes, Tarley,"

"Well, then," he raised his voice. "He's *your* problem now."

The monks led Par and Enio away. Enio struggled a few times, but was no match for the two men. Par choked back his tears. Everything passed in a blur. He was too numb to think. His legs lasted long enough to carry him across the grounds, up the stairs of the south tower, and to the room at the top, where he and Enio were locked inside.

CHAPTER NINE

ENIO KICKED THE heavy door and cursed under his breath. He went to one of two small, barred windows set in opposite walls. "Can't quite see the docks."

Par collapsed onto a pile of straw. "Gods, Enio. If I could change places with you—"

"Not sure I would." Enio crossed to the window that overlooked the town.

"Do you have to be so damn noble?"

"Noble, nothing. If they Reckon you, you might wind up like Buckets."

Par grimaced and took his point.

Enio strained to peer below the window. "Did you know there's a graveyard down there?"

"Yeah, parts of it are for poor people." As soon as Par said it, he wished he hadn't.

His friend tugged the bars. "If we could loosen these—"

"Then what? The drop is fifty feet onto gravestones and pointy statues."

Enio continued gazing out the small opening. Then he muttered, "How do you suppose they'll do it?"

"Do what?"

"Kill me."

Par's mind froze.

Enio continued, "I hope it's not burning."

"But… they could commute it, they said…" Par was grasping. "Maybe…"

"Life as a slave? I'd rather die. I hope it's quick. They do drownings sometimes. At least I'll get to see the river—"

"Shut up!" Par staggered to his feet, pushed past Enio and yanked on the bars. "Just shut up!"

Enio gripped his shoulders from behind, "Hey, easy!"

Par's rage seeped away. He slumped to the floor, his back against the wall, his face between his knees. Enio dropped beside him. They sat quietly, the only sounds their breathing and the cooing of pigeons on the roof.

At last, Enio spoke. "Hey, Par."

"What?" Par mumbled.

"Remember where we met?"

Par did. "On the abbey docks."

"Yeah. I finished unloading barrels from the cooper and headed inside."

Par raised his gaze from the dirty floor. "I was out sweeping, and I asked what you wanted."

"I said I was thirsty, and I wanted a drink."

"And I told you there was clean water inside on the right."

"And I said thanks."

Par nodded. "And went left."

"To the brewery."

Par looked at his friend. "By the time I got there, you had your mouth wrapped around a tap."

"Then Brother Gaius came in."

Despite himself, Par grinned a little. "Jumping mad."

"But," Enio said, "you covered for me. You said you told me the wrong way."

Par had.

Enio continued. "And I *know* you remember that time with Buckets."

Par smiled more. "Do you have to bring *that* up?"

Enio's face cracked into his wide, broken grin. "You came screaming down the hall like a chicken on fire. 'He's gonna kill me!'"

"I did not."

"You did!"

"He had a sword."

Enio laughed. "He had a broom!"

Par laughed, too. Once they settled down, he said, "That was the first time I really met Buckets. I'd seen him around, but you got me to talk to him."

"And you helped me get into the Lustering classes when no one else gave a damn."

Neither smiled anymore.

Enio went on, "So, don't go saying this is all on you. No one tells me what to do. We've helped each other when we've needed it. It's always been a fair trade."

After another silence, Enio got up. "Anyway, who do you think the gods hate more now?"

"This isn't a contest." Par meant it as a joke, and Enio chuckled. But once he'd said it, it didn't sound funny.

Enio moved back to the window, commenting on things he saw in the town. Soon, the thickness of the walls and the locked wooden door and the barred windows pressed again on Par's spirit.

At one point, Enio said, "I think I can see your home."

Par still sat on the floor, his arms curled around his legs. "Not anymore," he whispered.

✳

Par's emotional exhaustion landed hard. He slept much of the remaining day with a break at sunset for bread and water. He awoke after dark. A shaft of moonlight fell through the west window onto Enio, who snored softly.

All my fault.

The words wheeled through Par's head like vultures in a cadaverous sky.

Enio's in this because of me.

The moon's pale light brushed the cold stone floor. Par wasn't sure when he next slept. A single strike of the tower bell, probably the ten o'clock, marked the closing of the abbey's day. After another restless span, a further peal rang out. The midnight bells would follow, tolling a full twelve times.

At last, in the endless night, that sequence began.

The echo from the first bell faded into the darkness. Par heard a metallic clunk. The heavy door squeaked open. Buckets pushed his way into the room.

Both boys leapt up, Par never happier to see anyone in his life. "Buck—"

Buckets raised a finger to his lips. The hulking man closed the door and stepped into the moonlight.

"What—" Par began again.

And again Buckets gestured him to silence. Something seemed strange about him. The second midnight bell tolled.

Buckets moved to the window above the cemetery. He planted his sturdy legs against the floor and ran his large hands over the masonry. The third bell rang out. He grunted and strained. Sounds of cracking came from the stone as a glory kindled around the man's head. Par couldn't believe his eyes. Buckets was invoking!

The big man eased off as the third peal died away. On the fourth bell, he threw his weight at the wall. The portal plus several feet of surrounding masonry exploded outward, leaving a gaping hole.

Buckets turned back, smiling, his eyes sparkling like diamonds.

Par was speechless. Enio ran to the breach and looked out.

The fifth bell struck. Buckets lay his monstrous hand on Enio's shoulder, turning him around. A smile stretched across Enio's face. "Buckets, how—"

On the sixth strike, Buckets lifted Enio as if in a bear hug. With no warning, he tossed him through the hole and out of the tower. Enio flailed as he disappeared into the darkness, his yells drowned by the reverberating bell.

Par's heart nearly stopped. "Buckets, no!"

The seventh bell tolled. The man turned.

Par backed away. "You don't know what you're doing. We're too high!"

The eighth bell sounded. Buckets kept coming.

By the ninth peal, Par had backed against the far wall. Why was Buckets doing this? Had their friend come to end their misery?

On the tenth bell, Buckets snatched him up.

"No... no..." Par struggled, but Buckets hauled him to the breach.

The eleventh bell tolled. As it echoed away, Par heard something he'd never heard in his life.

"Trust me."

Buckets had spoken.

Par stopped fighting and met the man's eyes. They were warm and reassuring. On the final bell, Buckets hurled him out of the tower and into the void.

Par's stupor broke, but too late. The air rushed through his hair. He clawed at the darkness, but there was nothing to grab. He squeezed his eyes shut and waited for the end.

But the end didn't come. Instead, something soft stopped him. He opened his eyes. He was floating in mid-air, several feet above the gravestones. Enio stood on the ground below. Some invisible hand lowered Par to the ground, unharmed.

They stood among the many headstones and obelisks of the abbey's outer cemetery. Behind Enio, sharply outlined on the surface of a tall, flat monument, glowed a luminous figure made of patches of spectral light.

Par's eyes widened.

Enio took his arm. "It's the Father Abbot. He's come to help."

"Father Abbot?" Par said, trying to wrap his mind around everything. The apparition resembled a stained-glass saint. "Are you… dead?"

"A reasonable assumption," replied the old man with a voice that seemed to come from a crystal bellows. "However no, not yet."

Chapter Ten

THE IMAGE OF the Father Abbot glittered on the monument as if painted by rainbows. He pointed farther down the high abbey walls. "Look."

In a window overlooking the parapets stood a figure leaning on a staff, a golden aura silhouetting its body.

Par turned again to the vision before him. "You're a reflection?"

"Close enough." The Abbot's voice shimmered like wind chimes. "The abbey is distracted with midnight beseechments, but the watches will soon be out. We have precious little time."

Whatever invisible birds had brought Par safely to the ground now seemed trapped in his stomach. He glanced anxiously around.

"And I must apologize for the Prior's inflexibility," the Abbot continued. "Oh, I don't believe him a cruel man, but he's an up-and-comer in the Hierarchy. Everything by the book. He, in effect, runs the abbey now. All that's left for me is a bit of teaching, and managing the topiary."

The old man fell silent a moment. "What was I saying?"

"We have precious little time," Par prompted.

"Quite right. And Enio, I'm afraid the abbey will add the

destruction of property to your crimes." The Abbot motioned to the broken hole in the south tower. Buckets stood in the breach. He saluted, and stepped back into the darkness.

"But I didn't—" Enio began.

Par interrupted. "Before he tossed me, I heard Buckets speak."

"A temporary condition," said the Abbot. "Sadly, it will soon pass."

"You did something to him?" Par asked.

"With his permission. His only regret is not being able to spend time with you and his brother while his mind remains elevated. We both agreed that was best."

Par worried for their big friend. "Will he get in trouble for helping us?"

"Don't worry, son. He hasn't been able to invoke in years, and the ability will pass with his memory. Even under a Confessor he'd be unable to provide any evidence of his help." The Abbot peered at Enio. "But a boy who's been trading in strange sigils on the river? It will be easy to accept that Enio had a few more invocations stashed away to facilitate your escape."

Enio smiled. "That's pickles and cream with me."

The Abbot glowed with pride. "We timed it with the midnight bells. I needed to catch each of you the instant you were out. One on the six, one on the twelve. Clever, don't you think?"

"Brilliant," Enio said.

Par nodded. But there was something he needed to know before they ran off to gods knew where.

He stepped closer to the image. "Father Abbot, can you tell me why I can't invoke? Am I cursed? Am I... unworthy?" The word left a bitter taste.

The Abbot squinted. "That is the question. First, let me assure you that while the average young person has no end of things for which they could atone"—he glanced at Enio, who remained expressionless—"the gods have better things to do than decide who can light up a fire sigil. I am convinced they are not the reason behind your problem."

Par wasn't sure if he believed this or not.

The Father Abbot spoke to Enio. "Would you keep sentinel? I have something I must discuss with Parynius."

Par saw the same question in his friend's eyes that must be in his own, but he nodded to Enio. Enio shrugged and slipped away among the headstones.

The Abbot turned again to Par. "I think we can rule out the usual reasons, such as exhaustion or a passing illness. Nor are you feeble of mind. I assume you have never attempted a forbidden sigil?"

"Never."

The Abbot's face seemed to darken. "Par, would you allow me to briefly enter your mind?"

Par had been the subject of a Confessor sigil once before—when the abbey searched for whoever had carved obscene words on the north gate—but that sigil was only for truth-seeing. This sounded disturbingly more intrusive. Still, if it might reveal his problem…

He swallowed and nodded.

The spectral image of the Father Abbot seemed to extrude off the surface of the monument. His eyes burned wide and bright with some new fire. And when the Abbot spoke, his voice came like a command from the gods. "Tell me truly, Parynius, do *you* know why you cannot invoke?"

It didn't matter whether the Abbot was invoking to see a deception, or compelling Par to speak the truth. Par would have answered the same. He met the Abbot's extraordinary gaze and felt his own eyes tear up. "By all the gods, Father Abbot, I do not."

The intensity increased. Par's most private self was being spread out. His thoughts, his hopes and fears, lay open for the world to see. His soul was naked in the night, caught without shelter in a winter blast. He shivered and dropped to the ground, trying to cover himself. *Is this a Reckoning?*

When he felt he must cry out in despair, a light reached through his winter. With it came a friendly warmth that pushed away the cold.

No, Par. The thought came from the Abbot. *This is only a Reckoning's barest threshold.*

The intensity faded, and the presence retreated. Par was on his knees, sucking in the night air, his palms pressed against the hard ground. Tears streamed down his face.

"Forgive me," came the gentle voice of the Abbot. "There was no time to explain the procedure's depth."

Still trembling, Par staggered to his feet and dried his eyes, thankful that Enio was not around to see.

The image spoke again from the monument, dimmer and somehow wilted. "I searched as deeply as I dared. And I saw—"

Hooooahhh. Hooooahhh. The sound of a sick owl drifted from the tombstones.

The Father Abbot raised his eyes. "Good gods. What unnatural—"

Par pushed through his indignity. "It's Enio. But what did you find?"

"I'm not certain. For an instant… a shadow near your soul."

"A curse?" Par gasped.

Enio reappeared and pointed to the north tower. A light shone atop the wall.

"We're out of time," said the Abbot. "Par, a Reckoning can be a beneficial medicant. But something in that ministry has changed since my time in the capital, particularly their interest in curses. I don't know what they did to Tommy, but he's not alone. Nevertheless, I believe a Sigil Master is your best hope for answers."

The light on the wall disappeared.

"Then what do I do?" Par urged.

"You must flee this place. Seek a man—a merchant—named Alexander Vex. He will lead you to a Sigil Master outside the Rule of Eloria. Look in the city of Banes in the Borderlands. Tell him I sent you."

"Leave Eloria?" Par's jaw dropped.

Enio smiled. "Leave Eloria."

"This land is no longer safe, for either of you."

Flee his country? It hit Par like a brick. He couldn't invoke! How would he survive? His thoughts reeled. Should he submit to the Reckoning after all? If it changed him—if he were no longer Par, or if it left him like Buckets—maybe his family would take care of him. The idea he could go back *home* nearly restarted his tears.

Two new lights appeared, this time on the grounds outside the wall.

"Someone's coming," Enio said.

Par stared at the lights. He could shout, run to them. Then he'd be in the abbey's hands, and he wouldn't have to run anymore.

The terror of the Reckoning, however, would not relent. It strangled the shout in his throat.

The lanterns started toward them.

"Let's get out of here," Enio hissed.

Par glanced again at the image of the Father Abbot, shifting panes of delicate glass on the flat stone. Par felt like glass, too. A move in the wrong direction and he would shatter.

Voices came from the lights. The watch moved faster.

Enio yanked Par's sleeve. "Come on!"

He turned to Enio, and his friend's face made the decision. Par was responsible for Enio's crime, no matter what the Prior said. Surrendering wouldn't change that. Maybe this Alexander Vex could help them both.

As Par started off with Enio, he addressed the dimming countenance on the monument. "Thank you, Father Abbot."

The crystal voice came now as a wheeze. "Hurry boys. I fear I need a long rest—though I don't think the Prior will mind having me out of the way a while. The gods be with you, Enius Marius and Parynius Ignatius." The image faded.

Par ran with Enio through the cemetery. They circled the south tower and raced into the moonlight. The hill dropped to the river. Lights flashed above as the watch invoked their lanterns and sent out strong, straight beams. But the boys made it to the docks, and into the *Sea Dog*.

They floated silently with the current. Shouts faded in the night. The canoe drifted down the Greening to the southern edge of town. Par watched the lights there as long as he could—the lights of the place where he'd been born and lived his whole life.

His hand went to his chest, to his Lustering medal. He gripped the last thing he had of his home and his family, and the reminder of his unworthiness before the gods.

Then the lights were gone.

PART TWO

FLIGHT TO BANES

Chapter Eleven

THAT FIRST NIGHT on the Greening, Par jerked awake to every croak and hoot. He ducked whenever the canoe passed a riverside shack where a late candle burned or a restless horse neighed. At last, the eastern sky glowed with the dawn. Their boat had lodged in a clump of reeds along the western bank. Even with his best friend huddled before him, Par had never felt so alone.

He nudged Enio. "You awake?"

Enio yawned and sat up. To the west, wild fields swept to rolling hills that darkened with the forests of the Urdel, even to the distant white-capped Ults. Trees blocked the view to the east, but cows lowed somewhere beyond.

Enio jumped to his feet, nearly capsizing the canoe. "We did it!"

Par grabbed the sides. "Hey!"

Enio laughed and settled back. "We've got our Lustering medals. We've got the *Sea Dog*." He threw his arms in the air. "We're free!"

Par forced a grin to hide his anxieties. A water wheel loomed down the left bank. "Where are we?"

"That's Old Winkle's mill. I haven't been much past here, but I'd guess we're two or three days from Bishop's Landing."

"Is that where we're going?"

"That's where the river's going."

It was a very normal scene, and painfully alien. Everything smelled wrong. Even a cricket seemed to chirp out of tune.

Par turned to his friend. "You're handling all this pretty well."

"Why not? We talked about leaving after we were Lustered."

"But to just lose everything…"

Enio shrugged. "The way I see it, there's nothing I have someone can't take. And someone *will* take, sooner or later. It's better not to get attached to things. You set yourself up for misery."

Par nodded.

Enio gestured toward Par's seat plank. "I'm hungry. My bag's under there."

Par tugged out a ragged woolen sack and a bulky leather bag.

His friend pointed at the leather one. "That's not mine."

"From Buckets?" Par unwrapped the ties. "Blankets, food, cups… hunting knives?"

"I'll show you how to use them, city boy."

Par huffed. "I can use a knife." He could—for eating. He withdrew a fist-sized leather pouch. It jingled. He undid the laces. "Money!"

"Money? Let me see."

Par handed it over.

Enio poked through the little bag. "Coppers and silvers. Two, three mitres. Buckets and John are always finding loose change around the abbey." He pulled out a folded slip of pink paper. "And a Cardinal Note."

"A Cardinal Note? How much?"

Enio held it up to the light and gasped. "A hundred! Buckets doesn't have this kind of money."

"Must be from the Father Abbot. By the way, I've never seen invocations like he did last night."

"Me neither. Like a story of the saints."

Par had studied the stories, for all the good it had done him. "Maybe, but mostly light and sound and something to catch us."

"So if I got those sigils I could do them too?"

Par snickered at an image in his mind. "Saint Enio?"

"Has a ring."

"Like a cracked bell."

They both laughed. Par felt better, though he still wasn't ready to tell his friend about the Abbot peeling his mind back like an onion.

Enio tucked the note into the pouch and returned it to Par. "Keep that safe. It's more money than I've seen in my life. What should we do with it?"

Par stuffed the pouch into the larger sack and found a small bundle of dried meat. He removed two strips. A hundred *was* a lot of money. They could pay for new clothes, places to stay, even High healings. Without looking up, he said meekly, "Maybe it's enough to get your teeth fixed."

He waited for his friend to respond. When Enio didn't, Par raised his head.

Enio gave him an absurdly exaggerated smile, the jagged teeth along the side of his mouth bright in the morning sun.

Par smirked and threw a meat strip at him.

Enio caught it. "Nah. Nobody can crack a rocknut like me."

"Whatever we decide, where do we spend it? Won't people be searching for us?"

"Maybe." Enio tore into the dried meat, chewing thoughtfully. "But I know another thing people on the run can use."

"What?"

"Help."

"You know someone at Bishop's Landing?"

"Not exactly." Enio peered down the river. "We'll stay clear of the hamlets and farms and keep to the west bank—there's more weeds there to hide. Tonight, I'll watch for a Chogan barge."

Par raised his eyebrows. "I hope not the people who gave you that Arcanan sigil?"

Enio snorted. "Don't worry. I helped a guy hide out once. He thanked me with the sigil and a few coppers."

This plan sounded sketchier all the time. "We're in enough trouble. Can we afford to get involved with—"

"With who?" For the first time today, Enio wasn't smiling. "People look down their noses at anyone and everything on the river. But they still buy their spices and things, don't they? They still need them to deliver their stuff, load and unload it and keep it dry and say, 'Yes sir' and 'Yes ma'am,' and treat them like the High Fondiscate, don't they?"

Par sighed. "I didn't mean anything."

Enio picked up a paddle and shoved the canoe out of the reeds. "Well, river folk get a reputation sometimes. But they're just people, trying to make their lives like everyone else."

Par grabbed the other paddle. They maneuvered into a good current. Soon, the silence made him uncomfortable. Whenever they stopped speaking, Par thought of home.

He asked, "So, what do we do now?"

"I said I'd watch for the Choga."

"No, I mean, after today, or tonight, or this week. What are we going *to do*?"

"Didn't the Father Abbot tell you to find someone?"

"Yeah. Alexander Vex." Par had burned the name into his memory. "In the Borderlands, in Banes."

"Then I guess that's what you're going to do."

Par hesitated. He hadn't actually asked Enio if he'd come with him to find Vex. "What about you?"

Enio patted the side of his precious canoe. "Me and *Sea Dog*, we're heading to the Silver Sea. The Borderlands are west along the coast. So I guess you're stuck with me a while."

Par relaxed, grateful he wasn't going it alone. "How long to the sea?"

"By canoe—a week, at least."

They rowed quietly after that, past the reeds and beneath the willows that sulked over the cloudy water. Par tried not to think of anything but the river and the steady plunk of the paddles, but scenes of the last day crawled through his head—the Prior's condemnation of Enio's unholy sigil; Par's father giving him up to the abbey; the Abbot's revelation of a "shadow." Could they find this Alexander Vex a whole country away? Would Vex be of any help? Would Par be of any help to Enio?

Well, one thing was certain: Par wouldn't be the one slowing them down. With a bracing breath, he drove his oar hard into the water and thrust the canoe faster.

"Hey," Enio said over his shoulder, "take it easy."

"Why?" Par said. "Don't have the buttons for it?"

"Oh, we'll see who's got the buttons." Enio dug in his paddle and they shot ahead.

Par puffed and panted as they splashed down the river. The workout felt good. His life was forward now, not back.

Chapter Twelve

ALL DAY THEY continued down the river, stopping only to stretch their legs. At sunset, Enio guided them onto a sandbar at the mouth of an inflowing creek. Par broke out their gear and dipped a cup into the murky water. "Is it safe to drink it straight like this?"

"As long as you're careful where you scoop." Enio bit off a piece of jerky. "Want me to clean it?"

Par nodded.

Enio invoked over the cup and stirred with his finger. The tip came out greenish-brown. "Try now."

Par sipped. "Thanks."

Enio wiped his finger on his pants. "That's why they call it the Greening."

After a light meal, Par spread their blankets on the sand.

"Don't get too comfortable," his friend said. "Some boats sail through the night. Let's watch awhile."

Par leaned against the *Sea Dog*, convinced the mosquitos were personally out for his blood. When vessels floated past, the two hid behind the canoe. About an hour into the night, small lights appeared upriver.

Enio got to his feet.

Par reached out. "What—"

"Shh." Enio crept to the lip of the sandbar. "It's a merchant barge. Chogan, I think." The hair on his head began to glow—a weak glory as he invoked in the darkness. He stretched his right arm above his head and snapped three times. Sparks jumped from his fingers. Par had seen this before, like a student learning the fire sigil, but Enio was hardly a beginner.

"What are you doing?" Par whispered.

"River talk."

Three similar sparks flickered from the distant boat's deck.

Enio snapped twice more. "All right, let's go."

They threw their provisions into the canoe. "What was all that?" Par asked.

"The Chogan 'can I get a ride' signal. They're honor-bound to respond—after dark."

"Why only then?"

"A merchant barge isn't licensed as a passenger vessel. So you only ask at night."

They pushed into the river and paddled toward the boat. Par worried again about the reputation of the Choga. He phrased his question delicately. "This *is* a good idea, right?"

"Unless you've got a better one."

The barge approached like a beast of shadow in the night. A stout silhouette called over the deck rail, "Ahoy! Who goes?" Lamplight hit the canoe.

Enio raised his hand high over his head, fingers curled but no sparks this time. "Enio, brother of Iorgas, brother of Terod, brother of Loam."

Par had never heard those names. Was his friend bluffing their way onboard?

Enio whispered, "Lift your arm like mine, but don't wave."

There was no time to ask why. Par raised an arm.

The voice above came again. "Loam, you say? Then Agron welcomes you aboard the *Sweet Carmina*, Enio, brother of the Choga."

A rope ladder clattered over the side. Enio tethered their canoe to corded loops along the hull and spoke quietly before climbing. "The Choga have their own ways. I'll do the talking."

All Par could do was follow. Calloused hands hauled him over the deck rail. In the yellow light of hanging lanterns stood a burly man with shaggy black hair and a full beard strung with beads. Two more bearded men, tall but thinner, loomed nearby.

Enio thrust his arm forward. "Sweet sailings and fair landings, Agron. Thank you for your hospitality."

Agron took it at the elbow. "Aye, family is always welcome. And who might this be?"

"This is Par, brother of Enio."

Brother of Enio? Par's heart picked up a beat. Enio was lying his shirt off.

Agron held his arm to Par. "Sweet sailin's and fair landin's, brother of Enio."

As Par grasped it, Enio patted his back. "It's Par's first time under the hospitality of the Choga."

"Indeed?" Agron leaned down. Par held his breath. But Agron broke into a toothy smile. "Well, you're just in time for our evenin' meal, brother of Enio."

Par allowed himself to breathe. Worried he might violate some protocol, he kept his reply simple. "Thank you, sir."

Lamps hung above the rails—a few at the bow, and others at intervals along the sides, carving circles of light on the deck and around its large central mast. A cabin structure enclosed the entire back third of the vessel. One of the thin men disappeared toward the bow. The other clambered up wooden steps over the cabin.

Agron led to a door near the stairs where a small, curtained window glowed with a cheery light. He pushed opened the door, and before Par could see in, he was hit by such a rush of aromas his head spun. Pungent cinnamon, roasted garlic, sweet grilled onions. He stepped inside, his mouth watering.

The warm, cramped room was full of chattering people busy around a central table. A thin woman with fair hair scuttled from steaming pot to steaming pot along the sideboards. A stout, middle-aged woman with curly brown hair alternated between checking ovens, tossing pans and shooing away two toddlers, one blond boy and a girl with long dark tresses. Three men, one stout like Agron and the others younger but well muscled, carried chests from the cupboards with metal plates and utensils to the table.

Agron closed the door. "Family, we have guests. Enio is a brother of Iorgas, of Terod, and of Loam. And we have the great honor of bein' the first Choga to host his brother, Par."

The little girl let out a meek "Mama?" The fair-haired woman hushed her.

From the back of the cabin, the stout woman hustled up with a large wooden spatula. "Oh, look how small they are! I'll warrant they could use a good meal."

Agron eyed Par up and down. "They do pitch a bit on the young side."

Enio lifted his Lustering medal out of his shirt. "Old enough." He nudged Par.

Par showed his, too. This was his first time using it to pass as a free adult. What if he were challenged?

Agron gave it only the briefest glance. "Aye, old enough." He addressed the others, "First, we must welcome Par to our family."

Par looked to Enio, who nodded with enthusiasm.

Agron found a gourd in a cupboard, popped its cork and poured a syrupy brown liquid into three short wooden cups. He handed one each to Par and Enio.

Enio whispered, "It's insulting if you don't drink it."

Agron held up his cup. "Our family welcomes you aboard, Par brother of Enio, and bids you accept the hospitality of the Choga."

This was Par's first genuine encounter with the world outside St. Livius. He stood straight, determined to get it right. Inside him bloomed that same cheer he'd felt when celebrating his Lustering with John and Buckets. He toasted with the others and took a fast slurp.

His happy feelings imploded.

The vile fluid was the worst thing that had ever been in his mouth—going in or coming out. He squeezed his eyes shut and gagged.

Enio elbowed. "Drink!"

Par swallowed. It oozed down his throat like slime. He took another gulp. Merciful gods—the second time was worse than the first. It tasted like some putrid, rotten...

He gagged. His stomach lurched. *I'm going to vomit in front of everybody.* Par sent up a quick prayer for the Chogans not to rob him before throwing him over the side.

All at once he was surrounded by whoops and cheers.

Par opened his eyes.

"Enough, enough!" Agron laughed in gulping breaths. The two other cups sat on the table, still full. Enio was rolling on the flooring, laughing too.

Agron bellowed to the room, "If our hospitality is good enough for Par, brother of Enio, he's good enough for us."

Enio struggled to his feet. "They do it to everyone the first time," he gasped. "I got down four swallows before puking. Losing it doesn't matter as long as you accepted their hospitality."

"Aye, Enio," Agron said, and ruffled Par's hair.

Par tried to smile but only managed a grimace. "What in the purple hells *was* that?"

Agron emptied the cups back into the gourd. "Fermented mud-maggot juice."

"Fer—" Par's stomach heaved again. He took a deep breath and swallowed.

The stout woman moved around the table with a basket of bread. "Nothin' better for the bum corks." As she passed, she gave Par a swat on his backside. He squeaked.

Agron waved his hand. "All right, now. Let's drop anchor to supper."

Par put a hand on his stomach, not sure food was such a good idea.

Enio leaned in, "You have to eat. It'd be an insult not to."

Par glowered. If they got out of this in one piece, it would be Enio going over the side.

But Enio draped an arm over his shoulder. "Welcome to the Choga!"

CHAPTER THIRTEEN

P AR JOINED ENIO at the table beside the two children. His stomach settled more quickly than he'd expected. After a few exploratory spoonfuls of a vegetable stew, he dove in, eager to get the taste of fermented maggots out of his mouth.

The gathering became full of laughing, arguing, even snips of song. Par wasn't sure how to react, but Enio joined in the fun. Soon, Par did too. The fish and vegetables were flavored in ways entirely new to him. Except for the pickled fire root—which he swore burned a layer off his tongue—he loved it all.

During the meal, he learned that two of the men at the table were cousins of Agron by blood. The third was a hire, like the deck men. Lemma, the stout woman, and the fair-haired Tangera were both Agron's wives.

"You've got two wives?" Par couldn't help asking. This was forbidden in Eloria.

"Three," huffed Lemma, "if you count this sow-belly of a raft."

"At least *Sweet Carmina* never gives me lip," Agron tossed back, and everyone laughed.

After a while, the two men on deck swapped in for their meal, and the rest drank weak ale and told stories of their times on the river. Par delighted Agron's children with a simple table trick involving a balanced fork and knife—until a slight sway of the vessel toppled it. The children took the collapse as part of the fun.

As the night wore late, Agron said, "Not that it's my business, but are you two haulin' anywhere particular?"

"To the coast," Enio said. "And then—"

Par knocked Enio's foot, not wanting to discuss the Borderlands or Alexander Vex. "We're still figuring our options, now that we're Lustered."

Agron smiled. "An excitin' time for two young kippers. We're bound for Argent. You're welcome to keep aboard. But we've got ports to make first."

"No rush," Enio shrugged.

Par suddenly wondered if they *should* be rushing. They still didn't know whether they were being chased. "What's our next stop?"

Agron pushed up from the table. "We berth at Bishop's Landin' tomorrow, and we best be rested. There's space in the hold, if you don't be mindin' the cargo."

They made their goodnights. Agron directed them down to a wooden cavern crammed with crates and barrels. The air hung thick with spices. The bags from the *Sea Dog* were there. They also found a pile of empty sacks, and a corner to make their beds.

"You could've warned me," Par said as they built woolen nests.

"About what?"

"That maggot juice. I could've braced myself."

Enio grabbed two blankets from their leather bag and tossed one to Par. "That wouldn't have been fair." He turned back to his bedding.

Par frowned. Enio was so worried over the fairness of a drinking ritual that he wouldn't spare Par its torture. Yet the guy had cheated in front of the High Altar and lied to the faces of the Prior and Abbot. Par didn't understand his friend sometimes, but he let it go. "Lots of crates. What cargo are they carrying?"

"You have to ask?"

"Besides cinnamon."

Enio glanced around. "Other spices, teas, dried fruits from upriver. Boots and leatherwork, too—they make a lot of nice things in Choga province."

"And big families. How can Agron have two wives?"

"At port, he'll introduce the younger one, Tangela, as someone's sister. Choga is about as far north as you can go and still be in Eloria, and it's hard to tell who's related to who. They're all about relationships and trust."

"Is that why I suddenly became your brother?"

Enio grinned. "I said they had their own ways. I'm a brother of the Choga, and you're a brother of Enio. That got us on board."

Par nodded. "And in the canoe, that arm-raising thing?"

"A wave means danger, or a stranger. Only a brother of the Choga knows a still arm means safe."

Par spread out his blanket. "Well, you were right about them being helpful."

Enio hesitated. "Agron, anyway."

Par heard an unease in the words. "What do you mean?"

"It's *his* vessel, and his job to walk the line between Chogan obligations and the Rule. The others, the hires, they'll follow his lead. But they're not his blood family. So who knows?"

A new worry crept into Par's mind. "Would it help if we paid them? We have a little money."

"They know. By now they've searched our bags."

Par started. "Searched our bags?" He reached for their leather sack.

Enio laid out his blanket. "They didn't rob us, if that's what you're thinking. You can't blame them for looking. It's Agron's neck if we're smuggling."

Par found their little leather satchel. It was still full of coins, plus the Cardinal Note. He felt a pang of guilt. "Sorry. It's here."

"We'll offer them something before we say our goodbyes. It's the right thing to do since I'm a brother of the Choga."

Par sat on his bed and unlaced his boots. "Do you think," he paused, "it will be a problem if they find out I can't invoke?"

"I doubt they'll need you to light any candles. Don't bring it up."

"I wasn't. But they didn't do much invoking themselves. Do Chogans use invocations less?"

Enio stretched out on his bedding. "Same as most. But I bet the crew can fill a sail when they need to." He made a cavernous yawn. "Agron said we've got a big day tomorrow. Go to sleep."

Par lay on his makeshift mattress, head to head with Enio. The vessel barely rocked or creaked as they sailed down the river. Par was no longer in a familiar world, but despite Enio's warning about the hires, he felt safe among the Choga. Agron had welcomed him to his table, maybe even into his family. And the Chogans were loose with their words around him; a bit rough, but kind underneath. So different from his own family, especially over the past couple years. He could get used to this. Maybe he didn't have to go to the Borderlands.

Par whispered, "What do you think they'd do if they knew? About my secret?"

Soft snoring was the only reply.

CHAPTER FOURTEEN

Hands shook Par awake. He squinted into the dim light of the hold. "What—"

"Hurry!" Enio bolted past the barrels and up the stairs.

Par pulled on his boots. Had the gods brought him some new hell? As he stood, the floor heaved. He staggered and nearly fell. A very solid crate bumped him upright.

He weaved his way to the steps and stumbled through the door at the top.

Enio stood at the deck rail, his jagged teeth flashing in the sun. He made a grand arm sweep. "We're here!"

Par stopped at the rail, and wonder took him.

The wharf seemed a small city in itself. Rows of piers stretched along a bay tucked off the river's east side, populated by vessels of every shape and size. Workers rolled barrels, hoisted crates, pushed carts and shouted commands to donkeys, horses and each other as they moved their cargo along the great harbor. Blocks of warehouses stood farther back, many of three stories or more—taller than any Par had ever seen.

The energy of the crowds, the smoky-sweet smell of the boats, the screech of the gulls—it was overwhelming. A wide causeway sloped up among the warehouses. Carved on a massive arch in large splendid letters were the words *Bishop's Landing*.

Agron arrived at the deck rail. "First time?"

"It's fantastic," Par whispered.

"Aye. I expect you're itchin' to explore it."

Enio leaned over the rail. "Try and stop me."

Agron laughed. "I'll be wantin' some time there myself—later." He turned and bellowed to the crew.

The deck snapped to activity. Two crewmen dropped a gang-plank onto the pier. One ran down to a dock-side pulley crane. Another to one of several smaller buildings where a sign read *Inspector*. The rest gathered to remove a section of the deck that opened into the hold. Then they scurried around as if the boat were on fire, yelling, "Lash this!" and "Hoist that!"

Enio nudged Par. "Now we pay for the biscuits." He dove in to help.

Par followed.

His friend was absolutely in his element, working hand to hand with the others. But Par seemed in everyone's way. After a few commands and rebukes, many to mind the coamings—whatever a coaming was—they gave him the job of scrubbing the cabin and upper deck. The work was hot and exhausting, but it felt good. He enjoyed being useful again, with no thought about his worthiness before the gods.

At noon, the bustle wound down. Par found Enio ladling water from a barrel. "Sorry I couldn't help more."

Enio shared his drink. "You did plenty. Besides, no one expected you to know the ropes."

Par lowered his voice. "You said they weren't licensed to take on passengers. Is it a problem we're out here?"

"There's no passage violation while we're docked. We're only a couple river rats helping with the cargo."

Par grinned. "That's me. Par the river rat."

"Aye!" his friend laughed. "But before we set sail, we'll duck back below."

They joined the others for a midday meal of cold meat and fruited cakes. Agron said the ship would freight after lunch. Since the afternoon involved dealings with the public, he suggested the two make themselves scarce.

Par knew what that meant. Enio would insist they explore Bishop's Landing.

As they prepared to leave, Par eyed the wharf, intimidated now by the sights that earlier had seemed so enticing. "Is going into the city the best idea? We don't know the customs."

Enio pulled his Lustering medal over his shirt. "I've wanted to see this place my whole life. Come on." He bounded down the gangplank.

Par unveiled his own pendant and walked slowly off the *Sweet Carmina*. His friend grabbed him and dragged him across the wharf.

They passed beneath the great arch of Bishop's Landing. Beyond the warehouses, the causeway became a wide city street, loud with carts and horses and pedestrians. Bright white buildings lined the way as far as Par could see, many with intriguing storefront windows, others guarded by stately pillars, and a few with lofty towers. Vendors yelled and promoted their foods, their goods, and their entertainments.

"Wow," Enio said, his smile as wide as Par had ever seen. Enio's spirit of adventure was infectious. Yes, they were in a strange city, surrounded by the unknown, but the newness of it all was thrilling. Par was in a bigger world, and part of it.

They stopped to get their bearings. Enio dug a few coins out from his pocket. "Where should we go first?"

Across the street stood a man dressed in a loose green-and-white robe that billowed as if in a breeze. Yet there was no wind. His hands were spread out before him and between them, in mid-air, danced small cutout shapes.

Par pointed. "There."

The man's face was thin with a beard like an old goat. The paper characters were of colorful clowns, whimsical animals, and funny-looking monsters. They dangled from a string tied in a loop. As the performer moved his hands, the loop rose and fell untouched, and the characters twirled in the air currents.

Par stopped before him. "What are those?"

"My wind puppets," the man said. A basket of them sat to his side. "Two silvers a loop." He made a flourish with his hands. His string of figures drifted higher and hovered above Enio's head like a crown.

Enio eyed it suspiciously, then laughed.

Par nudged his friend. "I want to get one."

The wind puppets moved again and settled in front of Par. A slight breeze tickled his nose.

Enio turned away from the man and lowered his voice. "Are you sure? I don't know any wind sigils, and you can't invoke."

"You don't have to remind me. And yes, I'm sure." Par reached for the coins.

But Enio held them back. "All right. But I'll do it. We don't want to look like country clods in front of the puppet guy."

Enio bargained the man down to one silver five. Par selected a loop from the basket. He hung it around his neck and they continued along the street.

All day they explored the city, up and down, sampling pastries and exotic foods. Par especially liked a treat in which a woman added fruit syrups to boiling water, invoked it to ice and crushed it into thin bark cups. They tossed coppers to the entertainers, and a few times were chased away laughing as Enio made rude noises.

After a day full of gawking at grand buildings and statues and fountains, of pressing faces against store windows and of trying on hats and a dozen other diversions, they turned their feet back toward the wharf. Par couldn't remember a better day.

At sunset they spied the wind puppet performer gathering his wares. Par paused and waved, but the man hurried off, glancing back several times before disappearing.

Enio cleared his throat. "First I can't get you off the boat. Now I can't get you back on?"

"Sorry. Coming."

The causeway was nearly empty in the growing dusk. They walked down past the warehouses.

"I wonder," Par said, "if we could stay here. You could teach me to work the docks and—"

Large, muscular arms grabbed them both and yanked them into an alley.

Par yelped and struggled.

"Hey—" Enio began.

"Quiet!" It was Agron. His eyes were like saucers, and his nostrils flared. "Get further back."

They moved deeper into the shadows. Par caught his breath. "Agron, what is it?"

"You little bastards," he hissed. "I should keel haul you both."

Par's mouth hung slack. A dark foreboding grew in his heart.

"You should've told me." Agron peered again to the street. "You should've *told* me."

"Told you *what?*" Enio asked.

But Par already knew.

Agron leaned close, his face twisted into a scowl. When he spoke, he kept his voice low, but it rumbled like thunder. "That you're wanted criminals, *that's* what."

CHAPTER FIFTEEN

Agron seethed like a steaming kettle. "Do you have any idea what the penalties are for transportin' criminals?"

Enio frowned. "Why would a Chogan care—"

"When it puts—" Agron's voice spiked. He caught himself. "When it puts my family at risk."

Enio lowered his eyes. "Well, I didn't think—"

"Aye, you didn't."

Par tried to explain. "We had to run. We—"

"Don't tell me the details." Agron took a steadying breath.

The three crouched in the shadows. Par felt like a bug about to be squashed.

But Agron's voice softened. "Listen. They're lookin' for you, askin' around. You've got me in a hard spot, Enio brother of Loam." The big man rubbed his beard. "My honor as a Chogan tells me to keep you hid. But the Rule says I should toss you to the authorities. In the eyes of my crew, it's my duty to do just that and split the reward."

"There's a reward?" Enio asked.

Par elbowed him.

Agron shook his head. "I surely don't want to. My family has taken to you both."

Par had taken to them, too. He lifted the wind puppets from around his neck, the animals and funny monsters drooping from their string. "Whatever happens, Agron, I bought these for your children."

Agron grasped them in his meaty hand. He studied the figures for a long moment, then crushed the cutouts and tossed them away. "I can't."

"But—"

"Whoever sold these might remember, and if the authorities found my children with them…"

Par sighed. "I understand."

Agron kept silent for several seconds. "All right. Here's the best I can do."

Par leaned in.

"Nothin'."

"Nothing?"

"I can't haul you back aboard, you can see that. And I won't turn you in." He jabbed a sausage-like finger at them. "But if I'm caught with you in my sights, I'll have no choice but to chase you down. The crew and the Rule would demand it. Understand?"

Par nodded.

Agron glanced around. "Stay here. About mealtime, get to the *Carmina*. I'll bring the watches in for a drink. Take your canoe and go."

Enio held out his arm. "I'm sorry, Agron. I hope I'm still a brother of the Choga."

Agron ignored the arm, hooked his hands behind their necks and brought both boys to his forehead. "Aye, lads, you are. Sweet sailin's and fair landin's, brothers of Agron." He released them and lumbered to the end of the alley, paused, and disappeared around the corner.

Enio settled against a wall. "We screwed up."

Par joined him. He couldn't remember deciding not to tell Agron of their escape from the abbey. Even after he realized he could trust Agron, he'd left that call to Enio. But he had no right to blame his friend. Another secret, another disaster. "The Prior didn't waste any time sending out word. I wonder how far downriver they're looking?"

"Or off river."

Twilight darkened into night. The town bell helped estimate the hour. Few people passed the alley, except for an occasional figure with a lantern. Each time, Par held his breath until the light had gone.

When meal time came, they slunk out, darted from crate to crate, and crossed the wharf. They hid behind a stack of barrels near Agron's vessel. A lone man walked the top deck.

A second figure appeared. "Any sign of our river rats?" It was Agron's voice.

"None, Cap'n."

"Well, come inside for a drink. Been a profitable day."

"The men are wantin' that reward, Cap'n."

"Aye. But if we see them kids, we get them quiet, hear? Unless you want to share the dole with every jack on the wharf."

The two figures disappeared.

Enio whispered, "Let's go."

They slipped into the chilly waters and pulled themselves along the pier to the hull of the *Sweet Carmina*. The *Sea Dog* hung on the far side, now hoisted up to the rail.

Enio tugged on a tie rope. "I need to get to the rigging. Lift me."

Par braced himself and helped Enio reach the deck.

The seconds passed. Par peered beyond the bay to the dark river. He shivered in the cold water and felt a weakness growing inside. The abbey was still searching for them. They'd have to move faster. Be more careful. They couldn't get help from another Chogan barge and—

A whack of rope sounded above, followed by the squeal of wood on wood.

"Crap!" Enio's yell shattered the night.

Par wheeled. The *Sea Dog* plummeted toward him. He threw himself hard against the hull. The empty canoe crashed into the water, missing him by a nose.

A man called from the deck. "Who goes?"

An instant later, Enio sailed over the rail and plunged into the water. "Get in!" he sputtered.

They lunged into the boat and paddled hard across the bay.

"Who goes?" the voice repeated. A beam of light hit the canoe.

Another shout. "The boys!"

"Quiet." It was Agron. "Release the moorings and hoist the mainsail."

"Paddle *faster*," Enio gasped.

The canoe reached the mouth of the bay and turned downstream.

"Line for a blow!" Agron commanded.

"They're invoking on the sails." Enio sounded panicked.

"Blow, mates. Fill those sails!"

A roar came from behind, the sound of a gale wind. Men stood on the deck in the ship's lights, arms raised. The sails billowed as if storm-filled. The *Sweet Carmina* surged across the bay.

Par spun, searching for some option. They couldn't outrun Agron. And taking off on land this near the city would get them just as caught.

Up ahead, a smaller stream flowed in from scattered trees in the west. He pointed. "There!"

"But that—" Enio began. Then he shook his head. "No choice."

Agron's vessel reached the bay's mouth and turned into the river. The canoe angled into the side stream. It wasn't very wide, about twice the width of the *Carmina*.

"The water here is too shallow for them," Enio puffed.

The crew's shouts faded below the splash of the paddling. The *Carmina*'s sails slacked.

The boys rowed as long as they could, deep into the night, until their arms gave out. At last, they pulled the *Sea Dog* onto a dark, sandy shore.

Par collapsed next to the canoe. "Think we're safe?"

Enio dropped next to him. "Maybe Agron's waiting us out. Let's catch our breath and keep going."

Par laid back on the sand.

In another moment, he was asleep.

Chapter Sixteen

Prior Dogam brooded over a stack of papers in the candlelit private dining room. Across the table sat the elderly Abbot, wrapped in a woolen blanket and crowned with a red nightcap. The venerable figure slurped a spoonful of chicken broth into his withered mouth.

The Prior tried to ignore this ongoing disturbance. He read the next requisition.

For approval. Three barrels of oats. The brown kind, not the other kind.

He scribbled his signature and moved the document to his out pile.

Slurp.

The Prior took a patient breath and raised his eyes. "Feeling better, Cornelius?"

The Abbot wiped a napkin across his pale lips. "A bit. Thank you, Dogam."

"Two days asleep. You had us worried. Many wondered if this was your time of passing."

"I've often wondered that myself."

The Prior focused again on his work. Since he'd arrived at the abbey, the place had drowned him in this administrative nonsense. Worse, his plans of advancing in the Hierarchy were wildly off schedule. He all but ran the abbey now, though in the eyes of the capital it was still under the Abbot's care. And Cornelius simply refused to retire.

Or, frankly, to die.

Next on the stack was a request to replace the far left row of potherbs in the south gardens with nasturtiums, to help with an aphid problem.

Signed. Out pile.

Slurp.

The Prior's jaw tightened.

A knock came from the door.

Thank the gods. "Yes?"

The plump face of Brother Gaius peeked inside. "Sorry to bother you, Prior, Father Abbot."

"Not at all," smiled the Prior. "What can we do for you?"

The monk carried a wooden cage. "A navigaunt just arrived." Inside lay an unmoving hawk, its feathers crooked and torn.

The Abbot coughed. "Dead? A dire flight?"

The Prior opened the cage. "Well, let's have a look." He removed a finger-sized bone tube attached to the bird's leg. The capital imposed stiff penalties for flying a messenger bird so fast and hard that it died—even the filthy pigeons.

"By the way, Gaius," said the Abbot, "how's the wife? Your first baby, I hear."

"Much better, thank you. In fact—"

"That will be all." The Prior nodded at the cage. "Please dispose of that, Brother."

"Of course, Prior Dogam."

The Prior shut the door. He opened the tube. A tightly rolled parchment slid out. "It's a message from Argent."

"Not another dictate, I hope."

"No. It's in response to my last report." The Prior read. "'Blessings and greetings, Prior Dogam Secundus of the most precious Saint Livius Abbey. Regarding your escaped young miscreants, the circumstances are decidedly serious. The Hierarchy will take up this matter personally. Without delay, please send a few small items owned by these persons, the more valued by them the better. Thank you and please give our regards to Father Cornelius. Your most humble servant, Cronus Ikliam Horphesus, High Sigil Master, Quantificate Supreme, Keeper of the Hearths, Compass of the Realms.'"

"Oh, dear." The Abbot's spoon sagged into his soup.

The Prior frowned and paced along the table. "Why is the capital getting involved? Granted, Enio's invocation from the Profana—and before our *altar*, no less—was a serious transgression. But I've notified the surrounding towns, even to Bishop's Landing, sent the perfunctory reports to the capital, and dealt with the matter according to the Rule."

"The ways of the Hierarchy are often inscrutable," the Abbot said. "I assume they are requesting those personal items for some form of Location sigil. But I hate bothering the parents of those boys again. They've been through enough."

"I see no choice." The Prior settled back into his chair. He squeezed the small canister and stared at the stack of papers waiting for his signature. At last, he'd been noticed by one of the most powerful members of the Hierarchy, the High Sigil Master himself. But not for efficiency or leadership skill. In fact, for exactly the wrong reasons.

He gritted his teeth. "Dammit."

"Don't get your linens in a twist, my boy. No one could have predicted these events."

The Prior glared at the Abbot. "A Confessor would have. If

you'd implemented *any* of my suggestions, such as mandatory Confessions for the students—"

"Let's not punish the rest. This was an isolated incident."

"Or mandatory Confessions of the congregation. Par's father obviously suspected the boy had issues."

The Abbot waved this away. "All fathers suspect their sons have issues."

The Prior rolled the tube back and forth across the tabletop, searching for another reason for the capital's involvement, anything beyond his own incompetence.

As if in rescue, the Abbot raised a finger. "Perhaps catching the boys is not the Sigil Master's true objective."

The Prior stilled the tube. "What do you mean?"

"You know the Hierarchy and its layers."

"Please speak clearly, Cornelius."

The old man stirred his broth. "They could be testing you, our young, soon-to-be, Father Abbot."

The Prior hadn't considered that, though it didn't help with his anxieties. "Explain."

The Abbot set aside his spoon and glowered. "Let's not be coy. We both know your coming here a year ago—"

"Two."

"—was to prove yourself a capable administrator. Even an adequate politician. It's clear you have little love for monastic life."

"I take my responsibilities most seriously."

"Quite. But you'd not be the first to use such a place as a stepping stone. I've been around the block, you know."

"I'm sure you have. What are you suggesting?"

The Abbot slapped a bony hand on the table, sloshing his soup and waggling his jowls. "Show them you're not just some sycophant. That you can see beyond the Rule and the budgets and the paperwork. Do more than what is asked. Do what is *right*."

The Prior smiled at the man's frail indignation. "And what is *right* here?"

The Abbot arched his woolly eyebrows. "Dogam, I'm surprised. It's the most basic precept of the Hierarchy. Take care of those in your charge! Don't let Argent swoop in and usurp your responsibilities. Find those boys before they do. What the higher-ups are truly looking for is your competence and judgment, not two runaway children."

The Prior rubbed his chin. Cornelius might be a doddering old man in a backwater abbey, but he had his moments. "Let's say you are right. And once I've got them?"

For a moment, the Abbot remained silent. His lips tightened, and his face seemed troubled. At last, he said, "The important thing is getting to them first. But remember, they must be more scared than they've ever been in their lives. So bring them back here—gently, Prior—and let me handle things after that. Even if our speculations are wrong, it will give us time to make supplication to the Fondiscate for mercy in Enio's case. Things went too far with him."

"But the Rule—"

The Abbot sighed. "Let's not argue that now."

The Prior let it go, but the Father Abbot had raised an interesting possibility. Maybe someone was vying for the council seats the Prior had his eye on, and this was the capital's way of filtering candidates. This could be a blessing in disguise.

"All right. How?"

The Father Abbot scratched his nose. "Two days and still no word? Start at Bishop's Landing."

This required more thought. "You must be tired, Cornelius. Let me help you to your room."

"I'm fine, thank you. And I apologize for not kicking off again. Soon enough, I promise."

"You should not speak so."

"And your plans, Dogam?"

"Tomorrow I will meet with the boys' parents to acquire the requested objects. Then I will go to Bishop's Landing."

The Abbot nodded and returned to his soup.

The Prior's thoughts remained on the message. Argent was over a hundred leagues away. Even if the High Sigil Master tried to find the boys himself, the Prior had time and distance on his side.

But then what? Should he turn them over to the Father Abbot, or present them instead to High Master Cronus?

There would be time to decide. Before leaving for Bishop's Landing he had paperwork to finish. He lifted another document from the pile.

As evidenced by the attached survey, the pigeon droppings are again out of hand. I am requesting more resources...

Signed.

Out pile.

Slurp.

CHAPTER SEVENTEEN

When Par woke, Enio was already up, brushing weeds off the *Sea Dog*. Fat, gnarled oaks crowded the river banks.

Still sore from their escape, Par shuffled to the canoe. "Had breakfast?"

"Not yet." Enio tossed a vine into the water.

Par searched the canoe for their food. "Our bags!"

"What?" Enio looked in. "The money!"

"And the blankets. And everything else." Par slumped against the rim of the canoe.

Enio joined him. "Crap."

Par peered down the river. "Do you think anyone's following?"

"A patrol might be."

"Agron would still tell?"

Enio rubbed his chin. "I bet he could've caught us right off, but he stalled a few extra seconds. That gave us the time we needed. The crew, though—they'd expect him to tell."

Par wasn't so sure. "Maybe Agron kept the crew quiet so they could find us first and collect the reward."

Enio looked doubtful.

"Plus," Par added, "then the crew could keep our stuff, including the Cardinal Note."

His friend grinned. "Now you're thinking like a river rat."

Par forced a smile. "Either way, let's put more distance between us and them."

"Yeah, about that. You realize where we are?"

Par glanced again at the thick trees guarding the shores. His eyes widened. "The Urdel woodlands?"

"The edge."

Par had once mocked its tales of mysterious creatures and strange doings. But standing on its very threshold, he saw nothing funny. He took an unsteady breath. "We should keep going."

"But—"

"It will give us time to work out our next steps, in case someone's following."

Enio hesitated. He nodded.

Their progress was slow—save their strength, Enio said. Par knew it was because their arms still hurt from their escape. The river continued west under thickening trees. Par caught movements in the branches—squirrels, he hoped. The tangle was too dense to be sure. Other times, a cryptic bird or animal call challenged them from the banks. He or Enio would jump and laugh nervously. At least the first few times. Then they just hunkered down, continued to listen, and to watch.

By late morning, Par's nerves were frayed from the noises and movements and unpleasant smells, few of which he could identify. Suddenly, the *Sea Dog* bumped to a halt. The water had become too shallow.

They pulled onto a thin beach. Enio peered up and down the stream. "We have to go back."

"We can't. Even if Agron never told the authorities, news of a reward will be all over the Greening by now."

"What choice is there?"

"We have to go on foot."

Enio blinked. "Sorry, what?"

"The Borderlands are south whether we take the Greening or cut through the Urdel."

Enio raised his hands like he was calming a mad dog. "Wait. We're tired and I'm hungry. Let's find some food so we can think."

They gathered a few root vegetables and greens from along the water, which was fresh enough to drink. The roots were tasteless, and the greens, bitter, but the meal restored their energy. Still, after they'd eaten, they'd come up with no new options.

Enio stared again down the river. "I hate this plan."

"Me too, but I don't see any other way." Par took a breath and tried to summon some optimism. "Should we hit the trail?"

His friend stood still a moment, then moved to where his little boat waited on the sand. He pushed it onto the water.

Par called, "What are you doing?"

"You think I'm going to let the *Sea Dog* rot in this place?"

In an instant, Par's mood crashed. They'd have to abandon the *Sea Dog*. Enio loved that canoe, probably more than anything in this world.

"Um," Par tried. "If we carried—"

"It won't fit through the trees," Enio said in a tone like cold steel. He stepped into the stream beside his boat.

Par looked downriver, groping for another option. "If we took the Greening at night—"

"No, you're right. They'll be after us."

Par didn't know what else to say. He stepped forward. "I— want me to help?"

"No!" Enio barked back.

Par froze.

His friend's voice dropped. "I'll do it."

Enio waded up to his knees, dragging the *Sea Dog* with him. He stopped midstream, holding the canoe against the current.

Par stayed quiet. His throat was so tight no words would have made it out if he had any.

Enio gripped the boat with both hands. He was trembling. The only sound was the lap of the water against the wooden hull. At last, he said in a soft, cracking voice, "Go to the sea, *Sea Dog*. That's where you belong."

He let the canoe slip away.

Par watched his friend for what seemed a long time, neither of them moving, past when the little boat had disappeared beyond the trees.

Enio's shoulders shook once more and stilled. He wiped a sleeve across his face and returned to the shore.

Par reached out a hand. "Enio…"

"Let's just go."

With his head bent, Enio walked past. The heavy shadows beneath the trees swallowed him up.

✳

Par followed Enio into the Urdel. The spaces between the trees soon filled with thickets. Thorns caught their clothes and clawed their hands. Even the roots seemed to grab at Par's ankles. Sometimes, a reeking marsh, or a wall of impassable branches, or a blood-curdling screech forced them to another route.

When they stopped to rest, Par tried to get his friend talking. "Maybe we should have kept along the stream."

Nothing.

Par tried again. "Of course, that went west, and the Borderlands are south."

Barely a grunt.

"Assuming we're still going south. Can you tell?"

Enio shrugged and started out again.

Par let it go. He felt awful that Enio had lost the *Sea Dog*, but the silence made the going that much harder.

The canopy was so thick that sunlight rarely reached the ground. Late in the day, it became too dim to continue. Par dreaded their first night here, and the only clearing they found was dank and smelled like mold. They settled down with no blankets, no food and no talk. After the trials of the day, Par cared mostly about sleep. It came quickly.

The next thing he heard was the crackling of burning wood.

Enio sat before a small fire. A pale glow through the trees told of early morning. The aroma of roasting nuts filled the air—a welcome change from the rest of the musky forest.

Par sat up, groaning at a stiff neck.

Enio glanced over. His black hair was mussed and his clothes rumpled and torn. "I'm cooking rocknuts," he mumbled.

"Great, thanks," Par rasped and cleared his throat. He crawled closer to the fire. Actually, a fire might not be a good idea at all—what if the smoke attracted something? But at least Enio was talking again. Par didn't want to throw a blanket on his mood.

Par coaxed a few of the nuts out of the coals, searching for something cheery to say. "Did I ever tell you my rocknut story?"

His friend shook his head.

"Well, when I was little, I was in the smithy with my dad. I got to playing around the tool bench and knocked over some big iron thing. It fell on my hand and snapped my wrist."

Enio winced. "Ouch."

"You're not kidding. I wailed my head off. Dad rushed me to the abbey for a High healing. They fixed me up." He rotated his wrist. "We took the long way home through the center of town. Dad bought a bag of raw rocknuts and let me hold them. I'd take one out, hand it to him. He'd invoke to crack it open, and we'd share."

Par bit into a warm roasted nut. "These are good."

Enio poked the embers, sending a spray of sparks into the muggy air. "I like them raw, too."

Par grabbed an uncooked one. "Anyway, we passed an old woman sitting by the courthouse. She was a beggar, ragged and dirty. She held out her hand, and I offered her a nut. But Dad stopped me."

Enio looked up. "Why?"

"He said she was feeble or unworthy of the gods, so she couldn't invoke to open it. He cracked the nut, and I handed it to the woman. She ate it without a thank you or a smile. As we left, I started to cry."

"I'm sure she was grateful."

"That wasn't why I was crying. Dad asked. I said I couldn't invoke either, so I must be feeble and unworthy, too."

Par hadn't recalled this story in a long time. He'd only told it to cheer Enio. Now, a lump grew in his throat. He rolled the raw nut between his fingers. "Dad told me I was still too young, but I'd gotten scared. I thought I might have to leave home and be a beggar." He forced a smile. "I guess it's pretty stupid."

"It's not stupid."

Par let the nut drop to the ground and brushed off his hands. "Turns out I was sort of right."

"Well, don't tell anyone, but sometimes I don't think you're feeble at all."

"Oh, thanks." Par eyed his friend for a moment. "I'm sorry about the *Sea Dog.*"

Enio sighed. "Lasted longer than most things."

Par nodded.

"It's just—I promised my little canoe we'd go to the sea one day."

"It will."

"You think?"

Par closed his eyes and made finger gestures in the air. "My invocation says it's so."

"I can change my mind about that feeble thing."

Par looked again at his friend. "Well, what's stopping it?"

Enio took a deep breath. "You're right." He picked up the raw nut and smiled, his broken, ragged side teeth peeking out. He shoved the nut between them, and with a growl cracked it open. "See? You don't always need an invocation to get to the good stuff."

After they'd eaten, they buried the fire and continued on. Par breathed more easily with Enio in better spirits. But the journey remained tough, and a gloom lay on the forest, as if the sky above the canopy had clouded over.

That afternoon, the ground began to climb, and drop, and climb again. They moved among high mounds and tree-covered ridges. The foliage thinned on the taller rises and they were able to get their bearings. As Par had guessed, the sky was heavy with clouds.

At last, they camped partway up a hill. Par gathered kindling into a small pile. "Any idea how far we've gone?"

"Who knows?" Enio invoked to ignite the wood, but the wind had picked up and nothing caught. He tried several times, then kicked at the sticks and sat back. "This is so slow. Getting through will take weeks."

Thunder rolled in from the south.

"Rain's coming." Par sniffed the air.

"Do we have enough cover?"

As Par studied the sparse canopy, a booming crack and a flash of lightning shook the forest. He nearly jumped out of his skin.

"Crap!" Enio squatted with his hands over his head.

A chilly drizzle began. They hunkered near the trunk of a spreading tree.

The storm built as night fell. Thunder beat the hills. Shards of lightning split the black sky and filled the world with a thousand stark shadows—each time making Par shiver to his bones.

Then, in one flash, he saw a shape—a person standing on the next ridge, arms high.

Par shouted. "Someone's there!"

"Where?" Enio yelled.

Another blaze blasted the hill. Par saw it again. He swore the shape looked right at him. Then it was veiled by the night.

Enio leapt to his feet. "What in the purple hells was *that*?"

With the next flash, the apparition was gone.

The wind and rain tapered off. "Aw," Enio sank back down. "It's only a tree."

"But it looked liked—"

"It looked like a tree," Enio barked. "What else could it be?"

Par didn't answer. He'd seen fear in his friend's eyes. That hadn't been a tree. In fact, it reminded him of someone invoking before an altar. Someone like…

Prior Dogam?

But he was back at the abbey, leagues away.

Wasn't he?

Par settled onto the damp ground. He kept awake for quite some time, hoping that the distant rolls of thunder stayed distant, and that the far off, hideous howls of unfamiliar animals stayed away, too.

All the while, he kept his eyes wide open, fixed on the next hill.

CHAPTER EIGHTEEN

THE NEXT MORNING brought a damp freshness to the woodlands. Their pile of kindling sat dismal and soggy, so they made a breakfast of raw nuts. The specter from the storm still haunted Par. Had he really seen anything? In the daylight, it was just another tree-dotted ridge. If he mentioned that it might have been the Prior, Enio would call him crazy. Par pushed the image from his mind.

Maybe things weren't so bad. They were making progress. He'd get better at wilderness survival, better at finding food. Besides, he'd just spent his second night in the heart of the Urdel. Who from St. Livius could say that?

They continued their journey. The hills dropped again into forest. As before, the dense growth and sudden drops and endless brambles slowed them pitifully.

By midday, in an effort to cheer themselves, their talk turned to food. Par was going on about the wonderful spread at the abbey potluck, and the desserts he'd never tried.

He paused, waiting for Enio's response.

None came.

Par stopped and looked around.

He was alone.

"Enio?"

A chill ran down his neck—not only at worry for Enio, but at being alone in the Urdel.

A voice shot from the bushes. "Hey, Par!"

Par spun. "Where are you?"

Enio poked his smiling face through a thicket. "Cherryberries."

Par's dread evaporated. This was fantastic news—he didn't think he could face another nut. A grove of bushes with purple berries spread beneath a circle of trees. He picked a berry and eyed it. Then took a nibble.

The juice, as from a young cherry but with no pit, ran like syrup down his throat. Still, it wasn't as sweet as he'd expected. "We're sure these are cherryberries?"

"You only know farm berries. Things grow different in the wild." Enio popped another into his purple-stained mouth.

That sounded reasonable. Enio was the outdoorsman. Par finished the berry and studied his stained fingers. "Are these ripe?"

"More for me if you don't want them. But I've eaten things on the river—"

"Don't tell me." Par ate another.

Partway through their feast, a gentle rustling stirred above them. Yet there was no wind. Par looked up.

Hordes of dark shapes with long black wings hung among the shadowy branches.

A berry dropped from Par's mouth. He nudged Enio and motioned upward.

Enio whispered, "Don't. Move."

"What—"

"Nightgads." His friend slowly squatted. Par dropped to his haunches, too.

Enio went on, "I've heard stories. If they see us, they'll attack, get into our hair and lay eggs. Those won't come out until they hatch and the babies suck on our brains and we go crazy."

Par gulped. "What do we do?"

"First, cover our heads."

Enio eased off his shirt, his eyes glued on the trees. Par wrapped his own shirt around his head and tied the sleeves under his chin like a bonnet.

"All right," Enio said. "Real slow, crawl back the way we came."

Before they had gone two shuffles, Enio groaned and doubled up.

Par's own stomach twisted into a heaving cramp.

"Dammit!" he hissed and clutched his burning midsection as he scowled at Enio. "Those *weren't* cherryberries."

Purple stains spread from his friend's mouth and lips. Along with the turban, he looked so ridiculous that Par would have laughed, except for the pain tearing through his own bowels.

A chitter started in the trees. Par again eyed the black shapes. They seemed to vibrate with agitation. He tugged his friend. "We have to keep going."

Enio grimaced, took a trembling breath and resumed crawling.

And when Par didn't think things could get any worse, Enio let out a loud squealing rip of flatulence.

He met Enio's terrified eyes. A frenzy thrashed overhead. A thousand yellow eyes blinked down. Ebony wings spread like a shredding nightmare.

"Run!" Enio cried.

Par staggered to his feet and lurched through the thickets. "You idiot!"

"Just run!" Enio gasped.

Par's stomach boiled as he bounded and stumbled through the trees. Then somewhere ahead, Enio screamed. The ground gave way. Par was falling, careening down a steep, oily slope. He smacked face first in thick muck.

His every gagging breath fanned the fire in his body. He struggled onto his back. Enio lay next to him, face in the muck, unmoving.

Oh gods. Par turned him over. They were both covered—and half sunk—in a gummy, greenish ooze. A putrid mist bubbled from its depths, and a sickly slime stung hot on Par's skin. The stinging turned ice cold and went numb.

A wave of dizziness swept over him. He tried to steady himself but fell back with a sucking splat. He brought his fingers to his chest, to his Lustering medal. Then Par could no longer move. His eyes stared up the marshy rise to the wall of brush that had hidden the drop.

Something moved among the leaves.

The world was dimming. He was passing out. After everything he'd gone through—his years of labor at the abbey, his struggles before the gods, and now his hope for help at Banes—was this how it ended? Killed by a stupid berry?

The leaves parted. A face appeared. It was the face of a woman, an angel, come to bear him to the Higher Realms. Bright green eyes and golden hair shone in the sunlight.

Par's world fled down a black, spinning tunnel. The last sound he heard came from her lips.

Two words.

"Holy sticks!"

Chapter Nineteen

THE FATHER ABBOT sat in his favorite high-backed chair. The tired padding fit him in just the right places, and this spot in his dining room caught the full measure of the warm afternoon sun. Perfect for reading and letter-writing—and mending socks.

He finished darning a red one and snipped the thread. The work was meant to distract from his worries. It hadn't helped. Two days had passed since Prior Dogam left for Bishop's Landing—nearly a week since Par and Enio had fled. He prayed Dogam found them before the capital did. Even if the Abbot were wrong about Argent's Reckoners and they could safely treat Par's condition, Enio did not deserve execution for an ill-cast sigil in aid of a friend.

A rap sounded at the door.

"Yes?"

Brother Gaius stepped in. He stood straight and held in his stomach. The sight was comically formal.

"Hello, Brother Gaius. What is it?"

The monk cleared his throat. "May I present the High

Sigil Master, Cronus Ikliam Horphesus, Quantificate Supreme, Keeper—"

A tall man in a gold cloak pushed his way in. "Thank you, Brother."

The Abbot barely believed his eyes. What in the purple hells was Cronus doing here? Twenty years had passed since the Abbot had last seen his face. Now it was the face of the Rule and of the man whose letter spurred the Prior to Bishop's Landing. The Abbot hoped against hope this visit didn't concern the boys. It certainly wouldn't be a social call.

"Hello, Cornelius." The Sigil Master handed his cloak to the monk, revealing an immaculate white robe lined with red and black sigils. The severe, imposing figure seemed to be in the prime of middle age, though he wasn't much younger than the Abbot. Jet-black hair flowed to his wide shoulders. Dark, intense eyes glowered under a thick brow, but his long face hung pale and slack, as if laden with years.

The Abbot pulled himself together. He dismissed the monk. "Goodness, what a surprise. I would have dressed, had I known you were coming." He smoothed his brown house robe and pushed back his straggling white hair.

With a flair of vestments, the Sigil Master took the chair opposite. His gaze fell on the pile of darning. "Why not use a weaving invocation?"

"I've been under the weather."

"So I've been informed. It's been many years. Knees still a bother?"

"The older I get, the more things bother me. And you, Cronus? Sour stomachs still giving you trouble?"

The High Master delivered a practiced smile that stretched his long face longer. "High Master Cronus, please."

The Abbot smiled back. "My apologies. To what do we

owe this honor, High Master Cronus? Have you come to check on Buckets?"

"I'm sorry, who?"

"Tommy, the veteran you treated for a war curse. You've required status on his condition ever since you placed him here. We, of course, appreciate your concern."

"I have the highest regard for our war-ravaged and wish to keep informed of his progress. But—"

"There's been little change." The Abbot was genuinely concerned for Buckets, but this line of conversation also kept the topic away from Enio and Par. "If I recall, the Sorcerer Tomot cursed him. I've always wondered what form his treatment took."

The Sigil Master seemed to study the Abbot. "You never finished your training as a Reckoner, did you, Cornelius?"

"I believed healing hearts more to the spirit of the Rule than meddling with memories."

Cronus's face remained unreadable. "His treatment was extensive. I've not the time to tutor you in the specifics."

"But you did not heal him."

"We removed his curse."

The Abbot frowned. "And what of his burns? I once tried to heal them myself and concluded they were too far past their incident. But I'd never seen anything quite like them."

"I have spent my career studying curses. They are rare and cryptic things. Further invocations were inadvisable."

"Yes, but—"

The Sigil Master waved him into silence. "I've come to see Prior Dogam about your two missing boys."

The Abbot's hopes shriveled. "He is away."

"Where?"

"He's gone to Bishop's Landing to search for them."

"I see. Any progress?"

"None as yet." The Abbot kept a placid face. At least the capital had not caught them.

"Unfortunate," the man said. "The items he supplied to help locate the boys—I found them ineffective."

"Indeed? If I recall, we sent along Par's Lustering candle, a miniature of the goddess Má, and some socks."

"Perhaps these were not as precious to him as you thought?"

The Father Abbot shook his head. "Who can tell the mind of a boy? But the abbey awarded Par that statuette in a history contest. His parents said he prized it. We weren't sure of his attachment to the candle, but everyone loves a good pair of socks." The Abbot had guessed these things were nothing special—except for the statue, which the Prior had insisted on including. "I'm sorry we provided nothing for Enius. His father went on a drunk and dumped the boy's things into the river. If we trawled—"

"I've no time." The man's voice lost its diplomatic patience. "Before I arrived, I visited your town and used the boys' blood relatives as components in a Location invocation."

The Abbot started. He didn't know what that entailed and nearly lost his composure. "You did not harm—"

"They are fine. The connection between Enius and his father was insufficient, but Par's to his family held strong. Nevertheless—"

"Perhaps he is too distant?" Hope rekindled in the Abbot.

Cronus folded his hands and closed his eyes. "My Location sigil is supremely powerful."

"I see. Never a worry where you parked your donkey?"

"Careful, Abbot."

The Abbot regretted his joke. This was serious. If the capital got hold of Enio and convicted him of heresy, they'd execute him. "Forgive me. Well, if there's anything else—"

The man's eyes flashed open. "There is." He rose from his chair.

The Abbot turned his attention back to his socks, bracing

himself for what would come. "I'm puzzled how you travelled so quickly from Argent. Did you make the trip alone?"

The Sigil Master stopped at his side. "Cornelius, look at me."

This was the moment the Abbot feared. He looked up, his eyebrows peaked in candor. "Yes, High Master?"

"Tell me of those boys."

"There is little to tell." The Abbot sensed the delicate touch of a truth-seeing sigil. This he could handle. "Par cannot invoke. We only recently found that out. It set off this entire chain of events with Enio. We detained them both, but as you know, they escaped." So far, all true.

Cronus bent nearer. "And where are they now?"

Before the Abbot answered, he felt a second invocation, behind and simultaneous with the first. His thoughts were being looked into, probed, as softly as a moth's wing brushing a flower.

While he feigned to be considering the Sigil Master's question, the Abbot even more delicately enlightened a sigil of his own. The letter from Cronus had put him on edge, and he'd saved his strength over the past few days, in case a time came when he'd need his full reserves. He was still weak. He prayed he was strong enough.

The Abbot blinked with a child's innocence. "Par and Enio were last seen traveling south on the river, hence the Prior's trip to Bishop's Landing."

"Do you know where they are going?"

"I haven't the foggiest."

The Sigil Master's invocation spidered through the Abbot's mind. The Abbot put up no obvious resistance, letting his conversations with Prior Dogam stand undefended.

His own sigil stood in a dull, cluttered corner of his memories, a tired place of mostly forgotten friends, bits of a hymn he liked, his last trip to the latrine. From there in the shadows, his invocation wafted like invisible incense through his thoughts, wrapping in the dim palls of failing age his last meeting with Par and Enio. *Old man. Too weak even to manage a weaving sigil. I pray the boys are all right. How many socks still needed darning? Where are my good shoes? What time is it? Someone really needs to get on those pigeon droppings—the south windows alone…*

While he kept such thoughts circling through his head, he carefully peeked into the Sigil Master's own. The man was quite skilled, and the Abbot could search little without risk of detection. But two things stood out, and they chilled him. He drew them in quickly and pushed them down deep, away from his consciousness.

The effort to keep his own sigil active was exhausting. He fast approached the point of collapse, but he steadied his breathing, gazing mildly at the Sigil Master. His vision darkened. At least he had no perspiration to hide—he was too drained even to sweat.

Not a second too soon, the Master retreated from his mind. "I must continue on. Your people won't mind arranging transport, I trust."

"Continue on?" The Abbot hid a trembling hand in his sock pile.

"To Bishop's Landing."

"Damn!"

"Excuse me?"

The Abbot lifted a finger to his mouth and sucked a puncture wound from his needle. "Sorry. I'm a bit rusty at this."

"Have one of your monks do it."

"It's everything I can do to bat away the housekeeper." The Abbot was at the limit of his endurance. He needed to end this inquiry. "But very well, Master Cronus. Safe travels."

The man opened the door. "I'll give my regards to Prior Dogam, shall I?"

"Please do." The Abbot couldn't resist one last poke. "Oh, and Cronus?"

"Yes?"

"Could you use some extra socks?"

"Goodbye, Cornelius."

The door closed. The footsteps died away. Only then did the Abbot quench his sigil and collapse. His breathing came weak and labored. Brother Gaius peeked in, but the Abbot waved him off. He needed to think.

Groaning as he left his chair, he retrieved paper and pen from a cupboard and stumbled back to the table. He needed sleep. But first, he must warn Prior Dogam that Cronus was in pursuit, and of what the Abbot had learned from the Sigil Master's mind. Until now, he dared not tell the Prior—or anyone—that he'd sent Par and Enio to seek help outside Eloria. Yet everything had just changed. He must persuade the Prior to speed the boys to Banes.

The pen hung between his fingers. No. Anything the Abbot told the Prior, Cronus would extract. Whatever happened, he could only pray that the Prior's better angels prevailed.

He formed a new plan.

Ever since the Abbot awoke from his convalescence after helping the boys escape, he'd been thinking about Alexander Vex, the man he'd directed Par to find. A man he'd once called a friend— long ago. It had been a desperate decision, but he'd seen no other choice. The Abbot had hoped to work through his uncertainties about Vex before sending him a message, begging for his help. Now, after the things he'd glimpsed in the Sigil Master's mind, he could wait no longer.

One was a phrase: *Vigil Immortus*. The Abbot didn't understand its significance, yet it confirmed something the Abbot had begun to suspect: Tommy's burns weren't from the war. Good gods, what was Cronus doing to those suffering a curse?

The second thing he'd learned chilled him the most.

The capital didn't care two figs about capturing Enio for heresy.

Cronus acted alone.

And he wanted Par.

Chapter Twenty

A savory, smoky smell tickled Par's nose.

He opened his eyes.

Woven branches bent over him like a tent or a bower. A blanket of velvet-soft leaves covered his body. He tried to lift his head, but the world reeled and dropped him back.

To his right, light leaked through a curtain of vines. Enio slept to his left.

"E—" Par tried, but only managed a coarse murmur from a dry throat.

The last thing he remembered was falling into that stinging swamp, and a face breaking through the bushes. He'd grabbed his Lustering medal, and that had been that.

He reached for it again.

The medal was gone.

Crap. That was his ticket to travel. At least in Eloria.

A sweet humming came from outside. The scent of food. Par's stomach grumbled. He nudged Enio, but only received a grunt.

With a deep breath, Par pitched himself toward the light.

Another wave of dizziness hit. He lost his balance and tumbled through the vines.

He rose to hands and knees on the edge of a drab clearing. Sunlight bled through somber trees onto the weedy earth. Several paces away, a figure in a dark green cloak crouched near a campfire.

Par staggered to his feet. His head began to clear. "Who—"

"Par," Enio hissed from behind.

The figure by the fire stopped humming and turned. The hood fell away. A young woman stared back—the one he'd seen when he'd passed out.

She grinned. "Oh. Good morning."

Long yellow hair framed her slender face. She had a strange smile that seemed almost too wide for her head. Her eyes, especially, caught his attention. Large and soulful, they didn't match the friendless of her greeting. They reminded him of a sad animal—or a desperate one.

"Par!" Enio repeated louder.

"What?"

"You're naked."

Par looked down. He was naked. He peeked up and froze like a deer in sudden lamplight.

The woman nodded toward the edge of the clearing. Their clothes lay across a row of large rocks. She shifted her gaze to the fire.

"Par!"

"I heard you!" He covered himself, took two dignified steps, and leapt behind the rocks. Once hidden, he peered again into the clearing. She still wasn't looking. Their clothes were clean, and the rips repaired. He found his Lustering medal on its gold chain. A knapsack he didn't recognize sat nearby.

While he dressed—as fast as possible—the young woman said, "Aren't you two a little big for wood sprites?" Her voice was strong and lyrical.

Par cinched up his pants. "We're not wood sprites."

"You don't say. And whose bright idea was it to eat weir berries?"

He pulled on his shirt, then looked at their woody tent. Enio frowned through the vines.

"And if that wasn't enough," she continued, "I had to get you out of that muck and clean you off before it numbed you out forever."

Enio yelped. "She *cleaned* us?"

The woman smiled up from her work. "Every nook and cranny."

"Oh my gods, Par." Enio pulled his head back like a frightened turtle.

"There's gratitude," she said. "A rip shouldn't mind who mends it. My pop told me that."

A delicious odor wafted from the coals. Par had never been so hungry. His stomach growled louder.

"Appetite's returned?" The woman poked something in the embers. "Good. I treated you for the berries, but you never know."

Par watched her, unsure what to do or say, but the enticing aroma called to him. He couldn't remain stand-offish forever; he took a step closer. "Um, I'm Par."

"Nice to meet you, Par. I'm Alehilani."

"Elahe…"

"Lani is enough. Who's the other one?"

Par glanced back. His friend was peeking out again. "That's Enio."

Enio mouthed, *My clothes!*

Par waved at him to be quiet.

She peeled open a smoking packet of leaves. It was stuffed with little fish, heads and all, juicy and sizzling on a bed of roasted vegetables.

He swallowed a little drool.

"Par!" Enio called.

"They're on the rocks."

"That's not funny!"

Lani removed another tantalizing packet from the embers.

Par sighed. "Excuse me a second." He gathered Enio's clothes and pendant and brought them to the bower, squatting near the entrance while his friend dressed inside.

"I couldn't hear everything," Enio said. "What'd she say?"

"Her name is Lani. She saved us from the swamp and treated us for the berries." He winced as his stomach complained again. "Hurry, will you?"

Enio finished dressing and Par led him back to the fire. They sat across from this strange person. She seemed not many years older than them.

"Here, help yourself." Lani gave them each a cupped leaf with food. Par couldn't resist and dug in. Enio sniffed it and wrinkled his nose.

The fare was plain and unseasoned, but it melted in Par's mouth and he squeezed his eyes with pleasure. After a few wonderful bites, and sips of cool, sweet water from a gourd, he remembered his manners. "Thanks for this and helping us yesterday." He nudged his friend.

"Thanks," Enio mumbled, who'd begun to eat.

She crunched down on a little fish, bones and all. "Actually, two days ago. You slept through yesterday."

Par swallowed a morsel. "We must have been pretty bad off."

She laughed lightly. "Weir berries and a wither bog—you got a double. I came looking when I heard you running around like maniacs."

"We were being chased," Par said.

Lani squinted. "By what?"

Enio spoke through a full mouth. "Nightgads."

"Hold on. You were being chased by nightgads?"

He swallowed and nodded. "They were going to lay their eggs in our hair and—"

Lani giggled.

Enio scowled. "What's so funny?"

"Nightgads are gentle, sedentary creatures. And they don't lay eggs. Their young are born live."

Par glowered at Enio—who'd also said the berries were edible. "Are you kidding me?"

Enio tossed his chin. "Well, how does she know so much about it?"

She shrugged. "Comes with the territory."

"What territory?" Enio huffed.

With the slender fingers of one hand, Lani caressed a patch of moss among the weeds. The ground wasn't as dull as Par had thought. Tiny flowers ran in striking, many-colored veins among wispy young grasses. The trees rose straight and noble with a spreading grace. Sunlight shimmered like burnished gold through the canopy. Each rustle of the leaves seemed to whisper a secret. Par listened closer.

The crystal notes of a stream reached his ears. The songs of birds rang through the branches like silver flutes and bells, and countless jubilant insects chanted and warbled and crooned. Rich aromas blossomed in the air, filling his senses with the freshness of life and the woodland sweetness of decay.

Par had never experienced such life, such kinship with the earth. It was as if the world had been out of focus, and for the first time he saw it clearly. Everything glowed with an intensity so vivid, so vibrant, that Par was torn between leaping up and joining it or collapsing in worship. In absolute awe, he turned to his companions.

Enio seemed similarly taken. Lani beamed with the very eyes of springtime. A faint glory rippled through her hair. But the glory wasn't golden as were all others of Eloria, or silvery-pale like Enio's Arcanan fire-fly.

Hers was a lustrous emerald green.

"This territory," she said, her eyes fierce and bright. "The territory of a nymph."

Her glory faded. The splendor of the forest dimmed with it, as if clouds had hidden a perfect dawn.

Enio scrambled away from the campfire and rubbed his eyes. "She's a forest witch!"

Lani snorted. "Forest witch? Hardly."

Par gripped the grasses between his fingers, straining to hear again the music of the forest. His voice trembled. "Please, bring it back."

She shook her head. "I'm sorry, but humans can't handle too much of the élan, and I don't want to risk attracting the dun."

He didn't understand, but his sweet desperation ebbed. Par gazed again at the familiar plainness of the woodlands and sensed echoes of what he'd experienced, among the leaves and behind the rocks. It had left him thrilled but sad, as if he'd finished a cup of some divine nectar.

Enio's warning finally registered. Forest witch. Par studied her. She didn't look like a witch. At least she wasn't warty and ugly and green. Well, her eyes were green—as had been her glory.

"Was that…" he began, unsure whether he should back away with Enio. "Was that an invocation?"

Lani seemed to consider. "Yeah, pretty much." She poked at her food.

Enio stood and pointed an accusing finger. "Witch."

She peered at Enio. "You asked how I knew about the nightgads. I'm a nymph. This was the quickest way to answer without beating around the bushes."

"A nymph?" Enio puffed, and his arm dropped. "You don't talk like any nymph."

Lani brought one of the little fish to her mouth. "Known many nymphs, have you?" With an enthusiastic chomp, she bit off its tiny head.

"That's not the point!"

Crackling sounds came from her mouth as she chewed. "No, you're right. Most nymphs keep to themselves. But my pop was human, like you guys."

Par had heard old stories of strange beasts—and stranger unions—within the Urdel. Until now, he'd thought they were tales to scare children. "So you're half nymph?"

"You got it."

"Still a witch," Enio said flatly.

Lani spoke to Par but jerked a thumb at his friend. "What is *wrong* with that guy?"

Enio seemed ready for a fight. But witch or not, she had saved them. Maybe Enio was getting defensive after being called out on the nightgads and the berries. And, of course, there was the loss of the *Sea Dog*.

Par sighed. "He's had a hard week."

"Could be the berries got to his liver." She reached toward him. "Want me to—"

Enio jumped back. "Stay away from my liver!"

Par caught a sly, sideways wink from Lani. He was beginning to like her.

"Par," Enio said, "let's get out of here. She's—"

"She's what? And go where? We're probably alive because of her."

Lani swallowed her last bite. "No *probably* about it."

Enio crossed his arms. "Well, why *did* she help us?"

"Actually," she said, "I think you helped me."

Par raised his eyebrows. "How?"

"You got me off that ridge."

"But we didn't—"

"It was stupid of me, going up there in the first place."

Par remembered her standing on the hilltop, silhouetted with lightning. "What were you doing?"

"Communing. Trying to force a decision. You'd think I'd learned by now—you don't force the élan." She popped the remains of a speckled tail into her mouth. "Then I saw you under that tree, huddled like two scared squirrels. So I decided to keep an eye on you. Good thing, it turned out. Where did you say you were going?"

"We didn't," Enio snapped.

Par answered at the same time. "South."

She frowned and poked at the fire, stirring the ashes. "The élan—sours—there. At least, that's what the nymphs say. I've never been."

"The élan," Par said. This was all a lot to take in. "You mentioned that earlier. What did you mean?"

"Hard to explain. The great dance. The energy of life. You guys would call it the animals, nature, that sort of thing."

Par had no better word for that surge of life, but he'd been taught about the gods of nature. "So is the élan the Goddess Gê?"

"It's not a god. It's the élan."

"But maybe the name—"

Enio interrupted. "Can we skip the history lessons?"

Par nodded. "Anyway, is there a problem going south through the Urdel?"

She shrugged. "Like all things, it finds a balance. But it's not a balance for people. The dun is more active there."

"The dun?"

"Another part of the élan. Or its shadow. It likes places where the balance is off."

A shiver went up Par's spine. The Father Abbot said *he* had a shadow. Could that be the dun?

"Are you all right?" Lani was staring hard at him.

Par forced a smile. "Fine." He still hadn't told Enio of his shadow. This wasn't the time for that, either. "Lani, can we avoid the bad parts?"

"Like I said, I've never been." She looked west. "You could swing along the mountains. That's quite a distance."

He couldn't imagine surviving long enough to get to the mountains. "But we could go south, right? It's possible?"

She dusted off her hands. "Well, you won't make it by yourselves. We should get started."

"Now hold it," Enio said darkly. "What do you mean, *we?*"

"Par and I are going south. Stay if you want." She walked across the clearing to the bower.

When she was out of ear shot, Enio whispered, "Let's get out of here. We can't—"

"We can't make it through the Urdel on our own, Enio. Do you have a better idea?"

"Anything is a better idea." He eyed her. "She wants something. We don't know anything about her."

"She didn't know anything about us either, but she saved us from the wither swamp and took care of us for two days."

Enio squinted. "Some animals like their food alive."

Par was getting a little tired of his friend's attitude. "She's not an animal."

"Whatever she calls herself, she's a forest witch. They bewitch people."

"And *you* know all about those things? Like you knew about the nightgads and the weir berries?"

"Don't be thick. Be-*witch*, forest *witch*—it's right in the name."

Par just shook his head. "Now who's being thick."

Lani brushed her hand over the woven branches of the bower. Each untwined and bent back upright, their roots still planted, and settled among the bushes as if they'd never been disturbed.

Enio tried again. "I don't trust her. Let's—"

Par pushed the point. "Remember that speech you gave me about the Choga? People trying to make their lives like everybody else?"

"But she's not like everybody else." Enio sighed. "And do you have to remember everything I say?"

Par almost smiled. "It's hard not to."

"Then remember what I'm saying now. This is a mistake."

"So we'll be even in our mistakes." Par waited for Enio's comeback. None came.

Lani returned, poured her water gourd onto the ashes and stirred them again. "Alrighty, troops. Let's move out."

CHAPTER TWENTY-ONE

LANI FINISHED RESTORING the campsite to its natural state. She grabbed her knapsack and strode into the trees.

Par nudged Enio. "Come on."

His friend grunted and followed.

Ahead, a stream cut through the forest. The water sparkled like bright glass in the early light, and graceful willows stood back from the edges. Lani knelt on the bank and made playful splashes with her fingers. "Guys, I want to introduce you to Little Sirisa, daughter of the High Lake Sirice. Sirisa, meet Par and Enio."

Par stopped a few paces back, unsure how to respond.

"Well?" Lani prompted. "Don't be rude. Come say hello."

"To the river?"

"Yes, to the river. We'll be traveling together. She's going south, too."

There seemed no harm to it, so Par left his companion and squatted beside Lani. "Well, all right… Hello, Sirisa." He dipped his fingers in the cool water. It was deep and crystal and he could almost taste it.

Lani cleared her throat. She was looking past his shoulder.

Enio threw up his arms. "Now she's just messing with us!"

Par had no sympathy for his friend's frustration. "Any more than you and Agron with that maggot juice?"

"I don't believe this." Enio dropped his arms and shuffled to the creek. He stooped and slapped the water. "Hi."

The splashback hit him in the face.

Par snorted.

"She likes you," Lani chuckled.

Enio scowled and wiped off.

The waterway wasn't very wide. Par peered downstream. "We're following this?"

Lani pointed farther along the shoreline. "Over there is a mess of good reeds. We can weave them into a boat."

Par remembered the *Sea Dog*. He glanced at Enio, worried this might set him off again.

Instead, Enio peered thoughtfully at the stream. "Well, it's deep enough. We'll need something to tie a boat together. Vines, maybe."

"We'll see." Lani brushed off her cloak and walked down the bank.

Par lowered his voice. "Do you think we should tell her we're going to Banes?"

Enio huffed. "Are you kidding? No."

"Saying we're going *south* doesn't mean we'll wind up anywhere near it."

"She's probably never even heard of Banes."

"Maybe not, but—"

"I bet she can't build a boat, either."

Par grinned. "Then you can show her how." He followed Lani.

She'd removed her cloak and boots, rolled up her simple cotton trousers and waded into a muddy shallow. She yanked out a reed and tossed it onto the shore. "Can you guys trim these?"

Par picked it up. "We don't have any knives."

"In my knapsack."

He dropped the stalk and checked the bag. Among extra clothes, dried fruit, and other small bundles, he found a leather sheath wrapping a simple stone knife.

Enio stepped next to him. "Give it."

Par hesitated, worrying about his friend's attitude toward Lani. But he'd never known him to be violent—well, not dangerously. He passed Enio the blade.

Lani tossed up another stalk. Enio knelt to the growing pile. "These might work for the hull. But we'll need something stiffer—branches—for a framework."

"Can you find a few?" Lani said.

Enio began slicing off the root straggles. "We're in a forest, you know."

Par felt like an extra wheel. "What can I do?"

Lani tossed another one. "Help me pull these out."

Par looked at Enio.

"Go ahead," Enio shrugged. "There's only one knife."

The reeds were harder to extract than Lani made it look. Enio caught up on the trimming and found a few thin branches he felt were fit for the framework. Par sometimes noticed him sneaking peeks at Lani and himself.

Par smirked. Enio must have a thousand questions, just like Par, but his friend would never give her the satisfaction of asking. Par decided to be the good guy. He spoke to Lani loudly enough for Enio to hear. "You said you invoked on us. What was that?"

"For starters, I didn't really invoke. I can't do invocations."

That took Par completely by surprise. "You can't invoke—?" He nearly added the word "either" but stopped himself in time.

"Nope. That was an enchantment. And it wasn't *on* you. I coaxed out the clearing's élan."

"An enchantment?"

Lani wiped a sheen of sweat from her forehead. "You guys know about invocations, right?"

Par had never gotten one to work, but it wasn't for lack of studying. "Sure. It's a supplication to the gods to enlighten a sigil."

"The nymphs call sigils, twines. Your invocations appeal to the gods. Nymph enchantments commune with the élan. Arcanans use incantations, conjurations, which are something else entirely."

Enio spoke from among his work. "If she's not a witch, how does she know so much about that stuff?"

"My pop told me. He was from Arcana."

Par froze. Arcana was the enemy of Eloria. Of the gods. Was she Arcanan?

Lani sighed. "My pop told me about your wars. He was in them for a while."

"Your father fought—"

"No, he was a scout. His group was exploring the Cryilla Ridges looking for passages around the Urdel. As you guys found out, the woodlands can be deadly. Most of his party didn't make it. My mother found him, barely alive. Long story short, they fell in love."

She stood and stretched her back. "I think we've got enough."

"Get her life story?" Enio said as they approached the trimmed reeds.

Lani examined the heap. "I hate secrets."

"Me too," Par blurted before he realized the irony—he knew enough about keeping them. For a moment he worried Enio might point that out.

He didn't.

"All right," Lani said, "let's lay out the frame."

Par kept back. Enio began arranging the branches and reeds flat, like a squashed canoe. Lani followed a little behind, nudging the shape into something more circular. Enio didn't seem to notice. Par tried not to laugh.

"What about tie-vines?" Enio said as he worked a corner.

Lani nodded. "Oh, that's right. You said we might need those."

When she made no further effort to go look for any, Enio rolled his eyes and stood. "Fine. I'll get some." He stepped into the trees.

Par began to follow. Lani stopped him. She put a finger to her lips and whispered, "Hurry."

She continued to shift the reeds. Par had no idea what difference the shape made. Maybe this was Lani's idea of a prank? Well, Enio could use some lightening up. So he helped. They made a large circle, laying the reeds over the branches, crisscrossed and close together.

"Thanks, Par. This next part I'll do alone."

An emerald glory again circled Lani's head. She brushed her hands over the branches and reeds. They writhed like snakes. Par yelped and jumped back. The entire mass twisted and entwined. This was some kind of weaving enchantment! He'd seen such invocations to knit cloth, but nothing on this scale.

Enio returned from the forest with an armful of vines. He stopped short and let the bunch drop. "Hey!"

Lani was panting. "Whew—I'm all enchanted out. What do you think?"

Enio darted over, scowling at the new construction. "That's not a boat. That's a bowl."

It *did* look like a big, shallow bowl, large enough to hold all three of them.

Lani caught her breath. "The people around the northern lakes call it a coracle."

Enio nudged it with his foot. "There's no bow, no rudder, no seats."

"No kidding," she said. "But it's perfect for the Little Sirisa."

Enio shook his head and pointed toward the river. "Think Little Sirisa would like some matching cups and saucers?"

Her voice came patient and soft. "Why don't you ask her?"

"You're the one who talks to rivers. How did you meet? Get lonely and have tea parties with the ponds?"

"You know a lot about boats." Her eyes shone with an easy kindness.

Par reached for his friend's shoulder. "Enio—"

Enio twisted away from Par's hand. "Damn right. And rivers and—"

"You've seen a river's heart, haven't you?"

Enio winced. His mouth stayed open, but nothing came out.

Lani continued, "You've touched it."

Par looked from one to the other, a dread building in his chest. Was she using another enchantment? But no glory wrapped her head.

Enio still only stared.

She smiled. "Did you ever tell it?"

A tremor, like a coming storm, darkened Enio's face. Par thought he might actually punch her. Worse, the knife was still tucked at his waist. Par tensed, ready to jump him.

But Enio shook himself. With a grunt, he marched to the other side of the coracle. "Crazy witch," he muttered.

Lani stayed where she was. "It's all right, Enio. If you loved it, I'm sure it knew."

CHAPTER TWENTY-TWO

PAR LEANED CLOSE to Lani. He kept his voice low. "What did you do to him?"

She shook her head. "Nothing. The way the élan moves around your friend, I can tell he's been in communion with a river. I didn't mean to upset him."

Enio knelt near the coracle, tugging on the woven reeds and mumbling to himself.

Par thought it best to give him some space. "Lani, you said the nymphs keep to themselves, but that your pop was human. Is he around?"

"No, he's gone. And the dun took my mom when I was born."

"The... shadow?" Par chilled again at the memory of the Abbot's examination, and of his report of the shadow near Par's soul.

She nodded. "My parents got me away, but not before it attacked my mother. The dun is drawn to places where the balance is wrong—the unnatural. I guess half-nymphs qualify."

The thought that Par himself might be unnatural made him

squirm. "Well, you seem all right to me," he said as lightheartedly as he could.

She chuckled. "That's the nicest compliment I've ever gotten from a wood sprite."

Par smiled. He glanced at Enio, who was now inspecting the underside of the coracle.

When he turned back, Lani had gone pale. "Lani, is something wrong?"

"No, I—" She staggered and slumped to her knees.

"Lani!" Par dropped beside her.

Her breathing had quickened. She put a hand on her forehead. "I think I overdid the enchantments."

"How can I help?" He caught Enio looking, too.

"I just need to rest a minute." She waved him off. "But you asked about the dun."

"If you need to rest—"

"It's all right."

Par sat next to her, hoping it was nothing serious. He had no idea what to do if it was.

She took a deep breath and went on, "After that, Pop and the other nymphs agreed it would be better to raise me in the forests rather than with the humans. But when nymphs get to a certain age, we go off alone to search for the *chela élande*—the heart of the élan."

Par's anxiety faded. She seemed more herself again. "The thing you said Enio saw?"

"No, everything in nature has a heart. The *chela élande* is the mother of them all. It opens to nymphs in different places—a river, a mountain, something. When it does, we come into our full abilities, and stay there the rest of our lives. When my mom was young, she met it at a lake and became a lake nymph. I've been wandering for two years." She shrugged. "So far, nothing."

"How long is it supposed to take?"

"A few weeks or months, until we find our place of communion. I'd nearly given up when you saw me on the ridge." Her voice tinged with sadness. "I figured if the lightning wanted to take me, that was all right."

Par wasn't sure he understood. Maybe she meant some mystical connection to the storm. Or maybe she was just ready to give up. He thought back to his years of hiding his failure at invocation, his unworthiness before the gods—his father turning him over for the Reckoning. He could relate.

Her eyes brightened. "Anyway, like I said, the nymphs warned me away from the south. When you said you headed that way, I thought I'd tag along. Maybe it's time I looked there anyway—I might get lucky."

She rose from her knees. Par reached to help, but she stopped him. "I'm fine now, thank you."

Enio stood and crossed his arms. "If this thing doesn't sink right off, I'll need something to steer it." He poked among the leftover branches and vines.

Par watched the two, unsure what else to say.

Lani seemed to sense this. "You guys get ready. I'll pack up my knapsack."

She walked into the trees. Par was still a little worried at her collapse, but she seemed better now. So he helped his friend gather material.

Enio was the first to speak, mocking Lani's words. "You've *seen* it. You've *touched* it." He peered after her. "Who does she think she is, anyway?"

Par let the comment go. His mind had turned again to the dun.

To the shadow on his soul.

✳

Lani returned with her bag and tossed it into the coracle. They hauled the boat to the stream. The Little Sirisa took them eagerly.

Par nudged Enio. "Sweet sailin's and fair landin's. Aye, brother of Par?"

Enio grunted.

They floated through the day under a sunny sky. Their prospects of getting through the Urdel now looked promising. Enio spent the time fashioning two stout paddles. Par mostly talked to Lani, and he found his new friend fascinating. She told him of the things she'd seen in her travels—thundering, cloud-wrapped waterfalls; secret glades that whispered your name; sanctuaries of soaring trees as solemn as cathedrals.

Par told her of his own home and of the abbey. She seemed to hang on every word.

Late in the day, ahead on the riverbank and almost hidden in the brush rose a flat stone, about as tall as a person.

Par pointed it out. "That looks manmade."

"It is," Lani said. "Pop showed me others. Left by the ancient humans who drove the nymphs deep into the woodlands."

Par remembered something about that from the Histories. "After the first people fled the Gardens of Gê?"

"That's what Pop said."

"Your dad knew about the Goddess Gê? He believed in the gods?"

"Sure. Some Arcanans pray, too. But they don't invoke the gods."

"Why not?"

"Even if you don't accidentally call down a pestilence or something, they say relying on powerful beings can lead to slavery."

Par's beseechments had gotten no attention at all from the gods, but he became defensive. "We're not slaves. And look at the Arcanans. Without the gods, they're like children with no way to tell what's right or wrong or—"

She held up her hands. "Hey, I'm not taking sides."

Enio cleared his throat and rocked the boat.

Par jolted. "Hey!"

Enio pointed to the stone. "The day's almost gone. Let's camp there." He guided the coracle to the shore.

They hopped out. Enio went straight to the monument. It was broken across the top. He brushed its moss and dirt. "The markings are worn off." He peered past it. "There's more."

"Guys," Lani said, "let's not get too far from the banks. Remember, I've never been this way."

"Hey." Enio pushed aside the brush. "If you want to come with us, you need to keep up. Right, Par?"

Par called after him, "All right but, yeah, let's not go far."

They followed Enio through the foliage. The monuments continued in an indefinite line. Most had fallen into rubble, but a few stood intact, taller than Par's head. Worn shapes covered their surfaces, sometimes of people and animals or strange writing.

Par stopped at a tall one cracked down the center. A skull etched inside a circle stared back at him. Rays as from the sun radiated out from that, pointing to eight other oval carvings, like towering stones looming around it.

"Remind you of anything?" Par asked.

Enio shook his head. "Should it?"

"John's story about Buckets."

Lani moved closer. "Buckets?"

Par relayed the chief part of Buckets' story, and of him being taken to a circle of stones surrounding a frightening pit where he said he'd seen the sun.

Lani ran her fingers over the skull. "The blasted land your friend saw reminds me of the tales of the Devastation."

"Huh," Par said, "I hadn't thought of that." He'd learned different versions of that saga in school, sometimes as a war between the gods, or as a morality tale against disobedience. Each had ended in a great wasting of the Gardens and a turning away of mankind.

They investigated a few more stones until the sunlight became dim.

"We should get back," Lani said.

Par nodded, and she disappeared into the trees. Before he could follow, Enio gripped his shoulder.

"We need to talk," Enio hissed.

"Coming?" Lani called.

Enio's eyes were insistent.

Par wanted to talk to him anyway, convince him they should tell her where they were going. "Go ahead," he shouted to Lani, "we need to use the… go to the… you know."

Enio removed a wad of twigs from beneath his shirt. It was crudely shaped, with vestiges of arms and legs and a clump of a head. He glanced after Lani and kept his voice low. "I found this in her bag. It's a witch totem. See? That's how she's bewitching you." He handed it over.

Par sighed. He was sick of this. He squinted at the ridiculous thing. "Is this supposed to be me?"

Enio snatched it back. "What's wrong with it?" He repositioned a twig.

Par ground his teeth.

His friend stopped and raised his eyes.

Par couldn't hold it in any longer. "How stupid do you think I am?"

"All right," Enio hissed, "I made it. But I'm trying to get us through this place alive."

"So is *she*."

"Par, we hardly know anything about her."

"We know plenty. She told us—"

"What if she made all that up?"

"You're the one making stuff up!" He slapped the totem out of Enio's hand.

Enio flinched and tensed.

Par stiffened, too. Then shook his head. "What's *wrong* with you? She's not dangerous."

"Says you. But I still don't trust her. I'm trying to help—"

"You're *not* helping." Par lowered his rising voice. "Listen, we've got a long way to go, and we need to be a team. So whatever you think you're doing, just—cut it out, all right?"

Without waiting for a response, Par turned back to camp, trying to calm himself, grimacing all the way. He already had enough worries, with this shadow-thing near his soul, and running from the Prior, and the dangers of the forest. He didn't need Enio's idiocy on top of everything else.

A few minutes after he'd reached Lani and the shore, Enio emerged from the trees. He paused near the stone and gave a slight smile. He seemed a little embarrassed. Maybe Par had gotten through to him.

Par's hopes rose further when Enio made an effort to be more helpful. He cleared away brush and rocks. Lani found a clump of blue, potato-shaped vegetables along the banks. When she said they cooked best on sticks, Enio volunteered to make a fire.

As the potatoes cooked, Par noticed Lani was trembling. "Lani, what is it?"

Her eyes were no longer those of springtime, but of winter. "I'm not sure."

Par leaned closer, almost shivering himself at her expression.

The trembling eased. She shook her head and her face returned to normal. She picked up a skewer and gave a tight grin. "Probably just the damp."

CHAPTER TWENTY-THREE

Prior Dogam staggered high atop the Governor's Tower of Bishop's Landing. He grabbed the parapet to keep from falling and becoming a fresh stain on the pavement.

High Sigil Master Cronus caught his shoulder. "Careful, Prior. It's a long way down."

The Prior steadied himself. After the deep penetration of his mind, what could he say now that Master Cronus didn't know? The Prior's aspirations in the Hierarchy and frustration at being stuck at the abbey; his hope, now dashed, that finding the boys was a test of his potential; and his thrill, and intimidation, at meeting the High Sigil Master himself—all laid bare.

Cronus released him and stood before the city's lighted panorama. The streets, washed gold under the evening lanterns, still bustled with commerce. "Have you visited this tower before, Dogam?" The man's robes trembled in a breeze like water about to boil.

"No, Master Cronus."

"Neither have I. It's quite a pleasant view."

The Prior braced for the High Master's next words. Perhaps to demote him from the abbey or to berate him about his failings.

Instead, Cronus said, "I don't begrudge your ambitions, Dogam. I find them admirable."

"Thank you, sir." The Prior's tension eased. The Father Abbot's maddeningly brief message that Master Cronus was coming to take up the search was bad enough, but the Prior hadn't expected this mental excavation, especially without the normal approvals and oversights. Still, he knew better than to challenge a man of such authority. And he might have a chance to present himself as a competent, faithful servant.

Cronus continued, "You've made the right decision in aiding me, Prior, rather than finding the boys for Father Cornelius."

The Prior caught himself before objecting. He wasn't aware he'd chosen either way. "I'm sorry I have not captured them, Master Cronus, and saved you the trip. And I'm sure the Father Abbot meant no disrespect in suggesting your letter was merely a test."

"Dear Cornelius." Cronus gazed over the city. "He never could get his mind around the big picture. No, this matter is of much more import."

"I can certainly understand that Enio's crime warrants the Hierarchy's attention."

"Enio is not my concern. It is Parynius."

The Prior startled. "Par? But what of Enio's unsanctified sigil?"

Cronus spoke in a patient cadence, never looking at the Prior. "There is a bakery in Argent that makes delicious cherry tarts. It's a widely known secret that the family invokes some unsanctioned, passed-down sigil that puffs them just right."

"Well, yes, I understand the exceptions for family tradition. But Enio used an unholy sigil from the Profana."

"Such trivia does not interest me, much less the transgressions of an underage reprobate."

The Prior stared in disbelief. Performing such a profane sigil before an altar seemed the most egregious crime imaginable.

Cronus went on, "Did you ever suspect anything odd about Parynius?"

"Odd?" The Prior recovered his composure. "Not until he confessed that he has never invoked."

The High Master's profile was gargoyle-like in the dusk. "Curious, don't you think, that none of Par's prized belongings were effective for my Location sigil?"

The Prior's heart skipped a beat. Did the man think he was protecting the boys? "High Master, I assure you I did my best—"

"I am not accusing you of anything. You would not still be standing before me if I were."

The Prior glanced toward the parapet, briefly wondering if that was meant literally. "Then perhaps Par is too distant?"

"Not for me."

"Or he has… perished?" The Prior grimaced. Regardless of the trouble the boys had put him through, he hoped it hadn't come to that.

"Considering the recentness of that demise, there would still be a trace."

"May I ask, High Master, why is Par of such interest?"

Cronus paused. "I am sure someone of your aspirations knows of the capital's interest in curses?"

"Only that there is research."

"But you are aware of the power of a curse."

"Certainly their duration."

"Their duration is their power," Cronus said. "Such invocations continue long after their sigils are spent. They are, however, rare and obscure."

"And forbidden," added the Prior.

Cronus nodded. "This makes curses most difficult to study."

Something clicked in the Prior's mind. Time to step carefully, but this might be an opportunity to demonstrate shrewdness. "Is it that you wish to use Par's... curse... as a weapon? To prevent an enemy from invocation, as it prevents Par?"

"No, Dogam. The best way to prevent an enemy from invocation is simply to kill them."

The Prior frowned, deflated by the obvious answer.

Cronus turned to him. The Prior was not short, but the Sigil Master loomed even taller. "I've seen enough to believe you a good man, Dogam, and that I can trust you."

The Prior straightened. "You honor me, High Master."

"And so for now, I tell you this. The boy's curse must be singularly potent to confound my Location sigil. Derivations of such sigils ensure that no spy or assassin comes near our seat of government. Imagine our peril if someone circumvented these measures—especially during a time of war."

The Prior's stomach tightened. He looked into the man's heavy eyes. "War approaches?"

"The Treaty of Banes is failing. Arcanan vessels sail nearer the Boundaries every year. Fortunately, some of us have been making preparations."

"When will his Eminence inform the people of the coming hostilities?"

The Sigil Master's voice seemed to darken. "Our Fondiscate has led Eloria in the peace. But he will not act until changes have been made at the highest levels."

Changes at the highest levels? The Prior realized he stood at the precipice of more than just this tower. He took a step back from the edge. "I imagine Reckonings have progressed since my assignment to the abbey."

"Please, Dogam, say what you wish. I know you have a soft spot for those boys."

The Prior did, in fact, admire them. Par for his resourcefulness in hiding his problem for so long. And Enio for his raw ability to conjure an Arcanan sigil, so unholy a thing. Few adults raised in the ways of invocations were capable of it.

"I hope Par's Reckoning won't be too…" He wasn't sure of the most politic word to use.

The Sigil Master didn't help. "We must do what is necessary to understand and treat his curse."

The Prior winced. If the High Master could perform such a powerful Confessor invocation here, on him, without the oversight dictated by the Rule, what might he do to Par?

Such a question, however, had a whiff of insubordination. If the Prior hoped to gain any advantages from this interview, he could not allow it to end on that note. "How may I serve further, High Master?"

Cronus faced the river, the forests and distant mountains beyond. The last embers of sunset charred the fringes of the ashen clouds. "First, I must find the boys. You believe they still travel together?"

"Most likely, yes."

"Good. Please hand me the item."

The Prior retrieved a leather satchel from near the parapet. He undid the clasp and handed the Sigil Master a flat, cloth-wrapped object. "I prepared it as you instructed. Will it be enough?"

"If it is as precious as you claim. The Location sigil should give direction, though not distance. We must invoke it periodically as we travel."

"We?" This was the first the Prior heard of his continued involvement with the search.

"Yes, Prior, if you agree to accompany me. I sense you have a persuasive way with the boys, even a trust. And I need them to trust me. It will make any… Reckonings, easier."

Of course, the High Sigil Master could force the Prior to come, but this might be the Prior's ticket to a position in the capital. And if his presence eased Par's Reckoning, all the better.

Besides, if it took him away from the abbey, even for a while, it was a blessing.

The Prior bowed. "I live to serve, Master Cronus."

"Excellent." Cronus removed the material to reveal a short, rough plank of wood. "Watch closely, Dogam. Serve me well, and one day I will bestow this sigil upon you."

A thrill ran through the Prior. Few in Eloria were authorized to possess such a sigil.

From the Sigil Master's head flared a brilliant glory, like an untimely dawn. The wood absorbed and reflected this light, pulsing like a heartbeat. A sudden ray flashed to the southwest like an accusing finger. The Sigil Master's glory dimmed. The plank lost its glow.

He handed the board back. "This will do nicely. I have much more to tell you on our journey, Dogam. The issue with Parynius is dire beyond what you can imagine, and beyond what I dare mention here. For now, let us find a navigaunt. I need to send a message."

The Prior re-wrapped the small plank, covering up again the words *Sea Dog*.

CHAPTER TWENTY-FOUR

Par stoked the campfire on and off through the night. Enio woke once and said it wasn't cold enough to bother. In truth, Par couldn't sleep. The changes he'd seen pass over Lani still worried him.

In the morning, he helped her prepare yesterday's leftovers. Enio sat to the side and practiced the rockshoot sigil John had bestowed upon them at the abbey. Par had forgotten about that.

Enio picked up a pebble and a faint gold glory twinkled around his head. The little stone shot into the stream.

"Hey, Par. I almost got it across. Depends on how you hold it."

Par frowned—that rock had really moved. "Is it safe to practice that here?"

"We need to protect ourselves."

As Par turned back to the fire, a piercing screech sliced the air. A blur shot past and thudded into the standing stone.

Lani gasped and fell back. Par fumbled his skewers into the fire. "Dammit, Enio!"

"That wasn't me." Enio rushed over.

A dark stain smeared the monument. A hawk lay on the ground, twitching.

Lani rested a hand on its heaving breast. The swell of its lungs slowed and stopped. "Poor thing. There was nothing I could do."

Enio pointed to a small canister poking from its feathers. "Is that a navigaunt?"

Lani gently stroked the creature's head. "Navigaunt?"

Par nodded. "The Navigator Guild uses sigils to make birds deliver messages."

"They force them?" Her face darkened.

Guilt warmed Par at something he'd never questioned. He cleared his throat. "But I've never seen one die before. Do you mind if we, um, check the message?"

Lani sighed and eased back the wing.

Par untied the canister from a crumpled leg. He unrolled its narrow parchment, and his heart nearly stopped. "It's from the Prior."

"He's *still* after us?" Enio leaned closer. "What's it say?"

Par read it out loud. "'My Dear Enio and Par. Greetings from Prior Dogum Secondus of the Abbey Saint Livius. I trust you are safe. I am with High Sigil Master Cronus himself. He has taken a personal interest in Par's wellbeing, and promises if Par turns himself in, no charges will be pursued against Enio.'"

Enio huffed. "What a guy."

Par kept reading. "'We know you are in the woodlands bearing south. When you reach the Crescent River, follow it to Jod. We will meet you there. Boys, you need not run anymore. This is in everyone's best interest. Remember, I have never lied to either of you. Safe travels.'"

He took a shaky breath and handed the message to Enio. "Do you think we should?"

"After what he did to us? To me?"

"But he said—"

"Forget it." Enio glanced at Lani and tossed the message into the fire.

This was a lot to take in, and Enio clearly didn't want to tell Lani about their troubles or plans. Fortunately, she'd never been very nosy.

Par poked a stick into the campfire, still stunned at the message. "My food is burnt."

Lani scooped up the hawk. "This is our breakfast now."

Par's appetite evaporated. Cooking a navigaunt seemed wrong, almost like eating the neighbor's cat. But he said nothing as she plucked the feathers and roasted it. He even nibbled a few bites, in case it was insulting not to. It tasted like chicken gone bad.

All the while, he thought of the Prior and the High Sigil Master. They'd promised to forgive Enio's heresy, yet mention of Par's Reckoning was glaringly absent. Fear stirred again in his heart.

As they finished the meal, Enio went to the edge of the river and peered downstream. "I guess now we walk."

Par moved beside him. "Why?"

Enio pointed. The trees beyond thickened, bending low like a tunnel. "We could get stuck."

"What do you think?" Par asked Lani.

She brushed off her hands. "Considering my luck so far, I'll follow you guys. But it's a long way around."

With the Prior on their heels, Par wanted to waste no time getting to Banes. There seemed just enough room for the coracle. "I vote the river."

"All right," Lani said. "The river it is."

"Hey," Enio objected. "What about my vote?"

Par shrugged. "We each had a say. That way won."

"But she's not—"

"I'm not what?" Lani lowered her food.

Par determined to head off another conflict. He tapped Enio's shoulder. "Let's talk a minute." He gave Lani a sly wink. She resumed scraping meat off a slender bone.

He ushered Enio a little away. "Doesn't the Prior settle it? We need to get to Banes before he gets to Jod and starts searching upriver."

Enio kicked a knotty root. "This way is too jungly."

"Whichever way we go, it looks like he can track us. But if you want, I'll talk to Lani. Of course, it means we have to travel with her longer. And I'll need to tell her about Banes, and the Prior, and—"

"All right!" Enio hissed. "But if we get stuck, it's on you."

Par patted his friend on the back. "Remember, we're a team."

"Yeah," Enio said through gritted teeth. "Some team."

Par breathed with relief, and not only because Enio had agreed. He'd rather Lani didn't find out why he was on the run—that he was cursed, broken.

They unmade their camp and pushed into the Sirisa. Par sat with Lani in the back, Enio up front, struggling to guide them through the tangles and taking the worst of the sudden vines and low branches. With each whack or scratch, he grumbled louder. Par's unease grew at his friend's rising temper. Apart from anything else, it might draw unwelcome attention.

Lani barely moved, and then only to avoid a low branch.

"You all right?" Par worried at her growing silences.

"Just tired."

"I'm not surprised. You made an entire boat." Par said it to make her feel better—and himself.

Enio turned to them. "If you call this thing a bo—"

A tree limb knocked the back of his head. He yelped and grabbed his skull.

Par stifled a guilty laugh.

His friend raised his eyes. He wasn't smiling. "She did that!"

"What?" Par said it together with Lani.

"I know you can be thick, Par, but why can't you see it? She invoked on us once already."

"Lani said that was the élan—"

"And even if she didn't, you're not questioning *anything* she says."

"Hey," Lani snapped, "if you don't want to be around me, no one's keeping you."

Par looked at her with surprise. Her face had flushed. Maybe it was whatever illness or weakness she was fighting. Or maybe she'd had enough of Enio. He couldn't blame her.

"Right." Enio pointed toward the dense forest. "Just let us off at the next tavern dance."

Lani's voice was sharp. "We can drop you anywhere you want."

"Very funny. You've got us trapped in this… bilge bucket."

"Then make your own!"

"Don't think I couldn't!"

Par clenched his jaw. Why did Enio have to be this way? Something floated past—a dead fish, waxy and bloated. He grimaced and raised his eyes to the gods. Not that they had ever listened. While looking up, he noticed something.

He broke into the argument. "Hold on."

"What?" barked Enio.

"The canopy opened a little. What's happened to the light?"

The patches of sky held no clouds, yet hung like dismal rags with all the color washed out.

"Holy sticks," Lani whispered. Goosebumps crawled up Par's neck at the alarm in her eyes.

The craft slowed and stopped. The river stilled, black and unreflecting. There was no sound. The very air seemed to darken. Or rot.

Suddenly, Enio screamed. He swung his paddle at a sinewy black cloud that tried to wrap him like a cloak.

"Guys!" Lani grabbed her knapsack. "Use fire!"

A glory blazed gold around Enio's head. His paddle sizzled and ignited.

Lani's hair flashed with emerald brilliance. Her knapsack burst into flame.

Par shouted, "What's going on?"

Lani's eyes were wide with terror. "The dun!"

Enio and Lani swung their fires. The dun shredded, but didn't disperse. Then the craft jolted hard. The stream itself erupted into a black plague and surged over the boat's rim.

"Crap! Crap!" Enio lost his paddle over the side and clawed at his chest. The dun oozed over him like pitch.

Before Par could move, Lani screamed. The dun congealed into inky tendrils, wrapping her neck, pulling and choking. Her burning knapsack flew into the false night.

Par dove for Lani. He grabbed her and with all his strength pulled her away from the side. The dun shrouded her face. Her eyes dimmed, as if her life were being leeched away.

She went limp.

"No!" Par swiped at it. To his surprise, it dissipated as if it were a fog in a breeze.

"Par!" Enio yelped.

"Hold on!" Par had no clue why this was working, but as he moved his hands through the dun, it retreated from Lani's face and body.

"Help—"

Par turned.

Enio was gone.

"Enio!"

Par grabbed the remaining paddle. He thrust it into the black waters, calling his friend's name. As he readied to jump in himself, the paddle yanked. Par pulled.

Enio burst up, gasping and spitting. Par dragged him into the coracle. Enio crumpled, coughing up water. Lani was still slumped and unmoving. But the dun had gone.

Par checked Enio once more, then attended to Lani. She was unconscious and white as a ghost, but her hands were warming. Bits of sunlight flickered through the canopy. The trees seemed to straighten. The air again filled with the life of the burbling stream.

Par collapsed against the boat's side and took a moment to catch his breath. "Enio, you all right?"

Enio cleared his throat and sat up. He checked himself over. His eyes widened. "No, no, no…"

"What's wrong?"

Enio's hands fell still. "My Lustering medal. It's gone."

Par felt for his own. Still there. He checked the bottom of the craft and peered into the murky water. "Oh no, Enio. I'm sorry."

His friend sank back, his stare wide and unblinking. He trembled, as if he were about to scream or sob. Then all emotion leaked away.

Par held his gaze, wondering what to say, or what his friend was going through.

Enio's face hardened into a strange smile. He picked up the paddle and set again to moving the coracle. "What's lost is lost. No big deal."

It *was* a big deal. Maybe Enio needed some time. Par checked Lani again. She was still out, but her breathing was easy. "Think she'll be all right?"

"Probably." Enio kept paddling. "Lucky you saved her…"

For an instant, Par's heart warmed. However he'd done it, Par, the cursed, the unworthy, who couldn't invoke to save his life, had saved his friends.

Then he registered Enio's full statement.

"Lucky you saved her," Enio had said…

"… first."

✳

Par peered at Enio. "What?"

"It's not important." His friend guided their craft along the stream.

Lani groaned. "The dun…"

Par didn't have time for any more of Enio's nonsense. He laid a hand on Lani's shoulder. "The dun is gone."

"Gone?"

Par explained, skipping the part about helping her first.

"I don't understand." She was still very pale. "The dun comes only when the élan can't balance. But it hasn't bothered me since I was born."

Par hesitated, afraid to ask. "And why did it keep away from me?"

She shook her head.

Was it because of the shadow inside him? What if that shadow was the dun itself, the same thing that killed her mother?

He swallowed and pushed away the hideous thought. "Want to stop a while?"

"No. Let's put some distance between us and here."

Par nodded. "How about it, Enio?"

His friend made no response. Par let him be.

Lani slept as the Sirisa took them through the day. Par weighed Enio's brooding silence. The poor guy had lost his Lustering medal, a thing he'd worked so hard to get, yet he didn't complain any more about it. And helping Lani first? A snap decision. Maybe the real issue was Par's new friendship with her.

Was Enio jealous?

A guilty pride warmed him. No one had ever gotten jealous over his friendships before. Whatever Enio's problem, the guy needed to get past it. Par had lost his home. That still ached, but he wasn't sulking.

The trees gradually thinned. Birdsong returned to the air, and sunlight dappled the water. Soon, Par felt pretty good about himself. Enio had always been the one who knew what to do, and how. Sure, he was dirt poor, but that never stopped him from having ideas and plans. And confidence. Things that always reminded Par of his own unworthiness before the gods.

Now, he and Enio were equally at the mercy of the forest. Literally in the same boat. But Par had adapted better, made better choices.

Like trusting Lani.

His chest swelled with the aromatic forest air. On top of everything else, who had just saved all their lives? Par, *that's* who. He didn't need to see himself as somehow less than Enio, not anymore.

"Hey, Enio. Steer us to the left. There are fewer vines."

His friend steered them over.

Par sat back. He could handle Enio.

When Lani next woke, Par asked, "Any idea how much farther?"

She studied the passing trees. "Maybe another day."

"Great! Where will we come out?"

"I guess near the Crescent. Pop said it runs along the southern border of the Urdel."

Par had never agreed with Enio to keep their destination a secret, but if Lani knew of the Crescent, of the Borderlands…

"Lani, have you ever heard of Banes?"

She nodded. "Pop mentioned it."

"Yes!" Par let out a huge breath of relief.

"Par…" Enio's face darkened.

Par raised his eyebrows in a silent question.

Enio turned back to the river. "Forget it."

"Lani, how far to Banes?"

"Not sure. Couple days?"

Everything was coming together. "What else do you know about the Borderlands?"

"Neutral territory as far as your wars go, but I don't remember much. Eagle's Watch, Xol Tomot, Grey—"

Enio jerked to attention. "Did you say Xol Tomot?"

Par jolted too. That's where John and Buckets had fought the Sorcerer Tomot. Where Buckets had been cursed.

"Well," she said, "I'm not sure we can avoid the place."

Enio thrust his paddle hard into the water. "Who wants to avoid it?" The fire was back in his voice.

"What do you mean?" Par said.

"Xol Tomot." Enio made a tight grin. "That's where I get off."

CHAPTER TWENTY-FIVE

P AR HADN'T REALIZED Enio's problem with Lani had reached this level. To abandon them at Xol Tomot? "You can't be serious."

"You want to get to Banes, not me."

Par's mind flashed over the past few days. Maybe he should have listened closer to his friend's grumblings. Still, Par could use Enio's dream of sailing the sea to keep them together. After all, a good leader helps his people achieve their goals. "You need the coracle to get to the coast."

"I'll go to Xol Tomot, piss on the wall where they hurt Buckets. Then make my own boat."

Par sighed. He'd give Enio more time to work out his issues. "Whatever makes you happy. Let's stop for the day."

The forest here was no darker than usual. He helped Lani onto a patch of ground under a large oak. She closed her eyes and sat back.

Par called to Enio. "Can you find some wood?"

Enio shuffled into the trees.

Par watched Lani for a long moment. The late sunlight combed through her hair. He recalled the first time he'd seen her face, an angel above the wither swamp. She looked like an angel now.

She opened her eyes and smiled.

Par smiled back. "How you doing?"

She took a deep breath. "The dun must have done a job on me."

Even though Par had told no one of his shadow—not even Enio—he didn't want to keep that from Lani anymore. Maybe knowing would somehow help her. He'd stop short of telling her how it made him different. How he couldn't invoke.

He settled beside her and swallowed. "Before I left the abbey, the Father Abbot looked into my soul. He saw a shadow. Do you think it's the dun?"

"I've never heard of the dun living inside someone. No, that doesn't sound possible."

Par hoped she was right. He changed the subject. "Sorry about Enio. Like I said, he's had a hard week."

"Haven't we all?" Lani gave a slight chuckle.

"When you said he had a strong communion with a river, you were right. He loved the river near our home. It was pretty much all he had."

The humor left her face. "Did it upset him?"

"Don't worry about it."

Lani paused. "He doesn't like me, does he?"

"I think he's just jealous."

"Of what?"

Par rubbed the back of his neck. "That you and I are friends. He can be a little childish. Give him time."

"Yeah, give me time." Enio stood at the edge of the trees with an armful of firewood.

Par felt a stab of guilt at being caught talking behind his friend's back. He said nothing as Enio scratched out a shallow fire pit.

At last, Lani said, "Enio, I'm sorry if your river was private."

"I liked my river, it's no secret. And no one likes secrets. You both said so." He arranged the kindling, then brushed off his hands and knelt in front of the heap.

Par waited, but when Enio did nothing further, he asked, "Aren't you going to ignite it?"

"It's your turn."

"Mine?" Par stared at his friend.

"Sure. Let 'er rip."

"Um," Par glanced at Lani and back to Enio. "Why don't I find some river potatoes? Lani can you light—"

"I'm not up to it, Par," she said, "not after the dun."

Par scowled at Enio. Desperation began to simmer in his heart. "Enio, can I talk to you? Alone?"

"Let's talk here. We're a *team*, right?"

Before Par could reply, Enio slapped himself on the forehead. "Now *I'm* the one being thick. Par's cursed and can't invoke the gods." Enio poked a finger into the sticks and they burst into flame.

"Dammit, Enio!" Par jumped to his feet.

Enio did too. "I'm tired of these games. You almost got us killed."

"I what?"

"You forced us down this stream."

"But we all agreed—"

"And your 'shadow' story? You didn't think that was important to tell her until now? Or *me*?"

"But I *saved* you. The dun left when I—"

"And why was that, Par? Why did it take me but leave you?"

"How in the purple hells should I know?"

Enio stepped toward Lani. "I bet *she* knows."

Par blocked him. "Are you crazy? It grabbed her too."

Enio stopped an inch from Par's nose. "She wasn't the one it dragged over the side."

"Guys," Lani breathed.

Enio tried to push ahead. "You invoked it, didn't you?"

Par blocked him again. "Keep away from her!"

Enio pointed past. "You made us think it was after *you*! And you knew Par would leave me and—"

"I'm sick of this!" Par shouted. "She was closer. It was killing her!"

"Par," Lani said, "Enio's right."

Par turned. His mouth hung open. His arguments, his defenses, shattered like a dropped plate.

Enio stomped. "I *told* you!"

"No," Lani interrupted, "I don't mean me summoning the dun, or any of Enio's other craziness. But he's right about secrets. I said I hated them, and I've been the worst of all."

"What do you mean?" Par asked.

"Well, there's no easy way to say this." She turned to the fire. "The thing is, I'm dying."

For a moment, Par couldn't move. The word echoed in his ears.

Enio snorted. "Dying? I'll tell you what I think—"

"Nobody cares, Enio!" Par dropped at her side. He lowered his voice. "The dun hurt you that bad?"

"It surely didn't help. But that's not the reason."

"What then?" Par searched her eyes.

"I should have told you. But I was afraid—" She shook her head. "Let's be done with secrets. I've said that young nymphs go in search of the *chela élande*—the heart of the élan. This isn't just a coming-of-age ritual. A nymph *must* do this. And my time is almost up."

"But you're only half nymph." Par didn't know what else to say.

She smiled. "Hey, I'm not telling you for sympathy. Everything has its time. But by dun or by time, the élan balances things out."

"I'm sorry." His throat clenched.

"It's all right, Par." She pushed herself up. "Help me to the fire."

Par did. Enio stood aside. Par ignored him.

She settled on the sand, Par beside her. "I told you my mother and father were gone. Well, Pop is gone, but he didn't die. When it came time for my heart-walk, there was no longer a place for him with the nymphs. I had assumed we'd go off together."

"But you didn't?"

A sadness settled in her eyes. "One morning, he just left. I found a note that said how much he loved me, but he couldn't bear keeping me from my destiny. He said I had to go into the woodlands and find the heart. That my mother would have wanted that."

Par felt the familiar pang of missing his own family.

Lani went on, "I think I've always been split between looking for the élan and looking for him. Pop said he'd never go back to the lands of men—if captured, he might lead them to the nymphs. But I hoped finding you was my chance to see him again before…" She shrugged.

"We'll do everything we can to help."

Lani brightened. "Well, that's all the secrets I can think of. How about you?"

Par saw no point in hiding anything else. "Let's see. We're running from one of the most powerful men in Eloria. I'm supposed to have my head ripped open and fixed because I can't invoke. And Enio is guilty of high heresy and subject to execution. That's really about it."

Chapter Twenty-Six

Prior Dogam hurried across the wharf of Bishop's Landing. The air boomed with the shouts of workers preparing their vessels for a new day. Twice the Prior nearly lost the cheese pastries he carried in a collision. He waved off a brazen seagull who was begging him to do just that.

The High Sigil Master stood where the Prior had left him—beside a single-mast patrol boat and its captain, a stumpy man with a fat grey mustache and weathered eyes. The captain's expression was one of surprise and anxiety, as if a water wasp had landed on his wrist and he were afraid to flick it.

"You still don't seem to understand," huffed the man. "I sail under the authority of Master Simeon, Judge of the Doors. My duty—"

"Your duty is to the Hierarchy," Cronus said patiently. "I ask only that you reorder your normal route to take me downriver."

"But some other vessel—"

"I see no other vessel captained by such a capable man." The Sigil Master's voice took on a splash of syrup. "Or a man who can speed us along with the most alacrity."

Captain Humbard frowned behind his whiskers, but his double chins crinkled with pride.

"I assure you, Captain," Cronus leaned in, "your loyalty to the Hierarchy will not be overlooked. I will personally see that you are honored in Argent."

The Prior backed up the argument with a nod. Praise from the High Sigil Master—a few words to the right people—could be a boon to the captain's career. As hopefully they would be for the Prior's.

Humbard's mustache lost some of its disapproving droop. "Well, I suppose as long as the trip is along my route…"

"Thank you, Captain," said the High Master.

The man spun on his heel and waddled up the gangplank. "Look smart, mates! We launch in an hour."

A chorus of "ayes" echoed from the handful of crewmen.

The captain's wake smelled of rum. The Prior wrinkled his nose. "You believe this man a gifted sailor?"

Cronus kept his voice low. "Certainly not. But the other vessels are not fitted for sea travel."

"Of course." Once they reached the Silver Sea, there would still be the voyage west along the coast to meet Par in Jod. The Prior offered the Sigil Master a pastry. "Have you told the captain of our mission?"

"Only that we are pursuing two criminals, enemies of the state."

The Prior started. "But in your letter you promised to forgive Enio's heresy."

Cronus held the baked good flat in his palm and examined it at eye level. "The captain needs an official reason to take us aboard. Seeking two waifs in spiritual crisis will not suffice. In fact, I sent a similar message to the Governor of Jod."

"I don't understand. If their governor imprisons them—"

"Relax, Dogam. I keep my promises." He gestured for the

Prior to bring their few bags. "Our treaty with the Borderlands contains no articles regarding a child suspected of a cursement. But it requires they at least detain designated criminals. We cannot risk Par proceeding further south, perhaps falling into the hands of Arcana." He grimaced at the pastry, tossed it into the bay and continued up the gangplank. Vigilant seagulls tore the delicate item to pieces like wolves on a fresh kill.

The Prior knew little of treaties, but such knowledge might help him advance in the Hierarchy. His time with Cronus could give him insights into those subtleties.

He frowned at their bags, praying that this tutelage encompassed more than food service and baggage handling.

Within the hour, the patrol vessel was under way. Later in the day, the Sigil Master invoked again on the *Sea Dog* plank. The boys still headed south. Toward sunset, heavy clouds moved in. By evening, the sky grew darker still, and impish winds caused the crew to furl the sails and take only the current. Heavy rains came with the evening. The river roiled in the torrent. The Prior, the captain and the Sigil Master huddled outside the cabin doors.

"That's it," Humbard barked through the winds. "We have to find anchorage."

The Sigil Master roared back. "No, Captain. We will sail through the storm."

"The hells we will! High Sigil Master or not, I won't risk—"

"Say again, Captain?" Cronus raised a hand to his ear. "May we discuss this in your cabin?"

Humbard snarled through his whiskers and led the Sigil Master inside. The Prior tried to follow, but Cronus shut him out.

The Prior pressed against the door, shrinking from the rains. He could feel the eyes of the crew on his back, could almost hear the snickers at the High Master's secretary. His bag mule.

Shouts came from beyond the door, but he couldn't make out the words.

Then a scream.

Before the Prior could enter, the door flew open and knocked him back.

Captain Humbard rushed out, eyes wild, mouth frothing. He shoved past the Prior and disappeared up to the helm and into the downpour.

Cronus stood in the doorway, seeming almost pleased. He took the Prior's elbow and ushered him inside.

The cabin was comfortable for a patrol vessel, especially compared to the mere closets for the crew. A desk, lanterns, a padded chair, a small bed. The Sigil Master stooped beneath the low ceiling and went to the desk. "The captain is taking the helm and has volunteered his cabin for our use." He lifted a bottle out of a drawer. "Would you care for some wine?"

"That would be quite welcome, thank you." The Prior brushed off the rain splatter, wondering about the captain's change of attitude. Wind howled outside the walls, and rain drummed on the windows. The wine was a bit too sweet, but the Prior downed it anyway and took a second glass.

While Cronus thumbed through the captain's books and journals, the Prior settled on the bed. The wine, the rain, and the rocking of the lamps soon lulled him like a warm blanket. He settled back and closed his eyes.

A pounding on the door jolted him awake.

Cronus opened it before the Prior had left the bunk. The storm had passed, and morning light streamed in. A blushing young crewman, the ship's first mate, stood at the door. Fear twisted his freckled face. "It's the captain, sirs. Something's wrong."

They followed the crewman to the helm. Humbard was still at his post. Others stood nearby, eyes wide.

"He's been there the entire night," said the mate. "We found him this morning and tried to get him to lay off. He won't budge."

"Rest him on deck," Cronus commanded.

Humbard stood stiffly, gasping in shallow, broken breaths. His fingers gripped the wheel so tightly the men had to pry them off. The man's face was set like granite, and his swollen, bloodshot eyes never blinked.

They got him onto the deck. His chest heaved once more and stopped.

The Sigil Master studied him a moment and closed the eyelids. "I'm afraid Captain Humbard is dead."

The crew gasped as one, some making superstitious gestures.

"His heart," added the Sigil Master, rising from the body. He turned to the first mate. "What do they call you, son?"

"I, um—Willy, sir. It's short for Williped Ta—"

"You're in charge now, Willy. Have the body prepared. I will perform the blessing."

Willy nodded rapidly.

"And can you tell where we are?"

"Yes, High Master Sigil, sir. The Greening Delta."

"Excellent. When we reach the sea, turn us to Argent."

Prior Dogam's anxiety jumped. Not only had the Sigil Master made no effort to heal the captain, but Argent was in the opposite direction of Jod. What about their rush to find the boys?

The new captain and his crew whispered together. The Prior remained with the Sigil Master. "We're going to Argent?"

"We will make up the time. I have much to tell you when we arrive."

The Sigil Master gave the blessing over the body. It was formal and proper and it seemed to comfort the crew.

"Humbard was a fine man," Cronus proclaimed. "He was faithful to his duty and to the Hierarchy. He will be honored in Argent."

The words sent a shudder through the Prior. When they'd first met Captain Humbard, Cronus had promised the man that very thing.

Chapter Twenty-Seven

THE NEXT MORNING, Par barely got a word out of anybody. He woke Lani when breakfast was ready. "How you doing?"

"About the same."

"Feel like talking?"

She shook her head and nibbled her food.

He didn't blame her for being distant—now that she knew he was cursed and had a darkness inside. At least she was still civil.

Unlike Enio.

"Good morning," Par said as Enio came back from the bushes.

Enio passed without looking. "Shove it."

Par stopped himself before snapping back. Everything was a mess, and he didn't want to make it worse.

They continued down the Sirisa. The morning dragged on. Lani spent most of the time dozing. She seemed paler than yesterday. Bulbous, bald hills gradually replaced the forest. Later in the day, the hills ahead fell away. Sunlight sparkled on a river that cut through grassy plains, and the white-capped Ults rose in the far west. Par hadn't seen them since he'd left the abbey. A renewed homesickness spoiled his relief.

He swallowed his heartache. "The Borderlands?"

"It ain't Bishop's Landing," muttered Enio.

Par gently woke Lani. "I think we found the Crescent." He studied her carefully.

She sat up a little. "I think you're right."

Their own stream flowed into it. Lani made them thank the Sirisa and wish it well as it joined its brothers and sisters. Enio huffed, but didn't object. Par hoped that was progress.

The coracle drifted into the Crescent and glided along. Other creeks occasionally trickled in from the direction of the Urdel. Intermittent hills along the banks sometimes sharpened into rocky cliffs and hid the southern plains.

As the low sun hung yellow in the late evening sky, the coracle approached a river canyon bounded by high crags. Their stony crowns, obscured in shadow, gave the ominous impression of parapets. Before Par could comment on this, Enio barked, "Xol Tomot!"

On a hill ahead rose a keep, with a fat tower surrounded by looming walls. High windows threw back the sunset in an orange glint. A wooden landing jutted from the shore, and a run of steps zigzagged up the hill.

"Xol Tomot," Enio said again more softly, with a slight grin.

Par knelt next to him. They needed to get to Banes before the Prior and Sigil Master arrived in Jod and searched upriver. But Par had never hoped to see an old battleground from the Grey Wars, and Xol Tomot had a special meaning: it was where Buckets had been cursed.

As if in unspoken agreement, Enio steered the coracle to the aged landing. Squat pylons marked the corners where neglected ropes drooped from rusted rings. Par helped Lani onto the docks.

Enio tied the boat and scurried to the stairs.

Par called after him. "Where're you going?"

"Up."

Even if the keep were abandoned by man, there were still guests from the wilderness to consider. "What if there are, I don't know, bears or something?"

Enio ignored him and took the steps two at a time.

Bears or not, Par couldn't miss a once-in-a-lifetime chance to see Xol Tomot up close. "Wait for us!" He tried to usher Lani across the landing.

She stopped him. "Don't think I'm ready for a climb."

Par glanced at Enio's shrinking figure. "Well, I can stay—"

"Don't do that to me."

Par froze. "Do what?"

"Make me a burden. I couldn't stand it."

Par looked at her with new admiration. "Are you sure? If there are animals nearby—"

"Nymph, remember? I'll be fine. Besides, I'd like some private time with the Crescent."

Par reluctantly nodded. "I promise I won't be long."

She beamed a reassuring smile, sat near the coracle and began to chat with the river.

Enio had already passed two zigs. Par hurried after. With Lani staying behind, this was a perfect chance to get Enio alone, make sure he hadn't been serious about abandoning them. Par couldn't let him leave, especially if Lani's condition worsened. And things would be better from here on out, with Par calling the shots. He'd make Enio see that.

A broken stone balustrade shouldered the worn, dusty climb. After a few hundred steps, Par arrived panting at the base of the keep's silent walls. A tall iron door loomed before him. There was no sign of Enio. Lani sat far below at the edge of the docks. Par waved, but she didn't look.

He tried the doors. They wouldn't budge. He continued right, to the west corner, and peeked around. "Enio?"

A sudden flurry of crows leapt from the parapets and sent his heart into his throat. The birds cawed, circled once, and disappeared.

Par leaned against the wall and gathered his wits. The view was breathtaking. Vast purple plains swept below him. The Ults stood stark and white under an angry sunset. Dark lines cut through their roots—the Urdel, extending its reach.

He slid around the corner, running his left hand along the rough stone. Halfway to the end, the wall smoothed for several steps, but it offered nothing in the way of an entrance.

When he reached the far corner, Enio stepped around and walked right into him.

Par yelped, then laughed nervously. "We have to stop meeting this way."

Enio sidestepped him and walked on.

Par turned and followed. "Find anything?"

"More big doors, shut. No bears."

"Ha-ha," Par grumbled. "I found a smooth spot, but no openings."

Enio stopped. "Where?"

Par led him to the section.

Enio ran his hand over the stone. "A repair. Must be where Buckets' breached the wall." He unlaced his pants.

"What—" Par began, but remembered Enio's promise to piss on the spot where Tomot had hurt their friend from the abbey.

"Come on," Enio murmured. "We have to do it together. For Buckets."

"Right." Par undid his pants and stood shoulder to shoulder with Enio. As the sunset painted their soft shadows onto the weathered stone, Par honored their friend, beside his own friend.

"Good old Buckets," Enio said.

Par nodded. "Good old Buckets." His plan to lay down the law leaked away with the gentle tinkle of water.

Enio completed his honorific and laced back up.

Par feared he would walk away. "Wait until I'm done. That's the rule."

"I am."

Par had finished, but he continued to face the wall. "I don't want us to be mad at each other."

"I'm not mad." He didn't *sound* mad.

"It's all right if you are. I'm sorry you lost your Lustering medal. And the *Sea Dog*."

Enio sighed. "I told you. It's stupid to get attached to things. I'm… over it."

Par spoke softly. "Are you mad because I like her?"

Enio was silent a moment. Then, in a tone Par couldn't quite identify, he began, "Par, I—"

A voice bellowed from above. "I trust you two are planning to clean that up."

Par jerked. A man in long black robes stood on the battlements. His shaven face glowed ruddy in the setting sun, and his hair hung curly and white in the still air.

"Who're you?" Enio yelled. Par frantically laced his pants.

"I am the Sorcerer Tomot." The voice came gruff and commanding. "And *you* are trespassing."

Par stopped breathing. Tomot! They had to run. Now. But his legs wouldn't work.

Enio's mouth still did. "Tomot? You maggot! You hurt Buckets!"

The man's tone wavered. "I'm sorry, who?"

Before Par could react, Enio grabbed up a stone and rockshot it at the figure. It pinged off a parapet.

"Is *that* how we're doing this?" The man held up his arms. With a howl of wind and a billow of robes, his body rose above the wall. The atmosphere darkened. An explosion ripped through the air. Par was thrown to the ground.

He staggered to his feet, gasping. A patch of gravel between him and Enio had been blasted into a black scar.

Another crack and flash. Par saw it before it knocked him back—lightning, striking only inches away.

"Crap!" Enio scrambled up.

"Run!" Par grabbed his friend. They flew to the stairs. Every few seconds, another blast erupted at their heels. One shattered part of a railing.

Lani waved them on. "What's happening?"

"Tomot!" Par yelled.

They skidded onto the docks. Enio yanked off the tie rope. "Get in!"

The frightful bolts had ceased somewhere during their descent. Enio sped them away with the paddle. Par splashed with his hands to help.

At last, he dared a look back. A grim cloud of crows wheeled above the keep. A figure stood on the battlements, the Sorcerer Tomot, statue-like against the dimming sky.

CHAPTER TWENTY-EIGHT

Humbard's lifeless face haunted the Prior. The eyes were the worst. Like some crazed beast.

Or… a navigaunt on a dire flight? Had the Master invoked such a thing on the captain?

To accuse the Master of this horror would surely strain the man's trust, even bring another invasion of the Prior's mind. He couldn't risk that, not with the growing doubt as to whether he should continue to help the Master or bring this crime before the Hierarchy. And what if the Prior were wrong? He'd be throwing away his best chance at a distinguished career.

By midday they'd passed through the Greening Delta, reached the shimmering Silver Sea and turned east toward Argent. Rising cliffs overtook the shores. Late in the day, a crewman shouted, "Point ho!"

The shining spires of the High Temple soared above the eastern horizon, and the Prior's spirits rose with them. Soon, the boat rounded the towering cliffs of the Bay of Argent. The capital city broke upon his eyes like a shining vision of the Higher Realms.

Master Cronus moved to his side. "Have you spent much time in Argent, Prior?"

"Just for my training." In his time, he'd fallen in love with the city.

The offshore island slanted upwards toward the sea and ended in a thousand-foot wall of granite. The island's low, inland side, thick with piers and boats and wrapped by a high wall, connected across the bay to the mainland over a great causeway. With more cliffs shouldering the mainland town, the sight always gave the Prior the impression of a massive bowl, chipped to its base on three sides.

They sailed to the island near a wharf of multi-masted Navy ships, straight and trim, flying the flags of Argent—a triple-pointed crown. The ships seemed idle, with no urgency of war. Had the Prior misinterpreted the Master's words about the building tensions with Arcana? Maybe he was overthinking other things too. If nothing else, the delay to reach Jod gave him more time to work through his mounting uncertainties. If he were to abandon this whole affair, Argent would be his best opportunity. In that case, he'd destroy the remnant of the *Sea Dog,* so the Sigil Master could no longer track the boys. The Prior needed to decide soon.

As they disembarked, a shining black carriage with a noble horse was brought without delay to the Sigil Master. The Prior settled into the soft leather seats, inhaling the perfumed interior. How dignified this was, compared to sitting in a faraway abbey, watching an old man dribble soup. They clopped past the tall public gates and up through the city. The Prior's eyes rested on the verdant parks and stately lanes and stylish people. His fears of a war seemed far away, just an unpleasant dream.

At last they arrived at the highest point of the island. Backed to the drop-off of the lofty cliffs loomed the High Temple with its silver spires and massive golden doors. Compared to that, the Abbey Saint Livius was a shanty shack. Across a majestic central fountain stood the domed palace of their Eminence and Fondiscate, Pompeius Maxima Arcalus, girded with balconies that overlooked the graceful city and busy bay.

They entered the temple. Functionaries, dressed in the gowns of their lesser ranks, bowed and made way. The Prior nodded as he passed, trying to look humble. It wasn't difficult. The Sigil Master turned into a pillared side corridor and up a slim, ornate stair, and finally to the doors of the High Master's chambers. Inside, beyond a room of stark furniture with the feel of a private library, a balcony faced the sea. Its view, a thousand feet high, must be spectacular.

The Prior stepped that way, but the Sigil Master stopped him. "Over here."

They turned instead to a small, cupped alcove walled with books. The volumes of histories and sigils were more complete than the Prior had ever seen. "Beyond price," he whispered.

"Indeed, they are."

Prior Dogam noticed a thick black tome with the silver markings of the Profana. While he debated asking the Master about its place in the High Temple, a heavy pounding shook the chamber doors.

"Cronus!" shouted an angry woman.

"Melora?"

The Prior gasped. The Lady Melora, along with Simeon and Master Cronus, were the highest persons in the Hierarchy, under only the Fondiscate himself. To meet her would be one of the greatest honors of his career. Could an audience with the Fondiscate be far behind? Now he truly walked the halls of power.

Thank the gods the Prior hadn't abandoned his journeys with the Sigil Master. Besides, Cronus would probably get Par's cooperation whether or not the Prior helped.

The woman called again. "That's *Lady* Melora. Better yet, Lady Melora, Lord of the House."

The Master's tone was less than reverential. "What is it this time?"

Another heavy thump. "Meddling in the provinces without my oversight? We need to talk."

The Master lowered his voice. "I have to take this, Dogam. Wait for me."

"Of course." Would he get an introduction? He sniffed his robe, not having bathed.

Cronus left the alcove and gestured. A wall slid across its entrance.

The Prior reached out—too late. He was sealed inside. A strange blue light seeped from the edges of the floor. Then his small room began to descend.

Was this a private conveyor to the first level?

The chamber continued down.

To the cellars?

The air chilled as he descended. The Prior waited—there seemed no other option.

Finally, the room jolted to a stop. The wall slid back. A passage stretched ahead, lit by the same luminescence. The masonry looked ancient.

He stepped into the passage. Glass orbs in wall sconces glowed pale blue along its length. A steady light shone in their centers.

A scraping came from behind. The alcove had resealed. The Sigil Master had told him to wait, but did that mean here, in this dim hallway? Perhaps, but the Prior had lost patience with shut doors and walls and postponed explanations. He walked forward.

Narrow corridors opened on either hand, then cell-like rooms with cages that hung from high ceilings. A dungeon?

Hoary wooden doors slipped by. Before he picked one to investigate, the hallway ended in a thick stone door. Carved on its surface was an eight-pointed star. It stood cracked open. He peeked in and froze, barely believing his eyes.

A ghostly orb several paces across floated in the large, round chamber. Golden sparks twinkled across its surface, like stars in the night sky. A low black rail surrounded the sphere. Scattered tables and chairs were positioned around that.

The Prior didn't know how long he stared at the lights before a hand touched his shoulder. He barely flinched. "What is this?" he whispered in awe.

"An outpost of the Vigil," said the Sigil Master.

"The—"

Cronus ushered him into the room. He carried a carafe with a bottle and two glasses and placed it on a desk. "It is time for our talk, Dogam."

✳

Cronus touched the spectral surface of the globe. A point of light expanded into a cluster. "This is Argent."

The Prior recognized it, lights like fireflies sparkling in the shape of the island capital and the mainland town. "A map?"

"More than a map. The Monitor shows every active invocation within fifty leagues."

The Prior caught his breath. "I did not know the Hierarchy could create such things."

"It can't. The Monitor is over a thousand years old."

"Before the birth of Eloria?"

Without warning, Cronus gripped the Prior's head and broke into his mind. Unlike at Bishop's Landing, the Master entered not as a Confessor, sifting through thoughts and memories.

He came with the power of a Reckoner. The power to make changes.

The Prior resisted, but the High Master's will was supreme. It crashed upon him like a hammer at the forge. He found no retreat. He steeled himself for what would come.

White pain came. And with the pain, a voice.

This is a great honor, Dogam. Embrace it.

Images exploded in his mind, fragments of strange thoughts and visions. They seared into his memory. He thought he screamed.

The pain drew back. The images knitted together. A land unfolded before him, a blooming paradise of bright fountains, splendid towers, and magic. Glories blazed upon the heads of the people. But not golden alone. He saw the divine invocations of the gods used side by side with the profane incantations of Arcana.

These were the Gardens of Gê, the birthplace of humanity from legend.

The vision changed.

A magnificent man with the bushy red hair of a lion stood in a ring of fire. Knowledge came to the Prior along with this vision. Somehow combining the different magics, the mage Ridiax created a portal, an impossible doorway to the Higher Realms, that he might ascend among the gods. But he lost control. With a piteous cry, the man was swallowed up as by the heart of the sun.

The inferno spread across the paradise, leaving behind only dust and ash. The Prior had no means to look away. He struggled not to faint at the death and devastation. Other fearsome mages, survivors, labored together and pushed back the fires, finally containing the blazing rift—the Immortus—in a black pit ringed with obsidian monoliths.

The images faded. The Prior reeled. His head thundered with each driving heartbeat. He lay panting at the Master's feet.

Cronus helped him stand. "You'll recover in a moment, Dogam. I've made no changes to your mind, except to share these memories. I received them when the Vigil recruited me. As I now recruit you."

"Recruit—" He raised his leaden eyes.

"To the Vigil. Or what's left." Cronus uncorked his bottle and filled two glasses with a brown liquid. "After the mages contained the Immortus, they resettled the survivors far beyond their lands.

The people of the profane, celestial magics became the country of Arcana. The rest founded Eloria."

He offered a glass to the Prior. "An acquired taste."

The Prior's hand trembled as he lifted it to his mouth. He sipped and grimaced at the sour bitterness, like rotten fruit.

Cronus continued, "Of course, the formation of our countries took many generations. But by guiding our prejudices and laws and taboos, the Vigil Terrestria has kept the magics divided between Arcana and Eloria, preventing anyone from achieving such power again and causing another Devastation."

The Master's words began to take root. Prior Dogam spoke carefully. "The Hierarchy, the Fondiscate, has kept all this—"

Cronus laughed. "No, Dogam. They know nothing of these truths. Or of this Outpost. They hold the Rule precious, as a toddler might covet a favored blanket."

Regardless of the wine, the Prior's blood chilled at the scope of the deceit. What of heretics executed for using Arcanan magic? He'd consigned the boy Enio to trial for the same fate. If these things were true—and with the certainty that came with a Reckoning, he could not deny it—then his training, his ambitions, were a lie, a fool's quest.

Despair threatened to crush him, yet the High Master must see some larger purpose here. Some light in this darkness. "Why tell me these things? Is there some connection to Par?"

"To the point, Dogam. I like that. Can you walk?"

The Prior tried a step and nodded.

Cronus ushered him around the Monitor. "The other arm of the Vigil, the Vigil Immortus, was tasked with closing the rift contained by the monoliths. When I was recruited, before the Grey Wars, the Vigil had been at a dead end for centuries. Fools, all. They believed they might lay bare the mysteries of the Immortus, yet they'd kept the magics of Arcana and Eloria separate, consigning to oblivion the very knowledge that created it. But I have found a new path to its secrets."

"A new path?"

"Yes, Dogam. Invocations are futile near the rift. Yet I have discovered that not only can the Immortus be used to treat those suffering a curse, but the ways in which it affects a curse can be used to study the Immortus."

The Prior halted as he realized, "You want to study the effect of the Immortus on Par."

The Sigil Master waited.

"But why him? There must be others—"

"There have been others. But curses are rare things. When I discovered the boy's strange resistance to Location sigils, I became more intrigued than ever. His curse must be singularly strong. It may allow him unprecedented exposure to the flames of the rift."

The fiery visions returned to the Prior's mind, and the fate of Ridiax, the man who created it. A quiet horror grew in his chest. "What might this do to Par?"

"We must proceed with great care. I'd rather avoid another Buckets."

Buckets! Tommy, the man at the abbey with a ravaged mind and disfigured body, had been sent to Argent to have his curse treated. "His current condition is not a result of the war, but of the Immortus?"

"It is unfortunate, Dogam. But such is the outcome when a subject fights the procedure."

The Prior's heart sickened with the thought of Par, disfigured and feeble, stumbling through the abbey halls. "Could you not have overcome Tommy's resistance? A Reckoning—"

"A Reckoning would indeed have made him compliant. But it would have changed his mental landscape and contaminated my research. For the same reasons, I need Par as he is."

Many of the Master's past statements began to make sense—

why he needed the Prior to convince Par to cooperate, why he cared so little about Enio's heresy, and why he so easily dismissed the rule of the Hierarchy. But there was still something Cronus had not explained.

"At Bishop's Landing, you said we would soon be at war, and that Par's curse might put our country at risk. Was that true?"

Cronus shifted his eyes to the twinkling globe. "Our study of the boy may confirm such threats from his curse, but one thing is clear: we cannot sit around, century after century, hoping for some breakthrough with the Immortus. What if the monoliths weaken or fail while we wait?"

The Prior had no answer. No one alive could stop those devastating fires.

"And consider this, Prior. Without Par's help, I must continue the endless hunt for curses. War, however, forces curses from the shadows as people use them as weapons. As I've told you, changes have been made in high places. With very little effort—and for the good of our world—I could push our countries into such a war."

The Prior felt the blood drain from his face.

The Master turned his dark eyes on the Prior. "But with Par's help, that can be avoided. If his curse is the key to understanding the Immortus, he may be the last subject I'll ever need."

The revelations created a new agony. Cronus was asking the Prior to weigh an innocent boy's life against the safety of the world, against the specter and death of war. "And if I refuse my help?" He doubted Cronus would let him merely walk away.

The man smiled and laid a hand on the Prior's shoulder. "I will not force you, Dogam. I've searched your mind and seen your heart. You are a good man and understand the supremacy of our goal over all others."

The Sigil Master resumed their walk around the Monitor. "As in war, our duty is to sacrifice for the greater good. What more honorable, more sacred sacrifice, than one boy risking his life to save countless others? But as I said, the risks are minimized if he cooperates. So I need you to persuade him. It's for his benefit, and for all."

Cronus stopped at the far side of the Monitor. "I realize this is a lot to digest, but remember, the highest dictate of the Rule is to care for those in our charge. For members of the Vigil, this applies to Elorians and Arcanans alike. Our path is clear."

"What of the rest of the Vigil? Will they help?" The Master had called them fools.

"The rest… we two are all that remain. But I did not bring you here to simply expound on their History. Nor to show you the Monitor."

An archway in the back wall extended for a single pace and ended in solid rock. An ominous black step, covered with strange sigils, sat at its mouth.

"This is why we came. Another charm from long ago."

The High Master detached a black stone like a small idol worn by time from around his neck. He held it in the space of the archway. The sigils on the stone flashed, and the ones on the step answered. The passageway shimmered. A vista opened beyond.

It was as if the Prior looked through a door upon a city—but not Argent. Rugged walled towers rose before a crashing sea at the mouth of a great river.

The Prior had no words. As with the Monitor, he'd never seen such magic.

Cronus still held forth the black object. "The Threshold allows passage to anywhere the possessor of a keystone has ever seen."

The Master's cryptic statement on the patrol boat came back to the Prior, when they'd turned from their pursuit of the boys. He'd said they would make up the time.

This was how. The Threshold was their shortcut to Jod.

Prior Dogam stood stunned, trying to process it all. He'd begun this journey to get his career back on track and out of the abbey. Retrieving the runaways had turned into a perfect opportunity and brought him into a partnership with the High Sigil Master himself, a man who could lift the Prior to the peak of government.

Now, everything had turned upside down. His ambitions in the Hierarchy seemed trivial, only a child's fancy. But was there any going back? Was this what it truly means to walk the halls of power?

The Sigil Master motioned him forward. "If you please, Dogam. We have an appointment to keep."

The Prior took a breath and stepped through.

CHAPTER TWENTY-NINE

P AR'S HEART STILL pounded as Xol Tomot faded among the twilit cliffs. How could Enio be so foolish, running right up to its walls? They were lucky to be alive.

Lani had slumped in the coracle. He tried to rouse her.

She didn't move.

"Lani?" He felt her forehead. "She's hot." He shook her again. "She won't wake up. Oh gods, Enio—"

"Move." Enio pushed him aside. He invoked and touched her brow. She stirred, and her eyelids fluttered open. She smiled up at Enio. He stared for what seemed a long time before backing away.

She turned to Par. "Did I drop off again?"

Par sighed with relief and moved in. "Yeah. How're you feeling?"

"Better. What about *you*? The way you flew down those steps, I thought you'd break your neck."

"I'm fine." Her concern touched him, considering how weak she was herself.

Enio knelt at the front of the boat, guiding them along the river. "I'm all right, too, by the way."

Par spoke to his friend's back. "Don't run off like that again."

When no response came, Par again addressed Lani. "You should rest."

"Maybe just my eyes." In another moment, she was asleep.

Par checked her forehead. "She's all right now."

"Probably not for long," Enio mumbled.

Par's jaw tightened at the callous answer. "You don't know that. But—you can keep doing those healings, right?"

"I'm no Sigil Master. A couple times a day, and I'm out. Pretty soon, it won't be enough."

Par glanced back the way they'd come. "If we found the other nymphs…"

Enio kept paddling.

"Hey, are you listening?"

"We have no clue where they are. And they didn't help us with the dun."

He was right.

"So what do we do?" Par asked.

"Maybe someone in Banes can help."

"Vex?" Par looked hopefully at Lani.

Enio said nothing.

The canyon cliffs dropped again into intermittent bluffs. Except for the trill of insects and the slosh of water against their hull, the evening remained quiet. At least the Sorcerer Tomot hadn't chased them. They spent the night stopped along the banks, sleeping in the coracle.

The morning brought more endless fields and broken hills. With Lani always asleep and Enio keeping to himself, Par rarely had anyone to talk with. His worry mounted that the Prior would shortly discover they weren't going to Jod. Worse, they needed to find help for Lani, and soon.

"Can't we go any faster?" he tried once.

Enio grunted and dug in the paddle. "You want to get out and push?"

Par just shook his head. Talking with Enio had stopped being useful. The rift between them had grown into an abyss. Par didn't know how to bridge it and was tired of trying. So their few words concerned where to stop or find food. At least Lani didn't get feverish again. Par let her sleep, but another worry added to the rest.

She wasn't eating.

The following day arrived with low, somber clouds. Late in the afternoon, when he thought his spirits could sink no further, clusters of boats and docks appeared around a bend. Par jumped and pointed. "There!"

They'd found Banes. It was nothing like Bishop's Landing. A long wharf, splintered and grey, verged on the river. Dingy sailing vessels and skiffs lined the docks. Warehouses ran back from the boardwalk, none as appealing as even the most neglected in St. Livius.

Toward the middle of the wharf, a fat pier—the main entry port—jutted into the broad river. They guided the coracle to the banks well before that, to a landing that was little more than a few boards pressed into the mud. A short ladder hung from the boardwalk, and a foul smell seeped from underneath.

Enio climbed out and tied the boat.

Par rose on his toes to peer above the walk. Alleys and small lanes led deeper into the town. No towers or grand arches. A few taverns and inns wedged themselves between the warehouses.

"Lani?" He squeezed her shoulder.

She opened her eyes and squinted. "I'm sorry, do I know you?"

Par stopped breathing.

Lani gave a little laugh. "I'm kidding. Don't be so serious all the time."

Relief washed over him. Her humor helped. But the vibrant

life he'd seen when they'd first met was nearly gone. He forced a smile. "Welcome to Banes."

She sat up with his help, glanced around and looked at him again, confused.

He nodded. "Not much, is it?"

"I didn't want to say."

Par chuckled and helped her to her feet. "Enio, give me a hand."

His friend was nowhere in sight.

"Dammit. Where's he gone?" Enio had threatened to leave them. Had he finally done it? Anger flared in Par's chest, but he gritted his teeth. He had to focus on Lani.

Par helped her struggle up the short ladder to the boardwalk. Few people were at this end of the wharf. Near the main port, figures with carts or animals shuffled to and from the piers and warehouses, and the shadowy little lanes.

His spirits fell further when he realized they'd never made a plan for what to do once they got here. The Abbot's words echoed in his head. *Find a man named Alexander Vex.* How? Wander around and ask?

Lani sank unsteadily onto the boardwalk's weathered planks. Par helped her down and sat beside her.

She was silent a moment, catching her breath. "The river's beautiful."

The Crescent flowed wide and strong past the town but wasn't anything special. Par looked up and down the waterway, trying to see it through her eyes.

A grizzled man with a gaunt face shrouded in a frayed blanket passed nearby. Par met his eyes and shuddered at his toothless stare. The man moved on.

Lani leaned against Par's side. He wrapped his arm around her shoulder. Her breathing was shallow. He needed to find Enio. And Vex. But he couldn't leave her alone.

Despair threatened to choke him. He didn't know what to do. "I'm sorry," he whispered. "We should have stayed in the forest. The nymphs—"

"They wouldn't have helped." She looked toward the main port. "Are all cities like this?"

Par almost smiled, despite his worries. "Gods, no. You should see the towers of Bishop's Landing. Or St. Livius. The abbey is by the river, and it's full of monks trying to get closer to the gods. I liked to climb the bell tower. You could see the whole world from there. Well, I used to think so."

"I'd love to see it," she said weakly.

"You *will*. I'll take you. And we'll sail with Enio in a new canoe down the Greening to the sea. We'll—" He couldn't finish.

"It's all right, Par." Her voice had a quiet cheerfulness.

Tears formed in the corners of his eyes, but he would not break down. Not now. He needed help. Should he call out? The people didn't look friendly. And the Borderlands were not known for its kindness to the weak and vulnerable.

Lani shivered. He gripped her more tightly. If he couldn't find Vex, maybe he could bargain with the Prior to get her help. Would they still Reckon him? Would he even recognize himself after that? Or his friends?

He shook his head. Did it even matter anymore?

As he agonized over his thoughts, someone thumped up behind. "Crap."

Par spun.

It was Enio.

"Where in the hells—" Par began, fire returning to his voice.

"Look." Enio shoved a parchment into Par's hands.

Lani leaned in. "What is it?"

It contained both Enio and Par's images. The word *Wanted* stretched in large black letters across the top, and underneath that:

Parynius (Par) and Enius Marius (Enio)

for high crimes and heresy

by Order of the Land of Eloria and
under the Treaty of Banes.

Reward 100g

All hope of finding help evaporated. Par glanced around. "They've already notified this miserable town? Way out here?"

"Keep reading," Enio hissed.

Par did. It cited local contacts and dates and other treaty language. Then, near the bottom were the words that froze his eyes in their sockets.

Dead or Alive.

CHAPTER THIRTY

"They want us dead?" Par's tongue felt like it had been dragged through sawdust.

Enio pointed to another line. "They get a lot less money that way."

"Great." Par sensed Lani's eyes on him. He couldn't meet them. "Now what?"

Enio took back the parchment, crumpled it and tossed it over the rail. He began lifting Lani to her feet. "Come on. I found a room. I don't think the guy recognized my face."

"We don't have any money."

"Well, *I* don't."

Was his friend being thick? They'd lost everything escaping Agron.

Enio stared at Par's chest, and Par remembered—his Lustering medal. He thumbed it through his shirt. It was the last thing he had of his home and his family.

"Hurry." Enio reached out. "Before we get caught."

There was no choice. With a heavy heart, Par lifted it over his head.

Enio grabbed it. "Let's go."

They supported Lani at every step. Enio led them to a building fronting the river where a worn sign read *Rooms*, then to an ugly line of doors. "Wait here." He disappeared around a corner.

Lani rested against the peeling wooden wall.

Par watched the wharf from the corner of his eye. No one else came close. He touched his chest again.

"Was that pendant important to you?" Lani asked softly.

Par wanted to lie, tell her it was nothing, but he couldn't bring himself to do it.

She seemed to understand. "I'm sorry."

Enio returned with a rusty key and unlocked a door.

The tiny room smelled of liquor and sweat. They laid Lani on the narrow bed. Near its head was a wooden chair and a small table that held an empty washbasin and a cold, half-burnt candle. A cracked mirror hung on the wall, and the single window by the door was thickly curtained.

Par wrinkled his nose. "You couldn't get anything better?"

Enio dropped the key and a few coins onto the table. "Not if we want to eat too." He slumped to the floor, his back against the door.

Par checked Lani's breathing. She'd passed out again—all he could do was let her rest. He dropped into the chair. "Dead or alive? Why would they want *me* dead? You're the one who committed heresy."

"So much for the Silver Sea." Enio hung his head. "I should've stayed in St. Livius."

"They'd have executed you."

"What's changed?" he mumbled. "Except the *Sea Dog*—I wouldn't have had to..." He trailed off.

With all that had happened since they'd left the abbey, this was what Enio focused on? "Can't you let that go?"

Enio's eyes flashed. "I did *let it go*, remember?"

Par did remember, standing at the edge of the Urdel, watching Enio surrender the little canoe to the stream. But he didn't want to get into that. They'd barely gotten Lani from the coracle to the room. How long did she have left? "We have to find Vex."

"How?"

"I don't know!" Par shouted, overcome with frustration. He caught himself and sighed. "If we'd gotten here quicker—"

"And that's my fault?" Enio snapped.

"I didn't say—"

"I broke my back rowing that damn boat—by myself."

"Well, you're the river guy. I didn't think—"

"Par didn't think?" Enio huffed and looked away. "Fat chance."

Heat crawled up Par's neck. He'd worried himself sick, guiding their group, making decisions to get them safely from the abbey to Banes. "What are you saying?"

Enio spoke to the ceiling. "You're *always* thinking. Like how to cheat the Prior. Like how easy it would be to just cut through the Urdel." He turned back. "Like how you should be the one in charge."

The heat in Par's neck touched his face. He'd never said that— out loud.

Enio met Par's embarrassment with a tight grin. "It's pretty obvious you think you're better than me."

Par shifted uncomfortably. The chair squeaked. He changed the subject. "Well, I actually *was* thinking, that if we go on to Jod—"

"What?" Enio's eyes nearly popped from his head.

"Lani needs help. If we can't find Vex—"

"And if they execute me, that's just too bad?" Enio stood, pinched back the curtain and peeked outside.

"But the Prior promised to forgive you."

"To hells with the Prior."

Par had never known Prior Dogam to lie, and he needed Enio's help to get to Jod. "I'm the one taking the real risk here. What if they Reckon me?"

Enio let the curtain drop. He stared at Par before speaking. "What if a Reckoning is what you need after all?"

Par's mouth fell open. Despite their differences, Enio had always been on his side. "What's wrong with you? They'd go into my head and—"

"So what, if that's where your problem is."

The words landed like punches. "You didn't say that before our Lustering." His voice rose. "You said, 'Don't worry.' You said people invoke at different ages. That I'd—"

Enio threw his arms in the air. "When I showed you my fire-fly, you *begged* me to help. What was I supposed to say? Oh deary me, that might break a rule?"

Par shook his head. "Why did you have to use that godless sigil, anyway?"

"Yeah, you're right." Enio paced the meager room. "If I had just stolen a Lustering pendant, I'd be on the *Sea Dog* right now." He stopped and kicked the table leg. "I shouldn't have gone to the abbey classes, either. My fault again. Then I'd never gotten involved in this whole stupid mess."

Par surged to his feet. "It *was* your fault! You can't control yourself. If you hadn't hit Gorlo—"

Enio faced him. "That whole Lustering thing was *your* idea. Don't blame me because you didn't have the buttons to tell your father the truth."

"Don't be thick, Enio. My family—I don't expect you to understand."

Enio laughed. "Your family? They tossed you out like last week's fish."

"At least I had a family! At least they *tried* to help! Your dad—"

"My dad's a drunk," Enio smirked. "Who cares what a drunk does? But your dad knew *exactly* what he was doing."

"He—" Par stuttered, "My curse. He couldn't have me around—" Par had tried to forget his father turning him over to the Prior. But Enio's words brought back the memory, and it stabbed like a dagger. His eyes threatened tears. He blinked them back. "I thought you were my friend."

Enio hesitated. He looked away. "I've never said that."

The dagger twisted. Enio never had. "That's right—you've *got* no friends." Par spit the words. "And it's not because of your broken face. People are afraid of *you*! You're like a wild animal, like—"

"Admit it," Enio said. "Your whole family is better off without you." He glanced at the bed. "She would be, too."

Par looked at Lani's pale, unconscious face. Tears finally leaked down his cheeks. But they were hot. Boiling. "Better off?" he barked at Enio. "And maybe your mother—"

He stopped short. Enio rarely talked about his mother, or her death. Par felt a pang of guilt and lowered his eyes.

But Enio had started it.

The floor creaked. Par looked up. Enio stood right in front of him, glaring like a ghoul. Before Par could say another word, a fist slammed into his face.

Par bounced off the desk and crashed into the chair. Pain shot through his nose and mouth. And fury exploded in his mind. With a shout, he leapt at Enio and tackled him. Par flailed his fists, battering Enio's sides, his head, anywhere he found an opening.

Enio took the blows, but snaked an arm around Par's torso. They both squirmed and wedged into a knot of tangled limbs and straining muscles. Par had never beat him in a scuffle. Now, Par held nothing back. His arm clamped Enio's neck like a vice. "Take it back!"

"Or what?" Enio gasped. His legs wrapped one of Par's, bending it unnaturally.

"Or I'll choke you out!" Par squeezed tighter.

Enio gagged and jerked, wrenching Par's leg. Par howled and lost his grip. Enio yanked his head loose and sunk his broken teeth into the flesh on Par's side.

Par shrieked.

Enio pulled away.

Pain tore through Par's body. He gasped and scrambled backward.

Blood ran down Enio's chin. His eyes were wide, wild, and his fingers twitched and spasmed. A golden light flickered around his head. He was going to invoke.

"Go ahead!" Par wheezed, gripping his side and fighting to breathe. He had nothing left, in body or spirit. Except agony. "Do it!"

Enio's whole body shuddered. His eyes changed from rage to horror. He spun and bolted out the door.

CHAPTER THIRTY-ONE

PAR GRIPPED HIS side and groaned. Lani lay unconscious on the bed. She'd missed it all.

Enio was gone.

And good riddance.

With a heavy moan, Par pulled himself off the floor. Blood dripped from his mouth onto the desk. The key was there. He took it and locked the door.

He shuffled to the cracked mirror. His lip had an ugly gash. And when he'd hit the chair, he'd broken a tooth.

How could Enio do this? Or say those things? Who does he think—with all that's happened—

Par's thoughts wouldn't congeal. He stared at his reflection, split by the mirror's fracture, and he saw something deeper and more painful than the wounds.

Everything Enio had said was true.

He squeezed his eyes shut. It was Par's curse—no, his cowardice—that had driven him to get Enio to cheat during their Lustering. It was Par's desperation to reach Banes that had forced them deep into the Urdel. Because of him, Enio had lost his freedom, the *Sea Dog,* and nearly his life.

Par looked at Lani. If she hadn't turned from her own journey to help him, she wouldn't have been further weakened by the dun. Maybe by now she'd have found the heart of the élan.

His fight hadn't been with Enio. For years, he'd been fighting the truth about himself. Now he'd lost that fight. And he might also have lost the only other thing he had left.

Par unlocked the door. He didn't see Enio. Given Lani's condition, she'd be out for at least another hour. He stepped onto the wharf and locked the door behind him.

His leg throbbed. He limped to the rail and searched the river. Their coracle was still tied at the muddy little landing. Enio wasn't there.

Par's tears fell, bloated with grief, down to the dark water. He began to shake. He'd never felt so terrible in his life. And it wasn't from being beaten up by his best friend. After what he'd said to Enio, he didn't blame him.

It was best Enio had left. What could Par ever do to make things up to him? What reason would Enio ever have to—

A gasp sounded beneath the boardwalk.

Par leaned over the rail. Short wooden supports held up the framework.

He heard it again.

Par eased to his knees and onto his stomach. Pain screamed in his side. He pressed his palm on the wound and hung his chest over the edge, straining to see underneath.

Enio huddled there, in the mud, leaning against a support. His arms hugged his knees, his head drooped. Muffled sobs seeped through the low, foul-smelling gallery.

A dribble of blood ran from Par's nose. He sniffed it back.

Enio looked up. His face glistened in the reflected river light with the same expression Par had seen in the mirror—lost, friend-less, afraid.

In a sullen voice, Enio said, "Go away."

Par hesitated. Then, fighting through the fire that burned against his ribs, he took a breath and lowered himself down. He eased under the boardwalk and crouched in the mud a foot or two before Enio. Their breathing pulsed raw and ugly.

Par sighed. "I'm sorry. I shouldn't have said—"

"Look, Par," Enio dropped his gaze. "You were right."

"No, I—"

"Everyone's right," he mumbled. "I don't belong around people. I don't belong anywhere." Enio squeezed sludge between his fin-gers. "Except here, with the other rotten sucking mud-maggots."

Par eased closer. With a grunt, he sat beside Enio.

"I'm sorry," Par said again. "For what I said, for ruining your life." He paused. "Why did you run out? You were winning."

"I did win."

Par smiled a little.

Enio kept his eyes down. "I got scared."

"Of what?"

"Of what you said. I'm no better than an animal. I didn't want to…" He grimaced.

Par shook his head. "I didn't mean that, either."

"But Gorlo—"

"Gorlo deserved it. You did that for Buckets. For a friend."

"Well, that's what fr—" Enio chopped off the word.

Par raised his eyebrows. "Friends?"

Enio stayed silent.

"Why don't you ever say it?"

"You know why."

Par was sure Enio had never explained it, and asking the ques-tion had always seemed too awkward—until now. "Tell me."

Enio took a shaky breath. "Like I said, you shouldn't get

attached to things. You just set yourself up for misery when some-one takes them away."

He stared hard at Enio. The guy had experienced nothing but loss his whole life. Now it made sense. If Enio called Par his friend, it would mean they had an attachment. And for Enio that led to misery.

"Well," Par winced as pain stabbed again, "it can't be more miserable than we are right now."

Enio dragged a sleeve across his face and looked up.

"Is that why you hate Lani?" Par continued. "You're afraid she'll—"

"I don't hate Lani." Enio toed the mud with his boot. "She's pretty. And you're Lustered now—sort of. It's only natural you'd want to go off with her."

Par was such an idiot. "I do like her, Enio. But, no matter what happens, I would never just leave you like that."

Enio's eyes were wide and unblinking. "No?"

"Never." Par said it with more conviction than he had ever said anything.

Tears still sparkled in Enio's eyes, but they didn't seem as sad. He sniffled. "Oh, I forgot." He reached into his pocket and pulled out Par's Lustering medal.

Par gasped. "But the money for the room—"

"I just traded the chain." The pendant caught the river light and glinted in the shadows.

Par reached out, but stopped. "You keep it."

Enio gave a small laugh. "I'm not going through another Lustering to get you a new one." He pushed the pendant into Par's palm.

Par closed his fingers over it. Then he leaned in and hugged his friend. Enio hugged back. Unlike their hasty embrace as they had said goodbye in the abbey, Enio didn't flinch, and Par didn't pull away.

After a few more sniffles, they broke off.

"By the way," Par said, "you broke my tooth."

"Let me see."

Par peeled back his lip.

His friend eyed it. "I wonder if a healing could attach it again."

"I think I swallowed it."

"Later, then."

Par grimaced.

Enio shrugged. "It's *your* tooth."

"Never mind. Let's get out of here."

As they eased up from the mud, Enio said, "If you still want to find that Vex guy, I'm with you."

"Wherever we go—to Jod, or Arcana, or the Silver Sea—I'm not letting it be about me anymore."

"But your curse—"

"We'll figure something out. But we'll do it together."

Enio nodded. "Yep, we will. Let's get back. Lani must be missing me."

"Yeah," Par chuckled. "Plus, it stinks down here."

"Nah. You always smell like this."

Par smiled. "Shut up, Enio."

CHAPTER THIRTY-TWO

Par crawled with Enio out from under the boardwalk and onto the riverbank. They stopped to wash away their grime.

"Keep the water off the, um," Enio nodded at Par's bite wound. "When we get to the room, I'll see if I can do another healing."

"Thanks. But save it for Lani." Par brushed his clothes. "I just hope you didn't give me a disease."

Enio smiled his broken grin. "You should be more careful around wild animals."

"Ha-ha." Par noticed his friend's face was puffing up. "How's your eye?"

Enio touched it and winced.

Par frowned. "Sorry."

"Yeah." His friend stood up from the water. "Me too."

A bell clanged near the central pier. A sleek boat with tight sails was docking.

Enio pointed. "Look at that beauty. Think they'd give me a tour?"

Two men in white robes, the most stately Par had seen in Banes, stood at the bow.

His heart leapt into his throat. "Crap!" He tugged Enio out of sight.

"What—?"

"It's the Prior."

They peeked back up.

"And that guy with him," Par whispered. "I've seen his portrait a hundred times in the abbey. It's the High Sigil Master."

Enio's eyes were wide. "Now what?"

Par thought a moment. "Let's get closer."

His friend stared as if Par had lost his mind.

"I'm sick of all this running," Par said. "I want to find out why they're so damned determined to capture me."

Enio's bewilderment slowly drained from his face. The old smile returned. "Yeah. Let's."

They crept along the banks toward the boat, keeping just below the boardwalk, stopping when they were close enough to hear.

The Prior spoke. "You said there was also a Threshold hidden at Jod. Could not we have used that to get to Banes?"

"The Location sigil gives direction, not distance. We are most likely to find the boys by sailing upriver."

"When will you invoke again on the *Sea Dog*, Master Cronus?"

"The *Sea*—" Enio began. Par wrapped a hand over his friend's mouth.

"First," the Sigil Master said, "let us visit the mayor, or whatever passes for law enforcement in these godsforsaken lands. Perhaps they have arrested the boys."

"I pray that's all they've done," the Prior responded. "Those posters—"

"You've made clear your displeasure on that point, Dogam. Our Treaty with the Borderlands does not require their government to detain *petty* criminals, only those accused of high crimes, and so may offer a dead-or-alive reward. Rest assured the price we set guarantees Par will be delivered intact. But the boy is too valuable to risk him continuing on, perhaps even to the lands of Arcana."

The voices receded across the boardwalk.

"*Vamuable?*" Enio mumbled behind Par's palm.

Par removed it.

Enio eyed the boat. "They've got the *Sea Dog?*"

"It's too large to fit in that hold."

"Yeah." Enio sighed.

Par looked toward the town where the voices had disappeared. "We're out of options. Maybe I can make a deal. I'll turn myself in if they help Lani and let you go."

His friend rubbed his chin, either in thought or to ease a purple wound Par had put there. "I bet they'd agree. Keeping their word is something else."

"But—"

"Let's call that Plan B."

"We have a Plan A?"

"We have a Plan Vex. You go back to Lani. I'll start looking. Maybe I can find her a healer."

Par shook his head. "I'm coming with you. Lani's safe, and we'll get back before she wakes again. But we do better when we stick together."

Enio smiled. "Yeah, we do."

They darted into an alley. Enio asked directions from an old woman carrying something that squirmed in a sack. She pointed and said there was a healer near the town square.

Par glanced back as they headed that way. "I don't think she recognized us."

"The posters were new," Enio said through a swelling face. "Right now, we don't look very much like them."

They kept to the shadows and at last came to the central square, examining it from a dark corner. The tallest structure had high steps and a short bell tower. Over the doors of an adjacent building loomed the word *Court*.

Enio pointed to a posting board in front of the Courthouse. "I bet our pictures are on that. If we took them down—"

The Prior and the Sigil Master exited the Courthouse.

Par pulled Enio back. "Dammit."

The Prior opened a leather satchel and removed a cloth-wrapped object. He unwrapped a plank of wood and handed it to the Sigil Master.

"That's from the *Sea Dog*!" Enio surged forward.

Par held him back, groaning as the pain in his side spiked.

Enio grunted and eased off. He was breathing hard. If he lunged again, Par didn't think he could stop him.

The Sigil Master held out the plank. A powerful glory flared around his head. The board drank in the golden light and glowed. All at once, a bright beam flashed out and shot across the square. It hit Enio smack in the chest before it disappeared.

Enio slapped where it had hit. He seemed unharmed. "What the—"

"There!" shouted the Prior.

"Crap!" Par and Enio yelled together.

They bounded back through the alleys. Par had no idea what they'd do once they got to the room. Should they hide? Should they take Lani and flee in the coracle?

Several frantic wrong turns later, Par fumbled for the key and burst through the door. Enio locked it and jammed it with the chair.

Par checked on Lani. "She's still out."

His friend joined him at the bed and touched her head. A dim glory flickered from his own. Lani's eyelids fluttered but didn't open.

"It's all I can do," Enio said glumly.

Par put a hand on his friend's shoulder. "Thank you. You've done plenty."

A rap came at the door. They spun to the sound.

"Par." It was the Prior. "Don't be afraid. We won't hurt you."

Enio put a finger to his lips. He grabbed the candle-holder from the table and moved to the door.

"We know you're in there." The latch jiggled. "We just want to talk."

"Go to hells!" Enio yelled, brandishing the candlestick.

"Dogam, enough," commanded the harsh voice of the Sigil Master.

Par saw no way out. He swallowed hard. "Enio," he said softly. "I think I should—"

The door groaned. Its wood bulged weirdly inward, as if it were a sail filling with wind. The chair squealed and bent. Enio dug in his heels and pushed it back. "Par, help!"

Before Par could reach his friend, the door exploded, throwing Enio to the side. Pieces of the chair missed Par by a whisker and rained against the rear wall.

The High Sigil Master stepped inside. His face stretched into an ugly grin. "So. This is the infamous Par."

Par pushed himself up from the floor. The candlestick rolled near him. He grabbed it and stumbled forward. "Stay back, or—"

The Sigil Master gestured. Par flew against the back wall and hung there as if chained.

"Calm down, son," said the man. "The gods have smiled upon you this day."

Par couldn't move. Lani lay on the bed, her eyes closed, her face white. Enio was crumpled on the floor, moaning. With stunned horror, Par saw a dagger-sized shard of wood protruding from his friend's chest, surrounded by oozing blood.

The Prior stepped into the room.

"Prior Dogam! Please help Enio! And Lani, she's—"

Suddenly, impossibly, the wooden wall against Par's back was gone. He fell into empty air.

"No!" yelled the Sigil Master. His hands stretched out and his glory flashed bright.

The man's invocation caught Par's left arm. It yanked forward as if grasped. A similar force grabbed his legs from behind and pulled them back through the missing wall. Par stretched like a rope in mid-air. Searing pain tore through his side as he was dragged backward, and forward, and back again. The tug of war hit an impasse. Par screamed, stretched mercilessly in both directions.

A voice came from behind. "I'm sorry, Par!" It was familiar.

The view before him—the Sigil Master, the room, his friends—was in an instant replaced by a stone wall. He flew backwards and landed hard on a paved floor.

Waves of agony erupted from his left elbow. In a tortured daze, he reached for it. All he found was a bloody stump.

A man with curly white hair and a large nose bent over him.

"Tomot..." Par tried to squirm away. He had no strength.

"Yes." A silver glory shone around the man's head. "Sleep now. And you can call me Vex."

PART THREE

THE VIGIL

CHAPTER THIRTY-THREE

ENIO SAT CROSS-LEGGED, rocking back and forth. A layer of straw pricked his ankles. The squeaky chain suspending his cage above the floor scratched the silence of the surrounding stone cell.

A moan came from the adjoining cage. In the dim light of a high slit window, Lani stirred.

"Hey," he said. "You all right?"

She looked over. "Enio?"

"Yeah." He made a deep inhale. "I can smell it, you know."

"What?"

"The sea. I've never seen it. But I know it's out there."

Lani peered at the deep window. "Neither have I, but I think you're right. Where are we?"

"No idea." He examined the bare stone room for the hundredth time. Their cages hung an arm's width apart. A hallway ran past their barred chamber.

Lani turned around in her squat enclosure. "Where's Par?"

"Not sure. Something took him."

"Par's gone?" She got on her knees and gripped the bars, facing Enio.

Her sudden movement startled him. She seemed in better shape than at Banes. "Yeah. You were out cold. The Prior and the Sigil Master found us—damn near killed me when they blasted through the door. Then a tunnel opened behind Par and pulled him in and…" Enio hoped he'd imagined what he'd seen next— Par's bloody arm dropping to the floor, left behind.

"And what, Enio?"

He shrugged. "And I woke up here." He touched his chest. "They must have healed me before bringing us… wherever this is. You sure you're all right?"

"I think so." She slouched back, apparently still struggling with her weakness.

Enio raised to a crouch and called toward the hallway, "Hey, who's running this show?"

The words echoed away. A door squeaked. Foot-steps approached.

He glanced at Lani. "Better let me do the talking."

She nodded.

The High Sigil Master stepped before the cell. "I'm glad to see you've awakened."

Enio threw himself forward and sent his cage rocking. "Where's Par?"

"You saw, son. He was taken. He's not here."

"And where is *here*?"

"You're in Argent, boy."

"The capital?" How was that possible?

Prior Dogam stepped from the shadows beside the Sigil Master. "It's true, Enio. Master Cronus kept you asleep while we traveled."

Enio remembered nothing after Banes. How long had they been out? "Well, why in the purple hells are we in Argent?"

Cronus sighed. "Please do not swear in my presence." The man held a hand to the Prior, who passed him a woolen sack. The Master drew out a short plank with the words *Sea Dog* on its side. "I assume you recognize this?"

Enio jolted at the plank, at the words he'd burned there himself. "Where did you—"

"A fisherman at Bishop's Landing delivered an abandoned canoe to the port authorities. Prior Dogam identified it as yours."

"Great. Now you can give it back." Enio reached through the bars.

Cronus returned the board and the bag to the Prior. "Of course, Enius. And that will be only the first of our gifts—once you've helped us rescue Par from the Sorcerer Tomot."

"Tomot?" The last time Enio had seen the Sorcerer was when the man had thrown lightning at him.

"Yes. It was Tomot who took Par."

For the first time since he'd awakened, fear crawled into Enio's heart. He remembered a silhouette beyond that impossible tunnel at Banes. He'd dismissed it as a shadow—his eyes had been filling with shadows as he bled onto the floor.

The Prior spoke. "You can trust Master Cronus."

Enio snapped from his reverie. "And I'm supposed to trust *you*? The guy who locked us up in the first place? The guy who sentenced me to death for using a stupid sigil?"

"I did not *sentence* you," said the Prior. "But in hindsight, I did take the proceedings to an extreme. I hope to make up for that now. The High Sigil Master has agreed to pardon you."

"Is that what this is?" Enio kicked the bars. "A pardon?"

"Have a care," Cronus said. "You are no longer in neutral territory. This is the capital of Eloria. There is no better place for such a trial and sentence to be carried out."

Enio frowned.

The Sigil Master continued, "But why fret over something easily avoided? As I said, we need your help to save your friend."

"And why do you care about Par?"

"We care for every child in our country. But in this case, I want to help Par with the curse that has so plagued him."

Enio was pretty good at picking out a liar, and Cronus wasn't a very good one. But he always enjoyed giving a liar plenty of rope. "And how do we save him?"

"The Sorcerer Tomot is an Arcanan, an enemy of Eloria. He is also a very persuasive man. He will sway Par to his cause and prejudice him against mine. I need your help in turning Par back to the light."

Enio looked at Lani. She watched him with wide eyes. "And what about her?"

"I have no interest in forest witches."

That stung. Enio had used the same words himself. He turned back to the Sigil Master. "I still have no idea what you want."

"The time will come, Enius Marius, when Par must make a decision. He will either choose the light, or darkness and oblivion. My hope is you will help him make the right choice. We will speak more after you've eaten." Cronus turned away and paused. "I heard you escaped the abbey by using a breaching sigil. I do not recommend trying that this deep underground."

Underground? Enio turned to the window. He was sure the sea was outside their cell, somewhere.

"Of course," echoed the Sigil Master's voice, "I don't expect to gain your trust so easily. Later today, we will offer proof of Par's wellbeing."

When Enio turned back, both men had gone.

Lani raised to her knees. "Why do they want Par so badly?"

"Shh." Enio lowered his voice. "They might be listening."

They pushed their faces through the bars, as far as possible.

"I don't like this place." She dangled out an arm. "The élan is so weak in here."

Enio strained his eyes to the hallway. "They can't just want Par for a Reckoning. What do you think—"

With no warning, Lani slapped him across the face.

"Hey!" he yelped, and pulled back.

"What do I think?" she said, fire back in her voice. "I think you and I need to have a talk, Enio."

He winced. "About what?" He rubbed his cheek. The other side warmed, too.

Lani raised her eyebrows. "About pretty much everything."

CHAPTER THIRTY-FOUR

ENIO FROWNED AT Lani from his cage. "What are you talking about?"

She settled back in her straw. "You've done nothing but vilify me ever since we met."

Vilify? It didn't seem fair that a forest nymph had better words than he did. But he got the point.

"I get it," she said. "I embarrassed you in front of your friend."

"You didn't—"

"Please," she huffed. "The nightgads. The weir berries."

"Those—"

"Cleaning you."

His mouth snapped shut. He wasn't sure why that had set him off. She had just saved them from the wither swamp.

"You always put on a good show, Enio. Confident. Fearless. But that was no reason to treat me as if I were some evil"—her eyes glistened—"forest witch."

He winced again, slapped now on the inside. Cronus had used the same words. If she had said these things only a few days before, he'd have thrown them back in her face. After everything that had happened, Enio no longer had the heart.

He sighed. "You're right."

Lani was quiet a moment. "You couldn't know how much that hurt. Humans say it as they mock me and chase me off. You reminded me I belonged nowhere. That I had no friends."

Enio met her eyes. He'd often felt the same way. "Didn't you grow up with other nymphs?"

She gave a smile, but it was a sad one. "Nymphs aren't exactly what you'd call social. Even for them, they kept their distance. And the few humans I'd meet, once they found out what I was, acted like you. Par, though—" Lani sifted the straw. "He's always been friendly and kind. But I swear I wasn't trying to get between you."

"I know."

"You do?"

Enio nodded. "In Banes, while you were asleep, me and Par... we talked."

Lani smirked. "It was about time."

"Yep, it was." He chuckled, recalling their knock-down fight. Then he sobered. "I hope we haven't lost him."

"To Tomot?"

"Yeah." Still, that wasn't what worried Enio the most—it was Par's arm tearing off. He decided not to tell Lani. Instead, he sat up and reexamined their room. "Is there anything we can invoke on in here?"

"You mean to escape?"

"Why not?"

"I've always loved your spunk, Enio. Pop said I had that, too. We may be kindred spirits after all."

"River spirits?" Enio grinned at her easy acceptance of him. He could see why Par liked her.

"You never know." Her warm eyes beamed like sunshine in their dank cell. "But as far as escaping, any ideas?"

"Nothing yet. Walls, bars, window. And don't tell the Prior, but I don't have a breaching sigil. Would your weaving enchantment help?"

Lani held a hand over the straw. Not a strand moved. "Sorry. I'm not strong enough."

"It's all right." Enio tried to sound reassuring, but he continued to worry. The Sigil Master and Prior Dogam must have healed her some. It didn't seem to last.

A possibility occurred to him. "In Eloria, we can give someone else a sigil. Bestow it. We're not supposed to, but still."

"So can the nymphs."

"Can you bestow that one on me?"

"Maybe… but Pop never managed to use a nymph sigil. He said a person raised in one type of magic couldn't learn another. And I'm not sure a human can commune at that level with the élan. I mean, a real human, not like me."

Enio shrugged. "I've used an Arcanan sigil."

"Really?"

"Yep. So maybe I can use a nymph one."

"Are you sure? It may not be safe."

Enio puffed out his chest. "When has *safe* ever stopped me?"

A small laugh escaped her. "Well, if we're going to do this, let's do it now. While I'm—while I can."

"If you're too weak…"

Lani waved this away. "I'm good enough. Pull the cages closer."

Enio grasped her bars. She did the same to his. The cages swung easily on their chains, though he did most of the pulling. The bottoms angled together. He was able to touch his forehead to hers.

"Ready?" Lani asked.

"Ready. By the will of the gods—"

"Um," she interrupted. "We can probably skip that part."

Enio cleared his throat. "Right."

The sensation that came next was the same as every other bestowal he'd gotten. The shape that appeared in his mind was unremarkable, a squiggle that curved and looped around itself. But rather than a lustrous gold, the sigil flickered a fresh summer green. He expected it to flare into his mind, shining like a candle in a dark room. Instead it sputtered, weak and dim. He sensed Lani's struggle, and the sigil faded and shrank. With a shout, he threw his mind into the darkness and grabbed the sigil before it disappeared.

He broke contact. "Pretty sure I got it."

They released each other's cages. Lani slumped back, gasping

"Lani?" He stayed at his bars. The chains squeaked as the cages stilled.

She rested a hand on her heaving chest. "I'll be fine."

Enio didn't want to push her, but the best thing he could do was try to get them out of there. He waited for her breathing to steady. "All right. Now what?"

"You have to kindle it with the élan."

"How?"

"That's the problem. How did you use your Arcanan sigil?"

He thought back. "I didn't know it was Arcanan then. But the man said not to make a beseechment, the way we invoke the gods. He talked about energies and auras and spells…" Enio wiggled his fingers in the air. "A lot of mumbo-jumbo. I didn't really understand, and nothing worked."

Lani nodded. "Pop sometimes spoke the same way."

"But one night, I was in my canoe. The stars shone back from the water like a river of candles, and the moon was big and sharp, like the ones that almost burn your eyes." He licked his lips as the vision returned, strong and clear. "It was like the river and the sky had got all mixed up, and I was right in the middle, in the velvet. Then I remembered something else the man said, about balancing with the lights above, and the lights below. So later, I used that feeling—"

"Your river!"

He startled. "What?"

The excitement grew in her voice. "I need you to be back there."

Enio slumped. He'd tried to put the *Sea Dog* behind him, just another loss. But the memories had brought a heaviness to his heart.

Lani seemed to read his sadness. "I can see this is hard, but it may be your key to the élan. Think of your river—as clearly as you can."

After a deep breath, Enio closed his eyes. He thought of floating down the Greening in the *Sea Dog,* under fresh morning clouds, and beneath black skies choked with stars. He heard the soft clicking of insects, the songs of the waterbirds, and the voices the river made, each he could recognize with his eyes shut. The musky smells of fish came fresh and sour to his nose, with spring plants and mud after a flood, even the sweet rot of low water. He smiled at secret sandbanks hidden in the summer mists, and the rhythms in a rainstorm, and the croaking of toads and the crackling of river ice. Before he'd met Par, these had been his only companions—a million of them, but somehow one and the same.

"Beautiful." Lani's voice came gently to his ears. "Now, the light of the river. The vein of the élan. You've seen it."

Enio had never called it that. But he *had* seen it. Under a low evening sun or a bright autumn moon, the river caught their rays in a long filament. Sometimes that light hadn't seemed only a reflection—it ran deep, pulsing, beckoning him and the *Sea Dog.* She didn't need to tell him what to do next. He brought to mind her weaving sigil and let the river's vein flow straight into its heart.

The sigil in his mind flashed, a radiant emerald green, the green of every new leaf and sun-stirred pond and crisp forest scent he'd ever known.

He gasped. The experience overwhelmed him, like Lani's call-ing of the élan when they'd first met. He opened his eyes. His cheeks were damp, and not from sorrow.

"I think I did it." He lowered his gaze and wiped his face.

"Well, look at you," she said quietly. "My little river nymph."

Enio sniffled. "But I lost it." He looked back at Lani. "Should we start all over?"

Lani met his eyes and smiled. "I think we already have."

Chapter Thirty-Five

P AR STIRRED. A soft blanket wrapped him like a cocoon.
Was he back in that cozy little bower in Lani's camp? He
sniffed the air and grimaced—breakfast smelled like sulfur.
Something dark and terrible nagged at his mind. He retreated to
his memories of the élan, and the vibrant, living forest, and Lani
in its midst.

A pain flared in his leg. Another in his side. He twisted, gasping as the aches spiked. More ignited over his body. His happy
visions swirled into a dark cloud, then formed anew into the image
of Lani, pale and dying, and the Prior and the Sigil Master, and
Enio, blood oozing from his chest and—

"No!" Par's eyes snapped open.

A small stone chamber surrounded his simple bed. Sunlight
glowed outside a window. A narrow wooden door stood ajar.

He winced and tried to sit up. The movement was awkward.
He drew away the covers.

His left arm was gone from the elbow.

Par wailed in horror and leapt from the bed. He threw himself against the wall, clawing at it with one hand, trying to get away from this nightmare.

"No…" As his panic subsided, his sobs began. After all their struggles, they'd made it to Banes. He'd found Alexander Vex.

Gods. At what cost?

He choked back his tears and turned to the window. The river and docks of Xol Tomot stretched far below.

How had he gotten back here? As he focused on a distant hill, he brought a finger to his left stump, hidden now beneath a tattered sleeve. The arm didn't hurt, though bits of pain growled everywhere else. None compared to the misery of his heart.

Somewhere beyond the door, a throat cleared.

Par wiped his face. Vex, Tomot, or whatever the man called himself, must know of his friends.

His boots lay on the floor near a chair draped with fresh clothing. Par still wore his muddy, bloodstained shirt and pants, dried now. He ignored the new clothes and limped to the doorway on a throbbing ankle.

Stout tables filled most of the room beyond, covered with bubbling beakers, small statues of beasts, bowls of colorful powders and dozens of strange utensils. Cabinets, packed with scrolls and books, rested between tall windows in a curving stone wall. Opposite the windows, a stuffed armchair rested before a cold fireplace. A man in a red house coat sat there, straining his neck in Par's direction.

Par took in a fortifying breath and strode into the room. With a determined voice he began, "Where—"

He'd misjudged his strength. Two steps in and he stumbled.

The old man hurried over and caught Par before he fell. "Easy, boy. You've lost a great deal of blood."

Par allowed himself to be helped to a slender wooden chair at a table. This person was the same one from the walls of Xol Tomot. Up close, he was shorter than Par had judged, not much taller than himself. Strings of beads and baubles, along with a tiny hourglass, hung around his neck. His eyebrows were black, in contrast to his white wooly hair.

The man settled next to Par. Towels and a basin of water crowded the table's other contents. He scanned Par up and down. "You woke sooner than I'd expected. I heard a scream, but it wasn't your first."

"You're Tomot?"

"Tomot is more of a job title. Vex will do."

Par struggled to organize his thoughts. "Where are my friends?"

The man's face tightened. He reached for the basin. "They're with Cronus."

Then Enio and Lani were really gone. Par held back fresh tears. His voice wavered. "Why didn't you save all of us?"

"Son," the man said impatiently, "I couldn't even save all of *you*."

Par's gaze fell to his torn sleeve, his missing arm. He squeezed his eyes shut.

"But be assured," the man added, "Cronus won't harm your friends."

A flicker of hope touched Par's heart. He looked again at the sorcerer. "How do you know?"

"He has them to barter with, so he'll use his powers to keep them healthy. And believe me," Vex placed his fingers into the basin of water, "that man's abilities are profound."

Par's hope burned brighter. He gritted his teeth. "Then tell him I'm ready to bargain."

"Don't be a fool." Curls of steam began to rise from the water. Vex removed his hand. "But you'll see your friends soon. Cronus has proposed a parlay."

"What? When?"

"Once I've attended to your remaining injuries. After I fought off Cronus, it took everything I had to keep you this side of the Higher Realms." He reached for Par's wrist.

Par pulled away. "I want to see my friends."

"Stubborn, aren't you?" Vex sat back. "Look, I'm sorry I chased you and that other boy away. I wasn't expecting visitors, and I value my privacy. After you escaped your abbey, your Father Abbot sent me a message. But he directed it to Alexander Vex in Banes, not here. You're back at Xol Tomot, by the way."

"I noticed. But Lani and—"

"A trusted friend in Banes forwards such messages. As soon as I got it, I searched—"

"I don't care!" Par's patience was gone. Blood rushed to his head. "How do we help Enio and Lani? When—" The room reeled. He steadied himself, took a deep breath.

While he was distracted, Vex's hand shot out and snatched his wrist. "Gotcha."

Par tugged once and yelped. It hurt too much to resist.

"Stop fidgeting." The man moved his fingers over the bruised skin. A glory twinkled around his head. A silver one.

An Arcanan one.

The man might call himself Vex, but he was still the Sorcerer Tomot. Why would the Abbot send Par to him? The stories from the abbey rushed back. "If the Father Abbot knew you were Tomot, then he knew you cursed Buckets."

Vex paused his work and sighed. "I was under attack—this keep of Xol Tomot is strategically located, and both sides come after it during hostilities. I did not use my defense to kill, only to cause chaos to allow the escape of my..."

An agony entered the man's eyes. Par had seen it before—in Enio. It touched Par's heart. "You lost someone?"

Vex was silent.

"I'm sorry," Par said.

A brief smile touched the man's lips. It was the first Par had seen from him, but it was sad. "We were to marry." He released the wrist. "Better?"

Par flexed it, getting his thoughts back on track. "The Abbot said you'd help me find a Sigil Master."

"I suppose that was your Abbot's way of hoping I'd aid you, while he kept my identity as Tomot a secret. Or the *Sorcerer* Tomot, as you in Eloria call an Arcanan Sigil Master. It's a long story, and we've no time for it. Incidentally, my curse on Buckets would have worn off. I never imagined Cronus would use him for his accursed experiments."

"Experiments?"

"Hold still." Vex touched Par's lip. Another pain evaporated. "Do you know what Cronus wants with you?"

Par touched a tongue to his tooth, still broken. "He sent us a navigaunt message in the Urdel, but it didn't say much."

Vex moved his attention to Par's scalp. "Given the Abbot's surmises, it is your curse that interests Cronus. For one thing, it has the curious side effect that Location magic cannot find you."

"Then how did the navigaunt find me—ouch!"

The man sat back. "How's that?"

Par patted his head where he'd banged into the desk at Banes. "Better."

Vex bent toward the swollen ankle. "Cronus must have developed a way to impel a messenger bird in combination with a Location sigil. He's quite clever. I expect he didn't send it to you, but to one of your companions."

Enio, Par realized.

The man finished with the ankle. "Remove your shirt. I noticed several bleeds under there."

Par tried, but he couldn't work the laces. He suddenly recalled helping Li, his classmate with the palsied hand, tie his laces before the Lustering ceremony. Par wasn't sure whether to laugh or cry at the irony.

Vex helped with the shirt. "I'm sorry about your arm," he grumbled. "It was that, or give you up to Cronus."

Par saw his stump clearly for the first time. The skin was smooth and round. Healthy and horrible. "Would that have been so bad?" he wondered out loud.

"If I guess right, disastrous. I won't know until I've finished the examination that Cornelius began."

"Examination? You mean…" The memory of the Abbot gazing into his soul made Par shiver.

Vex didn't seem to notice. "Blue blazes boy, you put up a mighty fight." He moved his fingers over the wounds on Par's side. "Though I've never known Cronus to bite anyone."

Chapter Thirty-Six

Par flexed his ankle. It was healed. So were his other wounds—except the arm. Vex dabbed a towel into the basin of hot water to wash off the scabs and dried blood, but Par insisted on doing that much himself. Then Vex sent him to change into the clean clothes.

The simple tan shirt had buttons instead of laces. This made it easier to fasten with a single hand. The left sleeve had been modified to not only close at the end, but could be buttoned snuggly against his side. His stump arm felt better held still like that—he hadn't known what to do with it.

He returned to the main room. Vex waited near a door past the fireplace. He checked the small hourglass around his neck. "It's time to see your friends."

Par knitted his brows. "You said Cronus had them."

"Yes, in Argent." The man disappeared through the doorway.

Argent? That must be over a hundred leagues distant. Still, Par followed, the need to see Enio and Lani burning in his chest.

They descended the tower's tight spiral stairs. Par concentrated on each step—he no longer trusted his balance. A chamber opened out at ground level, empty except for crates and boxes, and with a wide oak door set between the windows.

Par stepped toward the door.

Vex stopped him. "This way."

Tucked behind the last turn of the stairs was a dead-end space. Vex invoked—or conjured, or whatever Arcanan Sigil Masters did. A tile slid back in the floor, revealing more steps. Par followed downward. There were no windows. Pale blue orbs set in wall sconces lit the way. He eyed them suspiciously. Their muted light shone steady, not like flame.

"How do you know the Father Abbot?" Par spoke as they walked, eager to hear a human voice in the strange light.

"We once worked together."

"In Eloria?"

Vex grumped. "Sorcerers don't go traipsing around your country, not if we value our heads."

Par was ready to drop the topic, deciding he wasn't going to get anything more.

But the man continued, and his voice took on an almost cheerful energy. "Near the end of the Grey Wars, your country sent Cornelius to Banes to assist with the treaty negotiations. He and I had many philosophical discussions there—some of which would have gotten us hung by our respective governments."

His tone dampened. "He left, however, when I tried to recruit him."

"Recruit? To Arcana?"

The stairs ended in a stone hallway, dim in the blue light.

Vex ushered Par along. "No. To the Vigil. Keep up, please."

They passed thick wooden doors and rooms barred like cells. The Vigil? It was frustrating how the man never fully answered a question.

A stone door engraved with an eight-pointed star loomed ahead. Vex pushed it open.

Par stopped and gasped. A fantastic globe of light filled the circular room, hovering in mid-air, sparkling with stars.

"This is called a Monitor," Vex said. "It's older than either of our countries and tracks all the spells—or invocations—being cast in the lands around." As the man gestured, the patterns grew and shrunk and the entire surface shifted and spun.

Par's stomach lurched like he was getting boat sick. He grabbed the doorframe.

"You get used to it," Vex said. "Come along." He continued around an encircling rail.

Par's nausea passed. He followed.

An empty stone alcove was set past the rail in the far wall. A fat ebony step sat at its entrance, carved with sigils.

Vex grasped an irregular black stone among the baubles around his neck. He nodded toward the step. "That's a Threshold. It's how I rescued you." He peered at Par. "Perhaps you should hold on to something."

In sudden panic, Par gripped the nearby rail. The entrance to the alcove shimmered. A breeze brought the smell of salt. Then a scream—gulls. A vista opened before them, as through a doorway. A cliff towered before the sea. Three tall spires at the top sparkled in the sunlight.

Par eyes widened. "Is that Argent?"

The cliff came toward them—no, their doorway somehow flew toward it. Par's stomach rolled at the motion, and his missing arm throbbed, but he couldn't look away.

The vision settled midway down the cliff, before a tongue of rock. Several figures stood in a cleft near its back, all but concealed among vines and creepers.

Par's heart leapt. "It's them! Go closer!"

The movement stopped short of the cliff, separating them from the ledge by a long drop to the sea.

"This is as close as I dare," Vex said.

"Enio! Lani!" Par shouted.

Lani was awake, leaning against the wall. Enio stepped forward and waved heartily. Par was about to wave back when he remembered—the Chogan signal. When they'd first approached Agron's barge, Enio told him to hold his arm high and still. He said still meant safe, and wave meant danger. Was Enio sending a warning? Par raised his good arm in a motionless greeting to signal he seemed to be in safe hands.

Two men loomed behind his friends—Prior Dogam, and High Sigil Master Cronus.

Enio called out, "Your arm!" Lani covered her mouth.

Par shouted back. "We're going to get you out of there!"

"Par!" his friend yelled again. "They want—"

A glory flashed around the Prior's head as he spoke something in Enio's ear. Enio's mouth went slack.

Cronus stepped forward. "Hold on, Par. You will be safe soon."

"He's playing you, Par," Vex mumbled. "It's one of his talents."

"Two days, Vex," bellowed Cronus. "Dawn, at the Immortus." He gestured. The scene dissolved back into an empty alcove.

"No!" Par reached out. His hand touched only the cool stone wall beyond the Threshold. He spun to Vex. "Can you open it again?"

"There's no point. Cronus will have taken his prisoners inside."

"Can't we use this to rescue them?"

"My Threshold won't open inside his Outpost. It's shielded against such magics, as is mine. That's why Cronus cannot snatch you away."

Par felt deflated, cheated by such a short meeting. But thank the gods Enio and Lani were alive.

Vex stroked his chin. "Cronus wants an exchange in two days, at the Immortus. At least he's anticipating my demands."

"The Immortus?"

"I still have much to tell you. Briefly, I can't use magic anywhere near it. Neither can he. We'll be on equal footing."

Par knelt down and ran his fingers over the cold ebony step. "We just wait?"

"There's a bigger problem. I won't give you over to him."

"But my friends—"

"You must understand, Cronus wants your curse."

"My curse?" Par almost laughed. Something he'd wanted to be rid of his whole life? And now, he could trade it for his friends? "Well, let him take it and good riddance!"

The man's face darkened. "I cannot allow it."

"Why?"

Vex turned to face the large globe of lights. "Cronus has been using curses to study the Immortus, a terrible thing of great power. He must believe your curse is a key to understanding it. And if he gains that power, I fear he plans to dissolve the governments of Arcana and Eloria and remake them in his own image."

"He could do that?"

"And worse. Such a change could not be done without great upheaval, without war—the two cultures have been separate too long. Countless lives would be lost so he could rule. It would be the end of the peace. And given the destructive powers of the Immortus, perhaps the end of everything."

This was too much to grasp. Yet there was one small, selfish part that still echoed in Par's ears. "Can Cronus really take away my curse?"

"His knowledge of the Immortus may allow it, as it allowed him to rip out the curses of others. As he did with your friend Buckets."

Par started.

The man nodded. "Buckets' injuries were your High Sigil Master's doing, not mine. Your fate could be the same. Make no mistake, Parynius—Cronus is a monster."

Buckets'—Tommy's—melted face, his enfeebled mind, rose again before Par's eyes. He swallowed hard. "Then what do we do?"

"I think you know."

A chill ran throughout Par's body. He did know. It was the reason the Abbot had sent him here. Vex needed to reach deeper into his mind, into his soul, beyond where even the Father Abbot had gone. The place of Par's shadow. To search out the nature of Par's curse. The reason the gods did not listen.

Vex turned. "I'll be upstairs. Come for lunch when you're ready. Later tonight, we'll take the next step."

Par remained, watching the twinkling lights. According to Vex, each was an invocation, or perhaps an incantation. None of which Par could ever do.

For the first time, however, his life was worth something. At least in trade. And whatever Vex discovered about Par's curse, would the man still, as he had said, refuse to bargain with Cronus? What, then, of Enio and Lani?

Par closed his eyes, burning the image of the ledge in the Argent cliff into his memory. Vex had emitted no glory, silver or otherwise, when he'd grasped that black stone around his neck and opened the Threshold. If that did not require an invocation, perhaps Par could use it himself.

Vex wanted him to wait two days.

Meanwhile, the Threshold waited, too—with his friends on its other side.

CHAPTER THIRTY-SEVEN

ENIO STOOD ON the tongue of rock, searching the sea's horizon. When the Prior whispered, "Quiet" in his ear, Enio's mouth had shut off. Then the doorway in the sky had winked out, taking Par with it.

Relief washed over him. Par was alive—even though his arm really was gone. And while Enio had used the Chogan wave to warn of the danger he and Lani were in, Par instead signaled he was safe.

But how was Tomot was *safe*?

Lani groaned. She slumped against the passage wall.

Enio rushed to her side. "Help her!" he barked.

"Of course." The Sigil Master reached a hand to her head. She inhaled deeply. Her eyes sparkled brighter than Enio had ever seen.

Cronus stepped back. "Satisfied?"

"Satisfied? After what you did to Par? You chopped off his arm, you onion-eyed goat."

"That was Tomot's doing. If he had not taken him—"

"If you'd let him go!"

Cronus sighed. "You do speak your mind, Enius. Let me

speak mine, for I have not the art to reason with children." He gestured to Lani. "It's plain she still requires my help. Do not force me to use her as a lever against you."

Enio grimaced. If he'd possessed a sigil to shoot fire from his eyeballs, Cronus would be a smoking cinder.

"Enio," Lani said softly. "Don't listen to him."

The man continued. "Yet that is all I ask. Simply listen to what the Prior has to say. Is that such a burden?"

Enio didn't want to do even that, but did he have a choice? He glanced at Lani—maybe he could make a deal. "Tell you what. You see how much Lani likes it outside that cage. Let us come out here when we're not being enlightened by your lap dog," Enio tossed his head at the Prior. "Then he can talk his brown nose off."

The Prior frowned. Cronus seemed to consider.

"Come on." Enio swept a hand across the vista of the Silver Sea. "Where are we going to go?"

The man nodded. "I can be reasonable. We will try that— under supervision."

Enio figured this was the best he'd get. He left it there.

"But for now, Prior, please return them to their cell."

Though Lani could walk, Enio helped her anyway. The cell was not far—inside, past an iron gate and around a corner.

The Prior sealed them again in their cages. After he left, Enio sat back against the bars. Lani did, too.

"Feeling better?" he asked.

"Much." She turned to him. Her face seemed to glow. "The élan outside, Enio. It's different from anything I've felt before. So big and alive. And it was… singing."

Enio had heard nothing. "Like you showed us in the Urdel?"

"Yes!" she smiled. Then shook her head. "And no. Something more urgent. As if it were calling to me." Her eyes glittered like starlight. "Do you think the sea holds the *chela élande*—my heart of the élan?"

"That thing you're searching for?"

"Yes."

"So far from the forest?"

"The élan is everywhere there is life." Lani closed her eyes. "It's so clear, Enio."

He stayed quiet. She'd once said when nymphs found the heart of the élan, they changed somehow and stayed with it. He watched her sitting in perfect bliss, and a new worry grew in his heart.

"Lani," he said, "if we get out of here—if they let us leave Argent—you'll come, right?"

She didn't seem to hear. Her breathing came so gentle, like a river lapping the shore.

Suddenly something occurred to him, and it nearly stopped his heart. Enio couldn't believe he'd never seen it before.

When her face was peaceful like that, and her hair a little messy, and a faraway, sad smile touched her face, she reminded him of someone he'd lost a long time ago.

She reminded him of his mother.

Chapter Thirty-Eight

When Par returned up the tower stairs, two things weighed on him. One was that Vex would be drilling into his mind, deeper than even the Father Abbot.

The other was whether, if it came down to it, Par could open the Threshold and rescue Enio and Lani himself. He needed to probe Vex about the second without giving away his intent.

The man had set a table with broth, brown bread, and cheese. He sat in his stuffed chair by the cold fireplace, reading a silver-edged book. Par settled before his lunch and began with the broth. He frowned—rocknut.

"Um," he tore a piece off the loaf, "how long was I unconscious after Banes?"

Vex didn't look up. "A day or so."

Par had assumed this because of his fresh wounds. But he faked surprise. "Only a day?"

"Or so."

"But how did Cronus get from Banes to Argent so fast?"

The man turned a page. "Through a Threshold, no doubt."

"Oh, I see." Par had guessed that, too. "There are more Thresholds?"

"A few. At Jod and the other Outposts. At the Immortus. The Citadel…"

"The Citadel?" Like the Immortus, it was another thing Vex hadn't explained.

"We're going there tonight," the man added.

"What? Why?"

"For your procedure. It was the home of the Vigil and is specially located for magics to work their best. Now let me study. I need to be at my best, too."

Par didn't want to dwell on this upcoming *procedure*. He swung back the topic. "Who built the Thresholds, anyway?"

"The Vigil."

"You keep mentioning them. I don't—"

The man clapped his book shut and glowered.

Par froze with his spoon above his soup.

Vex drew a deep breath. "I understand you like Histories."

"How'd you know?"

"Cornelius went on about you in his letter." The man shuffled a thick, drab-looking brown volume from his pile. "This will tell you of the Vigil's creation."

Par took the book, but he wasn't done with the Threshold.

He finished his soup and nibbled the cheese, giving Vex a little space before the next question.

"Is it far?" Par asked at last.

"What?"

"The Citadel."

"Very."

"Then we can go anywhere through the Threshold?"

Vex sighed. "Anywhere the key holder has ever seen."

The key holder. That sounded promising—as long as Par

didn't need to invoke. "I've always been taught that the target of an invocation must be present. How can you invoke to a faraway—"

"Son!" the man barked.

Par snapped his mouth closed.

Vex's raven eyebrows gathered like storm clouds. For a moment, Par feared they might shoot lightning.

But then they relaxed. "You're nervous about tonight. If I answer this, will you leave me in peace?"

Par nodded.

"Well, for one thing, remember that Cronus tracked your friend across great distances."

"That's right. How?"

"Cronus must possess some object your friend treasures. Anything dear to a person is always present to them."

Par supposed that made sense. Cronus had invoked over the plank from the *Sea Dog*.

"The principle of the Threshold is similar, but the magic is much older and stronger. In this case, it acts on the intimacy of a person's memories."

"And it's not an incantation? You just hold the stone and think of where you want to go?" Par winced at his own words. Had he given his plan away?

"Yes," the man answered. "Now, let me read."

Par exhaled with relief. If the time came, he'd sneak the stone key while Vex slept. Then he'd go to the Threshold and picture the ledge.

As promised, he left the man alone. Par finished eating, then wandered the tables, smelled the bottles and powders, and examined the statuettes, many of which looked like laughing devils. He knocked over a small scale, startling Vex, who warned if he didn't stop playing with things he might "set something off." The man didn't explain further, and Par didn't ask.

Finally, he took up the volume Vex had given him. "Well, I guess I'll get some rest."

"Par?"

"Yeah?" Par paused at the door to the small bedchamber.

Vex's voice was gentler than Par had gotten used to. "I... apologize for not being a very hospitable host. For many years I've kept mostly to myself."

A sadness touched the man's face. Par nodded, remembering his mention of a fiancée.

Vex crossed to a window. "After the Grey Wars, I threw myself into my work, both as Tomot, monitoring the Borderlands, and as Alexander Vex, traveling for my merchant business. In fact, the last guest I had here, outside the Vigil, was Cornelius."

"You said you met during treaty negotiations and tried to recruit him?"

"Yes. I brought Cornelius upriver on a little outing. We sailed to Xol Tomot, where I revealed I was also its infamous sorcerer. But before I could explain the Vigil, he decided he wanted nothing more to do with me."

"Because of what you did to Buckets?"

Vex nodded. "So I've since discovered. Remember, my curse was temporary and did not cause his disfigurement. I didn't know Cornelius had seen Buckets back in the capital after Cronus had finished with him, and that Cornelius blamed me—Tomot—for those injuries."

He paused. "Fate is funny that way. Not long after, the Vigil went silent. I've never heard from any of them again.

Par started. "What happened?"

"I've never found out. The Citadel sealed itself."

Vex turned from the window. "I tell you all this, because I've come to see your love for your friends, and theirs for you. When I said I would not turn you over to Cronus, I did not mean we'd abandon those you so care for. We will find another way."

The man grew quiet. Par wasn't sure what else to say. He simply nodded and continued to his bedroom.

"By the way, boy, it wouldn't have worked."

Par stopped. "What?"

"Your little scheme. Remember, there is also a floor hatch you can't open without me."

"But I—" Par steeled. "You read my mind?"

The man smiled. "It doesn't take a Sigil Master to see what you're thinking. You can be a bit obvious."

The man walked back to his chair. "Get some rest. Tomorrow we'll have a look inside that noggin of yours."

CHAPTER THIRTY-NINE

Enio sat in his cage, trying the weaving sigil on the straw. Lani said she sometimes saw a brief green bloom around his head—her word for a glory. She was probably just being nice. He couldn't get it to actually do anything.

"It's amazing you've been able to kindle the sigil at all." She watched him from her cage. "But for beginners, it works better on something more alive."

The sigil in his mind had become blurry. He looked at the high slit window. "I wonder how long they'll keep us?"

"Or Par."

Enio followed the dim light back to her cage. The resemblance to his mother had faded with the shift of shadows. But now he couldn't unsee it. He felt a little warm as she stared at him, and he looked away, embarrassed. He pushed these thoughts down, back into the shadows of his mind.

"Anyway," he huffed, "I'm hungry." He stood up as far as possible in his cage and yelled, "How about some food in here?"

A voice echoed down the hallway, "On my way, son."

He whispered to Lani. "Remember, let me do the talking."

"Yeah," she smiled. "That *always* works out."

Enio snorted.

Prior Dogam arrived. He unlocked the hallway bars with the brush of a hand, carrying a tray in the other. "I was preparing this when you called."

"About time," Enio said.

The Prior delivered cheese, apple slices, some kind of meat, and a gourd into Lani's cage.

"Hey"—Enio reached out—"where's mine?"

"She has yours and can pass it over. I feel I shouldn't put my hand too near your bars."

Enio gave a toothy grin.

The Prior backed away from the cages. Enio watched him as they shared their food.

At last, the man spoke. "I'm pleased you're both doing well after our healings."

Enio rubbed his chest where he'd been impaled. "I've had worse."

The Prior smirked. "Listen, son, I need to talk to you."

"So, talk."

The Prior turned to Lani. "*Sleep.*" His voice vibrated with the force of invocation. She slumped over in her cage.

"Lani!" Enio threw himself at the bars.

"She is fine. Our talk should be private. And the rest will do her good."

Enio sat back and glowered.

"I won't revisit the events at the abbey, for which I've already apologized. I need to persuade you to help Master Cronus. We need to strike a bargain for Par's release."

Maybe Cronus was right about one thing—it wouldn't hurt to listen. "Why does Tomot want him, anyway?"

"I'll explain more in a moment. But Par will prove little use to him. And Tomot can't keep him forever. Besides, I expect Par will insist on saving you. And you know how stubborn he can be."

Enio certainly knew that. "So what am I supposed to do about it?"

"If we simply bargain for your exchange, we might obtain Par, but Tomot will have filled him with lies and anger and resentment. In order for Master Cronus to have his best chance of dealing with Par's curse, Par must submit himself willingly, not grudgingly. He trusts you. You can convince him to trust us."

Enio pushed out his lower lip as if bartering for second-hand boots. "And if I don't agree, you'll break out the thumb screws?"

The Prior sighed. "Enio, if the Master wanted, he could Reckon you both, rewrite your personality and convictions. You'd believe exactly what he needed you to believe, for the rest of your lives."

A chill ran up Enio's back. He hadn't considered that. "So you get Par, and the Sorcerer Tomot gets us. That's a bargain?"

"If I guess correctly, you have no great desire to remain in Eloria. And Tomot has no use for your nymph friend. After the exchange, he will let her go."

Enio might believe this. Par had signaled the man was safe. And what if Tomot could help Lani?

"Well, you said you had more to tell me." He picked at a fingernail. "I don't seem to have any other appointments."

The Prior launched into a discussion of history and politics, mixed with sermons on the ethics of Elorian gods versus Arcanan delusions. Par would have loved it.

But Enio's eyes glazed over. Buried in this mountain of words, he saw two choices that tore him up inside. If he refused to help, they might let Lani continue to sicken. If he cooperated to save her, he betrayed Par.

They offered him a sword with two edges. Sooner or later, he would have to swing it.

✳

Late that day, Enio stood again on the ledge above the Silver Sea. An orange sun sagged toward the western mountains, and waves boomed against the rocks far below. A sheer cliff rose at his back, cloaked with vines and weeds. Gulls wheeled through the still air, screeching and crying.

He turned to the passage. "No matter where you go, you can't get away from the bird crap."

Lani sat against the wall, eyes half closed, face slack. The Prior skulked somewhere further up the tunnel, beyond the iron gate, giving them their privacy. The healings were losing their effect— she looked all squeezed out. During the hour they'd been on the ledge, she'd barely said a word.

Enio stepped toward her. "How you doing?"

"Can you feel it, Enio? The élan of the sea?"

He didn't. "Does it help?"

A brief smile touched her lips. "It's so alive, always changing. And ancient, with roots deeper than the mountains."

Enio tensed at her shallow breathing. If she got any worse, he'd call the Prior.

She caught him staring. "I'm sorry you had to make a deal to get us out here."

"Not much of a deal. The Prior talks. I listen."

"Anything important?"

"Same as the birds. A lot of noise. A lot of crap."

Lani chuckled.

Enio dropped beside her. "He tells me about Par. He says they can help with his curse."

"Why do they want him so badly?"

"The Prior says his curse might be important to preventing a war or saving lives somehow."

"And you believe him?"

Enio huffed. "About as far as I can kick him. I'm betting Cronus wants the curse for something else. And he needs me to talk Par into handing himself over."

"Knowing Par, he'd do it to get us out of here."

"Yeah. But Cronus also needs Par to trust him, or Par will end up like Buckets."

"Your injured friend from the abbey?" Horror crept across her face. "We can't let that happen."

"I know, but..." He dropped his head.

"But if you don't help them, they'll let me die?"

Enio didn't answer, caught hopelessly between betraying Par and losing Lani.

With a gentle hand, she raised his chin. "Thank you for getting me outside. The sea makes all the difference."

His face warmed. He took a deep breath. "Nothing like it."

"Can we go closer?"

Enio helped her the last few paces.

She knelt at the very edge. The low sun sparkled on the water and tinted the world gold. Her hair seemed soaked in its natural glory.

Enio stood a little behind, thinking again of his mother. A welcomed peace wrapped him. He remembered how he'd been afraid of Par going off with Lani. And before that, at their first meeting in the forest, of his own embarrassment at her taking care of them, and how he had acted so childish.

He smiled at himself and decided to tell her his thoughts—they might make her laugh. "Lani..." he began.

She remained completely still, facing the sea.

He moved beside her, and a jolt ran through him. Her eyes were wide, and her face had flushed. Her mouth hung open as if she'd seen a ghost.

"Lani? What's wrong?"

Her voice was filled with reverence, a whisper on a breeze. "It's come."

Enio followed her gaze. "What's come? I don't see anything."

"The *chela élande*—my heart of the élan."

"If you're getting sick again, I'll call—"

"But I don't want to leave you alone, Enio."

Her smile was so sad it pinched his heart. "What do you mean?"

"It's here. At last." She leaned off the edge.

"Lani!" He grabbed her arm to stop her from falling the hundreds of feet to the sea.

She struggled once and collapsed back.

He felt her forehead. It was burning up. He invoked the fever healing he'd used before. It did no good.

Lani smiled up at him. Her voice stayed low, but the old fire ran underneath. "Listen, you stubborn river rat. What do you think will happen when they realize they can't make you betray Par?"

Enio clenched his jaw.

She continued. "They'll use me against you both."

It was true. He still couldn't answer.

"Enio, if I'm wrong about the *chela élande*, I'd rather die this way, quick, in the arms of your beautiful Silver Sea, not like a worm withering in the sun. Or as a weapon against you."

He panicked, looked up the passage, to the sea, to her. "No. Maybe they can heal you again. Maybe—"

"It's only a matter of time, Enio. We both know it. Please, let me go."

Enio stared into her eyes, dark crystal waters in an emerald pond. They begged him. He shook his head, took her shoulders and tried to help her stand. "Let's get back inside. They'll fix you. I'll agree to help them only if—"

"If you help them, you'll betray Par."

Enio knew that, too. He was trapped.

She heaved a deep sigh and raised slowly up with him. He tried to support her, but she stumbled and he lost his balance. Then she pushed him away. Before he knew what was happening, she spun and with a single stride leapt off the edge.

"Lani!"

Without thinking, Enio invoked the weaving sigil. It flared in his head like a green sun. Vines along the cliff came alive and shot after her.

One caught Lani's wrist and held her suspended against the rock face, below his reach. With the sigil blazing in his mind, he grabbed the vine and strained to pull her up. She seemed to struggle for each breath. But as he peered into her face, he saw only peace—as in the eyes of his mother.

"Please, Enio," she gasped. "It's where I belong."

He held on with all his might. "I can't let you die!"

Tears streamed down her cheeks. "Then let me live."

The Prior shouted from the passage.

Even if Enio's throat weren't too tight to speak, he had no more words. Everything she'd said about his choices was true. And he had no doubt, healings or not, that she would not last much longer.

Please. Her breath came so shallow she mouthed it like a prayer.

With agony choking his heart, he let the weaving sigil grow dim. The vine in his hands went limp.

Prior Dogam was at his side. The man invoked, but whatever sigil he used, Lani had dropped beyond its reach. She fell, a great bird diving toward the rocks.

At that instant, the last rays of the setting sun flashed across the water. The surf below exploded upwards in a fountain of brilliant emerald. Then it opened like an immense flower with petals of pure, perfect light. Lani plunged into its center. Even Enio's grief could not eclipse the wonder of the sight. It was the very heart of life—the heart of the élan.

A moment later, the fantastic petals closed and were swallowed by the sea. A shining green afterglow spread outward in a radiant wave, even to the horizon. And then the daylight, and Lani, were gone.

The Prior shook him. "What have you done, son? What have you done?"

"I think…" Enio cleared his throat and blinked away tears. "I think I saved her."

Then he grinned, wide and fierce.

"And screwed you."

Chapter Forty

Enio slumped at the back of his cage, staring up at the dark, slit window. The memory of Lani falling from the cliff played in his head.

Prior Dogam pushed a bowl of porridge into the cage and stood back. "I'm sorry about your forest friend, son."

Enio frowned at the bowl. "Her name was Lani."

"But we still need your help."

"Then you're stuck," Enio mumbled. "Why should I help you now?"

"Nothing has changed. Par is still a prisoner."

The Prior's ongoing arguments rose again in Enio's mind. He spun and slammed a fist against the bars. "I don't care about wars and wizards and curses! You say Par's a prisoner. Why would he need me to talk him into coming back? Or trusting you? And why would I ever want to, after what you've done to us?"

"Why do you keep blaming Master Cronus for things that are not his fault?"

Enio huffed. "What are you talking about?"

"We sent you a message in the Urdel. If you had followed our instructions and gone to Jod—"

"So instead you tried to kill me in Banes?"

"We didn't know you'd blocked the door, so the Master's entry was over energetic. But we healed you. And your forest—and Lani."

"So you could use her to force me to help you."

"But we didn't use her. And her death was… not our doing."

Enio winced, still not sure he'd done the right thing by letting Lani fall into the sea.

Prior Dogam sighed. "What can I do to persuade you?"

"Bring her back."

"Master Cronus dispatched a search, but they've found no trace of her body."

No trace? Enio's spirits rose a little. Then there was still hope that what he'd seen when Lani hit the water was not a mirage—that the heart of the élan had taken her.

He shook the bars. "Well, let *me* go."

"Then instead of Par trading himself for you, he would remain imprisoned by Tomot. None of us want that."

Enio wasn't so sure. Par had signaled he was safe.

The Prior's face became troubled. "The matter is serious, Enio. If you don't cooperate, I fear Master Cronus will apply other means."

"Such as?"

Cronus stepped into the cell. "Such as, enlightening your priorities." The man came beside the Prior. "The boy still resists?"

Enio kicked the bowl of porridge from his cage. It smashed across the floor. "Go jump in a wither bog."

"Master Cronus," the Prior's voice had a tone of urgency. "If I had more time—"

"Yes, you will have more time. But to use it effectively, we need more information. Join me. You will find this instructive."

Both men moved to the cage. Enio pushed back.

A glory grew from the Sigil Master's head. The man laid a hand on Prior Dogam's shoulder, then turned his gaze on Enio.

Those eyes stabbed into Enio's brain like hot knives. He threw his arms across his face and screamed.

Cronus tore through his thoughts. Enio flailed, helpless as his memories were dragged into the light and fouled by the man's presence. The Abbot and Buckets helping him escape from the abbey; Par disappearing through the strange tunnel at Banes; Lani pleading with the eyes of his—

No! Enio lunged before a barrier he'd spent years making impassable to friend and foe alike.

The man paused like a wolf scenting its prey. *What have we here?*

Enio squared off, ready to fight, keeping himself between Cronus and his most precious memory. *Not that one.*

Exactly that one.

The man pounced. Enio fought, screaming curses, spitting poisonous thoughts. Though bodiless, he bit and rent like a wild beast. Over and over, he drove the man away. Each time, Cronus returned stronger.

No! Enio fought with all his might and passion, but Cronus did not relent. Enio weakened with each assault. At last, with a soul-renting cry, he was blasted back through his mental wall.

His mother lay by the wagon on the muddy ground, her body broken and twisted. Enio screamed and screamed, trapped beneath the axle, reaching toward her. His father slumped at her side, lifting her, holding her. His mother's kind smile drifted toward Enio, under gentle eyes that never moved again.

A light went out in his mind—in his spirit. He opened his eyes. He was curled in his cage, shivering, whimpering like a whipped dog.

"Well," Cronus said lightly, "I think we will have plenty to work with. Let us retire to refreshment."

Cronus left the room. The Prior remained before the cage, his face ashen.

"Damn you," Enio gasped at the man.

The Prior seemed shaken. "I didn't think…" He cleared his throat and straightened his back. "It will be all right, Enio. Master Cronus said he wouldn't change anything within your mind. He said—"

"Get out!" Enio gathered the last of his strength and threw himself at the bars. "Get out! Get out!"

The Prior bowed his head and left.

CHAPTER FORTY-ONE

PRIOR DOGAM SAT in the cool evening air on the balcony of the Sigil Master's chambers. On the table, a brass lantern bathed the area with a warm, yellow glow. A tureen of fresh pears in spiced wine rested near his elbow.

He spooned a slice of the soft, blushing fruit into a small glass bowl, but couldn't bring himself to eat. His mind returned to Enio, locked five hundred feet below in the hidden Outpost.

"Stupid boy," he mumbled. "Why must he be so difficult?" It was such a simple request. Help them help Par.

Yet how could he get Enio to convince Par when he still had doubts himself?

A knock sounded on the doorframe. "May I join you?"

The Prior stood. "Of course, High Master."

Cronus waved him down and sat across the table. He helped himself to a bowl of fruit. "Being dragged through another's mind, especially one as rebellious as that boy's, can be draining. Were you able to keep up?"

"Not for most of it—though I recall the memory of his

mother." The image of Enio, curled and screaming in that cage, still turned the Prior's stomach.

Cronus sucked in a slice of fruit and seemed to swallow it whole. "I believe this memory alone is the leverage we need to guide him to the right decision."

Before the Prior asked how the High Master planned to do that, the man continued, "Did you notice his knowledge that Cornelius performed such a procedure on Par?"

The Prior started. "He what?"

"Yes. The Abbot discovered a shadow near Par's soul. That would have required a similarly deep invocation."

The Prior could not imagine the Father Abbot being so brutal. "I didn't know—"

"And it was Cornelius, along with the man you call Buckets, who helped the boys escape the abbey."

The Prior's mouth hung open. He felt like an idiot. *Damn you, Cornelius.*

The Sigil Master chuckled. "Your Abbot fooled me, too, Dogam. That fossil still has a few tricks under his old robes."

"I'll return to the abbey," stammered the Prior. "I'll begin an investigation—"

"It no longer matters."

The Prior took a breath. "I have been wondering, Master Cronus, that if the High Council were told the full story of the Vigil they might understand the urgency of your designs, both in light of the hostility of Arcana and the danger of the Immortus. They might help—"

"Those simpletons?" The Sigil Master shook his head. "Half the Hierarchy owes their positions to nepotism and bribery. Simeon, Judge of the Doors, is a fine example. A *cousin* to his Eminence. A child with a stick could better defend a border."

"What of Lady Melora?"

Cronus huffed. "Another groveling sycophant."

Sycophant. The Prior winced. The Abbot used the same term, warning to weigh what was *asked* against what was *right*.

Cronus noticed his disquiet. "Fear not, Dogam. Remember, I have examined your mind. It is you I need, not them."

Instead of celebrating this reassurance of trust, the Prior was gripped by dread. At Bishop's Landing, the Sigil Master had mentioned changes at the highest levels.

Had he meant the *highest* level?

"Surely, the wisdom of our Fondiscate—"

"Wisdom, indeed." Cronus smiled in a way the Prior liked less and less. "The Council gives the title of Fondiscate to the one closest to the gods. Long ago, this might have held some truth. Today, they automatically bestow it upon the political Eminence."

"Automatically?"

"The Eminence must rule the nation. Ruling a people by the authority of man only goes so far."

A chill ran up the Prior's neck. To suggest the Fondiscate acted without divine guidance was tantamount to heresy. And if Cronus thought so little of the sacredness of that office… "A coup?"

The Master's voice lost any warmth the Prior had gained. "Do not pretend to know my mind, Dogam. You'll understand when the time is right."

The Prior swallowed. Good gods. What had he gotten himself into?

Cronus continued. "What we do is for the good of all. But not for the eyes of all. The Council's involvement would disrupt my progress, and such delays increase the risk of disaster. You are now a member of the Vigil. Our end is to protect the people, whether they know it or not."

The man closed his eyes. The Prior took the moment to quiet his fears. After what he'd learned of the true history of their country, and of the dangers that threatened it, he must trust that the High Sigil Master knew best. As the Abbot had reminded him, the most basic precept of the Hierarchy was to take care of those in your charge.

He focused back on the tasks at hand. "You said you had everything you needed from Enio?"

"It shouldn't take many sessions to prepare him."

"For… a Reckoning?"

"That level of modification defeats my purpose. Par would not be persuaded by a stranger."

The Prior nodded, relieved. At least Enio would not have his inner self undone. "How, then?"

Cronus opened his eyes. "While you've rested, I've revisited Enio's mind. Between replaying the memory of his mother, dangling it above oblivion and pulling it back, he will soon be more than willing to say a few sincere words to Par on our behalf. You'll be with me as I continue this treatment, Dogam. I plan to train you in these techniques."

Few people were allowed access to such powerful sigils, and the Prior would be one. He hoped to become worthy of the honor. Still, his stomach would not settle. He had no desire to see Enio go through any of this.

Cronus went on. "Remember, Dogam. This is for the sake of untold lives, not merely a couple of children."

The Prior took a deep breath. "I understand. When will we begin?"

"When you've finished here, join me in my chambers."

"Yes, Master Cronus."

The Sigil Master left. The Prior spooned a spiced pear around the edge of his bowl.

Not about a couple of children.

Cronus was right, of course. It was about untold thousands of children, and everyone else who might perish if the Immortus remained unhealed.

But the words of the Father Abbot would not leave his mind. *Don't do what is asked. Do what is right.*

He shook his head. That proverb was fine for a backcountry abbey, yet there were pressures at work, stakes that the old Abbot could not possibly fathom.

The Prior picked up his bowl and walked along the balcony. He tasted the fruit. Sweet and luscious. Better than anything in St. Livius.

He breathed in the crisp air, trying to enjoy a beautiful evening, standing in the High Temple, far above the moonlit Silver Sea.

It was no use. He grimaced again at the image of Enio writhing in his cage.

With a shout, the Prior hurled the bowl over the railing. The glass glinted in the yellow lantern light. Fruit and wine slashed a great crimson arc across the sky.

Chapter Forty-Two

P AR SPENT THE rest of that day and well into the evening in the bedchamber reading the book of the Vigil's history. It covered a time he'd never been taught—a span between the stories of the gods and the founding of Eloria. There was a new telling of the Gardens of Gê, still a place of fantastic beauty and magic. But it also told of the mage Ridiax and of his disastrous attempt to ascend into the Higher Realms. Par ran his fingers over an image of a blazing pit surrounded by eight monoliths, the Immortus, the only thing left in the very center of the great Devastation. He had no doubt it described the place where Buckets had been taken and burned.

The bulk of the book detailed the history of the Vigil, founded by the ancient mages who restrained the Immortus. They built the Citadel and the Thresholds to relocate the survivors over their eastern mountains, ultimately establishing the countries of Eloria and Arcana. The book chronicled the centuries as old members died, and the Vigil recruited new ones. Vex had not been the first Sorcerer Tomot.

At last, he rubbed his eyes and lay back. As he pushed the

worries of his upcoming procedure from his mind, thoughts of Enio and Lani filled the void. When he slept, he dreamt of a beast of shadow, hunting him through the forests and over the hills, leaping from cloud to cloud.

Vex woke him sometime later. It was still dark. "Ready?"

Par's heart took off like a racehorse. "Will this be a Reckoning?"

The man wore long red robes. He stepped closer. "Arcanans don't call it that, though the goal is similar—to treat an illness of the mind or spirit, to adjust memories, or, sometimes, personalities. However, I won't change anything about you." He tapped Par's forehead. "Not until we know what's going on in there."

Par wiped his sweaty palm on his shirt. He dreaded going through such a soul-baring invocation again. Plus, his dream had brought an additional worry: in the Urdel, the dun had only attacked his friends. He feared what Vex might find inside him— that he was a vessel of the dun, of the shadow of death.

They walked together to the larger room. Vex gathered a leather-bound tome from the armchair. He handed Par a small sack. "Carry this, won't you?"

Par took the bag. It wasn't heavy, but it clinked. In silence he followed the sorcerer, down to the hidden floor tile, then to the Outpost, and finally through the thick door with the star. It seemed the longest walk of his life.

At the Threshold, Vex grabbed his black keystone. The space shimmered. Darkness opened beyond and a hot, stale breeze touched Par's face. He winced and recoiled.

Vex peered through the doorway. "Stay alert. The Citadel is outside the borders of the Devastation, yet still a place of curious forces." He held the keystone into the opening. "You first."

Par set one foot across the ebony step. Warm air crawled up his trouser leg.

The man cleared his throat. "We don't have all night."

One more step and Par was through. He emerged beneath

a full moon before a meager round building. An open doorway glowed with a strange curtain of blue fire. Narrow steps curled around the exterior to the flat roof, while a short wall circled the setting, forming the small paved courtyard where Par had arrived. It was too dark to see anything beyond that.

And it was all a little disappointing. Par had expected a Citadel to be somehow grander.

In the shadowy distance, he could just make out fang-like cliffs against the stars. The Threshold had closed. "How do we get back?"

"There are other Thresholds nearby." Vex moved to the steps.

Something flew past, right into the curtain of light. Blue sparks erupted, and a smoking cinder the size of an apple dropped to the pavement.

Par jumped. "What was that?" The thing on the ground looked half briquette and half scorpion.

"Hmm?" Vex glanced over. "Oh, the skarix are about. Beware the tiny ones—the smaller the deadlier. They won't bother you if you don't bother them."

Par brushed his hand through his hair and hurried after the man. "Was that a small one? Are there many of them?"

"One less."

Par looked forlornly toward the doorway veiled in blue. "We aren't going inside?"

"I told you before—the Citadel has been sealed for years."

They ascended the short stairs that climbed to the roof. There was no rail. Par pressed nervously against the building's wall. The top was bare except for a stone table, like an altar.

Vex took Par's bag. "I need a few minutes to set up. Don't wander off."

Par moved to the edge of the roof and peered into the moonlit night. As his eyes adjusted to the darkness, the view that unfolded knocked any other thoughts from his mind and brought him to his knees.

He'd assumed they'd stepped through the Threshold into some courtyard, but the small building they'd climbed was itself on top of a lofty tower. Other structures, some of them towers as well, rose from a sprawling fortification far below. In a gap of the courtyard wall—the tower's parapets—more stairs disappeared over the side. Par cringed at the thought of descending hundreds of feet that way. Again, he could see no railing.

The man had set his tome on the stone table. Par's gaze wandered further, opposite the dark cliffs.

An even greater awe struck him. A desolate landscape spread away from the Citadel, even to the horizon. Luminous yellow mists, sickly and pale, swept across the lifeless terrain, dissolving as mysteriously as they'd appear. It might have been an evil sea, except for its stillness, and the large, scattered mounds in its midst, like the graves of giants.

A flash caught Par's eye. Near the horizon, a storm roiled. Massive spinning columns like dust devils, lit by green internal fires, danced before it, seeming to stop and turn of their own accord.

This was the Devastation of legend, dead yet somehow not. The sight was more dreadful than he'd ever imagined.

"Almost ready," Vex said.

Par staggered to his feet. Vex had removed candles from the sack, along with ghoulish metallic holders. He was placing them at the corners of the table.

The grotesque landscape, the high stone altar under a witching moon, the air stale like a tomb long closed—it was every nightmarish story Par had ever heard. "Could you have made this any creepier?"

Vex touched a wick. It flared blood red. "I see nothing creepy about it. Now, would you mind hopping onto the slab?"

Even in the hot air, Par shivered as he approached the altar, determined to get this over with. The Father Abbot had sent him to Vex for this very moment.

Yet everything had changed since the abbey. The events of the last few days flashed through his mind. He decided that before he allowed this sorcerer—a man he had just met—to take him even further into his own darkness, he owed it to himself to be sure of one last thing.

He stopped a step away. "No."

Vex paused above the next candle and looked up. "I'm sorry. Did you say no?"

"First, I need you to answer a question."

The sorcerer peered at the moon. "If you must, but make it quick."

Par took a deep breath. "How do I know that Cronus is the monster you say?"

The candle ignited. The sorcerer's eyes flashed before the flame. Just when Par thought the man might explode in anger, instead Vex began to laugh.

Until this moment, a slight smile, tinged with sadness, was the most humor Par had seen from him. Par didn't know how to react.

"Oh, dear." The man caught himself. "Forgive me. I've spent so many years countering Cronus's machinations, I can't remember when I last asked myself the same thing. Still, he is the High Sigil Master of your country. It is a perfectly reasonable question."

Par waited. Enio had signaled danger, but his friend had been wrong before.

Vex moved to the third candle and adjusted its holder. "I assume you need something more convincing than Cronus capturing your friends and taking your arm?"

"Well, you captured me too. If you hadn't..." Par squeezed his stump.

"And what about the injuries to your friend Buckets?"

"I don't know. An accident? That's why I'm asking."

"It was no accident. But I'll get to the point. You read the book I gave you?"

"Most of it."

Vex lit the third candle. As he spoke, he studied its crimson flame. "Cronus was initially recruited into the Vigil Terrestria, the arm of the Vigil that monitored our lands and its peoples. He oversaw the secret Outpost at Argent as I did at Xol Tomot. Because of his talents, he was also welcomed into the Vigil Immortus, those tasked with sealing the rift in that black pit and ridding the lands of its menace. But he became frustrated with the Vigil's progress and recommended they use curses to better understand it."

"Why curses?"

Vex looked back up, his face red in the candlelight. "As I once mentioned, magic is useless near the Immortus. The chaos of energies, the sheer power of the rift, frustrates such attempts. Perhaps the mages of Gê could manage it, as they once joined together to push back those fires. Such mages, however, died millennia ago, and without magic, the Immortus is devilishly hard to study."

He glanced again at the moon. "But think of curses as sigil-shaped wounds, scratches on the soul. Cronus found that the curse itself often remained intact after brief exposure to the rift, or could even be removed with extended contact. He believed insights to the Immortus could be gleaned from this phenomenon. The Vigil agreed to allow him to study these forces on animals. But he expanded his experiments—to include people."

"People like Buckets?" Par clenched his fist.

"Yes. The Vigil discovered this atrocity and summoned him before the council. Cronus argued that closing the Immortus was foolish in the first place. He said they should harness its magic and use it for greater things. They might remake the entire world into a new Garden, a new paradise, with the Vigil at its head."

Vex moved to the last candle. "Well, even those marginally on his side abandoned him. He begged for one last meeting to make his case. So the Vigil called a great conclave."

"When was this?"

"Almost twenty years ago. Most of the members gathered here at the Citadel. Then, as I told you, the Citadel went silent. When I later came to check, I found it sealed. It's been that way ever since. Other than Cronus, I've never seen anyone from the Vigil again."

"And you think he had something to do with their disappearance?"

Vex lit the last candle. It flickered in a sudden breeze, refusing to go out. "I can't prove it, but it means there are none left to oppose him. If he didn't, it seems quite a coincidence."

Par nodded. It seemed that way to him, too.

The man now stood at the table's head, bathed in the red candlelight, the tome open before him. He stared at Par from under a heavy brow. "That's all I can tell you. Your heart must guide you from here."

"And if I asked," Par hesitated, "would you let me go free?"

Vex frowned. "I will not turn you over to Cronus."

Before Par could ask if he was as much a prisoner as Enio and Lani, Vex continued. "However, if you insisted, I'd let you go anywhere else through a Threshold. Yet I believe completing the procedure begun by Cornelius, determining what we're dealing with, may be the best way to protect the peoples of all the lands, not to mention saving your friends." He took one last glimpse at the moon and motioned toward the table. "We are out of time. Par, will you trust me?"

While Par couldn't be sure, his heart told him Vex was sincere. And Par trusted the Father Abbot, who had sent him to Banes. Besides, Vex's words had helped clear his head. This wasn't just about his curse. He needed to find a way to rescue his friends.

"All right." Par swallowed and stepped to the stone altar. "I'm ready."

Chapter Forty-Three

PAR TOUCHED THE thick stone altar. The candle flames danced in the wind.

Vex helped him onto the table. "I fear a storm. We must hurry."

Par lay between the candles. His chest rose and fell in trembling breaths. He stared at the bright moon encircled by a strange spectral halo.

The man bent over him. "Here we go, son." Vex furrowed his brow and closed his eyes.

Before Par closed his own, a silver glory burst from the sorcerer's head, as if the moon behind Vex had exploded in starlight. Dazzled at the power of the incantation, Par's eyes snapped shut. He slowed his breathing and tried to calm himself. He'd already been through this sort of thing with the Father Abbot. How much worse could it be?

Fingers touched his head. Next came that same invasion of mind he'd experienced at the abbey. But as with the Father Abbot, the presence was warm and caring. Par relaxed a little. His decision to trust Vex had been correct.

A foreign thought wafted through. *I will be as gentle as possible.*

Par's inner life was sifted through like a sack of barley. This time, rather than resist, he abandoned himself to the loss of privacy. Maybe it would make the procedure easier—or faster.

Yet Vex went deeper than the Abbot, lifting the lid from Par's memories and imaginings. Any hope of being prepared collapsed. Secrets Par had kept from his parents, from Enio, even from himself, recoiled from the stark light with nowhere to hide. The despair that had gripped him during the Father Abbot's invocation threatened to overwhelm him again.

Another thought from the sorcerer: *Our journey must go much further. Brace yourself.*

As Par tried to figure out how to brace his brain, a sudden acceleration seemed to toss him into the air. He panicked at the notion of arcing through the night high above the tower. He flailed for a handhold, but he had no body now, and no hands to grab with.

Memories marched in vivid parades—his first meeting with Buckets; breaking his wrist in his father's smithy; early birthdays; running naked from a bath. The acceleration increased. He flew through a crystal tunnel of blurring images and chattering people, shifting and crowding together, closer and louder.

It was too much at once. The chaos became unbearable. He screamed soundlessly, unable to stop them. And when he feared he must go mad, he shot as from a cannon into darkness.

Now there was no up or down, no fast or slow, no light or sound. An infinite night, unlike any that had ever been in the world.

Vex!

No reply, not even an echo. The void swallowed his every thought as if it had never been. He feared it would swallow *him*, as if *he* had never been.

His panic spiked. Had something gone wrong? Had Vex lost him in this emptiness between life and death?

Then, in the distance, a light. Par welcomed it like the dawn after a nightmare. It beckoned him, warm and friendly and radiant with life. Yet it wasn't Vex. He reached out. Yes, he must be dead. This must be the gateway to the Higher Realms.

But the light, the joy, fled. Again, a cold abyss swallowed him. He cried out in new despair. The tunnel of feelings and memories returned, then dimmed and slowed and disappeared. A hot wind slapped his face. The hard stone table pressed against his back.

His eyes flew open. The stars overhead shone pure and bright in the vaults of the night. He dared not move, afraid he might find he had no life in his body.

After a few slow breaths, however, the terrors of the ordeal eased. He groaned and sat up. The candles were burned down to their holders. How long had he been gone? He strained his neck around, his hair whipped in a heavy wind. There was no sign of the sorcerer.

A moan rose from beside the table. Vex lay prone on the stone roof.

"Vex?" Par climbed down. He knelt beside the man and gripped his shoulder.

The sorcerer's eyes flickered opened. "Remarkable."

Par helped him sit against the table, out of the growing winds. The man was pale and unsteady, but Par couldn't wait any longer. "Did you see anything?"

Vex lifted a trembling hand to Par's face, wiping away tears Par hadn't known were there. "I did."

Par leaned forward, his muscles taut, counting the man's every breath.

At last, Vex cleared his throat and gave a low chuckle. "You know, I sometimes envy the Elorian way of things. Sigils and invocations. Gods and souls. It's elegant."

Par frowned, hoping that the sorcerer hadn't lost his mind.

"The Arcanans, though, have a dozen names for everything. Sorcerers and wizards and magicians; sigils and glyphs and runes and magic and spells. What's worse, everybody uses the terms differently. Why, I remember a time—"

"Vex!" Par was about to exit his skin.

The man nodded. "Sorry—I'm struggling to find words you'll understand." He studied Par's face. "We went to the very brink of your soul itself. But I needed to be sure."

"Sure of what?"

Vex sighed. "Your Father Abbot's instinct—that you had a shadow near your soul—was very near the truth. Every source of magic, whether the gods or the cosmos or whatever else is out there, originates in the Higher Realms. That is where our material world has its root—its spirit, if you will."

Par ground his teeth. He was in no mood for a theology lesson.

The man continued, "Our souls absorb and transform those energies into what we in Arcana call the numena. It's what keeps us alive and holds the world together. Mankind has learned to use the excess we collect to empower sigils. But your own soul does not absorb enough extra numena to allow such empowerments to occur. The shell of your soul—its skin, so to speak—is just a bit more opaque, a bit more dense than normal."

"What?" Par yelped. Every theory of his curse, his inability to invoke, swarmed his mind like hornets. He staggered to his feet and searched the night. Gusts fluttered his clothes like tattered sails under a mocking moon.

"Son, are you—"

Par flailed his single arm in frustration. "I don't understand! Do the gods hate me or not? Am I cursed or not?"

Vex raised a hand. "Help me up."

Par calmed enough to help the man stand. His voice rose with the wind. "How did this happen? Who did this to me?"

Vex steadied himself against the table. "Like our bodies, every soul is unique. You may have merely been born this way. A Reckoning could never have helped you."

Born this way? Weariness finally landed. He shook his head and leaned against the altar. "I don't believe it. He was right, all along."

Vex took him by the arm. "Right? What do you mean? Who was right?"

"Enio." Par eyes met Vex's. "He always said I was thick."

CHAPTER FORTY-FOUR

V EX PUSHED THROUGH the winds and grabbed his tome from the altar. His red robes flapped like the flags above a battlement. "We must get off this tower."

Grit and sand whipped Par's face and stung his eyes. The candles toppled and rolled off the table. He reached for one.

"Leave them!" Vex hurried down the short steps from the rooftop.

Par scrambled after. "How do we get back?"

"There's a Threshold down the outer stairs!"

They'd have to descend the long stairway that wrapped the tower, with no rail, in this wind? Par's legs almost buckled at the thought. "You're not serious?"

"No choice!" Vex motioned toward the Devastation. The towering dust devils with their green burning hearts leapt and danced closer. Par shielded his eyes and staggered through the gale, trailing the Sorcerer.

Then, from somewhere through a blasting cloud of sand, Vex yelled, "Par, no!"

Par skidded to a stop. The wind ceased. In the chaos, he'd

stumbled into—and somehow through—the tower's doorway of blue fire. The room stood empty, except for a set of tight spiral stairs disappearing into the floor.

Vex stood outside. He tapped the curtain of fire. Sparks burst from the surface. He shouted through a cupped hand. "The opaqueness of your spirit must confuse the Citadel seals!" The wind rose further, muffling his words. "Outer stairs... too dangerous anyway. Find... Threshold and key... council chambers."

"What about you?" Par shouted.

"I'll... Xol Tomot!"

Par grimaced, hating to leave Vex alone, and hating to search this strange place by himself. As he was about to argue further, green fires, like demon eyes, rose above the tower wall.

Par pointed. "Look out!"

Vex spun. The sand swirled wildly, glittering as it scratched the blue veil. Tendrils from the green fires shot toward the man. A glory flashed from his head just as a tempest of wind and flame engulfed him. When it receded, he was gone.

"Vex!" Par yelled.

Four other blazing green orbs rose above the wall and shot toward Par. He jumped back, but with a horrific wail they retreated, repelled by the blue fire of the Citadel's seal. They remained above the tower, burning with ferocity.

Par could only hope Vex was all right, but there was nothing he could do. Grimacing, he turned to the stairwell.

After descending twenty or thirty steps, he came to a small round window, cloaked with the same blue veil. Several such windows later, an archway loomed near a landing. A hooded, white-robed figure lay before it.

Par froze. "Hello?" he whispered.

It didn't move.

He crept near and nudged it with his foot. The hood sloughed aside. A bone-clean skull stared out.

Par yelped and cringed, but nothing stirred. He swallowed hard, approached the figure and peeked through the arch.

A circular chamber opened beyond. At its center sat the statue of a noble swan surrounded by the low walls of a dry fountain. More corpses lay strewn around it.

Par leaned against the wall, steadying his breath. He noticed a distant, low-pitched hum farther down the stairs. Below on the steps, another body.

That decided it. He eased out of the stairwell. At least out here, if something attacked him, he'd have space to run.

Three hallways radiated from the chamber, their roofs ending in graceful points. The corridor opposite was the largest. He kept himself to the wall and eased around the dead fountain, away from the skeletons.

As he explored the long hall, stepping around more robed figures, the revelation about his thick soul at last overtook his thoughts. At least he wasn't a vessel of the dun. And Vex said it wasn't a curse. But did it matter? Knowing that this wasn't some punishment from the gods, just a natural part of him, didn't seem to help anything. Either way, he couldn't invoke. If the Hierarchy got their hands on him, they might turn his mind into a potted plant trying to fix something that couldn't be fixed.

The corridor emptied into another chamber like the first. A barren stone fountain in the shape of an apple tree sat in the center. Magnificent doors of white wood stood open to the right.

Par peeked inside.

An indoor amphitheater spread before him. More dead figures, sprawled and twisted, filled the room. The seats layered down five levels to a large round stage surrounded by a rail. That platform reminded Par of the Monitor at Xol Tomot, yet no globe of light hovered above it. Floor-to-ceiling windows filled the far wall, all glowing with familiar curtains of blue light. The storm over the Devastation blurred their views.

Was this the council chamber Vex had mentioned? The curving walls were painted with grand pictures of mages with flowing robes and thunderous brows. Another opening, dull and shallow with a single black step, interrupted the artwork.

A Threshold!

But he still needed a key.

His stomach fell. He'd have to search the corpses.

Par began with those closest to the Threshold. He whispered, "Sorry," to each before touching its robes. As he searched, he found many items—a hairbrush, a tin of old nuts, a totem to the god Oä. But no stone key.

He stopped and wiped his forehead. Everything about this funereal task depressed him, and the more he worked, the worse he felt. He had to speed things up.

A figure slumped near a lectern before the round stage. The robes were fancier, more colorful than the rest—purple with gold sashing. He tried that one next.

The body lay face down. Par mumbled his apologies and rolled it over.

A ring with a large ebony ornament, like a mirror, sparkled on the index bone. A rainbow pattern rippled across its surface.

Par leaned toward it, fascinated by the scintillations. He gingerly turned it to get a better look.

The surface flashed. Par jerked away his hand.

A chorus of moans rose from the ring. Then an image, a bearded face, contorted and pale, appeared on the surface. "It was Cronus!" the man gasped. "He's killed us all!"

The sounds and image faded.

Par knelt before the corpse, both amazed and sickened. Had he just listened to this man's dying words? If so, Vex was right. Cronus *had* wiped out the Vigil.

He again surveyed the carnage in the room. There were no slashed robes, no burns. Maybe Vex could figure out what had happened. Par slid the ring from the skeletal finger and pocketed it. As he disturbed the body, something on a chain dropped from the man's neck.

A keystone!

Nearly shouting for joy, he reverently lifted off the necklace, put it over his head and returned to the Threshold.

As Vex had done, Par stood before the opening, squeezed the stone and concentrated. Relief washed over him at the thought of getting far away from these horrors, back to safety and—

The Threshold shimmered and opened into the bell tower of the Saint Livius Abbey.

Par sucked in an astonished breath.

The sky shone bright and cheery with early morning. He heard the distant chanting of the monks and caught a whiff of rose-scented incense.

How long had he been away? So much had happened since he'd left—most of it bad. One step and it would all be behind him. He'd see his parents again, his little brother. Then he'd steal away and live with the Choga. Because of his thick soul, Cronus would never find him.

The sight gladdened him a moment. But with a sad chuckle, he shook his head. Returning home was a childish fantasy. He still had to help Enio and Lani.

Par turned his mind to the tower room at Xol Tomot. At first, nothing happened. Then he remembered Vex had said the keep was protected. He changed his vision. The image re-formed into the landing where they'd first docked at the sorcerer's keep.

Still Par didn't move. He glanced again around the council chamber, at the dead bodies. At Cronus's evil work.

Vex said Cronus wanted his curse. Unlike Buckets, Par didn't have a curse. He had something else, something he might not be able to use for bargaining. If not, what would happen to his friends?

And what if Vex hadn't made it back to Xol Tomot? Even if Par climbed its walls to get inside, he couldn't open the floor tile to the Threshold. He'd be stranded there, with no way to help anybody.

Par clenched his jaw and concentrated once more. The doorway shimmered and opened before the cliff-side ledge of the Argent Outpost.

He might still have no choice except to bargain with Cronus. Before that, there was one last thing he could try: rescue his friends himself.

A yawning gap still stretched between the Threshold and the ledge, high above the sea.

Par backed up as far as possible. With a terrified shout, he ran full speed at the Threshold, and leapt.

CHAPTER FORTY-FIVE

Par soared over the gap high above the Silver Sea. Brisk, salty air blasted his face. The calls of gulls echoed through the sky.

He landed full-speed on the stone lip of the Argent Outpost. His right arm flailed, but with his left forearm gone, he was unable to catch his balance. Par careened sideways toward the drop-off. He grabbed at the cliff, seized a vine and slammed into the rock wall.

One foot dangled over the precipice. He froze, afraid to breathe. Waves crashed onto the rocks five hundred feet below.

When his heart retreated from his throat, Par eased back onto the ledge. An ugly rope burn across his hand smarted as if stung by bees. His arm, the missing part, throbbed again, and he'd torn his shirt. He wiped perspiration off his face, but the sweat was mixed with blood from a cut on his forehead. That hurt, too.

A pretty rotten start for a rescue.

The passage where his friends had stood disappeared into the cliff. He crept into its mouth. Several paces in, a metal gate blocked the way. Darkness swallowed the tunnel beyond.

He shook the bars.

Locked.

Crap.

He shuffled back to the ledge.

The Silver Sea shimmered to the horizon. This was the first time Par had stood before Enio's lifelong goal. At the moment, it brought him little joy.

He turned to the cliff wall. It seemed to climb into the clouds. Fissures and cracks peeked between vines and creepers.

Off to his left, a rectangular crevice caught his eye. It looked man made. He saw another beyond that.

Slotted windows?

His hope reignited. Maybe he could use the scattered rock outcrops and fissures as footholds to reach one of the openings. He'd managed worse contortions cleaning the stained glass at the abbey.

Par peered again over the edge, gasped and drew back. But single-handed? One mistake and he'd be dead.

He tugged a vine, but it dug painfully into the burn in his palm. So he used his teeth to rip a strip of cloth from his torn shirt, wrapped the wound, and tried the vine again.

Better.

Just don't look down.

Par mapped out his first few moves and tested the closest jut. Satisfied it would hold, he squeezed the vine, clenched his teeth and took the step. The sea roared below like a hungry beast, and the gulls overhead seemed to curse him.

He repeated his maneuvers, edging along the jagged wall from one foot-sized ledge to the next. When he was almost within touching distance of the window, the outcrops ended. There were still cracks. They should be enough to get him the rest of the way.

He clutched a new vine and dug a foot into a fissure. It felt secure. As he readied for the final stretch, a screech blared in his ear. He gasped and nearly lost his grip.

Furious squawks filled the air. A large white bird with ink-tipped wings, red eyes, and a beak like a dagger hovered behind him. As if in chorus with its rebukes, baby chirps answered from a crack ahead.

"Shoo!" he yelled, trying to match the mother's anger. "I'm not after your children!"

But the bird attacked. Wings beat at Par's face. He couldn't swat the creature and still hold the vine. He tried banging at the mother with his head.

The bird dodged and jabbed its beak into Par's shoulder.

He screamed and squeezed his lifeline for all he was worth.

The creature clawed at his neck. Par pressed his face into the hard rock, protecting his eyes. The window was so close, but the bird wouldn't let him move. If it went for his hand…

"Help!" he shouted. "Help me!" He'd rather be captured than die. His straining leg muscles began to shake. The sea thundered below. He clung on in blind, sick terror, with the crazy thought that the last thing he'd ever smell was his own sour sweat. As if to mock him, a breeze chilled his skin, like death breathing down his neck.

The bird backed off. Par hugged the cliff, his heart pounding, afraid to move. He braced for the next attack.

Instead, a great hush filled the air. Even the waves had fallen mute. Par dared to look.

What he witnessed was astounding. It seemed as if every bird in the world had gathered into a towering funnel that stretched clear down to the sea. They circled without a sound. The foam and spray around the rocks no longer spit and thrashed like a wild animal. The water moved in a gentle swirl, slow and tranquil, like the birds. And where the sun reached the depths, the reflection glimmered back in a beautiful sparkling green.

Par's panic eased. He didn't know what was happening, but the gentle light below shone with a profound sense of peace. His breathing slowed. He stopped shaking.

In another moment, he felt more himself. He blinked away the vision and shook his head—this was no time for sightseeing. While the birds were distracted, he turned again to the window.

He used the vines to help him farther along the rough cliff wall and up to the sill. The baby birds cooed in their snug little hole.

The slotted window ran deep, like a short tunnel, but was wide enough for him to fit through. Half his body made it inside before the shaft opened out again, high in the wall of a room like a prison cell. A hallway passed beyond it, lit by a pale blue glow. The bars there stood open.

He gathered the vine into his little crawlspace and dropped the end into the room. Gripping it in his one hand, he braced his feet against the wall and tried to walk himself down.

It was working—until the bandage slid off his palm. With the eruption of pain he lost his grip, landed on his feet, and crumpled.

As Par sat on the cold stone floor in the dim light, wincing at a sharp new pain in his ankle, he was warmed by a small wave of euphoria. He'd made it into the Argent Outpost, along a cliff face, without an invocation, and with only one arm.

He almost laughed. Par might be "thick," but if nothing else, he could always join the circus.

CHAPTER FORTY-SIX

PAR LIMPED FROM the cell. His ankle stung from the drop, but his missing forearm burned like fire. Maybe because the mama bird had jabbed that shoulder.

To the right, a corner led back toward the outside ledge. There'd be no escape that way.

The next cell to the left was locked. Two cages hung from the ceiling. In one, Enio sat cross-legged, his head down.

Par leapt to the corridor bars. His friend seemed unharmed—which was more than Par could say for himself. He whispered as loudly as he dared, "*Enio.*"

His friend didn't move. "Par?" he muttered. "Is that you?"

Par smiled. "It's not the High Fondiscate."

Enio continued without looking up, "It's good you're here. They want to talk to you."

Something was wrong. Par glanced at the empty cage. "Where's Lani?"

"Oh, she's… she left."

"She escaped?"

"There's a lot I didn't understand." Enio took in an expansive breath, swelling his bent back and shoulders. "But they told me. They'll tell you, too."

"You didn't answer. Where's—"

"You want to protect the country from Arcana, don't you?"

A chill crawled up Par's spine. This didn't sound like his friend. "Enio, what's going on?"

"They say Tomot lies. They say they can help you."

"Enio, look at me."

"It can't hurt to listen, right?" His friend chuckled thinly. "Isn't that what they say? If you'd just—"

"Enio!"

His friend's face snapped up. The eyes were dull and hollow. Then they focused and widened. "Par?"

"Yes! What have they done to you?"

Enio brought his palms to his temples, but he never blinked. "They've been in my head." His voice trembled.

Par's heart almost stopped. He struggled to form the words. "Did they Reckon you?"

"I don't think so. But they keep going back. They..." Enio gasped and swallowed. His mouth contorted like melting wax. "They show me my mother, when she died. Cronus plays it over and over and—" The words choked off.

Par's insides twisted like Enio's mouth. His friend never spoke of his mother—he said it hurt too much.

Enio crawled forward. "Sometimes, I almost forget her face." He yanked on his cage bars, weakly at first, then with a violence Par had never seen. "None of it makes sense! Why should I have to convince you of anything? Why..." His energy left him. His fingers slid down the bars.

"What do they want?" Par hissed.

"They want me to—but you can't—but I don't know." He closed his eyes and dropped his head to his chest. "I don't know."

Par glanced up the hallway and back at his friend. "I'm going to get you out. I have to find the keys."

Enio lunged. His arm shot through his cage bars. "Don't leave!"

Par froze. It killed him that he'd have to leave Enio while he searched. Then he remembered his Lustering medal, now chainless, still in his pocket. Par dug it out. "Listen. I need to go for a little while. Here, catch this." He tossed it across the cell to his friend.

The throw was short, but Enio snatched it out of the air. He brought it to his chest.

"Hold that for me until I get back, all right?"

Par waited for his friend to say something, but Enio slumped in his cage and closed his eyes. His face again became unreadable.

With Par's every nerve on edge, he turned back to the hall. He passed other cells, but they showed no sign of Lani. He'd get Enio out first. Then they'd find her together.

The hallway ahead ended in a stone door carved with a star, the same design as the Monitor Room at Xol Tomot. Par prayed there was a Threshold behind it.

Before he could get close to check, the pain in his arm spiked. He fell against the wall, gasping.

Par caught his breath and found he'd halted near a wooden door. Something about it seemed odd.

No, not odd. Familiar?

He cracked it open.

An acrid odor hit him and he grimaced. Aisles of shelves with glass jars and tanks of every size stretched before him. A luminous yellow liquid filled the vessels.

Par crept inside. Many of the containers held the corpses of animals—rabbits, crows, dogs. Some of the faces were horribly twisted. Other jars were so small he couldn't tell what was in them.

Some kind of sick museum?

His pain exploded worse than ever. He collapsed to the floor, muffling a cry.

As the agony ebbed, he gritted his teeth and struggled to his feet. The tank before him contained an arm.

His lost arm.

He jerked back in horror.

The arm jerked, too.

Enio's voice echoed in the distance. "He's here! He's here!"

Par stumbled to the door. The Prior stood before Enio's cell.

Crap!

Par didn't wait to make a plan. He ran for the Monitor room.

As he gained the doorway, the Prior shouted. "*Stop!*"

Par was already inside, out of line of an invocation. He sped around the sphere. The Threshold was there.

He grabbed the stone around his neck. The doorway shimmered and opened. He dove.

"*Stop!*"

This time, the Prior's voice slammed into Par's mind and his muscles seized, but his momentum carried him through the portal.

He crashed onto his back on the river landing of Xol Tomot. Other than his heaving chest, Par couldn't move. Crows leapt from the corner pylons, cawing and screaming.

The Threshold closed. Par tried to call for help. His voice didn't obey.

Then the portal re-opened. Cronus loomed beyond the doorway. "Don't worry, son. We'll soon be together."

With a sudden gush of wind, Vex dropped out of the very air and landed between Par and the Threshold. The man's head blazed with silver light. "Come to surrender, Cronus?"

The Sigil Master offered him a wry smile. "You would do well to consider that yourself, but our next encounter will have to wait until tomorrow. At the Immortus."

The portal blinked out.

Par groaned.

Vex knelt beside him. A touch from the man's hand and Par could move. He sat up, his anger burning hotter than every pain and ache. He'd been so close! What was Cronus doing to Enio? What had happened to Lani?

Vex helped him stand. "It's time we made our plans."

"Plans?" Par growled.

Vex laid a hand on his shoulder. "To rescue your friends. To save the world."

CHAPTER FORTY-SEVEN

FROM A DESOLATE corner of his mind, Enio watched Cronus, followed by the Prior, tramp through his head as if they owned the place. Each time they'd come, he'd fought. And each time, the fight ended sooner than the last. But Enio was done. What was the point? Cronus had found everything he needed the first time.

When they once again pulled out, he curled into a tight ball at the bottom of his cage.

"Interesting." Cronus spoke close enough that Enio winced at the man's sour breath. "He doesn't recall whether he shouted to warn Par, or to alert you he was here."

It was true, and it killed Enio that he couldn't remember.

"Still, Master Cronus, he did attempt to persuade Par to our cause."

"And he deserves a reward. It is why, this time, I did not revisit his mother's memories."

Enio ground his teeth.

The Prior spoke again. "The boy is exhausted."

"Speak freely, Dogam. It is a waste of time to hide your thoughts."

"As you said, High Master, this is not about two children. But is there no other way? One that is less… severe?"

Enio jerked inside like a poked fish. Was the Prior trying to help him?

"The boy remains unharmed, Dogam."

"Yes, but—"

"And our guest must remember that if he does not persuade his friend to trust us, we can still Reckon Parynius to our way of thinking."

A Reckoning was Par's greatest fear. Enio would do whatever he could to prevent it. He knew Cronus was using that against him. Enio's brain was melting.

"Master Cronus, did you not say a Reckoning defeated your purpose?"

"It is a risk. But unless Enius embraces the truth, we will have no choice."

A shuffle of robes and the Sigil Master's voice receded. "I have other duties. See to the boy's needs if you wish."

Footsteps faded from the room. Was the Prior still there, watching? Maybe, but Enio didn't care. Nothing could rattle him after having his head turned inside out.

Until, in a gentle voice, Prior Dogam said, "Did you know, Enio, I once met your mother?"

Enio froze, but he couldn't help listening.

The Prior went on. "It was before the Hierarchy assigned me to the abbey. I happened to be passing through St. Livius. Cornelius put me up in the guest quarters. In the morning, he took me on rounds. It seems one family had a firebrand of a youngster who refused to chant his morning litany. Little Enius kept sneaking off to play along the river. Your parents feared this was stunting your spiritual development."

Enio stifled a snort.

"I suggested they try bolting the doors. But the Abbot told them not to worry. He said there'd be time for the litanies and the saints and the Rule, but people came to the gods in different ways. Eventually, you'd find your path."

The Prior's story brought Enio vague images of sitting on his bed with his mother, learning his prayers. He smiled, even while his insides twisted.

The Prior went on, "It's a shame what happened to her. Tarley was never the same. I suspect you get your stubborn streak from him, but you have your mother's eyes."

Enio sat up. "Then you can remind me what she looks like when Cronus takes her away forever."

"He's not—I've tried to explain the importance of what the High Master is doing. Though I admit his methods are somewhat unorthodox."

"Like torture?"

The man frowned, his face gaunt and pale.

"Look," Enio said, "You've told me all about your wars and curses, and how Cronus wants me to get Par to trust you so he doesn't end up like Buckets."

Before the Prior responded, Enio lifted a hand. "Don't worry. I expect it won't be long before I'll say whatever Cronus wants— even if I'd rather die."

The Prior stepped closer. "Things aren't as grim as you make them out. Master Cronus has much to offer."

"Like my life?"

"Like a chance to help thousands of lives. And, Enio, he can give Par his arm back."

Enio's eyes widened. He'd seen the abbey heal many injuries, but never restore a limb.

"It's true, son. Cronus recovered Par's arm. Isn't that worth a few words to your friend on our behalf?"

Enio rubbed his face. The Prior was right about one thing—he was exhausted. And the man was at it again with his arguments. Each new time, they became easier to swallow.

He rallied his little strength. "Let me ask you this: You've seen what Cronus is willing to do to me to get what he wants. What do you think he's willing to do to Par?"

"Par is of supreme importance. He could be the key—"

"You keep saying that. And how far will Cronus go? Do you think he'll stop at what he did to Buckets?"

Prior Dogam seemed to struggle for his words. "Sometimes, son, we have to do what is right, not—"

"A cage is right?" Enio tugged on the bars. "Torture is right?"

The Prior's face steeled. "You are not one to speak of what is right, Enius Marius, one who cast an Arcanan spell before a high altar."

"To help Par. But why are you helping Cronus? To protect the country? Bull. Everyone knows you can't stand the abbey. And he got you out."

"And where have your choices gotten *you*?" barked the Prior. "Inside a cell beneath the High Temple."

Enio gave a tight smile. "Seems to me, so have yours."

The Prior flinched. Light flashed around his head. He reached toward the cage. "You're upsetting yourself. Let me help calm—"

Enio moved back. "Stay away from me."

For a moment, the Prior loomed before him as the imposing figure Enio remembered from the abbey. Then the man's glory faded. "Very well. Are you hungry?"

"You know what?" Enio settled in his cage once more. "When you mentioned the abbey, you reminded me of something else."

"What's that?"

"How it smelled like roses and beer. Even the monks."

A faint smile crept across the Prior's lips. "The abbey's brewery did a fair business. I tried to convince the Abbot that with better distribution—"

"You smelled that way, too."

The Prior's nostrils flared. His nose dipped toward his shoulder.

Enio shook his head. "Not anymore. Now you smell like the incense at funerals. Same as your Master."

The Prior's eyes narrowed. "Call if you need anything." The man strode from the room.

Enio curled up and closed his eyes. It still bothered him that he didn't know whether he'd meant to warn Par or the Prior when he'd shouted. Which would have been better? What if doing what the Prior wanted was the only way to keep Par from Buckets' fate, and from a Reckoning?

He grimaced; he was slipping away. At one point or another, Enio had lost everything important in his life. By tomorrow, he might even lose himself.

But he had one small hope left. Par said he'd never abandon him. Enio would hold him to that promise.

In the silence of the cell, he slipped his hand into his pocket and felt the cold metal of Par's Lustering pendant. The rest of his memories had been looted. But with his last bit of strength—the last bit of *Enio*—he'd managed to keep this one hidden away, just for himself.

CHAPTER FORTY-EIGHT

P AR SAT BESIDE Vex on the bottom steps of the docks of
Xol Tomot. One by one, crows returned from the sky and
glided onto the pylons and rails. This was the very place
where he and his friends had first arrived in their coracle. A heaviness settled in his muscles and in his heart. His rescue had failed.

As he again breathed the sour-sweet river air, his head cleared.
His words came rapidly. "Cronus was in Enio's head. Lani wasn't
there, but Enio wouldn't tell me where she went. I'm afraid something's happened to her and—"

"Slow down," Vex said. "Let's take this one step at a time. So,
Xol Tomot was not your first stop after the Citadel?"

Par's face warmed. He shook his head. Vex had directed him
to Xol Tomot—it had been Par's crazy idea to attempt a rescue at
Argent. "I didn't know if you'd... made it back. I got worried I'd
be stranded here, with no way to help my friends." He groaned
as his ankle and his rope-burned hand throbbed. "How did you
escape the dust demons?"

Vex reached toward where Par rubbed his ankle. A glory circled the man's head. "I flew my way to another Threshold."

That explained it. Par had forgotten the sorcerer could fly.

As that pain faded, Vex examined a rip over Par's knee. "I swear, boy, you go through clothing faster than grass through a goose. Were you attacked in the Citadel?" The man ran his fingers along the tear. The scraped knee healed, and the fabric stitched itself. Then he tended to Par's wounded hand.

Par grimaced at the memory. "No, but it was full of dead people. Skeletons."

"Indeed?" The sorcerer frowned.

"Hold on." Par checked his pocket. The ring was still there. "I took this off one. Here, touch the middle."

Vex's eyes widened. "This is the ring of the Luminary—the Vigil's leader." He lifted the ring from Par's hand and examined the central black stone. It sparkled in the sunlight. When he touched the surface, the likeness of the bearded man Par had seen in it before reappeared, gasping in the same shaky voice, "It was Cronus! He's killed us all!"

A tremor crossed Vex's face. "That was the Luminary himself. And it confirms my suspicions. Cronus slaughtered the Vigil."

"Can we expose his crimes to the High Council of Eloria?" Par's hopes rose.

"Your reasoning has merit, young Par. While I waited for your return, I spent a good deal of time making plans, and considering to whom we might appeal. Contacting Argent and informing them of your Sigil Master's atrocities is, I fear, useless."

"Why? If we can prove he's a murderer—"

"Remember, though I live in the Borderlands, I am from Arcana. Who in your Hierarchy would believe anything I tell them? And the ring is not of Elorian origin. They'd view it as some godless thing, good only for the fire."

That was probably true. "What about help from Arcana?"

"Only another member of the Vigil could help us now." Vex hung his head. "And none are left."

Par shuddered again at the image of the bodies, their bony eye sockets staring up at him. He hoped never to see anything like that again.

He lowered his voice. "How do you suppose Cronus killed them?"

"I'll examine this message for clues." Vex pocketed the ring and stood.

A gaunt bird with greying feathers cawed before the sorcerer.

"Not now, Cornelius." Vex shooed it away.

Par had to smile a little. "You named one after the Father Abbot?"

Vex turned up the stairs. "Tell me more of your journey."

As they climbed the hill of Xol Tomot, Par detailed all he'd seen in the Citadel, and how he'd scaled the cliff at Argent and found his friend—and his arm in a jar.

As they reached the summit, he finished his tale.

Vex stopped before the keep's iron doors. "You realize the recklessness of your plan." It was a simple statement of fact.

Par couldn't argue. "I do."

A crow cawed from on top of the wall.

The sorcerer lifted his head, the sunlight deepening the wrinkles in his face. "But I admire that you tried. We should never give up on our friends."

Par followed his gaze. It was the bird Vex had named Cornelius.

"And going forward, I hope you'll trust me a bit more." Vex gestured, and the heavy door groaned and opened.

They entered the keep and crossed the empty courtyard to the tower. Par had already allowed Vex inside his head, even to his soul. Par did trust him. Plus, Vex had been correct about Cronus. The lives of Par's friends, not to mention his own, seemed now to rest in this sorcerer's hands.

And speaking of hands... "What is Cronus doing with my arm?"

They entered the tower and climbed the staircase. "Given what you've told me of the other containers in that room, perhaps it's part of his Immortus research."

"But the arm moved. I… felt it."

Vex was silent for several steps. "With his Elorian healing skills, and what Cronus has learned since he's been a member of the Vigil, it's possible he plans to offer to reattach it."

Par halted. "That's possible?" He rubbed his stump. He'd never, even in his most hopeful moments, imagined he might get his arm back.

"If so," Vex disappeared around a spiral, "it would come with a heavy price."

A vision of the sprawled and twisted corpses at the Citadel returned to Par's mind, and he understood the price.

While Enio might be freed, Par would become the servant of a monster.

Chapter Forty-Nine

Back in the wizard's high chamber, the central table had been cleared of its bubbling beakers and curious powders and utensils. Books and parchments now covered the surface.

Vex stood before a cabinet. "Your shirt is beyond repair. I'll find you a fresh one later—an advantage of owning an import business. But after your ordeal, you must be famished."

Par gripped his stomach. He hadn't realized it until now.

From the shelves of the cabinet, Vex produced a plate of cold meat and a bundled fruit cake. He handed them to Par, then sat at the table and bent over the tomes.

Par settled and ate, expecting him to keep talking.

He didn't.

At last, Par couldn't wait any longer. "You said you've been making plans."

"Yes," Vex said, still hunched. "Even before we traveled to the Citadel. But recent developments have changed things."

"How?"

"For starters, you don't have a curse."

With everything that had happened since the ritual atop the Citadel, Par hadn't had much time to digest this. It hit him again now. His years of helping around the abbey, his constant struggles under the eyes of his teachers and parents, his endless appeals to the gods—all for nothing?

He grimaced. The Abbot had been right. The gods weren't judging him. At the Citadel, Vex seemed to say that the sources of magic were equally available to everyone, like the lights from common candles. Par's soul just had poor eyesight.

"Well, at least I don't have the dun," he mumbled.

"Why do you say that?"

Par explained his encounter in the Urdel, and how the dun had avoided him.

"Interesting," said the sorcerer. "I suspect you confused it the same way you did the Citadel seals."

It made as much sense as anything, but something more pressing came to mind. "If Cronus finds out I don't have a curse, will he still trade me for Enio?"

"Curse or not, your condition may still aid him in better understanding the Immortus, in harnessing it." Vex pushed his book aside. "However, since you can penetrate the Citadel, we are presented with a new opportunity."

Par wasn't sure where this was going, but at least he still had value to Cronus. "So what do we do?"

Vex spread out a parchment. "Let's start with your High Sigil Master's demands. Whatever we plan, it must be done tomorrow at the Immortus. That's where he'll be the most vulnerable."

The parchment showed a circle surrounded by eight slim rectangles and letters in a language Par didn't recognize. "That's the Immortus?"

"Strictly speaking, it's the rift to the Higher Realms opened by the mage Ridiax. What we call the Immortus blazes forth from the highest of those realms. Our world, our magic, even the gods derive their existence from its emanations."

Vex gestured to the rectangles. "The monoliths hold back the pure, unfiltered energies of the Higher Realms, lest they flood through the rift and destroy everything in a final Devastation."

A chill ran through Par's body at the power, the death held in check for so many centuries. He touched a finger to the circle. "How big is it?"

"The pit is wide enough to admit a man lowered in a long cage."

"Like Buckets." Par frowned.

Vex continued. "The monoliths stand back from the pit, each one as broad as the gap between."

"Is it near the Citadel?" Par hadn't seen a circle of stones from that high rooftop.

"Many days beyond. At the very center of the Devastation."

"So we'll open our Threshold to it."

"Near it. Our Threshold won't open close to the monoliths." Vex gestured to the spaces between the stones. "By the way, each gap is itself a Threshold. That's how we'll leave the place—if everything goes well."

If everything goes well. The words echoed in Par's ears.

Vex tapped inside the diagram. "One thing this doesn't show. Wooden platforms and scaffolding fill the area—everything made of organic material. After a few days, metal goes funny there."

"Funny?"

"Soft, eroded. Don't ask me why." He slid open a drawer beneath the tabletop. It made an unnerving screech. "My first plan was to keep things simple."

The man withdrew two bone knives. He laid them on the table. "My magic doesn't work near the Immortus. But these will."

"Knives?"

"Remember how good I was with the lightning bolts."

"But you kept missing us."

"On purpose—despite how much your friend deserved repayment for impelling a rock at me. But practicing my lightning from the outside wall is very conspicuous, and inside it's rather hard on the upholstery. So I hone my aim using knives. The skill transfers."

Par hadn't known what to expect when Vex confronted Cronus at the Immortus, but he felt let down by the current plan. "You really think you can defeat him with just a knife?"

"To be honest, no. People generally don't simply fall over when struck. And with the intervening scaffolding, I'd have only a slim chance for a kill shot. That's where my second plan comes in."

Vex retrieved another item from the drawer—a small glass vial containing a putrid-looking green liquid.

Par cringed. "Poison?"

Vex swirled it in the light. "And fast-acting. A few drops on the blade and I won't need to hit his heart."

"But you said the scaffolding—"

"Never count out luck, son."

It was as if they treaded a mental bridge with rickety boards, but Par wasn't on the best ground to argue the dangers of recklessness. "What if there's no opening?"

"Plan three. You'll have a poisoned blade hidden upon your person."

Par's eyes widened. "You mean, you want *me* to…" He made a little stabbing motion.

Vex nodded.

"Wait, now." Par could count his serious fights on his single hand, yet this sorcerer from Arcana wanted him to assassinate one of the highest men in the Hierarchy of Eloria? Could Par really kill someone? Even a murderer?

Vex frowned. "If all else fails, if Cronus takes you, you'll be close. Remember what's at stake—and that he had no pity on the Vigil."

Par swallowed, his throat gone dry. "I hope to Oä there's a plan four."

Vex put away the vial. "There is. And it's my best one."

He laid a dusty black tome across the parchment. "The mages who contained the Immortus realized that one misstep in their attempts to close the rift might make matters worse. So they also created what we call the Blink stones."

He flipped to a picture of an inky oval object, like a rotten egg.

Par touched the black Threshold key still hanging around his own neck. "The Thresholds, the standing stones—what is this black mineral they're always using?"

"That's beyond my knowledge. As I was saying, the mages made the Blink stones to test their theories. Used properly, they will briefly disable any one of the monoliths."

"What good does that do?"

"When the monolith goes dark, the Immortus flashes out in that direction. The mages would then test their newest magics against its reach." Vex leaned closer. "As you might expect, anything standing between the Immortus and that monolith is obliterated."

Par began to see the point. "So we need Cronus to move in front of one?"

"Yes."

Par had another thought. "Alone?"

Vex hesitated. "Ideally."

"Ideally?" Par yelped.

"This may be our only chance—"

"No." Par slapped the book. "Not if it gets Enio too."

The sorcerer's voice remained soft. "I did not mean him. But what of your Prior?"

Prior Dogam had always been strict, but had never seemed actually evil. Maybe Cronus was lying to the Prior, or had gotten in his head, like with Enio.

Vex seemed to guess his disapproval. "I am not thrilled about the idea. The letter from Cornelius urged me to give your Prior every chance to prove himself. But by now, it's obvious he has committed his fortunes to Cronus."

Par couldn't see himself making that sort of judgment. He just hoped things wouldn't come to it.

He changed the subject. "How many Blink stones do you have?"

"None."

"None? Then why—" Par's stomach dropped. "Don't tell me. They're in the Citadel."

Vex nodded. "I need you to return and get one."

CHAPTER FIFTY

PAR QUAKED AT the thought of returning to the Citadel. Demons of dust and wind had attacked them last time. The place itself was a tomb, filled with the remains of the men and women Cronus had murdered.

Yet a Blink stone seemed liked their best hope.

He swallowed and kept his voice steady. "When do I leave?"

Vex closed his book. "As soon as you're ready."

Par groaned and rose from his chair. He'd just gotten back from his ordeal at Argent.

The sorcerer held up a hand. "But the day is not so old, even far off at the Citadel. We can afford a brief respite. Two hours?"

It was better than nothing. Par shuffled to his little room and lay face down on the bed. His head swam with visions of Lani and Enio, of the Citadel, and tomorrow's confrontation at the Immortus.

He rolled over and stared at the wooden beams along the ceiling. He counted the cracks, but kept losing his place. So he flipped through the book of the Vigil's history, put it aside, and with a frustrated grunt shuffled to the window. Crows hopped and chased each other along the riverbanks.

Par felt tied down, locked up, with too much to do. He left the bedchamber, slunk past Vex to the spiral stairs and explored other parts of the keep. There were grim rooms with dusty furniture, faded portraits of people he didn't recognize, an empty stable and a weedy courtyard.

His silent wanderings only fed a growing despair—everything he'd tried to do to help his friends failed.

At last, going back up the steps he reached a door that opened onto the tower's rooftop. He leaned over the western parapets and watched cloud shadows drift across the plains and distant mountains.

Vex found him there. "Feeling better?"

Par shrugged.

"I realize life has moved very fast for you since your abbey."

"You could say that," Par mumbled. "I should have just gone for a Reckoning in the first place."

"Nonsense. Your Reckoners would have destroyed your mind trying to fix something they didn't understand."

"At least afterwards I wouldn't have cared about anything. Like my ugly soul." Par kicked the low wall.

Silence settled over the rooftop. Over the world.

Vex spoke softly. "In my time, I've looked into many minds. Believe me when I say there's nothing ugly in your soul." He paused. "Though regrets make it appear that way."

"Regrets." Par snorted. "I've got plenty."

Vex leaned next to him, elbow to elbow. "No matter how old we get, regrets are inevitable. All we can do is learn from them and try to do better."

"I've mostly learned how to be a better liar."

"You didn't lie to cause anyone harm."

Par hoped that much was true.

Vex continued, "Few see the totality of themselves as you did when Cornelius entered your mind. Or when I examined you at the Citadel. If there's one thing I've learned, it's never be afraid of the truth."

The truth. Par shook his head and tried to cross his arms, but realized he was no longer equipped for that gesture.

"Dammit." Tears dampened his eyes. He laid his single arm across the stone wall and dropped his face into his elbow.

A hand squeezed his shoulder. Par couldn't stop himself—he spun, clutched the sorcerer's robe and buried his face in its folds. "If I had just admitted my problem earlier"—he trembled, determined not to sob—"my friends wouldn't be in this mess."

Vex remained as still as a statue, then brushed a hand through Par's hair.

With a long sniffle, Par backed away. He wiped his eyes and forced an embarrassed grin. "Sorry."

Vex straightened, smoothing his robes. "Quite all—" His voice cracked. "Quite all right." He cleared his throat. "I've been told I'm not terribly good at explanations. If you have any outstanding questions, I'll do my best."

Par took a shaky breath and pulled himself together. There were so many things he knew too little about—the Vigil, the Immortus, Arcana. Nothing really seemed worth asking.

Crows circled the tower. They reminded him of something he'd puzzled about earlier. "You said you hadn't seen the Father Abbot since the Grey Wars?"

"That's correct."

"So why did you name a bird *Cornelius*?

Vex shifted his gaze to the crows. He didn't answer.

In a sudden flash, Par understood. "He was your best friend."

"Friend?" Vex made a small laugh. "I hardly think a sorcerer and an abbot could have much in common."

"Me and Enio, we're pretty different. But we get along great." Par had to smile. Usually.

"Well, for a short time, perhaps he was." Vex was quiet a moment. "Did Cornelius ever speak of me?"

"We didn't really have conversations."

"Of course."

"But you were the one he thought of, when he found out I needed help."

"His instincts were sound, as always." Vex sighed. "I should never have given up on Cornelius so easily. If I had swallowed my pride when he rejected me, tried to explain—"

"Maybe it wasn't your pride," Par said. "You'd been in a war. You'd lost people and didn't want to deal with losing any more."

The man gave a slight nod.

Par went on. "Besides, the Father Abbot's leaving wasn't your fault. You didn't know Cronus had burned Buckets at the Immortus, and the Father Abbot didn't know those injuries weren't from you. Blame Cronus, if anyone."

"Cronus does seem to be a common factor in our woes." Vex bent closer and lowered his voice. "I sense your Father Abbot's wisdom has rubbed off."

Par's ears warmed.

Vex patted his shoulder. "In any case my boy, it's time we got along to the Citadel. Are you ready?"

Par glanced once more at the white-peaked mountains. The Citadel was far beyond those, but as close as a step through the Threshold. "As ready as it gets."

They walked together across the tower.

"One more thing," the man added.

"Yeah?"

"Remind me not to call you *boy* anymore."

CHAPTER FIFTY-ONE

Par followed the sorcerer down the tower stairs. They walked without talking, but Par didn't mind. With his return to the Citadel just ahead, it was all he could do to keep his legs moving.

Vex led him into the Monitor room and stopped before the Threshold.

Par took a deep breath and squared his shoulders.

The Threshold opened and the familiar stale wind of the Devastation rushed in. They arrived back on the Citadel tower. The sandstorm had ended, and the blue doorway shimmered before them.

Vex stopped before the curtain of light. "I've been wondering about the Luminary's ring. Perhaps it will allow me to accompany you into the Citadel." He produced the ring from his robes, slid it onto his finger and touched the blue curtain of light.

Sparks erupted from the surface. Vex pulled back. "It was worth a try. You take it. Leave it inside." He dropped the ring into Par's hand.

Par again examined the ebony stone in its silver setting. "Why?"

"If our plans fail, the Citadel may be the only safe place for this record of Cronus's treachery."

The ring was too big for Par's slender fingers. He stuffed it into his pocket.

Vex motioned to the entrance. "Go all the way down. From there, use the first hallway on the right, then go left to the third stairway. Go up one level and around—"

"Wait." Par already had enough on his mind. "Can't you write it down?"

The man's eyes brightened. "Excellent idea." He raised a hand toward Par's face.

Par flinched. "What are you doing?"

"Writing it down. Trust me."

Par nodded and closed his eyes, resigning himself to another uncomfortable intrusion. But as fingers brushed his forehead, doors and hallways and fountains and stairs rolled gently into his mind.

"Wow," he whispered.

"There. You know where the vault is?"

Par did. He opened his eyes. "In the middle of a big room three levels beneath the council chambers."

"Correct. I've seen it only in passing. Another seal protects the vault. I'm hopeful it won't stop you." Wrinkles formed on the man's forehead between straggling white hairs. "And Par—remove only a single Blink stone. Nothing more."

"What if I find something else we could use against Cronus?"

Vex's expression remained stern. "It's tempting. But the Vigil stored powerful things in that vault. We can't chance Cronus getting his hands on them. One Blink stone is risk enough."

That made sense. Par nodded.

"Also," Vex continued, "there's no need to meet me back here—you now know the location of all the Citadel Thresholds."

Par searched his mind and found several, some inside and some out. "Got it." He waited a moment for the man to say something more, then stepped toward the doorway.

"But—" Vex began.

Par turned back.

"Don't return to the Threshold in the council chambers. A Threshold can be reopened many times, but will only allow passage—of body or magic—once per day."

"That's why Cronus didn't follow me from Argent?"

Vex held up a finger. "That reminds me. This time, please return directly to Xol Tomot."

"I will."

The man stared off, seemingly in thought.

Par gritted his teeth, worried if he didn't get going, he'd lose his nerve. "All right, then," Par said, and turned away.

"And—"

"And?" Par couldn't keep the exasperation out of his voice.

Vex's face softened. "Be careful."

Par warmed. With a slight smile, he said, "You too."

He stepped once more before the blue curtain of fire. The barrier of light allowed his fingers to pass unhindered. He took a deep breath, let it out and stepped through. With a last glance at the sorcerer—who gave an encouraging nod—he descended the spiral steps.

This time, he went all the way to the bottom. He traveled the elegant halls, thankful he passed very few skeletons. The bulk he'd seen were in the council chambers, and he didn't need to go that way again. But at the top of a grand stairway, he heard the same distant hum he'd heard during his first visit. Par had forgotten to ask Vex what it was. He chewed his lip, hoping that if it were important, Vex would have mentioned it. The noise increased the farther he got. He glanced over his shoulder, right and left, unable to pinpoint the source.

As he crept down the last corridor, the sound changed from an annoying hum to a ringing buzz. Close ahead loomed a high-arched entrance with open double doors—his destination. Another robed skeleton lay near the entrance.

Par peeked inside. A sprawling room of marble floors and towering columns spread before him. Tall, shallow alcoves lined the walls, each containing a majestic statue of a solemn man or woman. In the room's center stood an enclosed inner chamber, round and ornate like a private crypt. That was the vault. A curtain of blue light covered the single entrance.

The buzz became a roar. At last, Par found its source.

A domed roof covered the vault. A hive of gigantic proportions nestled on top, surrounded by a shifting fog.

Yet it wasn't a fog. An icy fear crept over his skin.

It was a cloud of insects.

Par held his breath and pulled back into the corridor. He'd seen one of those bugs before. Vex had called them skarix—dragonflies with scorpion tails. The man had said the smaller, the deadlier.

Great. Now what?

Vex had also said they didn't bother you if you didn't bother them. As Par glanced again at the skeleton near his feet, a new worry rose in his mind. Had Cronus's massacre of the Vigil brought on such a thorough decomposition of the bodies? Or had the skarix, perhaps trapped in the Citadel, developed a new appetite and picked them clean?

He focused on the vault. His breathing came faster. Should he sprint the distance? Or creep through the room and hope the skarix didn't notice?

He eyed the hive again. The swarm expanded, stretching like an arm—toward him.

Crap!

He bolted toward the vault. The arm split into long fingers reaching his way.

Par had no time to test if he'd be able to pass unharmed through the seal. He reached the vault, and with a last shout threw himself into the blue light. He crashed safely inside onto the hard stone floor.

The skarix hit the curtain with muted sparks. Their smoking husks rained outside like cinders.

Par lay panting, catching his breath. Then he raised to his feet. When he was sure the skarix couldn't follow, he took his first good look around the silent vault.

It was empty.

Chapter Fifty-Two

"No…" The word crumbled from Par's lips.

Bare stone shelves, caked with dust, wrapped the chamber. A short brick wall, like a parapet, surrounded a wide hole in the center of the floor.

More stairs? He peered over the rim. A simple shaft disappeared into darkness.

That was it. No chests of gold, no precious jewels—and no Blink stones.

Panic flashed through his body. He rechecked his internal map. This was the vault. Had it been robbed?

He gripped the edge of the low wall. "Hello?"

A deep, hollow echo.

Par removed his right boot and dangled it above the aperture. He hated to lose it, but there was nothing else in the vault, and he was desperate to know if anything was down there.

He let it drop. After another breath, he thought he heard a muffled thud, so distant it might have been his imagination.

Par couldn't think. His face became hot. The heat spread to

his limbs, his chest. His body shook. Not with a trembling sob. Not with fright. With blind fury.

"No!" He exploded at last, the frustrations of days, of years, breaking free.

"It's not fair!" Spit flew from his mouth. He shouted to no one. To everyone. To the gods.

He railed through the room, hammering the stone shelves, kicking the walls, screaming at the empty air. The Blink stones were their best chance against Cronus. And this had been *Par's* chance to do something useful. Something to actually help. But like his friends, his arm—his whole life—it had been snatched away.

The room rang with his anguish. If there had been anything there to smash, he'd have smashed it. Anything to hurl into that dark abyss would be gone.

At last, his rage exhausted, Par slumped to the floor. He sat panting, numb in mind and body. It really *wasn't* fair. Regardless of what Vex had said, Par must be cursed.

He let out a weak chuckle. What was he even doing here, so far from home, on the edge of a lifeless desert, trapped in this godsforsaken fortress built by men long dead? And why had the gods made him this way? Dropped him in the middle of such things?

The only response was his labored breathing. He hadn't really expected an answer. The gods didn't care about people like him. They never had. They befriended the saints, the pure and the wise. Par was just a boy with a weird soul.

He rocked slowly, back and forth, like a withering leaf before winter. Maybe the stories of the saints were just that—stories. Or everyone forgot the ones about the victims. About the people who tried and failed.

And died.

Par froze. It was a black thought. Yet here he was, deep in the Citadel vault—a tomb within a tomb.

He remained still, his breathing slow in the crypt-like silence. As he contemplated this chamber, as barren as his soul, an even more cheerless thought, like a lily over a fresh grave, bloomed in his mind.

Cronus had only kept Enio to bargain for Par. Vex had to risk his life to protect Par, to keep Cronus from acquiring the secrets of the Immortus.

Wouldn't it solve everyone's problems if…

He swallowed.

If Par died right there.

Gods, what a thing to realize. His very bones seemed to ice over. Still, it made sense. If this vault were indeed his tomb, there'd be no reason for Cronus to keep Enio. Vex wouldn't need to confront Cronus at the Immortus.

Vex's words echoed in his head. *Never be afraid of the truth.*

Was *this* the truth he'd meant? Had Vex become too fond of Par to kill him himself, so he'd sent him into the vault, to let the Citadel do it?

Par shuddered. So what now? Sit here and wait to starve? A leap into the well might be less agonizing. He looked to the doorway, at the skarix. Or step out there, give them one good meal?

He gazed up at the gentle light that illuminated the vault. A carven star spread across the domed roof. Pale blue orbs—like stars themselves—traced its sides.

It was lovely, peaceful—perfect for a tomb. He just didn't want it to be his. And did he really have the buttons to lay down his life, even for such a noble cause?

Perhaps it was cowardice speaking, but the more he considered, the more he wondered if his death fixed anything in the long run. It wouldn't guarantee that Cronus released Enio. The man might keep him, use him to bargain with Vex for some new thing. Cronus would still be out there—the High Sigil Master of Eloria, the murderer of the Vigil—torturing others, like Buckets, to unravel the mysteries of the Immortus.

Besides, while Par simply refused to believe Vex had sent him to such a fate, he had one more reason to live, the most important.

There was no way in the purple hells he'd just sit here while his friends needed his help.

The cold fear that chilled his heart thawed like frost in the sun. He rose and walked the chamber again, hunting for any speck or clue he might have missed. In the end, his only plan was to wait out the skarix. When they tired and returned to their hive, he'd rush out the door and through the halls to the nearest Threshold. He'd just have to be faster than the bugs.

He settled onto the low wall surrounding the well.

Clink.

A sudden rush of air threw up the back of his shirt. He winced at a blast of light, leapt from the rim and covered his head.

The commotion ended. He lowered his arm.

And gasped with wonder.

The shelves overflowed with jewels—rubies and emeralds and diamonds, trays of them, bags and chests. Never had he imagined such wealth. Not even in the High Fondiscate's palace.

As his eyes drank in the glittering treasures, he noticed that the well now glowed with an inner light. Where darkness had before hidden its depths, other levels, similar to the one in which he stood, layered downward, one after the other. No stairs or ladders connected them. On many he saw more boxes and chests. On others, scrolls and books—and they kept going.

Had the treasures come from the well? Had he somehow summoned them up?

Before he took the time to figure that out, he needed to search for a Blink stone, in case the treasures disappeared as mysteriously as they'd arrived. He dug through the chests and bags, one by one. Though he spent a good deal of time rummaging around, he found no rotten eggs.

Par returned to the well, walked around it, surveyed the many levels. Where he'd sat on the low wall, he'd smeared the dust. There was a faint image etched underneath—a small circle filled with triangles. This wasn't a sigil, he knew that much. Sigils had no sharp angles.

He pressed his hand on the spot.

Nothing happened.

Par found further designs. Dozens decorated the rim, each more or less geometric. Touching them had no effect.

He stepped back. Had he done something different last time?

Well, he hadn't pressed on the stone.

He'd sat on it.

Par inspected his dusty posterior. While he might have an unusual soul, he was certain there was nothing magic about *that* part. He shrugged and plunked this time on a square etched with spirals.

Clink.

A flash of light, a blast of air, and the shelves filled with glowing crystal orbs of every size and color.

But how—?

It struck him. He checked his pocket and found the Luminary's ring. That must have touched the wall through his pants and swapped out the levels.

The orbs now filling the stone shelves each rested in a silver cup. He approached a row of blue ones, the same as those that lit the Citadel halls and the star in the ceiling. He brushed one with his finger. The orb brightened a moment. The sides felt cool and smooth. Par poked an orange one. It flashed.

"Ouch!" He snapped back his hand. That one had been so hot it burned.

He scanned the array of globes, wondering what the other

colors did. As he sucked his stinging finger, he decided not to bother any more of them. None resembled a Blink stone.

He returned to the well, to the next design—an oval full of smaller circles. He touched it with the ring.

New items replaced the globes. Small bags, more chests, bottles. Some had strange writing. Others had labels he understood. Oils, herbs, sparkling powders. Par sighed, his patience wearing away, and began again, searching each chest and every bag.

Nothing.

This was taking too long. What else could he do? He stepped again to the well, scratching his head at the symbols. Triangles, squares, circles, rectangles. Then one caught his eye—a circle with eight tiny rectangles around it. The same as the picture Vex had shown him of the Immortus.

Par touched the ring to that.

The shelves filled anew. Nothing shone or sparkled this time. Scrolls and books populated many of them. There were dark jars of sooty powder, and others of yellowing bones. A few somber boxes sat among them. They seemed the best place to start.

At last, fortune made a rare appearance. After poking through two boxes of what seemed like broken black glass, he found one stuffed with cloth. He felt a lump, probed deeper, and caught his breath. Huddled in a bed of velvet was a nest of rotten eggs. Just as Vex had described.

"Yes! Yes!" His heart leapt and his body followed. He laughed with relief, then at his own laughter—it sounded a little crazed. After composing himself and wiping back his sweaty hair, he lifted out one of the stones and stashed it in his pocket.

As Par turned back to the doorway, he sobered. The skarix showed no sign of backing off. His victory meant nothing unless he found a way out. How could he get past those deadly insects?

An idea kindled in his mind. One thing that kept the bugs

away back home was fire—and while invoking a flame sigil was forever beyond his power, he bet he could make a torch.

First, he needed a stick. Par eyed a jar of old bones. No, too grisly. He found an ancient scroll on a single dowel, slid off the parchment and kept the rod.

Using the ring, he brought back the herbs and other bottles. He picked one he remembered from last time—some kind of oil.

Finally, he swapped back to the glowing orbs, locating the one that had scorched his finger. Par removed his shirt and tied it in a wad at the end of the stick. He doused his crude torch with the oil and pushed it onto the orange globe.

Come on... come on.

A thin wisp rose from the cloth, sweet and pungent. The smoke increased. The shirt ignited. He tilted the torch, helping it catch. Flames engulfed it.

He set the Luminary's ring on the last symbol he'd touched, leaving it behind as Vex had requested. The shelves emptied, as bare as when he'd arrived. Then, with his torch close before him, he stepped tentatively through the seal of light.

Sure enough, the fire worked. The skarix retreated like a fog before a breeze. Par crossed the chamber, guarding all directions, keeping the flames between him and the buzzing hordes.

The skarix brooded across the room, disorganized, hesitating.

He backed out of the grand chamber as fast as he dared, careful not to trip in his one boot. The cloud of insects became bolder and drifted forward. A few shot nearer, buzzing toward his face. Par's torch took care of them. The rest kept their distance, but followed him.

As he retreated down the hall, his impatience grew. He ached to turn and run, but was unsure when he'd be near enough the Threshold to outdistance the insects.

Suddenly, as he took the last corner, his attention still on the skarix, he stumbled over two skeletons in a last embrace. The torch flew from his hand.

The wings of the skarix thrummed with fresh energy.

But the Threshold was just ahead. He abandoned the torch and ran.

A glance showed the bugs in angry pursuit. They were still out of range. Par reached the gallery containing the Threshold. With a last triumphant look back, he leapt again onto the docks of Xol Tomot.

✳

The buzzing of the skarix cut off as the Threshold snapped closed. Except for a cricket chanting litanies in the early evening, all was silent, but the gloom could not smother Par's spirits. His chest swelled with the crisp river air—and with pride. This time, he'd returned victorious.

Vex sat at the bottom of the stone stairs near a dim lantern. His head had nodded forward, his wooly hair blanketing his shoulders like snow.

The sight touched Par. How long had Vex waited? Hours, probably. Par was starting to see him as almost family. Like an old uncle.

A playful mischief crept into his mind. He lifted the Blink stone from his pocket and edged up a step. Then he held out the egg-shaped rock and let it drop into the man's lap.

"Erk!" A silver aura snapped around Vex's head and a tiny ball of flame leapt from his hands.

Par fell back in terror. "Wait, it's me!"

The fire arced over the docks and disappeared with a sizzle into the river.

Vex glanced up and shook his head. "Blazes, son. Never wake a wizard."

"Sorry." Par settled next to him, his heart pounding. "But look. I got it."

Vex brightened the lamp and held up the stone. "And the ring?"

"Left it in the vault."

"Good, good." His voice was flat. He groaned as he got to his feet, lifted the lamp and turned up the stairs.

Par hesitated, confused. He'd expected enthusiasm, or relief, or *something*. "There were skarix. Lots of them."

"Skarix." The man said it as if he spoke of the weather.

"Isn't that what you called them?" The night air chilled Par's shirtless shoulders. He rubbed the skin and tried to sound cheery. "And wait until I tell you about the vault."

Vex kept walking. "It's been a difficult day. We could both use a good sleep, especially before tomorrow."

Par's spirits sagged. He wanted to tell all about his trip through the Citadel, and the vault, and the torch he'd fashioned to fight off the skarix, but he guessed the looming confrontation with Cronus had Vex distracted. So he kept quiet as they ascended the steps, the lamp casting shadows through the balustrade like giants crawling along the hillside. They reached the iron doors, and then the high chamber in the tower.

The sorcerer grunted into his chair by the dark fireplace, sounding every one of his many years.

Par left him without a goodnight and crept to his bedchamber. He sank through his worries into an exhausted, dreamless sleep.

CHAPTER FIFTY-THREE

SUNLIGHT SHONE OUTSIDE the window of the small bed-chamber. Par took in a deep, well-rested breath. He rolled over—and started. Vex sat in the room's single wooden chair.

"What—" Par stopped. The man's face was ashen.

Vex flashed a weak smile under heavy eyes. "You lost another shirt. I fashioned you a new one."

A simple brown shirt with a shortened left arm was draped over the end of the bed. Par put it on. "How long were you waiting for me to wake up?"

Vex pushed himself out of his chair. "We need to talk." He left the room.

Something was wrong. Another pair of boots rested by the door. Par slipped them on and followed.

As he sat where they'd made yesterday's plans, Par suddenly had a new worry. "Did I get the wrong stone?"

A thin black book rested on the table. Vex laid a hand on it. "No. And I'm sorry about my subdued reaction last night. Your deeds have greatly increased our odds against Cronus. But we must face the possibility we may still fail."

This wasn't an outcome Par wanted to consider. He sat back in his chair. "What? We've got the Blink stone. And we'll have your knives with the poisoned blades." He was reaching. That part had never sounded promising.

Vex rubbed his palm across the book's dark cover. "When we first met, I said I wouldn't turn you over to Cronus. And the stakes have risen even higher. You can access the Citadel, the knowledge and magic within its vaults. We now know what evil Cronus is capable of, and we must make absolutely certain he does not, through you, gain access to those treasures."

Par squirmed in his seat, uncomfortable where this might be going. "What else can we do?"

Vex lifted the book. Regardless of its worn corners, it had a severe look—hard, tight. "You remember the curse I threw upon your friend, Buckets?"

Par grimaced and nodded.

"I used it in defense, not to cause lasting harm. The curse would have worn off, I—"

"You already told me."

"Par, listen. This is important." Vex opened to a sigil wound so tight it was almost as black as the cover. "That curse has been passed down through my family, as such things are. This book explains the ways to use the spell. I've always cast it as a brief defense, a temporary blemish upon the soul. But it has another mode, one I've never employed."

Par's hopes inched up. Had Vex devised an even more effective attack?

The man continued, "With a deeper strike, the hysteria that overwhelmed Buckets does not manifest right away. However, as the hours pass, the curse grows as a bonfire from a spark. It consumes the victim's mind, condemning him to permanent madness."

Par didn't quite understand. "But you can't use magic at the Immortus, right?"

Vex met his eyes. "I do not mean it for Cronus."

"Then who—"

"You."

For a moment, Par couldn't react. Then a dry laugh escaped his lungs. It died into a smile creeping across his mouth. "Me?"

The man nodded slowly. "If Cronus takes you captive, he will discover you can enter the Citadel. Even if your condition does not aid him with the Immortus, he might use you to plunder the vault. Either way, the lands of both Eloria and Arcana would be lost."

Par's smile evaporated. He stared in disbelief—Vex was serious! "No..." Par shook his head, pushing the word through a constricting throat.

"We must deny him this, Par. We—"

"No!" Par stumbled from his chair. He'd twisted his entire life around the fear that the gods had cursed him, that he was unworthy, useless. It had driven him from his home and country. Now, after everything, Vex wanted to curse him for real?

Vex rose tall before him. "I know this is difficult. But our plans may yet succeed." He added an unconvincing optimism to his voice. "We'll save your friend, we'll defeat Cronus, and I'll remove the curse before—"

"Wait." Par backed away. "I'll go to the vault, find something else. You can make me a new torch—the skarix are still there, but I'll do it. And... did I tell you about the diamonds? Maybe we could buy Enio back, we—"

"I can think of nothing Cronus wants more than you."

"Then think harder! You're a Sigil Master, for Oä's sake!"

Vex slammed a fist on the table. "Don't you suppose I've tried? All night I tried!"

"I don't care!" Par spit back. "How can you even ask this?"

Vex stiffened. "I wear the mantel of the Sorcerer Tomot. I am the last of the Vigil. I have a duty—"

"—to destroy my mind?"

"This is our final line." Vex's voice wavered. "If we fail, if this curse takes your mind, you will be useless to Cronus. But you will have saved Enio, and all the lands."

The statement slammed into Par's brain like a hammer, shattering his arguments. He felt as if he were falling.

"There must be another... I can't..." His world reeled. He'd refused to give up his life in the vault. Was this any better? Overwhelmed, his legs gave out. He slumped to the floor.

A hand dropped on his shoulder. "I'm sorry, son. If there was any other way..."

Par tried to breathe, in and out. As his heart slowed its pounding, he remembered the things Cronus had done. To the Vigil, to Enio and Buckets, and who knew how many others. And Par realized the worst part: Vex was right. They couldn't allow Cronus to get to the vault. If their plans failed, the curse would make sure.

He swallowed, hard and deep. It took everything he had to raise his head and look into the sorcerer's face. "Will it hurt?" It was almost a whisper.

Vex's eyes glistened. "You'll barely feel a thing."

"Do it. Quick."

The man reached out. Par closed his eyes and braced himself as fingers touched his head. A flash shot through his mind, like silent lightning in the night. He winced, but Vex had spoken the truth, it hadn't hurt. Only an echo afterwards—thunder over his grave.

He opened his eyes. Vex knelt before him, his face soft.

Par tried to keep the trembling in his chest out of his voice. "So now I am among the cursed." It wasn't a question. It was a confession to the universe.

The man moved his hands from Par's head to his shoulders. "Not for long."

A few hours, Vex had said. Long enough to face Cronus. Long enough to help his friends.

Or lose himself in madness.

Vex returned to the table. He withdrew two small scabbards from the drawer. "I've treated the blades with the poison. We'll hide one under your shirt, in the back."

Par got to his feet, anxious to get this over before he went to porridge. "Why didn't you just curse me while I slept?"

"I wanted it to be your decision."

It was true—for all the man's powers, he'd waited until Par had agreed. "When do we meet Cronus?"

"Dawn." The sorcerer frowned at his hourglass.

"It's past that!" Par was now aware of every passing second.

"Not at the Immortus," Vex said. "But we leave now."

Chapter Fifty-Four

The simple leather scabbard fit the small of Par's back. Vex fastened the straps and showed how to remove the poisoned dagger safely. They descended to the Threshold. Vex stopped before the portal. He side-eyed Par.

"What?" Par leaned away, worried another shoe was about to drop.

The man spoke calmly. "I'm not overly familiar with your Elorian customs. If you know any appropriate prayers, now is the time."

None came to mind. Par shook his head.

Vex gave a slight smile. "Neither do I."

The Threshold opened. A stark grey landscape of ragged mists spread under charcoal clouds. All was still. Par stepped onto ebony sand. It had an ancient quality, like the remains of rotted stone. He wrinkled his nose at the now familiar smell, that of a tomb long closed.

The old sorcerer stepped beside him. He pointed. "There. The Immortus."

Par caught his breath. In the pre-dawn gloom, on a somber

plain devoid of hill or tree, towered a cluster of shadowy monoliths. A glow from inside the circle flashed like distant lightning.

Before Par formed any words, Vex moaned and staggered.

Par grabbed his arm. "What's wrong?"

"I thought I'd check if spells were still useless here." He took a steadying breath. "We wouldn't want to walk into a trap."

"And?" Par glanced around. Other than the standing stones, the landscape was barren.

Vex let off a low chuckle. "I tried to summon a simple breeze. The chaos of magics nearly knocked me senseless."

They started toward the Immortus, a few hundred paces ahead. The only sounds were their shuffling steps over the grim residue of the Devastation—and Par's own heart, a drum in his ears. There was no turning back. Their plans were in motion.

As was Vex's curse, deep within Par's soul.

He stifled a tremor as his emotions fought for control. Terror. Anger. Hope. In the east, the sun was rising, a pale orb behind colorless clouds. Elorians associated the sun with Oä, the most powerful of their gods. Par hadn't been inclined to pray to any of them earlier. Now, with the Immortus looming before him, he took a breath, and spoke in his head.

The Rule says if you want the gods to hear, draw near. This place seems like a terrible step in that direction—not that any of you ever listened to me before. But I hope you've seen what Cronus has done, and that you'll stop him from hurting anyone else. Especially Enio. He may not pray much either, but he only got involved to help me. He doesn't deserve any of this.

It wasn't much of a prayer, but it was the best Par could manage.

The sand under their feet thinned, revealing a smooth, dark surface like black glass. They stopped before the circle of monoliths, several times their height. Thick wooden scaffolding blocked the gaps, except for one.

"This is it, Par. Here we go."

Par gritted his teeth and ordered his legs to march forward. He walked with Vex through the opening.

The circle of eight monoliths reached to the grey sky like decayed teeth. Strange red sigils glowed upon their faces. A large pit glimmered and flashed beneath a shroud of scaffolding. The only access to the far side was through a long wooden cage suspended from pulleys and stretching across the center of the pit like a covered bridge.

Par wasn't close enough to see down inside, but it must contain the Immortus—the blazing energies from the Higher Realms. A sudden dread gripped his bones. This was where Cronus had experimented on Buckets, removed his curse, and burned his body and mind in the process.

Past the pit, beyond the cage, stood Enio.

"Enio!" Par lurched forward. Vex stopped him.

"Hi, Par!" Enio called back.

His friend was smiling. His clothes were bright, his face clean. Even his hair was combed. The plank from the *Sea Dog* hung around his neck.

Cronus stood behind Enio, Prior Dogam on the right, like in a family portrait. Ropes dropped from the scaffolds and wrapped a wheel next to the Prior. A lever rose from its side.

The three were before one of the monoliths. The Blink stone could make quick work of Cronus—but it would also incinerate Enio and the Prior.

Vex spoke first. "We've come to bargain, Cronus, not surrender."

Cronus laid a hand on Enio's shoulder. "It's good to see you too, Alexander—and you, Parynius."

Par winced as his stump began to throb, pounding as if the blood were struggling to escape. A slim wooden box tied with rope rested on the ground before the Prior. Par guessed what was inside.

Vex spoke again. "Give up this madness. The Immortus is beyond any of our powers to control."

"You underestimate the Vigil, my dear sorcerer. They've had millennia to probe its secrets, to understand the spells by which Ridiax created the rift. I am on the verge of completing their research. And now, our most worthy friend Parynius can help."

An awkward pride flickered in Par's chest. Nobody had ever called him *worthy* before.

"And why in blazes would I allow Par to help you, Cronus?"

"Is it your decision, Vex? Don't you think we should leave that up to him?"

Vex squeezed Par's shoulder. He lowered his voice. "Ask him what you want, son. Your choices will rule this day."

Cronus continued, "Par, you must feel caught in the middle of something you have no power to deal with. Of things you don't understand, or even care to."

Par grimaced. That was the understatement of the ages.

"And I expect Alexander has distorted my intentions. However, he is a tortured man. He's lost much in his many years, at last retreating from the world to live as a hermit. Such a path dries a soul and twists a mind. But we should not call men like him evil. Rather, let us pity them."

Par recalled Vex speaking of his lost fiancée, and of his broken friendship with the Abbot. How long had the man lived alone? So much sadness. Par kept listening.

"But let us focus on the present. I am the last of the Vigil, not the wretched man beside you. My goal is as it has always been—to tame the Immortus, to protect the lands. I'm sure Alexander's explanation of its dangers was sufficient for you to understand why. And I believe you can help."

Par took a deep breath. "I want to talk to Enio."

"Of course, Parynius. We can always trust our true friends. Enius, go closer."

Enio strode forward, up against the cage door on the far side of the pit.

Par moved to his own door and froze in terror at the sight beneath. A raging whirlpool of white fire spat and churned and seethed, as if the very stars had been torn from the sky and ripped to shreds. A distant roar rose from its depths, yet no heat. But he knew what the Immortus could do. What it had done to Buckets.

"Hi Par," Enio repeated from across the pit.

Par tore his gaze from the awful spectacle. Doors of latticed wood sealed each end of the tall cage, as at the ends of a short corridor. He tried to enter, to go to his friend, but the door was built to swing outwards, and the bottom of the cage hung slightly below the rim of the pit, blocking it from opening. A thin table inside sported leather straps.

He grabbed the wooden bars and pushed his face through. "Enio, are you all right?"

Enio's mouth stretched into its wide, broken smile. "Never better. Master Cronus and the Prior, they've explained everything. They only want to help."

Par eyed his friend's cheerful face, remembering how twisted it had been at the Argent Outpost. "You said they'd been inside your head. Showed you your mother."

"They…" Enio paused.

"A lovely memory," Cronus said from behind him. "Thank you again for sharing her with us."

"Oh, yeah," Enio nodded. "We shared."

Par frowned uncertainly. "What about Lani? You haven't told me—"

"She found it!" Enio's face beamed. "The heart of the élan."

Par's jaw fell. For a moment he couldn't speak. "What? Where?"

"In the sea. So you don't have to worry about her anymore."

This should be wonderful news. Somehow, it made Par's stomach heavy.

"Listen, Par. Why don't you come with us?"

Par looked past his friend. "And the Prior? He locked us up."

Prior Dogam and Cronus remained still, both watching Enio.

"Oh, that?" Enio chuckled. "He's apologized. And look." Enio held up the plank of the *Sea Dog*. "They found it on the Greening. They'll help rebuild it when we get home."

Home. Par sighed. Such a beautiful word.

"And there's something else." Enio turned to the Prior.

Prior Dogam removed the ropes from the slim wooden box. He lifted out a tall glass jar. Par's arm floated inside.

Par grabbed his stump. The pain had eased. He swore he even felt the fingers.

Suddenly, they moved. In the jar.

He moved them!

Par clenched and unclenched the hand, twisted the wrist, savoring every gesture. Each time it took more effort.

"Yes, Par," Cronus said. "I have preserved that which Vex caused you to lose. What you are experiencing is not magic, but your natural connection. Sadly, even now it fades. If I don't rejoin the arm soon, you will lose it forever."

"Cronus," Vex called, shifting to the side. Par guessed he sought to draw the man to a better angle for the Blink stone, or a poisoned knife. "We know what happened to the Vigil."

Cronus stiffened, but said nothing.

"You murdered them all. We have proof."

Prior Dogam's head snapped toward Cronus.

The High Sigil Master recovered his composure. "Indeed? And how did I accomplish this?"

"What matters is that you did it."

Par realized they had never determined how. Was the message in the ring enough to convict the man of such an atrocity?

Enio still stood before the cage, a stupid grin on his face.

"Cronus," Par called. "Will you let Enio go?"

"Of course, Parynius. But I do not believe Alexander is here without treachery. If I free Enio now, before you join me, can you say that Vex would honor your decision?"

Par hesitated. Once Enio was safe, Vex might use the Blink stone to incinerate the man. Doubts nagged his mind—a mind that faced destruction by Vex's curse. Was he still thinking straight? Had Vex been wrong about Cronus? Was there a way through this, where no one got hurt, where Par could avoid madness?

"Enio," Par focused on his friend. "This is the most important thing I've ever asked. Are you telling me the truth? Is it safe?"

Enio's smile never wavered. He inched his arm high above his head.

It was the Chogan wave. A still wave meant safe. That was the sign Par needed. He gave a relieved sigh and raised his own arm. In the shadow of all his fear and doubt, he would trust Enio.

Par kept his arm up a moment longer and lowered it.

But Enio didn't.

No one made a sound. Par stared at his friend, confusion growing in his heart.

Cronus broke the silence. "Very good, Enius. That's enough."

Enio remained unmoving, a statue with a sculpted face.

"Prior," mumbled Cronus.

Prior Dogam stepped forward.

And Par gasped as he noticed something else. Enio's hand was squeezed closed. A dark trickle ran down his wrist.

"Enio, you're bleeding!"

A tremor shook Enio's body.

Cronus pushed the Prior aside and grabbed Enio's arm. A glimmer dropped from the hand and clinked to the ground.

Par recognized it at once—the Lustering medal he'd given Enio to hold. His friend had held it so tightly it had sliced into his palm.

"Par," Enio wheezed, seeming to fight the words. "He's lying. Don't—"

Cronus spun him around. "Idiot boy."

Something seemed to shatter within Enio. Words exploded from his mouth. "Bastard! You ba—"

Cronus's fist hammered into Enio's face and sent him crashing to the ground.

"Enio!" Par cried.

Cronus stepped toward the motionless body.

"No!" Par shouted, fearing the man might shove his friend into the fires.

The Prior lunged before Cronus. "High Master, wait. We've failed with Enius, but he's no threat to you."

In an instant, Vex was beside Par. The man held forth the Blink stone. Enio had fallen away from the monolith, but Cronus still stood before it.

As did the Prior.

"No!" Par knocked Vex's arm just as the Blink stone flashed.

The Immortus roared like a furious beast. But Par had fouled Vex's aim, and the sigils on a different monolith blinked dark. White fires leapt from the pit, clawing at a section of the scaffolding. In the next instant, the sigils on that towering stone resumed their glow. The fires dispersed, like waves against a cliff. Sections of framing where the Immortus had passed were gone. They hadn't even caught fire. They simply sloughed away, raining ash.

Other parts of the scaffolding groaned and sagged. A beam fell, but the cage above the pit remained intact, hanging stable from its ropes.

Vex's eyes fell on Par with a fire of their own.

"I couldn't—" Par began.

The man's face cooled. "It's all right, son. I should have known you'd made up your mind about the Prior."

Par hadn't, until that very moment. Prior Dogam had been the assistant to the Abbot. He'd guided them in their Lustering training and schooling. Regardless of his strict ways, Par could never accept the Prior was evil, or a murderer—like Cronus.

The High Sigil Master now stood near Enio's body. "Why, Vex, you've acquired a Blink stone. How interesting. Any other surprises?"

"Why, Cronus," Vex called, "if I told you, it wouldn't be a surprise."

"Quite right!" Cronus laughed. He was covering something in his hand.

Suddenly, Vex cried out.

Par spun. Had Vex tried to cast another spell?

Vex fell to his knees and grabbed his neck, then slumped to the ground.

"Vex!" Par dropped beside him.

Cronus held an opened vial. "Did you know, Alexander, that with the proper combination of a navigaunt and Location sigil, it is not only messenger birds that can be compelled to seek out a person? For example, even the smallest of creatures—such as the skarix I prepared for you before we arrived."

Par jolted. The smaller the deadlier! He bent to Vex. The man's chest heaved. Thin red lines spidered from a spot on his neck. His eyes rolled in his head.

Par reeled to Cronus. "Help him!"

Cronus remained close to Enio's crumpled body. "I must admit, I am saddened at this outcome." He let out a deep, patient sigh. "Now, we must do things the hard way."

CHAPTER FIFTY-FIVE

PAR'S THOUGHTS RACED—THEIR plans had fallen apart. Vex lay dying beside him. Enio lay unconscious on the other side of the pit.

"Help Vex!" Par repeated. "Or I'll—" What *could* he do? He grabbed the Blink stone. "I'll use this."

Cronus lifted Enio's limp body and held it out like a doll. "Is killing me worth your friend's life?"

Par was fast running out of options, but he still had the poisoned dagger. He lowered the stone.

"Wise decision, son. Now, come through the cage. Dogam, if you please?"

The Prior, his face white, stepped to the wheel. He pushed the lever a notch and spun the ropes. With a heavy groan, the cage rose enough to clear the doors from the sides of the pit.

Par pointed. "Put Enio down first."

"Of course." Cronus held the body to the Prior. "Bind this."

Prior Dogam eased Enio to the ground, dabbing blood from the boy's face with his robe.

Cronus turned back to the cage. "My patience wears thin, Parynius."

Par entered his door. It swayed closed behind him.

Cronus waited beyond the far side. "I cannot stress enough my disappointment. I have spent considerable time explaining to Dogam and Enius the wisdom of my designs. All for your sake, Par."

The floor of the cage was tightly latticed, but the raging fires still showed beneath. Par looked away from the terrible sight. "Why me?"

"Did Alexander not explain?"

Par glanced back at the prone, moaning Vex.

"No matter." Cronus said. "Candidates for a Reckoning always interest me, since it is possible their condition is caused by a curse. I have used such persons to study the Immortus, but when my Location sigil failed to find you, I realized your curse's unusual potency. It may allow you closer exposure to the energies of the Immortus than any of my previous subjects."

Par inched through the cage toward Cronus. The Immortus flashed below, pricking like ants in his boots. "Then why all the lies to Enio? Why not just trade him for me?"

"I had hoped he would persuade you to my cause, and I needed his entreaties to be sincere. Yes, I might have simply Reckoned either of you to cooperate. But I preferred your mind to be pure, accepting, with no obstacles to my study. Alas, that opportunity is lost. I will have to make do with what I have. Waste not, want not." The man held up a hand. "That's far enough."

Par halted beside the table. It resembled a thin altar. Worn leather straps wove up through the wood.

Cronus knelt over Enio, checking the ropes the Prior had tied. "Dogam, please retrieve the Blink stone from our new friend. We don't want any more accidents."

"Yes, Master Cronus."

"Oh, and Dogam?"

"Yes?"

"Search him."

Par tensed. *The knife!*

The Prior entered the far side of the cage. He stopped before Par and held out his hand. "The Blink stone, Par."

Then he lowered his voice and spoke quickly. "Was Vex telling the truth? Did Cronus murder the Vigil?"

As Par handed over the stone, hope flashed in his heart. Maybe the Prior would help. "Yes," he whispered back. "And Cronus wants to use the Immortus to bring war and rule all the lands. We have to stop him."

Prior Dogam searched Par. "I've been a fool—my ambitions got the best of me. But there's nothing we can do. Cronus is too powerful." The Prior paused when he came to the hidden scabbard.

Par kept his voice low. "Not here, he isn't. It's a knife. It's poisoned."

The Prior met his eyes, then eased out the knife and tucked it into his own robes.

Cronus spoke from near Enio's body. "Is this some duplicity, Dogam?"

Par's gaze shot to the man. A rope now also leashed Enio's neck to a scaffold, as if he were a dog.

Cronus went on. "But perhaps your skill with ropes is as poor as it was with your persuasion. Nevermind. I've secured his bonds. Now, bring Parynius to me."

Par followed the Prior out of the cage and faced Cronus across Enio's tied and crumpled body. His friend was unmoving, but breathing. "All right," Par said. "I'm here. Help Vex."

The Prior dropped the Blink stone in Cronus's hand but held his position next to Par.

"Thank you, Dogam. Now Parynius, given that no matter what I say you will not willingly cooperate, why in the lofty realms should I bother with Alexander?" He examined the stone. "Except perhaps to end his suffering."

"No!" Par had one more card of his own to play. It betrayed Vex's plans, but it might also save the man's life. "Vex used Buckets' curse on me. If he doesn't remove it, I'll fall into madness. You lose him, you lose *me*."

Cronus's eyes widened. He looked across the pit toward Vex. "Why, I'd never imagined Alexander had the stomach for such a desperate act."

Par could only hope the Prior didn't use the knife until after Cronus healed Vex. Then he realized something. He peered darkly at the High Sigil Master. "That's how you did it."

"I'm sorry?"

"That's how you killed the Vigil. You loosed skarix into the Citadel." Par felt the Prior stiffen beside him.

"You are a clever boy! It wasn't as sophisticated as preparing a single one as I did with Vex. A cloud of the smallest, nearly invisible, which I insured were well aroused. Released through a Threshold and—" He paused. "But the Citadel sealed after that. How did Vex get his hands on a Blink stone?"

Par stopped breathing.

Cronus's face stretched into a horrible grin. "The same anomaly that allows you to avoid my Location sigil allows you to pass the seals. And"—his smile worsened—"to enter its vault."

"Yes!" Par exploded in anguish. Now, everything was up to the Prior. "Just help Vex!"

"Well, it seems you are more valuable than I imagined." Cronus stroked his chin. "Since Alexander set that curse upon you, it's true that only he can undo it safely. But remember, I successfully removed it from your friend, Buckets—with some unfortunate side effects."

"High Master." The Prior pressed Par back, stepping between him and Cronus. "You must not do that to Par."

"Remember whom you serve, Dogam. Secure him to the table."

The Prior turned to face Par. Again they locked eyes as he slid the knife from his robe. "I will no longer obey you, Cronus."

Prior Dogam spun, the knife out.

Cronus held up the Blink stone. "Drop it, Dogam, or I'll incinerate both you and your young charge."

The stone began to glow. The Immortus crackled behind Par. He and the Prior were near a monolith. Cronus was not.

Prior Dogam did not budge. "You would not kill Par."

"It would sadden me to no end, but I've managed without him until now. And you threaten me with a knife. If it is a question of my life or his, which do you suppose I'll choose?"

The Prior's hand wavered and dropped. The knife clanged to the ground before him.

Par's hopes crashed. That had been their final weapon.

Cronus kept the Blink stone out. "You disappoint me, Dogam. I had great things planned for you, for your career."

"Damn my career," spat the Prior.

"Indeed. Don't make me ask again. Please see to Parynius."

Prior Dogam turned, his face somber. "Par, I—"

There was a flurry of robes behind the Prior. With a sudden gasp, his chest arched out and his head snapped back. Par jerked away. The Prior dropped to his knees and toppled forward.

Cronus stood behind him—above the knife in the Prior's back.

Despair and pity tore at Par's heart. He reached for the Prior. "No…"

"Par," wheezed the Prior, "I'm sorry." Then he screamed. His body gave a great spasm. He rolled to his side and flailed, toppling and smashing the jar containing Par's arm.

Sharp pain shot through Par's side. The arm lay still on the ground. Yellow fluid ran into the pit and steamed away.

Prior Dogam moved no more. Cronus stood over him. "Upon

further reflection, Dogam, your usefulness ended with Enio's failure." He shoved the Prior's body into the Immortus.

Par watched, horrified, as it slid over the edge. The fires tore at it, ripped it apart, dissolved the flesh and bone in a black, acrid cloud.

He turned to Cronus, tears in his eyes, ready to fight.

Cronus had stepped closer. He held the Blink stone in his fist. Before Par made another move, Cronus slammed it into Par's head.

The world flashed off and on. Darkness. Movement. The smell of sweat and old incense. Something pinched Par's ankles and wrists. His head throbbed.

When his sight steadied, he lay flat on the table in the cage. He strained upwards, but leather straps held him fast. A warm trickle ran across his temple.

"Par!" Enio shouted.

Par turned his head. Enio struggled against his ropes.

"I'll deal with him later." Cronus tightened the strap across Par's neck. "But we can't lose you to that curse. I believe I can undo it. Even if I have to burn it out."

After an agonized cry of frustration and another heave of his body, Par's strength left him. He slumped down against the hard wood. The Immortus growled below. They had lost. At best, Cronus would Reckon him to slavery, force him to raid the Citadel. At worst—he didn't want to think about the fires beneath.

Par stared up, through the scaffolding, at the pale, uncaring sky. The clouds hung like shrouds. No rain fell, no weeping from the gods.

Cronus tightened another strap. "You know, it's a shame you failed your Lustering. I do hate dealing with the uninitiated."

Par squeezed his eyes shut, but had no tears left. Whether the curse took him, or the Immortus burned away his mind, it would be over soon. He thought of his home, his family. Of Lani. His times with Enio on the river. Their cheats at the abbey to hide that he couldn't invoke.

And how hard he had practiced that flame sigil! A simple spiral with an upward reach. There it was, in his mind. He drew it near.

Then, for the first time in his entire life, the sigil flared like the sun.

Like the Immortus!

His eyes snapped open. Par had never experienced such power. Vex said magic was too chaotic here to use, too overwhelming. But Par had a strange thickness to his soul. That must be filtering the energies, taming them.

He summoned the sigil again, as he had at the altar in the abbey a lifetime ago. When the sigil was ablaze in his head, he focused past Cronus onto an ankle strap. A tiny spot smoldered and went out.

Par grimaced—barely enough to light a candle.

"Par!" Enio yelled. "Hold on, I'm coming!" He ripped at the ropes with his teeth. Blood splattered his mouth.

"Cronus," Par begged. "No matter what you do to me, please, let Enio go."

"He is no longer your concern, boy. Or at least, he won't be for long." Cronus moved down the table.

Par took a breath. He didn't have much time. He directed his gaze higher, to the pulleys and ropes. Fat, dry rope. A terrifying idea came to his head. Could he burn them through, drop Cronus into the fires of the Immortus?

But Par would have to go with him.

Buckets' melted face rose in his mind. The odor of the Prior's incinerated body still lingered. Par's every weakness returned at once. His lost arm and exhausted muscles. His worthlessness before his family and the gods.

He shook them off, again summoning the sigil. This time, he

projected it overhead, to the rope that branched from a pulley to the corners of the cage.

Like the leather strap, barely a wisp. He was too weak. He had failed everyone again.

"Enio." Par strained to look over. His voice trembled. "I'm sorry I got you into all this. I hope to the gods that one day you'll sail the Silver Sea."

"No, Par…" Enio stared with wide, glistening eyes.

Suddenly, Par remembered something. "You know, you still haven't said it."

"Said what?"

"You still haven't called me your friend. Even at Banes you skipped around it."

"Are you kidding? This isn't the time!"

Par squeezed his eyes closed. He was wrong. He did have tears left. "I need to hear it. Please."

When he looked again, Enio had gone back to chewing his ropes.

Par almost laughed. At Banes, Enio had said you shouldn't get attached to things. That you just set yourself up for misery when someone took them away. Of course, Enio would never call him his friend. Par accepted that. But it made these last moments that much harder.

With tears blurring his eyes, Par took a trembling breath and called to Enio, "Sweet sailin's and fair landins', brother of Par!"

And when he'd resolved he had heard Enio's voice for the final time, Enio thundered out, loud and urgent, "Don't be thick, Par! I'm not your brother!"

Par gasped and locked eyes with him.

Enio gave his wide, broken smile, his face wet with more than blood. "I'm your friend."

At last.

The words sank into his ears. As they did, Par felt something move deep within his heart, and an unexpected, joyful warmth bloomed in his chest. For years, he'd struggled to feel worthy, valued, by the gods, by his teachers. Even by his family. Now he knew, he had been valued all along.

By a friend.

Par swallowed fresh tears. Bright tears. The warmth inside him grew. And a fresh determination filled him. He wasn't done. Not yet.

As Cronus adjusted the tilt of the table, Par searched the area, the monoliths, the scaffolding. And got an idea. If he had the strength—or the courage—to pull it off, he might only get one chance. He focused on his dying arm near the shattered glass and gritted his teeth, willing it to move.

The wrist spasmed.

He flexed the fingers, in and out, dragging the arm across the ground. He barely felt any sensation from it now.

"Cronus!" He gasped, hoping the man didn't notice what he was doing. "I'll be no good to you if you make me like Buckets."

Cronus finished his adjustments. "I will try to be more careful this time. But our cause is what matters. I am sure you can see that."

The arm drew near the wheel and lever. There were many notches. He only needed to manage one. With a quick breath and a shout, he convulsed the muscles. The arm jerked, twisted, and hit the lever.

The cage bumped downward, just a few inches, stopping as the lever snapped into the next notch. Par's arm fell away, numb.

Cronus staggered and grabbed the cage. "What—"

Par tried to move the arm again, but he could no longer feel it. The arm was dead.

Cronus shook the door. The bottom of the cage had dropped to its position below the pit's edge, blocking the door from opening.

He turned toward Par. "Very clever, boy. But where have your actions gotten you?"

Par snarled at the man. "What's important is where they've gotten *you*."

Before he lost his nerve, he brought to mind the flame sigil. The new warmth in his heart seemed to join with the invocation in his head, and the sigil exploded even brighter than the sun. A point of intense white fire flared into the rope above. It burst into flames.

"Par?" Enio said, his tone full of wonder. "Did you do that?"

"Yes!" Par laughed, almost crazily.

Cronus turned upwards. "Impossible!"

Par filled his lungs and shouted, "Am I Lustered *now*, Cronus?"

The man's face lost all composure. He raised his arms toward the burning rope as though attempting an invocation, but in an instant he grabbed his head and screamed. He fell to his knees.

Par locked his eyes on the threads as they burned, trying not to think of anything else. "See, Enio? See how far I lit it? More than your fire-fly!"

"Almost!" his friend yelled.

Par grinned a little, but his smile vanished when one of the rope's threads snapped. The cage jolted.

Cronus stumbled to Par's side. "If you did this, you can stop it. Put the flame out, boy! Put it out!"

Par shot a glance at the man. "The purple hells take you, you bastard."

Another thread snapped. The cage rocked again.

"No!" Cronus screamed. He leapt to the door, hammering at the bars.

"Listen, Enio!" Par stared at his friend, blocking out everything else. "Use Vex's Threshold key to open the space between a monolith. Get him help."

"Par, I can't lose you! You're my friend and I can't lose you!"

Par sighed gently and closed his eyes. If that was the last thing he ever heard, it was enough.

And he was so tired.

The final thread snapped. Par's stomach lurched as the cage crashed downward. He gritted his teeth, hoping that what happened next happened quick.

PART FOUR

BEYOND THE IMMORTUS

CHAPTER FIFTY-SIX

SEARING WHITE LIGHT burst behind Par's eyelids and ripped through his brain. The fires of the Immortus seized him. But it *was* over quick. Even as the Immortus consumed his flesh and bones and swallowed him in blackness.

A moment of screaming agony ended. The raging fires cooled and faded in the dark. All became silent and still.

He hung suspended in deepest night. The void felt similar to when Vex had examined his soul—a nothingness beyond life. This time, Par had no fear. His battle was over. Would the gods receive him? Or would his last thought dissolve into oblivion?

Then, far away, a shimmering, as the sun seen from beneath the waves. Par drifted toward it. His movement sped up. Faster and faster he flew.

At last he crashed through, into brilliant light and flashing color. He tried to focus, to make sense of what he saw. As the light coalesced, Par gaped in awe.

He floated among the stars.

Their countless hosts filled a velvet sky. Fantastic silver glories shone around each. Their rays spiraled out, twisting like sigils, unfurling into prismatic winds that reached into the night. Higher up, clusters of golden suns dazzled among the stars, some winking and pulsing in strange rhythms. At the very zenith of all blazed a single glorious orb, a more beautiful light Par had never seen. It must be the Immortus, the source of creation Vex had described. But all this splendor did not blind him—something resembling a bright cloud floated above Par, protecting him from the mighty lights and the ethereal winds.

He longed to go toward those stars, those suns, yet he had no arms to reach, no way to move. And something cold, like a dull pain, weighed him down. He turned his attention to where he used to have feet.

A bodiless vapor, oozing and rotten, clawed at him. The repulsive thing emitted waves of sinister thought. *No! The lands must have my Paradise! My Rule! A boy will not deny me this!*

It was Cronus.

Par had no legs to kick. No hands to fight. But the warmth that still echoed within him flashed with its own divine light. *The hells take you, Cronus!*

The brief blaze pushed Cronus away, plunging him toward a domain of great gloom. Dim storms of crimson and purple roiled there like glowing ulcers or burning wounds. He screamed and cursed as he fell toward that festering place of twilight and shadow.

Par stared in horror. It was the very realm of the purple hells. And while he could not be sure, before Cronus disappeared something seemed to flash up from those realms and snatch the man.

Peace slowly returned to Par's heart. Cronus was gone. Enio would free himself and help Vex.

Then a thought boomed from above. *Well done!*

Par started and turned to the sheltering haze between him and the remarkable lights. *Is that... a god?*

Far from it. My people called me Ridiax.

Ridiax? That name sounds familiar. Par was getting confused. *Am I thinking or are you speaking or—*

Wait. I'll make this easier.

The cloud breathed forth a ghostly shape. It solidified into a thunderous old man with the bushy red hair of a lion and wrapped in robes of royal blue. A pure white glory encircled his head.

"How's this?" the man said.

"I can see you—and hear myself!" But Par still didn't have a body of his own.

"Welcome to the Higher Realms, Parynius Ignatius."

"You know my name?"

"We speak soul to soul. Little is hidden here."

It hit Par—Higher Realms, soul to soul. "Then, I *am* dead."

"Not quite. Like me, you have disincarnated, surviving the passage intact."

"Intact?" Par examined himself more closely. He was just a glowing egg-shaped fog. Then he remembered where he'd heard the name Ridiax. "The mage who opened the rift?" Par found it again. From this side, it appeared as a churning spectral whirlpool.

"It was not my intent." Waves of regret flowed from the man. "The mages of Gê were far accomplished in their magic, but I sought a greater spell. The magics all peoples use in the material world, they channel through their souls. I wove a spell to lift my soul higher, toward more powerful energies, and to shield me, to prevent my destruction as I rose. But I could not maintain my ascension. I was not as strong as I'd believed."

A sad smile spread across his face. "Or as wise. I made it this far, but my portal, the rift, had not closed. The energies from this realm leaked through, holding it open. Worse, I realized I must not end my spell. If the shield protecting me fell, the full intensity of the Immortus would destroy me before I closed the rift and flood unrestrained into your world. Even the monoliths raised by the mages would not stop that much power."

"But wasn't that over a thousand years ago?" The Vigil histories had said the man was dead. Par couldn't imagine anyone living this long—or doing it alone.

"Indeed, though time passes strangely here. Yet this is my penance, existing between your world and the next, holding my shield in place, preventing another Devastation as had swept the fair lands of Gê."

The enormity of the man's mistake, and his doom, made Par shiver to bones he no longer had. He looked again at the silver stars and the golden lights wheeling overhead. "Are those the gods?"

"Some are, yes."

"Why haven't they helped you?"

"I've often wondered that myself." Ridiax grimaced. "They seem rather standoffish, if you ask me."

"Tell me about it," Par muttered. But he hadn't meant to say that out loud. He cringed and eyed the great lights, hoping they hadn't noticed.

The mage laughed. "Then again, perhaps they *have* helped, by giving me the strength to continue here. And by sending you."

"Me?"

"Yes, Par." Ridiax paused. "Your unexpected arrival has given me an idea."

Par shuddered. The man's voice had adopted that same tone as when Vex was about to propose something terrible. "Why me?"

"You might be able to take my place."

Par's thoughts seized up. He rattled them free. "What?"

Ridiax raised his hands. "Just for a moment. Long enough for your natural shield—that thickness in your soul—to filter the Immortus while I direct my magic to the rift and close it forever."

"My soul." Par understood. "That's how I survived the passage."

"And how your High Sigil Master survived with you." The mage shook his head. "It's surprising a man of such knowledge never realized the truth."

"What truth?" Par asked.

"There are no shortcuts to Paradise."

Par gazed again at the rift. The last mages of Gê had formed the Vigil millennia ago, dedicated to one day sealing it. And Par felt a new resolve as he remembered Buckets and the others Cronus had hurt—or like the Prior, killed, trying to harness its terrible power. Maybe at last Par could do something actually important with his life. Something great. Something—

The man seemed to catch his thought. "Par, when I was in the world, I should have used my powers to make it a better place, to help others. Instead, I focused on myself, on doing great acts of magic. And I learned sometimes doing *good* things is more important than doing great ones."

Par nodded, a little ashamed. "Sorry."

"Don't be. You've done some fine deeds this very day."

Before Par could reflect on that, something occurred to him. "Whatever happens, will we be trapped here?"

"That's a very good question. I have no idea. Interesting, is it not?"

That wasn't the word Par would have chosen. "What if I'm not strong enough? Would it get worse?"

"Things of true importance always come with risk. But I have had ages to study this place and reflect on my failure. If there is a problem, I'll sense it quickly and abort the attempt. But understand, I am not immortal. One day, my spell and I must end. Let us not waste this opportunity."

"However," he continued with a tinge of mischief in his voice, "as your friend Enio might say, if you don't have the buttons for it…"

Par could only smile inside. "Who doesn't have the buttons?"

"Excellent. Your heart is as stout as your soul. Prepare yourself."

Ridiax again disappeared into the luminous cloud eclipsing the Immortus.

Then Par remembered. Vex's curse! Was it still scratched upon in his soul? Would it affect Ridiax's plan?

But the cloud was upon him.

As Par struggled to call out, to warn Ridiax, a swarm of sigils crashed through him. Then the light of the Immortus slammed into his mind like a conquering tempest.

He rallied and pushed back at the nearly overwhelming blast.

Good, Par. Keep it up!

The light grew more intense. The stars and suns wheeled around him, searing his soul—joy and hate and fury and love. All together and increasing.

Par shouted in despair.

Then, an explosion of blinding radiance. A voice echoed from its heart. *Farewell, Parynius Ignatious. And thank you!*

Ridiax was gone. For a moment, fantastic sigils swam and sparkled before Par's eyes. Then the chaos faded. He lay on cold, bare stone.

Hands grabbed him. "Par?"

Enio's bloodied face replaced the storm of sigils.

Before Par could respond, his mind fell again into darkness. This time, it held only peace.

CHAPTER FIFTY-SEVEN

WHEN PAR AWOKE, a burnt and disfigured face loomed over him. One bright blue eye shone beside a dead one. The mouth twisted into a grin.

Par gasped. Then recognition hit. "Buckets?"

The hulking man gave his familiar joyful grunt. Before Par said another word, arms like tree trunks wrapped him up.

Par hugged too, squirming free before he suffocated. "Buckets, what are you doing here?"

And where was *here*?

A small chamber surrounded Par's long, low bed. Cheerful sunlight glowed through a latticed window. A tapestry of the saints, the odor of beer and roses, and a pile of socks on a small table told him this was not Xol Tomot.

The abbey?

Opposite the window, a door flew open. In burst Enio, and Par's heart swelled.

With a single bound, his friend was beside him. *Crack* went a bed slat. The three became a new mass of hugs and laughter.

At last, they sat back. Enio beamed his broken smile. "*You* hugged Buckets."

The large man now stood at the foot of the bed, still grinning.

Par raised his brows. "Why shouldn't I?"

Enio pointed. "You *hugged* him."

Par shook his head and followed Enio's finger. It aimed at Par's arm.

His left arm.

Par barely believed his eyes. It was back! He lifted both hands to make sure he really had two. The last he'd seen of his missing limb was as it fell dead near the pit.

He stared at Enio. "You saved it?"

His friend frowned. "That disgusting thing? Gods, no. Oh, and your tooth is fixed."

Par ran his tongue along the tip. It was smooth, like before Banes.

Enio dug into a pocket. "But I *did* save this." He held out Par's Lustering medal.

As at Banes, Par reached for it and stopped. When Enio had been locked in that cage at Argent, Par had given him the pendant to hold. It had helped his friend break free of whatever Cronus had done to his mind. "You keep it. It's done you more good than me."

Again as at Banes, Enio shoved it into Par's hand. "They gave me a new one." He lifted it from under his shirt. The medal glittered from a bright gold chain.

Par squinted at the pendant resting in his new hand. "What's happened? I don't understand."

A voice came from the doorway. "Admitting ignorance is always a good beginning." The Father Abbot stepped into the room. A hooded monk followed and shut the door behind him.

The Abbot crossed to the bed. "I'm thrilled to see you awake."

Memories rushed back. Par's eyes widened. "Where's Vex? Did he—"

"I'm fine, thank you." The monk pushed off his cowl. It was the sorcerer.

Another weight dropped from Par's shoulders. "Thank the gods," he breathed.

The Abbot's expression turned serious. "Enio told us of his time with Cronus, as much as he remembers. What has become of Prior Dogam?"

Vex and Enio had been unconscious for that horror. Par met the Abbot's troubled gaze and spoke the words sadly. "Cronus killed him."

A heavy silence fell on the room.

Par went on, "But not before the Prior tried to save us. He smashed the jar and freed my arm." Par liked to think that the man, with his last breath, had done it on purpose.

The Abbot closed his eyes. "The news grieves me to hear. For all his impatient ambitions, Prior Dogam had a good heart."

Vex stepped beside the Abbot. "Enio says you invoked a flame sigil and took Cronus with you into the Immortus. Do you feel up to telling us about that?"

Par did. He explained everything that had happened, and what he'd seen in the Higher Realms, as best he could. Enio made him repeat the part where Cronus fell into the purple hells.

As Par described the closing of the rift and the storm of sigils, Vex and the Father Abbot seemed to exchange a secretive glance. Par paused, but they said nothing. "Then I saw Enio. I don't know what happened next."

Enio hopped from the bed. He swung his arms and acted out as he talked. "After the cage fell, I chewed through the ropes to get to Tomot."

The sorcerer held up a hand. "While I am in your country, please refer to me as Vex."

Enio ignored him. "But then the Immortus exploded like lightning hitting a river melon, and *bam*, it was gone. Just a shallow sort of bowl in the rock where it had been. You were out cold at the bottom. I dragged you over to Tomot—"

"Vex," repeated the sorcerer with more emphasis.

"—but he was hardly any help at all."

"Cronus had attacked me with a skarix." Vex added. "It's a deadly—"

Enio waved him quiet. "*I'm* telling this."

The man grimaced.

Enio turned back to Par. "Anyway, I found the keystone like you said—I'd seen Cronus use one before. I thought of the abbey and whoosh! So, here we are."

Buckets laughed and clapped. Enio bowed.

The Father Abbot spoke. "Enio opened the Threshold into John and Tommy's room. Thankfully, they were out with their morning duties. I quake at the thought of Tommy being woken by the Sorcerer Tomot."

Par glanced from Buckets to Vex. "It's all right you're together now?" Vex had cursed Buckets during the Grey Wars. But Buckets' happy face remained untroubled.

"In fact," Vex said, "we'd never seen each other up close. And it was Cronus who tortured him at the Immortus, not me."

"Speaking of the Immortus…" Par held up his restored arm.

The Abbot slid a chair from the table and sat beside the bed. He reached out and cradled the wrist, examining it. "Alexander and I have a theory."

"Yes," Vex added, "unless Enio wants to explain that, too."

Enio scowled.

The Abbot continued, "Par, when you disincarnated, you lost your entire body. It formed anew when you returned. Some propose that everything in the mortal world devolves from the Higher Realms. Your arm may not have been missing long enough for your soul to adjust, so when you came back, the process recreated it."

Enio sat again next to Par. "Like your tooth."

"What about Vex's curse?" Par assumed it had not activated, and he had not gone mad.

Vex took up the explanation. "Once Cornelius healed me of the skarix venom, I examined you carefully, but found no trace."

"Passing between the realms healed it, like my arm?"

"That knowledge is beyond me," Vex replied. "Perhaps it disappeared with your exposure to the Immortus itself."

"Or," the Abbot released Par's wrist, "it was healed as a last gift from the mage Ridiax."

Par started. "The thickness to my soul—is it fixed too?" He focused on a candle on the small table.

Nothing happened.

Vex shook his head. "No Par, you are as you've always been."

"Oh." He sighed and lowered his gaze to hide a fresh disappointment.

The Father Abbot laid a gnarled hand on Par's shoulder. "Don't dwell on what you were born with—the gifts you were given or the things you've lost. What matters is what you do with what you've got. The choices you make."

Par took a deep breath and nodded. He'd always felt that way about Enio. It was time he believed it about himself.

He nudged Enio with an elbow. "And the friends."

Enio nudged him back.

Par looked again at the wise old Abbot. "So what happens now?"

"Vex has filled me in on your time together. First, it's best you don't speak to anyone of the things you've seen and learned. Of the Vigil, the Outposts, and Cronus."

"Why not?"

"We can't risk Eloria or Arcana discovering the magics in those Outposts, or—Oä forbid—the Citadel, and using them against each other."

Par nodded. That made sense.

"Also," added the Abbot, "the Hierarchy needs to maintain confidence during these unstable times. Cronus, our High Sigil Master, has just disappeared. I must decide how, or if, to communicate to the Hierarchy what has happened."

Enio huffed. "The sooner I forget that guy, the better."

"Very good. And Par, one more thing. If the Hierarchy again discovers your inability to invoke, I fear you would still be a candidate for a Reckoning."

Par's stomach tightened. "And Enio's heresy—"

"That," the Abbot said, "I can fix. A few words in the right ears. A big mistake, and so forth."

Par relaxed a little. That was good news for Enio, but it didn't help him. "Then, besides trying to avoid a Reckoning, what about me? What do I do?"

Vex leaned closer. "I have a proposal. The sigils you saw in the Higher Realms—do you remember any of them?"

Par closed his eyes. Myriads came to mind. "Plenty, why?"

"Par," said the Abbot, "when we bestow sigils, it is, as you might say, a soul-to-soul transaction. When you were in the Higher Realms, you were pure soul. So any sigils you remember were, by definition, bestowed upon you."

Par's eyes snapped open. "I have those sigils inside me?"

"It seems so."

"But what good are they? Ridiax closed the Immortus. That's the only place I've ever invoked. So I can't use them. I can't even bestow them."

"Indeed," Vex said. "Yet the knowledge you have of their forms, their compass and gyres, would be very interesting for me to study. And perhaps with help from the tomes in the Citadel—"

Par tensed. "You want me to go back to the vault?"

Vex raised his hands. "Only if it's safe. But I would like you to return with me to Xol Tomot for another reason. Even though the Vigil's task of closing the Immortus is done, we also kept watch on the lands to prevent a new rift. I must now decide how to proceed with that mission, and I believe it's time I no longer did it alone. And by accompanying me to the Borderlands, you would no longer be in Eloria, and so be safe from a Reckoning."

The more Par considered the idea, the better it sounded. "What about Enio?"

"He is also welcome—if he promises not to shoot any more rocks at me."

Enio snorted.

"In fact," the man continued, "for one raised in Eloria to invoke an Arcanan fire-fly spell, not to mention a nymph enchantment, is quite unusual. He is worth further study, too."

The Father Abbot pushed his chair back and stood. "Well, Alexander, let's leave these two to get reacquainted. Par, we'll discuss more of your journeys, and of your future, later."

The Abbot led Vex and Tommy from the room.

Par turned to his friend. "What do you say, Enio? Ready for another trip?"

Enio shrugged. But then his face lit. "I haven't told you what Cronus did after he took me at Banes." He jumped from the bed and began.

A worry formed in the dark of Par's mind. His friend seemed to be avoiding something. The unease faded as Enio told of his time with Cronus and the Prior.

And especially of Lani.

Chapter Fifty-Eight

Two days later, Par sat in the abbey gardens on the end of a stone bench. The summer sun warmed the back of his neck and brought sweet and musky smells to his nose. Not far away, monks tended a row of nasturtiums.

Enio arrived down a path and sat at the other end of the bench.

Par waited several awkward seconds before speaking. "They here?"

"Yep."

Another silence before Par spoke again. "Changed your mind?"

"Nope."

Par sighed. "Vex is a good guy—once you get used to him. And you've still got time to decide. I don't leave for a couple weeks."

His friend closed his eyes and breathed deep and slow, as if taking in the garden. "I saw the Silver Sea, Par. I heard the waves, felt the wind, smelled the salt in the air. But couldn't touch a drop. I have to go. I owe it to the *Sea Dog*."

"Xol Tomot is only a few days from the sea. We—"

"And I have to know what I saw was real."

Par was arguing uphill. He'd told Enio of his perils along the cliff face, and the strange green light below the waves. He hadn't known then that was where Lani had disappeared. Enio's account of her and the heart of the élan left little doubt the light had somehow come from her.

Now Par felt torn. Vex had taken a Chogan barge to the Borderlands. At month's end, he'd open a Threshold to the abbey and transport Par back to Xol Tomot. Par would begin his new life there, with Vex, out of danger of a Reckoning.

But Par wanted to search for Lani, too.

He tried one more time to get Enio to come with him. "Maybe Vex can help find her."

"Then get him to help. I'm going to the Silver Sea."

Brother Marcus arrived from the temple. "They're waiting."

Par held Enio's eyes a moment, but saw no compromise in their dark glints.

Beyond the garden, a slim door took them inside. Their boots echoed down the empty corridor. Enio kept his voice low. "Figured out what you're going to say?"

"The Abbot told me not to be too specific."

"You know what I mean."

Par did. He clenched his jaw. His father had given him up to the abbey when Par confessed he'd never invoked. Now Par would face him again.

They arrived at the Chapter Room. Enio patted him on the back and Par stepped inside.

The last time he'd been in this immaculate chamber with its long wooden table, velvet chairs, and bright high windows was when he'd confessed he couldn't invoke the gods. It was the last time he'd seen his father.

The man stood at the far end of the table, his large back to the door. His mother was beside him. The Father Abbot stood with the two, holding their cooing baby in his arms.

Par had planned this out. He'd step into the room, his head

held high, and sit across from his parents. The Abbot would assure them a Reckoning had not been needed after all. Par was, in fact, now fully Lustered. That made him an adult, no longer accountable to his parents. Par knew he still couldn't invoke, but the Father Abbot said the fewer in on that secret, the better.

This was as far as he'd gotten in his mind.

The Father Abbot looked up. "Here he is, now."

His parents turned and Par froze. Before he managed to say anything, they shouted his name. His mother rushed forward and grabbed him, planting kiss after kiss on his head.

His father, a bear of a man, lumbered over, rubbing the back of his neck. "We didn't understand, son. I should never—"

"Edwin," the Abbot had followed with Par's baby brother. "You did what everyone thought was best—at the time."

Edwin nodded. Then began to blubber. "Oh, purple hells." He grabbed Par and lifted him off the ground. "I'm so sorry, son."

Par's game plan fell apart like a wet griddle cake. He started to cry.

His father lowered him back to the ground and cleared his throat. "Well, I'm glad everything turned out all right. The Father Abbot tells me you're Lustered now. So that's the end of that."

Par wiped his nose and faced his parents. He swallowed and took a breath. "No, it isn't." The Abbot had told him to keep quiet about his invocation problem. Par certainly wouldn't shout it from the rooftops. Still, as far as his parents were concerned, he was done with the lying.

He steeled himself. "The truth is, I never—"

"Par"—his father held up a hand—"you're Lustered now. The gods have proven you worthy. You don't have to explain anything."

"But—"

"The things I said last time. I was upset. And afraid."

"And stupid," said Par's mother.

"And stupid," chuckled his father. "But believe me, son. Even if it were true that the gods never answered your invocations, you've *always* been worthy to us."

"That's just it, Dad. I—"

"Always." His father laid his thick hands on Par's shoulder. The smith's eyes smoldered with intensity.

Par saw it in his face. His father knew. He wondered if his parents had always known.

"Now," said his father, "let's sit down and you can tell us about your journeys."

The Abbot had coached Par on this part. Speak of his time on the river with the Choga, his visit to Bishop's Landing, and of how he and Enio had gotten lost in the Urdel. Tie it up with a final meeting with the Prior. Everything true. But beyond that, vague.

They sat together. His mother took the baby from the Abbot. "And don't forget Enio, dear."

"Oh, yes." His father cleared his throat. "That boy—"

"He's my friend."

His father nodded. "It didn't make sense to me before. But the Father Abbot tells me he helped you, kept you safe."

"Well," Par's smile on the outside was a shadow of the one inside. "We helped each other."

"He seems the capable kind. Is he around? I'd like to thank him personally. He's welcome in our home any time."

Par looked back at the doorway.

Enio had left.

CHAPTER FIFTY-NINE

ENIO WATCHED PAR join his family and warmed when they
hugged. Par would be all right.

Then Enio backed away and disappeared down the
corridor. Maybe he'd head to the docks, see what was new on
the Greening.

As he turned into the blocky sunlight of the west hall, he
pulled up short. A gaunt, grey-haired man stood a few paces away,
mumbling to himself. It was his father, Tarley. The man's hair was
trim and neat. Besides his first well-groomed appearance in years,
he seemed different in another way—smaller.

Tarley looked up. His eyes glistened like oily water.

Enio clenched his fists. The old rage rose inside at the years
of misery he could never forget. At his father turning him in to
the abbey for a pocket of coins. He felt an urge to rush the man
and tear him apart.

But something held him back. His anger collided with the
memories that Cronus had used to torture him—the overturned
wagon, his mother dying. Enio trapped and screaming. Of his
father, cradling her and sobbing.

Tarley cleared his throat. He spoke in a thin, shaky voice. "Just coming to see you, boy. I, uh, hear you did good."

Enio's blood kept below a boil, though not by much. He spoke with a steel tongue. "I'm not a boy. I'm Lustered."

"Sure," his father nodded. "That's a fine thing, then."

"What do you want?" Whatever it was, Enio might enjoy telling him to look for it in the purple hells.

"I wanted—" The man sniffled and looked toward a window. "I know that after your ma died, we didn't do too well together."

"Is that what you call it?" Enio almost laughed.

His father kept his eyes away. "Well, after you ran off, I got real bad. Threw myself in the river, they say. Don't remember much, but the abbey cleaned me up. Got me right."

Enio had no time for this. For him. He shook his head and began to leave.

"Wait." The man dug into a pocket. "You dropped this when you left. Found it the other day in the floor boards."

Tarley approached. He held out a small wooden object.

The breath caught in Enio's throat. It was his mother's comb, the last thing he'd had of her. He'd lost it the night he fled his father and returned to the abbey to warn Par.

Words jumbled in his head. Emotions in his chest. His jaw tightened. He lowered his gaze to the hard stone tiles.

Tarley's shadow stopped at his boots. "Here, take it."

Without looking up, Enio put out his hand. The comb fell into his palm—a yellowing piece of carved boxwood, worn smooth where his mother had held it to comb her hair.

And his.

He squeezed it with sweaty fingers. Footsteps retreated.

Enio shot his eyes at the back of the slumped figure walking away. "When Ma died, you got mean."

Tarley froze mid-stride.

"And rotten." Enio's voice came louder. Something twisted in his stomach. "It wasn't right. Ma wouldn't have liked it—or you."

The man turned. Enio could take him, if he wanted. Pay back this pitiful excuse for a father. This pale, weak old man with tears on his cheeks.

Instead, before Enio could stop himself, he tossed the comb in an easy arc. "You keep it," he muttered.

It floated through the sunlight. The man scrambled to snatch it with both hands, as if grabbing a lifeline. He held it to his breast. Then he swallowed hard and opened his mouth to say something.

Enio spoke first, his voice flat. "You better go."

They eyed each other a moment longer. With a nod and a hint of a sad smile, the man left.

The chanting of distant monks drifted through the shadows, passing like an elusive waft of incense. Enio's pounding heart slowed. He didn't feel angry now, not exactly. He couldn't tell what he felt, or why he had given away his mother's comb.

Why he hadn't torn his father apart.

Enio took a different route to the docks. In a few weeks, he'd leave for the Silver Sea and never have to see the man again. Enio didn't need the comb, anyway. His mother would always be inside him. He nodded to himself. That was why he'd tossed it back. Just charity for a bum. Like his mother used to give.

At the docks, he helped load a long skiff with barley bundles, and the owner offered him a ride downstream. Enio accepted. Before he left for the sea later this month, he had things to do.

He dragged his fingers through the cool green waters. Sagging willows slipped along the eastern bank. Insects buzzed the little boat, but he hardly noticed. His thoughts stayed stuck on the meeting in the hall.

His father seemed different in one more way. Less bile in his bitters, as the brewers said. Memories of the past marched through Enio's mind. Of the monster after his mother died.

And of a time before, of a man who'd taught him to fish.

Enio thanked the boatman and hopped out near the warehouse district. As he headed to the salvage yards, he realized one thing *had* changed.

He might never be able to forget his father. He knew he'd never forgive him.

Now, at least a little, Enio thought he understood him.

Chapter Sixty

THE FIRST FEW nights, Par slept at home. It squeezed him like too-small boots. So instead, he stayed at the abbey. He spent most of his days in the library anyway, a cluttered, modest chamber near the Chapter Room. Before Vex left for Xol Tomot, he'd set Par the task of trying to match the strange new sigils in his head to those in the books. Regardless of the tedium, the month passed much too quickly.

Now, as noon approached, Par sat alone at the library's single desk, before parchments and pen, sketching glyphs. He wasn't getting much done. This was his last day in St. Livius. When the sun reached its zenith, Vex would open a Threshold from Xol Tomot to the abbey's bell tower. Par would step through and leave his home behind.

His chair creaked as he shifted restlessly. He closed a book and studied an unlit candle on the corner of the desk.

What the hells. It's worth a try.

Par put down his pen and wrapped his fingers around the cool beeswax. He closed his eyes and brought the flame sigil to mind.

The faintest poof broke the silence. He looked up. The wick had ignited.

Par gasped and his eyes began to widen—until a snicker sounded just outside the door. He frowned over an embarrassed smile. "Not funny."

Enio stepped in, carrying a smoldering candle. "It was a *little* funny. Twenty feet, by the way." He put it aside and sat on the edge of the desk. "How goes the sigiling?"

Par dismissed his futile experiment, happy to see his friend before they parted. "Slow. After a while, they all look the same. What have you been up to?"

Enio shuffled through the parchments. "For one thing, the Abbot is curious about how I can juggle three different sigil magics."

"Divine, Arcanan, and élan?"

"Yep. He's never seen that before. Says it's wrong to dig around in people's brains, but since I'm already messed up, he's fine with it."

Par cocked an eyebrow. "He said that?"

Enio shrugged. "Well, he asked if he could take a look. Didn't matter to me."

"What'd he find?"

"Nothing."

It was Par's turn to snicker. "I could have saved him the trouble. It's pretty empty up there."

"Ha-ha—magic pants."

Par shook his head—he should never have told Enio about sitting on the vault symbols. But he let it go, not wanting to waste their last moments together. "Speaking of the mysterious mind of Enio, how did you keep my Lustering medal a secret from Cronus? When he got into your memories—" Par stopped. He hadn't meant to open old wounds.

But Enio's voice came light. "My ma's memory went deep. I guess so did our friendship. Maybe too much for him."

Par liked the explanation. He accepted it.

Enio pointed to the latest sketch. "That one looks like a smashed pastry."

Par rubbed his eyes. "I'm think I'm going sigil-blind."

"Said your goodbyes?"

"Yeah. The Abbot told my parents I've got a sponsorship to travel and study the Histories, be a teacher someday. Close enough to the truth, and it keeps them from worrying. Plus, Vex says I can visit through the Threshold."

Par still hadn't said goodbye to Enio. And when Enio left for the sea, Par wouldn't know where to visit him. He rested his gaze on his friend. "I wish—"

Enio leapt off the desk. "I want to show you something."

Par stood, too. "But—"

"And close your eyes." His friend waited at the door.

"Enio, we don't have time—"

"Just do it."

Par sighed and did.

Enio took him by the arm and half pulled him down the corridor. "If you look, I'll knock you into the Higher Realms."

"Been there," Par answered without a beat, but he stumbled along with his eyes shut.

They turned a corner. A musky river breeze marked this as the west hallway. Some paces later they stopped. Enio positioned him and stepped away. "Now."

Par stood at the same window where he'd panicked and prayed before their Lustering ceremony. Below were the abbey docks. This time, instead of the now-lost *Sea Dog*, a larger vessel floated there. It looked like a miniature version of a Chogan merchant barge, with a single mast toward the front and a cabin structure in back. Railings wrapped the deck except where a break let out a gangplank.

His friend grinned like a maniac. "What do you think?"

It dawned on Par. "That's yours? You bought a boat?"

"Bought, hells. I built it."

Par's jaw almost dropped off. "You—"

"Well, mostly on top of salvage. Used Lani's weave for some things, and the rockshoot from John to hammer. Come on." Enio raced toward the stairs. Par stayed on his friend's heels— Vex could wait.

They reached the docks. The sail was furled and two lines tied the boat to pilings. Par bounded with Enio across the landing and stopped near the ship's bow, where the words *Sea Dog* were burned into the side. It was the original plank from Enio's canoe. They ran their fingers over the old wood with reverence, as if the letters were carved in gold.

"It's beautiful, Enio. But why not *Sea Dog II*?"

His friend patted the hull. "It's the same boat. The *Sea Dog* just grew a little. Follow me."

Enio led him up the gangway and halted when they reached the top. "Boots."

"What?"

"I don't want to scuff it." Enio kicked off his shoes.

Par leaned against the rail and removed his, too. Though smaller, the deck was laid out like the *Sweet Carmina*, with a square hatch behind the mast. Lanterns hung from the rails at intervals. Stairs ran up over the cabin.

His friend strode across the deck. "I'll give you the tour. Watch the coamings."

Par still wasn't sure what a coaming was, but bolted after Enio. Two strides later Par jammed his toe into a slight raised ridge around the deck hatch. "Crap!"

Enio stopped by the rail. "I said, watch the coamings."

"*That's* a coaming?" Par winced and rubbed his toe.

But Enio was off again. "Come see the cuddy."

The cuddy was the cabin—small, but enough to fit cabinets,

table and chairs. They peeked below into the dark hold. Par could only make out a few barrels and boxes.

At last, they climbed the stairs to the top deck and stood behind the wheel. His friend pointed at the different ropes and explained what each one did. They fell silent until Enio breathed, "Sweet, right?"

The vessel was marvelous, even if it was patched-together salvage. "Sweet as peas and twice as nice."

Enio beamed.

"But how did you pay for the materials?" Salvage was cheap, but Par didn't think his friend had a copper to his name.

Enio fiddled with lines that draped from the mainsail to near the wheel. "Those baubles Vex wore turned out to be worth something. He gave me a few when I hooked him up with a Chogan ride to the Borderlands. Still got a couple left."

Par nodded. At least his friend had some money. It made seeing him go off alone a little less worrisome.

Enio changed the subject. "I bet you're wondering how I sail this by myself."

It was a good question. "How?"

"While I steer, I use Lani's weaving enchantment to work the tackle. Watch."

He gripped a rope. It vibrated as if it were alive. The sail unfurled. He worked another. More lines quivered and snapped. The sail twisted and swelled with the breeze.

Par watched, amazed. Then he noticed they were inching away from the landing—the lines holding the vessel to the pilings had been released. Before he could join Enio on a run downstream, the abbey's noontime bell rang out.

Time to meet Vex.

"Well, it's grand, Enio." The joy leaked from his voice.

"Yep. Stocked and ready to go."

An emptiness began to fill Par's heart. "When do you leave?"

Enio held his head high and peered down the river. "Now."

Par exhaled sadly. Then it sunk in. "Now?"

"That's right. I'm kidnapping you."

Par glanced to the diverging dock. "Enio, be serious."

"Never been more."

The tone of his voice. His face. He *was* serious.

Par gestured at the abbey. "I can't just leave. Vex expects—"

"Yes, you can. You've let others shape your life long enough. We both have. But we're Lustered now. It's time we made our *own* lives."

Par longed to take Enio's side, but he found himself arguing. "I still can't invoke. I'll be safe with Vex."

Enio nodded. "Yeah, probably. But is that what you really want?"

Par didn't answer.

His friend glared downstream and spoke softly. "I know it isn't."

"You know what I want?"

"Same as me. Find Lani."

For an instant, the sounds of the river, the birds, the creaking of the ship, all vanished. His friend was right—that was exactly what Par wanted.

The real possibility of going off with Enio bubbled in his stomach. He made a last half-hearted objection. "What about your plan to sail the Silver Sea? Sail the world?"

"I will, Par—after we find Lani. But I never wanted to go alone. I wanted us to sail it together."

The words smashed through Par's last barriers like Buckets breaching the tower wall. His heart warmed. "Really?"

"Yes, really. Don't be thick."

Regardless of the risks, the prospect of searching for Lani— and of his own purpose in the world—made Par's spirit soar. He glanced again at the bell tower where the sorcerer would, at any moment, open the Threshold. With a feigned yell in that direction, Par decided. "Help. I'm being kidnapped."

Enio broke into his wide, crooked smile. "Better yet, enlisted as a new recruit of the *Sea Dog*."

Par began to salute, but started as he realized something. "Wait, my bags and—"

"Everything you packed for Xol Tomot is in the hold."

Par eyed his friend. "Sneaky."

Enio offered his arm. "Well, once a river rat…"

Par took it, feeling the same joy inside that he saw on his friend's face. "Always a river rat."

They pulled each other and hugged.

After a few hearty back slaps, Par rallied to his new state of affairs. "All right, then. Let's swash some buckles!" He grabbed the wheel.

"Do what, now?"

"You know. Swish the bucklers and—"

Enio nudged him aside. "Better let me drive."

The vessel slipped past the squat hill of the Abbey Saint Livius. Enio guided them into the current. "Since you're part of the crew, you need a title. Second mate."

Par frowned. "Why not first mate?"

"You gotta work up the ranks."

"What? That's the dumbest—"

"Hey, I can drop you to ensign." Enio rubbed his chin. "Ensign Magic Pants."

Par scowled, but his spirits would not be dampened. Enio stood behind the wheel, as straight and tall as any river captain. With his fierce gaze ahead and his dark hair tossed by the breeze, he reminded Par of a horse at full gallop. It felt good to see his friend finally chasing his dreams.

And to chase his own.

Par filled his lungs with the boundless, fragrant air of his new freedom. The sun warmed his shoulders, and a sense of adventure wrapped him like a magic cloak. Maybe that great orb in the sky *was* the god Oä, watching over his children. And the veiled moon and stars were strange windows to celestial power. And the shining ripples on the river, like sunlight dancing in a spider's web, were hints of the élan as it surged and pulsed through all living things.

He smiled contentedly. Even though he'd been to the Higher Realms, he still had so much to learn. But there was one thing he knew for certain: he'd explore these mysteries with his friend.

Par flexed his new arm and stepped behind Enio.

Right after he made him promise never to utter the words *magic pants* again.

Epilogue

THE FATHER ABBOT rested his bony hands on the bell tower's parapet. Pigeons cooed in the rafters. Far below, the Greening River sparkled like a road paved with emeralds.

Suddenly, the birds squawked and fluttered into the mid-day sky. The Abbot turned. A ghostly doorway had opened in thin air behind him. Beyond loomed a man with curly white hair, dressed in a shimmering blue robe with silver stars.

The Abbot smiled. "Right on time, Alexander. Nice outfit."

Vex remained on the far side of the Threshold, smoothing his garments. "Thank you, Cornelius. I wanted to welcome Par properly."

"About that. I'm afraid we have a bit of a hitch."

"Oh? Should I try later?"

"I doubt that would help." The Abbot pointed to where a small sailing vessel drifted downstream. Two tiny figures wrestled across the top deck. "It appears Par has had a change of plans."

The Threshold swung like a giant eye to follow the Abbot's finger. "He is not coming back?"

"I suspect not."

"But Par can enter the Citadel. With his help, we might even unseal it. The treasures, the knowledge and magics locked in the vault—"

"Alexander," the Abbot said patiently. "Cronus has pushed the lands near to war. Do you want to risk either side gaining access to that power?"

Vex paused. "You believe it should remain sealed?"

"I do."

The uncaptained boat veered dangerously toward the shore. A figure dove for the ship's wheel.

Vex nodded. "Your concern is valid. I have considered it myself. But Par and Enio now know many of the Vigil's secrets. If we are to let them travel free, should we at least not have them Reckoned?"

The Abbot flashed an angry glance at the sorcerer. "To even suggest—"

The sorcerer raised a hand. "Forgive me. I fear I have misused your terminology."

The Abbot squinted at the emphasis on the word *your*.

Vex went on. "However, some of their memories could be a risk, even to themselves. With their permission, those could be diluted. I was not suggesting we fundamentally change who Par and Enio are."

The Abbot's gaze fell again on the vessel as it swerved away from the banks. "Who they are is the very thing that demands they go in search of their lost friend. And that they do it together."

"But the sigils in Par's head—"

"As long as he cannot bestow them, they remain merely a curiosity. And wherever life beckons, if they are to use their talents wisely, they must understand their world. It's time they got out there and explored it."

The boat gradually straightened. The two small occupants now stood shoulder to shoulder at the helm.

Finally, the Abbot let out a long sigh. "Well, there go our two Sigil Masters."

"Sigil Masters?"

"Perhaps, one day. The sigils in Par's mind, though dormant, may be the most powerful since the Gardens of Gê. And while I didn't want to swell Enio's head, it's quite rare for an individual to manage both an Elorian invocation and Arcanan spell. But a nymph enchantment besides? It's unheard of."

"True, though the notion of High Sigil Master Enio gives me the shivers."

The Abbot stifled a sudden cough.

"And I can't say I am not disappointed," Vex grumbled. "Such potential."

"Is that the only reason for your grief, Alexander?"

"Is it not enough? I am the last of the Vigil. I had hoped…" He paused. His tone softened. "You're right. I will miss Par's company. And with the Immortus closed, perhaps the world has no more need of the Vigil. Or of a crusty old sorcerer."

A sudden gust billowed the single-masted sails. The boat lurched forward.

The Abbot turned to Vex. "Speaking of the Vigil, perhaps it's time for a change there, too."

Vex shook his head. "I don't understand."

"A new Vigil. One which continues to watch, yet also works to bridge our differences." The Abbot's voice darkened. "Or at least, avoid a war."

"A monumental task for one man, Cornelius."

"What about for two?"

Vex raised his dark, bushy eyebrows. "You?"

The Abbot frowned. "Why not me? I've considered retirement for some time, but I'm not so old that—" He stopped and shrugged. "Well, perhaps I am. But as you said, you're no spring chicken either."

Vex cleared his throat. "I take your point."

The Abbot stepped toward the Threshold and examined its boundaries. "Then it's decided. How do I get through this thing?"

"You would leave now?"

"At our age, there's no time to waste."

"But will not the abbey worry where you've gone?"

The Abbot lowered his voice. "Brother Gaius waits for me below. Can you imagine his shock when he sees I've disappeared from the highest point of the abbey? He'll say I've ascended to the gods."

"Quite an exit."

The Abbot chuckled. "I'll revisit in a day or two and turn the abbey over to him. And I'll bring you back Par's sketchings. Until then, let them wonder. A little mystery is good for the soul."

Vex seemed to consider. "Well, I'd hate to have just fixed the place up for nothing." He held his arm out through the Threshold.

The Abbot took it and stepped to Xol Tomot.

They remained at the portal. The boat's sail bobbed above the treetops like a flag borne by an army on the march.

The Abbot spoke softly. "It weighs on my heart that Prior Dogam could not be with us. Perhaps he was right. If I had turned the abbey over to him—"

"Do not blame yourself for his choices, Cornelius. You are a beloved abbot. Your monks would not have let you retire had you tried. Besides, we all have our regrets. Chief of mine was the loss of our friendship so long ago."

"Loss? When a gift is in the giving, it can never be lost."

"Still, I fear those of our years are past developing such dear relationships."

"Oh, I don't know about that, Alexander."

With a flash of sails through the trees and a distant snatch of song, Par and Enio at last disappeared around the river's bend.

The Abbot placed a gentle hand on the sorcerer's shoulder. "After all, we've had two very good teachers."

The End

Dear reader,

I hope you enjoyed the story of
The Sigil Masters as much as I enjoyed telling it.

You can continue the journey with Book Two, *Dark Reckoning*

Sweet sailin's and fair landin's

Rick

About the Author

Rick Duffy writes to discover new worlds and wander from the familiar. He grew up on the boundary of street-lit suburb and shadowed forest, reading second-hand fantasy and science fiction books often out of order. He now writes them himself (in order) and is best know for his award winning The Sigil Masters.

Rick lives in Colorado, is never far from a biking trail or a cup of tea, and hopes we all find time everyday to explore.

Connect with him at rickduffy.com

www.ingramcontent.com/pod-product-compliance
Lightning Source LLC
Chambersburg PA
CBHW030829110726
47900CB00006B/1810